THE ARGENTINE DOCTOR'S HEART

BY
MEREDITH WEBBER

SMALL TOWN MARRIAGE MIRACLE

BY
JENNIFER TAYLOR

Praise for
Meredith Webber and Jennifer Taylor:

'Medical™ Romance favourite Meredith Webber
has penned a spellbinding and moving tale
set under the hot desert sun!'
—*Cataromance* on THE DESERT PRINCE'S
CONVENIENT BRIDE by Meredith Webber

'Stirring, poignant and heartwarming,
THE SURGEON'S FATHERHOOD SURPRISE
is another triumph from a much-loved writer.'
—*Cataromance* on Jennifer Taylor's
THE SURGEON'S FATHERHOOD SURPRISE

MELTING THE ARGENTINE DOCTOR'S HEART

BY

MEREDITH WEBBER

To my Argentinian relatives,
the wonderful Daniela and Damian, with thanks

First published in Great Britain 2011
by Mills & Boon, an imprint of Harlequin (UK) Limited,
Eton House, 18-24 Paradise Road, Richmond, Surrey TW9 1SR

ISBN: 978 0 263 88593 4

Harlequin (UK) policy is to use papers that are natural, renewable and recyclable products and made from wood grown in sustainable forests. The logging and manufacturing process conform to the legal environmental regulations of the country of origin.

Printed and bound in Spain
by Blackprint CPI, Barcelona

‘It’s impossible that you stay here…

‘Find a hotel in the city. I will visit you both there. You spring this on me with no warning, but I’ll not deny my child. I will make arrangements, speak to lawyers, see she is—’

‘Financially secure?’ Caroline spat the words at Jorge, her fury a palpable force. ‘She needs your love, Jorge, not your money. Would that be too hard for you to offer her?’

Would it? He looked towards the child. Jorge found his heart was hurting again. Was the wall he’d built around his feelings crumbling so easily?

‘Come inside,’ he said at last.

Meredith Webber says of herself, 'Some ten years ago, I read an article which suggested that Mills and Boon were looking for new Medical™ Romance authors. I had one of those "I can do that" moments, and gave it a try. What began as a challenge has become an obsession—though I do temper the "butt on seat" career of writing with dirty but healthy outdoor pursuits, fossicking through the Australian Outback in search of gold or opals. Having had some success in all of these endeavours, I now consider I've found the perfect lifestyle.'

Recent titles by the same author:

TAMING DR TEMPEST
SHEIKH, CHILDREN'S DOCTOR…HUSBAND

CHAPTER ONE

THE anger that had sprung to fierce life when Caroline had read the article about the clinic in Argentina continued to burn within her as her plane crossed the Pacific Ocean. It simmered nicely as she struggled with a three-year-old through Customs in Buenos Aires and onto the local plane for the short flight north to Rosario, where one Dr Jorge Suárez had set up a special clinic for people of the indigenous Toba tribe who had settled in the city at the end of the twentieth century.

One Jorge Suárez!

Unfortunately, as the taxi took Ella along endless tree-lined boulevards and past wide parks, which she knew from the guide book she'd read on the flight were called *plazas*, the anger began to fade. Doubts rushed in to fill the space where it had been. The fact that Ella was asleep beside her meant Caroline had nothing but her thoughts to keep her company.

And the thoughts were *not* good!

What if Jorge *had* actually meant what he'd said in that devastating, humiliating, soul-eroding email sent from France four years ago? What if she was wrong in assuming he'd sent it because his beautiful face, and probably his whole body, had been scarred and, proud man that he was, he'd feared her pity? What if he *hadn't* ever loved her, and she'd been nothing but a convenience, someone to be lied to so he could get her into bed?

She hadn't believed his words when the email had arrived; couldn't believe that the overwhelming, all-conquering love she'd thought they'd shared had been nothing more than a farce; their talks of marriage a sham. Frustration had been her strongest emotion at the time, frustration because she couldn't fly to his side and demand to know if his words were true. But news of her mother's breast cancer had come through only a week before his accident and she'd been on the long flight back to Australia when it had happened.

By the time she'd gathered her wits and had organised for her mother to begin treatment, he'd changed his email address, and letters sent to him at the hospital to which he'd been airlifted after the accident had been returned unopened. *That* was when she'd been forced to wonder if she'd been deceived by a master of the love game.

Two months later, while supporting her mother through debilitating radiation therapy, Caroline had realised she was pregnant. She'd searched the internet until she'd found his father's address in a suburb called Recoleta in Buenos Aires, and sent a letter to Jorge care of that address. After all, a man deserved to know he was about to become a father. That letter, too, had boomeranged right back to her.

The Spanish-accented voice of the cab driver—deep and rich, so like Jorge's—told her she was close to her destination and now doubt turned to panic.

Why had she done this?

How *could* she have been so stupid?

To have dragged Ella all this way on an assumption made from a very blurry internet photograph—was she *mad*?

Fortunately, though not so fortunate for the people who lived here, the taxi had turned off the tree-lined boulevard, down a suburban street then into a small lane between makeshift homes.

'Poor people who come from the north,' the taxi driver explained. 'The city builds them housing but more come before they can all have homes.'

The clinic looked exactly as it had on the internet, like an old corner store, painted white, and the small, brown-skinned people lazing around outside it might have been the same ones she'd read about in the article, mostly indigenous Toba people who lived in this over-crowded section of the big city of Rosario. The taxi stopped and though her stomach was knotted tightly and her lungs had seized so she could only gasp in short choppy breaths, she resisted the temptation to ask the driver to take her back to the airport.

Resisted, too, the panic that threatened to overwhelm her, reminding herself of the reason she had come.

Whatever she might feel—whatever might lie between Jorge and herself—her daughter deserved a father. Growing up without one herself, she had longed for someone to call Daddy. But worse than the longing—that hollow gap in her life—she knew how insecure it had made her around boys, and how uncertain she'd been about men.

Perhaps it even explained how easily she'd been seduced by Jorge's declarations of love…

Refusing to acknowledge such a dread thought, she forced air deep into her lungs, shook her daughter gently awake, paid the cab driver, and muttered, 'Here goes!' to herself.

Yes, her voice had quavered and, yes, she had a momentary concern about bringing Ella to this obviously overcrowded area of what had looked a beautiful city, but having come all this way for Ella to meet her father, Caroline was not going to be stopped at the front door.

The sleepy child grumbled slightly when her mother lifted her, but as the little arms locked around Caroline's neck, and the soft, thick, dark curls brushed her cheek, her tension eased, determination returning in its place. She was doing this for her daughter.

Jorge looked up as his helper and friend, Juan, came rushing into the room.

'Taxi with lady and baby outside. Lady with baby coming in.'

Juan's use of the word 'lady' was enough to tell Jorge that this was no ordinary visit. The woman obviously wasn't one of the local people for whom he'd set up the clinic, so a taxi dropping off a woman with a child—an emergency, surely.

He was moving towards the door of his office as these thoughts chased through his head, and a couple of paces past that he was at the front door of the clinic, staring in disbelief at the tall blonde woman striding up the front path, a small, dark-haired child nestled in her arms.

His first fleeting thought was that this would be a really good time for lightning to strike him, but when the cloudless sky failed to deliver instant incineration, and he doubted a tsunami would sweep him away—too far from the sea—he was forced to confront the intruder.

'Caroline?'

His voice made a question of her name but his gut, cramping uncomfortably, knew exactly who it was. Heat stirred in unfamiliar places, while his heart gave a bump in his chest and panic rattled his brain. Fortunately the doctor in him reacted with concern for the child and, automatically turning the good side of his face to the woman he'd once loved—once?—he let the doctor take over.

'What are you doing here? Is the child ill?'

His words halted her, but only momentarily, not enough for him to really study her, to see if she was still as beautiful as the vision he saw in his dreams.

Beautiful! She'd mocked him when he'd called her that, pointing out that her mouth was too big, her nose too thin, her eyes too wide apart, hair too fair—a dozen shortcomings listed as she'd shied away from his praise…

Caroline didn't answer. She continued down the path until she stood directly in front of him—close enough to touch if his arms had moved from his side, if any part of his body would have obeyed an order from his stunned brain.

She studied him, her face betraying nothing as she took in the scarring down his right cheek. Now his brain was beginning to work again and he realised she could only have found him through the internet and the article that had appeared on it had shown his photograph, scar and all.

'The *child*,' she said carefully, her voice so taut he knew she was as tense as he was, 'is your daughter.'

Dumbstruck! He knew the word yet had never understood its meaning until this moment. It was as if the lightning bolt that hadn't come earlier had finally arrived, spearing into his brain.

At that moment, the child raised her head from her mother's shoulder and looked around, smiling tentatively at him before shyly snuggling her face back into Caroline's neck. The denial he'd been working up to died on his lips. As a small child, his mother had so loved his curls she'd refused to cut his hair, and he'd seen the face that looked at him in photographs of himself as a toddler.

He had a child!

He had a daughter!

The knowledge bounced around in his head in the blank space where his brain had once been.

'Her name is Ella.'

Ella?

Caroline had called the child Ella?

Had she remembered it was his mother's name?

Of course she would have! And the naming could be part of an elaborate con. The child—Ella—had kicked against restraint in her mother's arms and was now on the ground, looking around her, eyes wide as she took in these new surroundings.

And unless Caroline had found a lover who looked

just like him, maybe Jorge had to accept the child was his.

His daughter!

Ella!

He squatted down, holding up a hand to stop Caroline who looked as if she might swoop on the little girl.

'Hello,' he said, using the deliberately soft voice he used not only for children but for new patients at the clinic.

Dark eyes stared at him, moving across his face, pausing, then a tentative smile danced around small pink lips, and she raised a hand in a small salute.

'Hi,' she said, and as he squatted, immobilised by the smile, by her voice, she stepped forward and put the palm of her hand against his scarred cheek. 'Sore?'

He couldn't speak, the lump in his throat too hard to dislodge. How could this be? How could he comprehend it? The child was his? *This* child, who'd touched his face with baby-soft fingers? He reached out, shocked to see his fingers shaking, and brushed his hand against the shiny brown curls.

'Not sore,' he said gently, unable to tell her of the pain in other parts of his body, in particular his heart.

The child smiled, and patted his cheek this time, then, in the way of very small and easily diverted children, she turned to check out her surroundings.

Glancing up, he saw tears in Caroline's eyes, but the reality of what she'd done took precedence over weakness, growing in enormity.

They couldn't stay.

He wouldn't get involved—couldn't get involved.

For the last four years he had pushed the world away, hating the pity he saw in people's eyes, happy only when he was working on a new project, doing something to help people worse off than himself, people who wouldn't care if he looked like Frankenstein's monster because he was willing to help them.

He knew it was pride—foolish, stupid pride—that had made him react this way—and if he hadn't known then his father had told him often enough—but it was the only way he could cope with his injuries and with the continued pain they caused.

But now he had a *daughter*?

The child—Ella—was watching the game a group of children were playing beside the clinic, and anger rose again. He turned back to the woman who had brought this cataclysmic shock into his life, letting his anger override the surge of attraction just looking at her produced.

'And you've come for what? Some grand display? Some macabre retaliation for me dumping you? You'd drag a child halfway around the world in order to punish me in some way?'

Now anger fired *her* eyes, Caroline's eyes, as blue as the skies over the snow-clad mountains in mid-winter—or so he'd thought four years ago….

'Not really,' she said, speaking calmly in spite of that anger flashing in the blue. 'I came to fulfil a pledge we made a long time ago. Maybe you remember it, although from what I've read you've taken it to extremes. One month a year, we pledged. One month a year we'd work somewhere in the world, treating people who didn't have the resources for the medical facilities most people enjoy. Until now I've worked my month a year in outback communities at home, helping set up different strategies to maintain good health. But when I read your clinic was always looking for volunteer doctors, I realised I could kill two birds with one stone.'

Although smiling was the last thing she felt like doing at the moment—in all the hundreds of scenarios she'd pictured of this meeting, Jorge yelling at her for dragging Ella halfway round the world had been the last—Caroline managed a smile, and waved her hand to where the taxi driver had dumped her large backpack and Ella's smaller, koala-shaped one.

'As you can see, I've come prepared. I'm here for a month,' she finished, and felt a rush of satisfaction at the astonishment—not to mention horror—on his face.

His face!

His poor face!

Although the photo had prepared her for the scarring, seeing it, the physical manifestations of what had happened, had hit her like a punch to her stomach. For something like that to happen to a man as handsome and proud as Jorge, it was unimaginable how he had coped.

It had seemed natural when she'd read about the injuries he'd sustained, and learnt that for a time he'd thought he might not walk again, that the first thing he would have done was deny his love for her. He would have pictured her reaction to his injuries, seen himself as a burden, her love as pity, and a man as proud as Jorge would never in a million years accept pity.

So he'd sent that email?

She'd been so sure, reading the article, that this had to have been the explanation for his rejection and, furious that he'd had so little faith in her, even more angry that he'd denied Ella a father, she'd begun to make plans to get them to Argentina as quickly as possible.

Seeing him now, seeing *his* anger, the doubts that had crept in while she had been in the taxi intensified, and nausea swirled in her stomach. Yet her body ignored his anger; *it* knew he was still Jorge—the man she'd loved, still loved, it told her.

His next words slammed against her, emphasising her body's folly, making it crystal clear that he was far from delighted to see her.

'You cannot stay. I do not want you here.'

His voice was flat, hard and furious, although the fury was thinly veiled, no doubt tightly reined in, in front of Ella, but Caroline was not going to be put off at the first setback, no matter how much this blunt rejection might hurt. Despite her body's automatic reaction to seeing him, she had no idea what would happen between Jorge and herself in the future but, whatever developed, she was determined Ella would know her father.

She ploughed on over his arguments.

'The article I read said you had accommodation for a visiting doctor and Ella's used to sharing my bed when we travel,' she told him. 'I figured, being a clinic, there are sure to be some trustworthy aides or patients who won't mind babysitting if Ella's a nuisance. In fact, I thought, as I'll be here, once you've introduced me around and shown me how you work, you can spend some time getting to know your daughter, maybe even think about introducing her to your father.'

She rattled off the words, hoping she sounded calmer than she felt, which was as if she'd somehow been dropped into a washing machine—churning, tumbling, swirling…

'You can't work here!'

The blunt statement brought her back to earth. That was good, as she was running out of words to cover the way she was feeling. On top of that, his flat declaration revived her fighting spirit and she wasn't giving in this time without a fight, no matter how much seeing him again was tormenting her body.

'Of course I can.' She shot the words at him. 'I've been learning Spanish for the last three years and although I don't know the Toba language, I assume, as they have been settled here for a couple of decades, most will speak a little Spanish. I have a visa, my medical qualifications have been approved by your medical association, and I have permission from…' she couldn't remember the name of the organisation '…something to do with the medical officer of the municipality of Rosario to do volunteer work at this particular clinic for the duration of one month.'

'This is *my* clinic!'

Even as the words escaped his lips, Jorge realised how stupid they would sound. He didn't need to see the smile twitching at Caroline's lips or hear her cutting 'Oh, really?' to know she'd read the pettiness of it, *and* realised it was totally out of character.

So she knew she'd rattled him but, then, that was what this stupid escapade must be about—rattling him.

In more ways than one, although she couldn't know that—wouldn't ever know that!

Uncertain where to go next, needing time to think before he said anything more—needing, more than anything, to get away from the woman who had reawoken sensations he'd never thought to feel again—he turned to see where the child, Ella, no, he couldn't call her that—not yet—had gone.

Although staying within sight of her mother, she had wandered closer to where the Toba children played. She watched the game, probably unaware of the sensation she was causing among the locals—a small stranger in their midst.

A *child*?

His child?

No! There was no time for wonder!

'You have done this deliberately,' he said to Caroline, letting his anger run free now the child was out of earshot. 'You have come here on some mad whim, dragged a child all this way, when a letter and a photo would have sufficed. So why, Caroline? To punish me for not loving you?'

She stepped back as if he'd struck her, then straightened for the fight. He'd seen her fight before, but usually with him, not against him, fighting for the rights of others, fighting for what she called a 'fair go' for people who couldn't fight for themselves.

'And you'd have opened the letter as you did all the others, including the one I sent telling you I was pregnant?' Sarcasm curled like wisps of smoke around the heated words. 'Or should I have written "Photo of your child" on the envelope so you didn't just scrawl "Return to sender" on it and pop it back into the mail?'

She paused then stepped closer, her voice softer, the faint hint of the lemon shampoo she must still use moving in her silvery hair, floating in the air towards him.

Momentarily distracting him…

'You, of all people, know how I felt growing up without my father,' she continued. 'You were the first person I ever opened up to about how inadequate I'd felt all through my teens, and the foolish things I'd done to win boys' attention. This is not about punishment, Jorge, neither is it about you and me, or about the past. I've come because I thought you should know Ella exists, but more for her sake than for yours, because the one thing I don't want for her is to grow up without knowing her father.'

She took a deep breath, as if the words, and perhaps the emotion behind them, had emptied her right out.

And remembering, he knew it could have, for he'd known her for six months before she'd talked about not having a father…

Yet even sympathy for her didn't stop the disappointment that had seeped into him as he'd listened to the honesty of her explanation. Could he possibly have been thinking she'd come because she still loved him?

How likely would that be when his farewell email had been so deliberately cruel?

'You should have written!'

It was weak, pathetic even, but all he could come up with as he struggled to regain some mental poise, even to find renewed anger, anything that would turn her away from here.

But in place of an objection, what flew into his mind was something she'd said earlier—something about staying here!

With him!

She intended to invade his home so she'd not only be working near him but living near him as well, her body a constant reminder, a constant distraction, a constant tease...

Now the anger came.

'It's impossible that you should stay here. Find a hotel in the city. I will visit you both there. You spring this on me with no warning, but I'll not deny my child. I will make arrangements, speak to lawyers, see she is—'

'Financially secure?'

She spat the words at him, her fury a palpable force.

'Do you think for one moment that's what I want? Your money? As it happens, Ella is already financially secure. The father I never knew died and left me more than enough money to keep her in luxury for her entire life, but I want Ella to have a father, Jorge, and I thought, by coming here, maybe over a month we could work out some way for that to happen.'

She stopped for breath again then added even more fiercely, 'She needs your love, Jorge, not your money. Would that be too hard for you to offer her?'

Would it?

He looked towards the child—Ella—who was laughing as one of the children kicked a tattered ball towards her. One small foot lifted and a shiny purple shoe kicked the ball back. The Toba children all waved their arms and yelled their approval of the young, curly-headed stranger in their midst.

Jorge found his heart was hurting again…

Was the wall he'd built around his feelings crumbling so easily?

Even considering it heralded danger.

'This is impossible! We cannot stand here, arguing. Come inside, not the clinic but my—my *home*.'

He emphasised the last word in the invitation to convince himself there was no shame attached to inviting guests into his rough adobe hut, but picturing it in his mind as he'd left that morning—an unwashed breakfast bowl and spoon on the sink; piles of books like mini-skyscrapers all over the floor; his bed unmade should anyone peer through the curtain that served as a bedroom door.

The child—Ella—surely would, though an unmade bed should mean little to her.

'We'll have *mate*, a kind of tea. Have you had time to try it?'

Now he sounded like a tourist guide, and though she was walking behind him, little Ella at her side, he knew Caroline had heard the falseness in his voice and was smiling as she replied, 'We've come straight from the airport so we've not had time, although I've heard of it.'

She'd answered like a polite tourist, although when she added, 'Of course, you used to tell me about it, Jorge, and long for a taste of it,' her voice was soft and he could almost believe…

Believe what?

That after four years she still felt something for him?

Imbécil! Was he so stupid that he was thinking this way?

They'd reached his hut. *His* hut? He'd thought of it that way since the project had begun but it was never destined to be his for ever, or even for much longer. Soon it would house volunteer doctors.

Volunteer doctors! The board set up to run the clinic had agreed they would still accept volunteer help when it was offered, as well as paying a permanent doctor. Caroline must have made the arrangement through the board and somehow dates had become mixed up, which would explain why he hadn't received notification.

He shook his head at the bureaucratic bungling that had thrust him into this situation and continued towards the hut.

At least now it had a front door, though not much of one, cut from a bigger, thick timber door one of his helpers had found in a second-hand yard. Cutting the door, like the other tasks he'd undertaken in building his hut, had reminded him how little he knew about manual labour—how easy and privileged his growing up had been.

'Great door!'

Caroline was smiling at him, running her fingers

along the rough edges where the plane had bitten too deep into the wood.

'All your own work?'

He fought the urge to smile back—and the even stronger urge to put his fingers over hers. To smile at her would be to lose, to touch her would be to surrender, and although he wasn't sure of the battle taking place, its rules or even the battleground, he wasn't going to lose.

'I built the hut with some of the unemployed young men in the area, so we could all learn the traditional way of building. We try to reuse wood where we can. We cannot stop deforestation taking place, not only here but in so many rainforest areas throughout the world, but at least we should be aware that we need not add to it.'

Her smile grew softer, gleaming in her eyes where anger had been earlier, and his heart bumped once again in his chest.

Danger—that was what the bump meant. It was as good as a flashing sign saying, Beware! He straightened up, feeling the skin on his body tighten and momentary pain. Pain was good as it reminded him that he couldn't let a smile breach his defences.

'Did the building project help the young men get work?' she asked.

She was worming her way into his confidence but he couldn't let a smile divert him, any more than he could let Caroline's apparent interest in his building project distract him from the fact that she was here to disrupt his life.

Yet politeness meant he had to answer.

'For some of them, it led to work.' He kept his voice

carefully neutral, and looked at a spot over her shoulder as he spoke so he didn't have to see the so-familiar curve of her cheek, the blue of her eyes, the silver of her hair, but he'd lost her attention anyway, the child coming dangerously close to the piles of books.

'Don't knock them over!'

Caroline's cry diverted his attention from battles, danger, smiling eyes and building projects, but it had come too late to stop Ella spilling one of his piles of books.

'Not reached the bookshelves-pages of your how-to-build book?' Caroline teased, kneeling to help Ella rebuild the pile.

And this time, perhaps because she was kneeling and might not see it, he *did* smile.

'Furniture is a different world, far too complex for an amateur like me to tackle,' he said, amazed he was able to have this ordinary conversation when his insides were churning and his mind battling to reject that this was happening. 'We were gifted some furniture, not a lot, but enough.'

Caroline finished tidying the spilt pile of books and stood up, leaving Ella wandering around the stacks in much the same way as a child might play in a maze. Although every sinew in her body was tight, the tension in the room palpable, she had to keep pretending—to keep up her end of what was really a bizarre conversation, given the circumstances. She and Jorge together after four years and they were discussing building projects!

Better than arguing, she told herself, but at the same

time her heart ached for the time when she and Jorge would have laughed together over this strained and formally polite behaviour.

Laughed, hugged, kissed, made love?

But it was her turn to talk, not think!

'Is there a big unemployment problem in the area?'

She left Ella with a warning not to touch things and crossed the room to the little kitchen nook, where he waited by the single gas ring for the kettle to boil. Picking up the gourd in which he had put the chopped-up leaves—were they called *yerba*? She tried to remember—for the tea, she turned it in her hands, cupping it and appreciating how snugly it fitted her hand, stirring the chopped dry leaves with the metal straw.

Eventually he answered, taking his turn in this painful pretence.

'It's a problem among the young people—the ones who choose not to go on to higher education,' Jorge replied, though his inner reaction to her closeness and his fascination with the movement of her hands had delayed his reply too long. 'In the beginning, working with the boys to make the mud bricks for the walls, I found it was a more satisfying form of physical therapy than working out in a gymnasium. Gradually it became a challenge to all of us, to build something with our own hands—something we could feel pride in. Yes, the hut is rough, the door is rough, but it is *our* hut and *our* door, and I, for one, cannot open it without a sense of perhaps not pride but satisfaction that I could, with only a little help, make myself a shelter.'

'You started by making the bricks?'

Disbelief and admiration warred in her voice but the shrill whistle of the kettle stopped the conversation. He took the gourd from her, turning it upside down a couple of times to move the finer leaves to the top, then tipping it from side to side. That done, he poured in cold water to saturate the leaves and let it sit a minute on the table. The mechanical movement of his hands as he made the *mate* gave him time to think—time to tell himself her admiration wasn't personal. She would be equally admiring of any man she knew had built his own dwelling.

Any man she knew?

He glanced at her left hand, certain he'd see a wedding ring.

No jewellery at all, but, then, she'd always shunned what she called fripperies. And if she'd married, Ella would have a father figure in her life, and there'd have been no reason for her to come.

He tipped the gourd once more so the leaves settled on one side of it, and carefully added the boiling water.

And while it steeped he shrugged off her admiration, making light of what had been a mammoth task.

'It's how people used to do it, and I cannot spend all my spare hours reading.'

'Spare hours,' Caroline replied. 'I remember them, though the memory is hazy.' She looked towards her daughter, then added, 'Not that I'd swap Ella for even one spare hour.'

The remarks bothered Jorge, for all he was trying to do was keep the conversation determinedly neutral—coolly polite, nothing more. She'd sounded wistful, as if genuine regret lurked somewhere behind the words.

'You have so little time?' he asked, dropping a silver straw into the *mate* then pausing for an unseen guest to try it before handing the gourd to Caroline.

She lifted the gourd, and sipped through the straw, grimacing slightly at the taste, or perhaps the heat of the drink.

'I pass it back to you, is that right?' she said, and, knowing she'd remembered something as simple as the *mate* ceremony of sharing made his heart go bump again, but though the barriers he'd erected around his heart were as rough as the walls of his hut, he knew he had to keep them intact, heart-bumps or no heart-bumps!

His mind tracked back to the previous conversation—the question Caroline hadn't answered.

'You have so little time?' he asked again.

It was all too weird, Caroline decided, standing in a little hut not unlike the one they'd shared in Africa—although that one had been round and roofed with palm fronds, not corrugated iron—with Jorge beside her, asking polite questions—exactly as it had been when they'd first met…

CHAPTER TWO

SHE shook off the memory and steeled herself against the attraction that still tingled along her nerves when she looked at him or heard his voice. Best to consider his question—to answer him.

Best to forget the past and all its joy and pain…

'I work, I come home, and I try to be a good mother. Like all working mothers I feel guilt that someone else spends more time with my daughter than I do, so I probably overcompensate. Then, when Ella goes to bed, there are always business things to take care of, or articles to read or write—you know how it is, keeping up with the latest developments, hoping you'll find something to help a patient you've seen recently.'

He turned to face her so the scar on his cheek was fully visible and it was only with an enormous effort she resisted the urge to lay her palm against his damaged skin, as Ella had done earlier.

'You said your father left you money. You must have no need to work.'

She smiled at him and waved her hands around the hut, pleased to have such a bland, harmless topic of conversation to occupy her mind and distract it from the suggestions of her body—suggestions like moving closer, touching him…

'And I'm sure you're not so impoverished you needed to build your own hut, so you, at least, should understand. A lot of people put a lot of time and effort to train me for the job I do. I wouldn't feel right to just stop doing it, especially when there are areas where doctors are still desperately needed. I've been working in an inner-city practice where patients are a mix of trendy twenties, urban aboriginals, homeless youths, prostitutes, Asian migrants and long-term street people. Probably not unlike this area you work in, although, from the article I read, most of your patients are the indigenous Toba people, so you don't get the same mix.'

Pleased with herself for answering as if the tension in the air between them wasn't twisting her intestines into knots, she kept going. Talking was better than thinking. Unfortunately for this plan, Ella chose that moment to knock over a second pile of books.

'Oh, blast,' Caroline said as she hurried towards the mess, but Jorge was there before her. 'I really should control my daughter better.'

The words were no sooner out than she realised how stupid they had been.

'Our daughter,' she amended, but knew it was too late. She was kneeling now, directly in front of him, looking into Jorge's deep brown eyes, eyes she'd once fallen right into and drowned in, losing her heart, soul and body to the man who owned them.

And because she was looking, she saw the pain, read

it as clearly as words written in white chalk on a black background.

'I'm sorry,' she whispered, though for what she wasn't certain.

For the lost years?

For him not knowing he had a daughter?

For hurting him by not showing enough love that he could have depended on it four years ago, depended on it enough not to have written that email?

Though surely pride had written that email—his pride, not her lack of love.

She didn't know.

He stood up without a word, walking back to the kitchen where the *mate* sat on the small kitchen table. Leaving Ella to restack the books, Caroline followed him, picking up the gourd and taking another sip, trying to get back to polite conversation because anything else was too painful.

'It must be an acquired taste,' she said, handing the gourd over to him and hoping he'd think she'd been considering *mate*, not love and the pain it caused as she'd sipped. 'And obviously very popular! We saw people drinking it everywhere—walking along the street in the city, even waiting at bus stops.'

'It is a custom not only in Argentina but all over South America.'

Caroline smiled but she knew it was a sad effort, memories of the past hammering in her head as they both tried gamely to keep the stupid conversation going.

'Strange, isn't it,' she said quietly, 'that we who talked about everything under the sun should be reduced to tourist-talk? But now that Ella has found her land legs after the journey, perhaps it is time for you to meet her properly.'

She turned, calling to her daughter, who'd selected a book with a red cover, settled herself into a tattered armchair and was reading herself a story from it. As it was almost certainly in Spanish and quite possibly a lurid medical text, Caroline wondered what Ella would choose to make of it. At the moment she was hooked on *The Three Robbers*, which also had a red cover, so possibly that was the story she was telling herself.

'Ella!'

The little girl looked up from the book as Caroline said her name.

'Come over here and meet Jorge properly.'

Caroline pronounced his name as best she could, although she'd never fully mastered the deep-throated 'h' sound that was more like an *x* than the English pronunciation of *g*.

Ella came to stand beside her, her lips moving so Caroline knew she was trying out the name.

'Hor-hay?' she queried, and to Caroline's surprise Jorge knelt in front of her and politely shook her hand.

'It is a hard name for you to say,' he told her. 'Perhaps before long we can find something else for you to call me, something easier.'

'*My* name is easy,' Ella, ever confident, ever up for a chat, told him. 'It was my grandma's name—the grandma I didn't know. I knew my other grandma but I don't really remember her very much because she went to be a star in heaven when I was only two.'

The child's innocent remark made Jorge glance up at Caroline and saw pain whiten her cheeks, the wound of her mother's death still raw, but the child—Ella—was talking again and he turned back to her, fascinated by the resemblance to his younger self, captivated by a small person who was now telling him about the big plane that had flown up in the sky.

'Not high enough to see my two grandmas who are stars,' she explained seriously, 'but too high to see down to the ground except when we went over some mountains before the plane came down again. Mummy says you used to go walking in those mountains and maybe when I'm a bit bigger I could go too.'

Not all the words were crystal clear but her story still came through, each syllable tightening a band around his chest, the innocent chatter of the child all but suffocating him.

'Mummy talked about me?' he asked, though he knew it was wrong to question a child this way.

'She told me lots of stories about her friend Hor-hay who worked with her in—'

She broke off to look up at Caroline.

'Where was it, Mummy?'

'Africa,' Caroline supplied, and the restraint in her voice suggested she'd have preferred to put her hand over her daughter's mouth to stop the revelations rather than helping out with the conversation.

'Afica!' Ella declared triumphantly, then she pointed at the gourd, still in Jorge's hand. 'Can I have some of that?'

He passed the gourd to her, letting her hold it but

keeping his hand on it as well. He was vaguely aware of Caroline's anxious 'Is it cool enough now?' but mostly he was swamped by unnameable—even unfathomable—emotions as, for the first time, he shared *mate* with his daughter.

'Yuk!'

So she didn't take to it, but that mattered little. She would, in time, grow accustomed to the taste.

In time?

Was he seriously considering getting involved in this child's life?

How could he, living as he did, virtually a hermit?

But even as the objection surfaced he remembered that his bare existence in this place where he felt most at peace was coming to an end—and soon. Nine days from now the local government was taking over the clinic, and he was returning to Buenos Aires to be with *his* father, to live with the man who had first taught him the strength of love.

Ella was telling him an involved tale about a doll Caroline had made her leave at home, but the words barely penetrated, his brain swamped by the revelation that peace might be achievable in other places if the right elements were in place—elements like a wife and a child…

Not without love, common sense reminded him. In his search for peace after the accident he'd tried relationships without love, and peace was the last thing they had brought him.

Impossible, too, that Caroline could love him. Not after the way he'd treated her. Uncertain of his future, thinking he might be an invalid for life and not wanting to tie the woman he loved to him, he'd deliberately worded that email to kill whatever love she'd felt for him, driving a spear of harsh, hurtful words into her heart.

Caroline's heart ached as she watched father and daughter together. With her usual sunny disposition, once Ella had felt comfortable in the hut she was chatting away to Jorge as if she'd known him for ever. If only she had! If only Jorge had been there to share the early joys and triumphs, though he'd have been there for the bad times too, in that case, the endless sleepless nights, the time they'd battled croup, her mother's death.

Don't think about that now—think positive, think forward. There are obviously two bedrooms in this hut, so I *will* work with him. One month isn't long but surely it will give me time to learn if what he said was true, or if it was his stupid pride that split us up.

'Caroline?'

His voice suggested he'd spoken while she'd been lost in her own determined thoughts, but she'd missed whatever question it might have been.

'Jorge?' she responded, feeling almost light-headed with the sheer delight of being close to him and saying his name again. Not that she could let such pathetic reactions show. She, too, had pride, and she wasn't going to fling herself at this man and be rebuffed again. No, time would tell her if any of the fire that had flared between them still existed, and until she'd seen some hint of his, she would have to keep hers well tamped down.

'I was saying you can't stay here, but there is a hotel not far away. It is clean, the food is excellent, and there is a big *plaza*—a park—with a children's playground just across the road. If you insist on this foolish notion of working in the clinic, there is a bus you can catch each day, a small commute.'

She found a smile, knowing it would hide the hurt caused by him pushing her away, although it was only what she'd expected.

'No, I'll stay here,' she said, picking Ella up to cover her hesitation before replying. 'The information on the internet said there was simple accommodation for visiting doctors and simple is okay with me. We've got a sleeping mat and sleeping bags. We'll be fine. Also, staying here, eating meals with you, Ella will get used to you and when you have time off, she'll be happy to be with you.'

Ella joined the conversation at this stage, putting her hand on Caroline's cheek to turn her face.

'Are we really staying here, Mummy, in this little house? With the kids outside to play with?'

Jorge heard the words and knew he'd lost the first battle of this war he didn't fully understand. But looking at the child clinging to her mother, he wondered just how hard it was for Caroline to be parted from the little charmer who was her daughter, to go to work and leave Ella in someone else's care.

And was he thinking this to stop himself thinking about the pair of them living here, sharing his house, his meals, always there, tormenting him with their closeness? It would be bad enough being near Caroline while they worked, but to have her in his home as well?

A totally inappropriate excitement sizzled to life

within him but he ignored it, using the image that confronted him in the mirror each morning to douse it. Most normal women would react with revulsion and although he doubted Caroline, who had seen the worst things people could do to each other, would be revolted, what he feared most from her was pity.

As if to remove himself from his thoughts, he reminded himself it was only for a couple of weeks—nine days to the handover and a few more days after that to settle the new doctor into the clinic. He crossed to the front door.

'I suppose if you insist on staying I can hardly throw you out. I'll get your bags.'

But once outside he simply looked at the bags, not wanting to lift them, not wanting to carry them into his home, fighting the anger rising once again at Caroline's intrusion into his life, for all it was probably justified.

Was his apparent co-operation prompted by a genuine desire to get to know his daughter, Caroline wondered, or was there some deeper ploy behind him giving in?

Whatever! At least he was gone for a while and she could breathe normally again. She gave Ella a hug and set her down, telling her she could go outside and play with the children, but not to wander off. She'd already checked she could see the children from the window, so she could keep watch unobtrusively.

A shadow darkened the doorway and she glanced across to see not Jorge but a younger man, carrying the two backpacks into the hut.

'Jorge remembered an appointment in the city, he was already late,' the young man explained. 'I am Juan, his assistant, a kind of nurse now but studying medicine at the university.'

Politeness insisted Caroline cross the room to shake his hand, but she couldn't help casting an anxious glance out the door at the same time.

'Do not worry about the little girl,' Juan told her. 'My grandmother is there, she watches the children all day. Some of them, their mothers work, but others just come to play. My grandmother says it keeps her young to be with the children.'

'I'm sure it does,' Caroline agreed, 'but it is a great kindness she does as well, for it's hard for mothers to leave their children to go to work. I know it!'

Juan smiled shyly and was about to back out the door when Caroline realised that with Jorge gone and Ella happily playing, she was at a loose end.

'Would it be all right if I visited the clinic?'

Before Juan could answer, Jorge appeared.

'Did Juan tell you I have to go? I'm sorry, but the appointment is with a government official and I'm already late.'

'Juan explained, and I was asking if I could visit the clinic.'

She saw the reluctance in his face but as the purpose of the article on the internet had been to attract volunteer doctors to the clinic, he could hardly refuse to let her work there.

'Your vaccinations are up-to-date?' he queried, impatience edging the words.

'Hep A, Hep B, typhoid and yellow fever. We've both had them, as Ella was able to handle them now she's over two, although I'm reasonably sure they were only precautionary.'

Ha! she thought, savouring a moment of triumph that he couldn't turn them away for health reasons.

Jorge hesitated.

'Go to your appointment, I'll be fine,' she told him. He frowned at her and turned away. He'd probably have liked to growl as well, although in front of Juan…

But when he and Juan had left, Caroline forgot about visiting the clinic and sank down into an armchair, taking a deep, replenishing breath. She was so far from fine she wondered if she'd ever reach such a place again. Physically and mentally exhausted, her body aching with the effort of pretending Jorge meant nothing more to her than the father of her child, she now had to wonder, seriously, if this was not the very worst decision she had ever made.

From the first moment she'd set eyes on him, all the love she'd felt for him had come rushing back. Oh, it had been there all along, in a dull ache somewhere inside her, sharper pain at times like Ella's birth, her mother's death, and silly times, like when Ella had taken her first faltering steps, but seeing him again, hearing his voice, watching as he moved his hands in conversation, the longing to go to him and hold him in her arms had been so great she'd only barely managed to hide it.

Or she hoped she'd hidden it.

She closed her eyes but his image was graven in her mind, chiselled as deeply as the gouges he'd made in the door. Thinking back over the encounter—surely there was a more appropriate word for such a cataclysmic moment in her life—she began to believe her doubts had been more realistic than her original excitement. Jorge had shown no sign—not a glimmer—of the kind of love she still felt for him.

So maybe the email had been the truth, not the hurtful outpouring of stupid pride!

Which left her where?

Her determination that Ella would know her father and that he should play some part in her upbringing remained. By working here with him, she, Caroline, could get a sense of the man he had become and perhaps make a feasible plan for the future. Part of her decision to come had rested on the fact that with her mother dead and her small estate finalised, she and Ella had had nothing to keep them in Australia. She'd accepted that if Jorge's life's work was here, then here was where they'd have to live.

Oh, she'd *hoped* for love, hoped she might be able to break through whatever barriers he'd built up to protect himself, but she wasn't going to beg or plead and in doing so make a fool of herself if his love had been a lie all along.

A sense of utter helplessness brought tears to her eyes, but she'd cried enough for Jorge in the past. Now was the time for action. Ella's future was more important than her own pathetic need for love, so she would have to focus on that—on finding a way to stay somewhere close to Jorge, so he could be a father to his child.

And you? her heart mocked. *You'll* be able to see him regularly and not reveal the love you still feel for him?

She'd *have* to! That was all there was to it.

And having made the decision, she went to the doorway where Juan had dropped their backpacks. She heaved hers onto her shoulder, picked up Ella's little koala pack and walked into what she assumed was the spare bedroom, blinking in surprise when she saw the elaborate, wooden, four-poster bed and the polished wooden chest of drawers squeezed in beside it.

Like the old but so comfortable leather armchair, bizarre furnishings for the simple hut Jorge and the young men had built.

Thinking of him toiling in the broiling sun, determination pushing him through the pain of tight healing muscles and recalcitrant tendons, she put her hand against the wall, feeling its warmth and with it the warmth of the man she'd loved.

Was he still there, inside the scarred skin and mended bones?

And if he was, would she be able to find him?

The cry came from behind the hut, not from the direction of the clinic, and the pain in the sound had Caroline reacting automatically. A child lay on the dry, rusty-red ground, gasping for breath, and, unable to understand what the excited children were telling her, she felt first for an obstruction in his mouth.

Juan came running from the clinic, speaking to the children, while a woman Caroline assumed was his grandmother herded the little ones together, taking hold of Ella's hand as she kept them back from the fallen boy.

'He just fell down, the children said,' Juan told her.

Pleased he was there to translate for her, she asked

if the boy was an epileptic—did he have a history of seizures? When the answer was no, she asked about allergies—did the children know if the boy had been bitten by something?

The child was breathing, but the harsh rasping sounds of his breath suggested it was an effort. Caroline lifted him in her arms and though Juan protested, she insisted she could carry him to the clinic, hesitating only long enough to turn to the woman who held Ella's hand and receive a reassuring nod in reply.

'I'm just going to give this boy some medicine,' she said to Ella, 'I'll be back soon. You stay with—'

'Mima,' the woman said, while Ella, who'd obviously been told, echoed the word.

'Mima,' Caroline repeated.

Inside the clinic she set her patient down on an already prepared table and began a proper examination. His blood pressure was low, and a redness appearing on his skin suggested an anaphylactic reaction, though to what she didn't know.

Juan had produced an oxygen mask and was fitting it to the child's face, before adjusting the flow.

'Do you know if you have epinephrine in the clinic?' Caroline asked her helper. 'The adrenalin solution used for anaphylactic shock.'

'We have adrenalin solution,' Juan told her.

He unlocked a tall metal cabinet on one side of the small room and delved around in it, returning to Caroline's side with a tray on which he'd placed a box of ampoules and a syringe, swabs and antiseptic and a little metal kidney dish, something Caroline hadn't seen for years. She checked the medication and the dosage on the ampoules before breaking one open and drawing up the solution. Asking Juan to tell the boy what they were doing, she took a swab from the tray Juan had carried and swabbed the boy's thigh, then slid the needle in, forcing the liquid slowly into the muscle.

'We'll give that five minutes and take his blood pressure again. If it hasn't improved, he might need more.'

Before Juan could reply there was a clamour outside and a woman burst into the treatment room, already near capacity with the patient, treatment table, a chair, the cabinet and two workers.

'This is his mother,' Juan explained, before speaking rapidly to the woman.

Caroline acknowledged the woman with a smile, but her attention was all on her patient. Was he breathing more easily now? Had it been so simple? She began a full examination of the boy's skin, beginning with the parts she could see as she didn't want to disturb him too much by turning him over.

'Ah!' She pointed to a raised red welt just below her patient's right ankle. 'It's a strange place, very low, for a wasp or bee sting, but perhaps you have ants here that cause this reaction.'

Juan seemed to consider this. He spoke to the mother once again.

'I do not know of ants that can do this and his mother says he has been bitten by ants before. But she says the boys have been playing near the jacaranda trees and sometimes bees crawl into the bells of the fallen flowers.

He may have angered a bee by stepping on a flower and accidentally stepping on the bee as well.'

'Ah!'

It seemed a logical explanation, and as the little boy was obviously more comfortable now, the drug must have worked.

'He will need to stay here for some hours,' she told Juan. 'Could you explain to the mother we need to watch him in case he gets sick again?'

Caroline had to wonder what Juan had said, for the woman seized both of Caroline's hands and pressed a kiss on each of them, her '*Gracias*' and '*Muchas gracias*' so fervent they would have broken through any language barrier.

'Is there somewhere we can put the boy where he'd be more comfortable and his mother could perhaps sit by his side?' Caroline asked.

'I will fix,' Juan told her. 'Are you one of the new doctors who are coming here to work?'

The question made Caroline realise that at no stage had Juan questioned her right to treat the child or her competency to act in the emergency. Obviously Jorge attracted enough foreign helpers for Juan to accept Caroline without question, which was a good thing as far as her campaign to stay was concerned. Knowing Jorge, she guessed that throughout his appointment part of his mind would be fixed on how quickly he could move Caroline out of his life. Now he'd had time to think, he'd have come up with some excuse or strategy, of that she had no doubt, but this was one battle she wasn't going to lose.

She left Juan to move the little boy, and took a look around. The room they'd been in was apparently the only treatment room, and in front of it was another room, little more than a lobby, where a few patients might be able to wait out of the sun. There were three chairs, a small table and tattered magazines, while all the walls were covered with posters, familiar in context although the messages appeared to be in a language other than Spanish. Probably the Toba language?

The posters adjured people to wash their hands, immunise their children, use sunscreen—or maybe it was insect repellent mothers were wiping on their children's arms. Another poster showed vegetables and fruit, piles of grains and milk, presumably suggesting good dietary habits—so nothing much changed in this wide world, Caroline decided as she peered into another small room that opened off the lobby.

It must be Jorge's office, for it had an old table and chair—obviously scrounged from somewhere—with papers piled across the surface of the table and more papers and files on top of the battered-looking filing cabinets that lined the walls. After visiting his house, Caroline wasn't surprised to see his medical textbooks in tall towers on the floor. In fact, she smiled, for although so much up-to-date information was available to doctors through the internet, she, too, liked to open a textbook when she was checking something.

Beyond the treatment room on one side and office on the other was a wide room that took up the whole of the back section of the building. There were three beds on one side and Juan was settling the little boy into one of these. An old man lay sleeping in the next one, while the third was empty. A stack of mattresses in the far corner on the other side of the room suggested that at times the 'hospital' could cater for more than three patients.

Juan must have seen her studying the stack as he came to her side and explained, 'In the worst of summer sometimes people come from far up north to visit their families who live here now. They come from their homes in the *bosque impenetrable*—the impenetrable forest—but their families have no room for them so Jorge says they can sleep here. Sometimes they are sick, even with TB, but they are afraid of treatment. Sometimes he can give them treatment, once he gains their… Is trust the English word?'

Caroline nodded, but she was thinking about Juan's explanation. She had read of the land covered with thorny trees and jungle where many Toba people still lived, a place where she could imagine armadillos still mooching along the ground and jaguars hiding on the branches of the trees, and where exotic birds still made their homes.

They must be tough, the Toba people, to have survived in that environment, and knowing that she understood a little more of why Jorge would wish to help the little community of them who had settled in Rosario but were having trouble making the transition to city life.

Having satisfied the city official that the handover of the clinic was proceeding according to plan, Jorge could hardly avoid driving back to the clinic. The handover might be going according to plan, but his life had been flung so far off track he wondered if he'd ever get it back to somewhere approaching normal.

He drove reluctantly out of the city, through the leafy suburbs towards the close-packed settlement of the Toba.

Where the woman he'd thrust out of his life four years ago awaited him?

He ran his fingers over the scarring on his right cheek, remembering his shock and horror when the bandages had come off, telling himself it didn't matter, knowing it did because the scars were only the visible signs of the damage to his body—damage that could well have been permanent.

Emailing her…

Now she was back, and he knew her well enough to understand that nothing short of an earthquake would move her, and as the region was relatively stable an earthquake was just as unlikely as the tsunami he'd wished for earlier. Not that he'd welcome either one—he'd not welcome anything that would put anyone in danger.

Perhaps he could pay someone to put a python in her bedroom—maybe even a giant anaconda. He sighed as he dismissed this new idea—knowing Caroline, instead of being frightened away, she'd strangle the creature and cook it for dinner.

Maybe—

Dios mio! Why was he thinking this way? Had the woman's appearance totally addled his brain? Was finding out he had a daughter turning him crazy?

Caroline was here, and here she'd stay, at least until she'd got what she'd come for.

Which was?

Estupido! The exclamation wasn't aimed at Caroline but at himself, for as he'd asked himself the question a jolt of desire had rattled his body. Of course she wasn't here to see him—well, not as the lover he had been, although memories of the love they'd shared, the passion, the heat and the fire set his body alight.

He could see her body now, shadowy as it had always been in the dim light of the small round hut, welcoming, enveloping, becoming one with his—sharing the journey to oblivion with him as they tried to blot out the horrors they had seen during the day…

CHAPTER THREE

FRUSTRATION reawoke his anger. Love-making would be the furthest thing from Caroline's mind. She had come to shock him into doing what she wanted, come without warning. Come to ensure her daughter had a father.

Could he do that?

Be a father to the child?

At least the questions diverted him from thoughts of Caroline's motives and the impossibility of love.

He had the greatest example of fatherhood in the world, his father having been behind him all his life, teaching him, encouraging him, backing him in all he wished to do, but most of all loving him with an uncritical and unstinting devotion. His father was the rock he'd clung to when he'd returned from hospital in France, broken both physically and emotionally.

Everyone should have such a father!

But could he emulate the man he loved—be as good a father to Ella as his father had been to him?

Somewhere inside him a determination to do just that was beginning to grow, but weighed against it was the fact that involvement with Ella would mean involvement with Caroline, and if seeing her once had brought such chaos to his mind and body, how would he react to being with her on a regular basis?

No, best he knocked the whole thing on the head right now. Caroline was beautiful. She'd find a man and marry, thus providing a father figure for Ella.

Some other man being a father to his daughter? Guiding her through life, winning her love?

A pain he barely understood shuddered through him.

There had to be an answer, and it was up to him to find it, and soon, before gossip, which, although they were separated by hundreds of miles, inevitably reached his father. Once his father laid eyes on Ella, she would be his princess, the answer to all his dreams, the one gift he'd wanted so badly from his son but had accepted he might never be given…

His father…

Maldici—n! His father wouldn't have to wait for gossip to filter south. In just over a fortnight he, Jorge, was due to drive south to live with his father, to resume his medical career—some as yet unknown medical career in the city of his birth, to give back just a little of the love and devotion his father had spent on him.

'You can't stay here.'

It probably wasn't the best conversation-opener he'd ever managed, and he was becoming repetitive, but Caroline's arrival had put his own imminent departure right out of his mind, but remembering—remembering other things as well—he knew he had to get rid of her.

Now!

Her reply was a slight raising of her eyebrows as she glanced up from the book she held on her knee.

'My spoken Spanish is probably better than my reading of it, but I can follow enough of this account of the Toba people to know they were a very fierce tribe. They were never assimilated into the general population as other tribes were?'

She was doing this deliberately, changing the conversation to something she must know held his interest, and for a moment he nearly fell for it, explaining to her what he knew of the early European settlement of the northern Grand Chaco area and the Toba people.

Until he remembered why she was doing it. Diverting him.

He changed the conversation back to where *he'd* begun it.

'I won't be here myself in a couple of weeks,' he told her. 'I began the clinic to do something for myself as well as for the local people, and now the government is taking it over. My job here is done and I'm moving on.'

'Ah!' she said, setting down the book and looking up at him, her eyes snagging something in his chest. 'I wondered when Juan accepted me so readily. Then something he said made me think that perhaps you had some more permanent arrangement with other doctors, rather than relying on people giving up a short period of time.'

She looked as if she had more to say, but she'd already puzzled him enough.

'You were speaking to Juan? Did you go over to look at the clinic?'

She smiled—he wished she wouldn't do that—and stood up. He wished she wouldn't do that as well, because it brought her closer and he could feel the connection that had always been between them zinging in the air already.

'I should have told you when you came in,' she said, heading for the door, 'but you had a patient while you were away. Anaphylaxis. A little boy. I've kept him in. His mother's with him.'

Could that be true?

Of course it could!

Like strangling a snake, this woman could do anything and was usually around when any kind of anything needed doing. The grumpy thoughts dogged his footsteps as he trod behind her to the clinic. The little boy was fine, his mother far too effusive with her praise of Caroline—a trained monkey could have given an epinephrine injection.

Jorge wasn't sure why her competence was making him so angry. It couldn't possibly be because his libido was at war with his brain. He headed for his office, knowing she was following because every nerve ending in his back was standing to attention—probably saluting, if nerve endings could salute.

'Did you make a file? Write it up?'

'Juan did that for me,' the aggravating female replied. 'I didn't think my Spanish was up to it.'

'Why learn it at all?' he asked, and realised immediately he should have kept his mouth shut. All he was doing was giving her more reason to show her wonder-woman skills.

'I learned it for Ella. I've been sharing what I know with her, but it's not the same as having her grow up in a bilingual family, hearing both languages all her life. It's so much easier for children to learn at a young age—I see three-year-olds in the practice at home chattering away in Arabic or Vietnamese, then talking to me in English. By the time they're five most of them can act as translators for their parents if it's needed.'

He wanted so much to hate her, but how could he when every time she opened her mouth she revealed more that was good and worthy?

And best he didn't think about her mouth, the way his body was behaving. Best he not be beguiled by those lips and memories of what they had done to him in the past.

He wasn't angry now, Caroline realised, not *angry* angry, more grouchy—put out—as well he should be.

He'd had a tendency to grouchy, usually when unable to achieve miracles for the people they treated—unable to stop the wars and famines that made so many people's lives so insecure, their health so fragile.

Back then she'd found ways to divert him when the impossibility of it all had got him down—but though her body might ache with memories of those diversions, this wasn't the time to be considering them. Especially as her own anger at him for treating her as he had—for doubting her love—still burned beside the love inside her.

Yelling at him, bringing all the hurt out into the open,

would be a diversion, but what would it achieve—more distance between them when what she needed was some kind of neutral ground where they could work out a satisfactory arrangement for their daughter? Besides, apart from the grouchiness, he was handling this massive disruption in his life so smoothly she'd lose ground if she didn't match his…aplomb? She didn't think she'd ever done aplomb before but she hoped that was what she was managing.

There remained the issue of a diversion. She'd try a practical one.

'Should I find somewhere to buy some food? You weren't expecting visitors, particularly not a child. Ella will eat practically anything but I can't expect you to be feeding us.'

She saw anger flare again.

'Of course I will feed you,' he snapped. 'You are my guests, even if totally uninvited ones.'

'And unwelcome ones?'

She couldn't stop herself asking, although she knew the answer was sure to hurt.

'Definitely unwelcome. You've deliberately staged this—this reunion—' he spat the word at her '—to cause me maximum emotional disruption and physical inconvenience. The only worse way you could have played it would have been to go to my father's home. Perhaps you didn't think about that?'

Stricken by his words, Caroline could only stare at him, until her own anger came to her aid.

'You think I did this out of spite? Planned this deliberately to upset you? And why? To get back at you for having dumped me? For having ignored my letters and left me with a child to bring up on my own? Believe me, Jorge, I was over that a long time ago.'

'So why come now?'

She opened her mouth to tell the truth—to say she'd read about the extent of his injuries, seen his photo, seen the scars, and knowing him had guessed he'd pushed her away deliberately, believing her pity would be more hurtful than the pain of losing love.

But that would be tantamount to admitting she still loved him, and from his reaction to her arrival any love he'd ever felt for her was long gone.

So she told a lie, well, a partial lie, following right on the heels of the one where she was over the hurt he'd caused a long time ago…

'I could afford it now,' she said. 'Suddenly I had the money to take time off work and travel. Letters hadn't worked so I decided maybe seeing Ella would persuade you to become involved in her life.'

'You had no money before? You always worked? And how did you manage when Ella was a baby? Did you not breastfeed her?'

Well, as a diversion for his grumpiness it had certainly worked, but grumpy didn't begin to describe how the switch in conversation and those rude questions had made *her* feel.

'It was before my father found me and made up for twenty-eight years of neglect by leaving me his money,' she snapped. 'I *had* to work to keep us but, yes, I was breastfeeding. My mother, when she was in remission, cared for Ella. It's not that hard these days to freeze pouches of milk so there was a supply for Ella during the day.'

She gave him a glare she hoped was as cold as the pouches of frozen milk, mainly because his probing had reawoken the guilt she still felt at not being able to spend more time with both her baby and her ailing mother.

He'd been leaning against his desk and now he stepped towards her and for a moment she thought he was going to touch her—maybe even kiss her—though that, of course, was nothing more than wishful thinking.

As it turned out, he stopped just out of touching distance and said quietly, 'I do regret not being there to help you. I regret not opening the letter that would have told me of the child.'

And because her body had tensed for the kiss—as if!—she snapped again.

'Her name is Ella! It shouldn't be too hard for you to remember. And now it's getting late—it's been a big day. I need to sort out food, rescue Mima from her, and get her bathed and into bed.'

Now he did touch her, catching her arm as she spun away from him, the abrupt halting of her movement spinning her back so she landed up against his body.

His body—as hard as she remembered it—solid, chunky almost, the kind of body that would be a bulwark against anything the world could throw at her.

But that had been then, when she'd believed their love so great their souls had joined.

One slight move now and their lips would join. The air grew thick and still between them, desire throbbing in her body,a moment in time, stretching, stretching to forever—then he steadied her and stepped away, going behind his desk, sitting down, looking at the note Juan had made about the boy.

Had she imagined the shift in the atmosphere when he'd touched her? Imagined it because she'd have liked to think their mutual attraction still existed?

'I must find Ella,' she muttered, and backed out of the room, only to remember something and have to return. 'I didn't speak to the boy's mother about future bee stings or the danger they could be to him. Will you talk to her about having something on hand if he's stung again?'

Jorge looked up at the woman who hovered in his doorway. A few minutes ago he had nearly kissed her, the impulse brought on by a simple touch—his hand going out to halt her—and now he couldn't remember why. Something to do with her going shopping? Or had he been about to apologise for something?

He had no idea because the touch had set fire to something inside him and heat had sizzled in the air around them, thickening it like unseen smoke.

Well, he could forget about sizzle and thick air between them, she'd made it very clear she was over him long ago, yet she'd hesitated before answering that she couldn't afford to have come sooner and he'd sensed that might only be part of the truth.

Estúpido! That was what he was, to be feeling disappointment about these revelations. He'd deliberately worded his email to hurt her sufficiently that she wouldn't rush to his bedside and make a martyr of herself caring for him. Not that there was much of the martyr in Caroline, she was far too practical for that, and speaking of practical, he should go home and check what food he had. Maybe someone *would* have to go shopping.

At least a trip to the market would take him out of Caroline's orbit for a while.

With that decided he headed back to the hut, to find Caroline stripping the extremely grubby clothes off an extremely grubby small child.

'I played with the kids, Hor-hay,' Ella told him. 'Mummy should have changed my shoes first so my good shoes didn't get dirty but Mummy says we can clean them, and I can kick the ball a very long way.'

He looked at the naked child and felt a pang of some indescribable emotion deep inside him. Part ownership, although he knew no one could own another person, and part pride, that he had helped create this perfect little being, and part something else—wonder was the closest he could come to it.

'I have a big tub outside the back door where I do the washing. Do you want to have a bath in that?' he asked, pleased now he'd insisted on building his hut in the old way with the bench and tub outside. Beyond it he'd put in a shower, but the tub was where the local people bathed their infants.

'Will you help?' Ella asked. 'I can do my tummy and my legs and toes and arms and fingers, *and* my ears.' She threw a glare at Caroline as she added the last bit and he realised it must be a source of argument between them. Was she enlisting his aid against her mother? Could three-year-olds be so manipulative?

'Manipulator *par excellence*,' Caroline said drily, rolling the dirty clothes into a ball. 'Watch yourself!'

'I can do ears if you need help,' he told Ella, who was practising the new word she'd just heard. 'Manpitor,' issued from the small lips, the determination in her practice so charming, so delightful, his chest went tight with pain.

Again!

'I'll boil some water for the bath,' he said, needing to get away for a minute while he took stock of his feelings. It was okay to fall in love with his daughter, he told himself, but now he'd admitted that he found fears rising in the joy—fears for her safety, fears for her health, nameless fears…

The trouble was, falling in love with anyone, particularly a daughter, hadn't been part of his life plan. *His* life plan, carefully considered over months of difficult operations, painful treatment and rehabilitation, had been to avoid all emotion in the future. To cut himself off, not from feeling for others, from empathy, but from personal emotional involvement. His father's love he could handle. He could even cope with Antoinette's fussing for she'd been their housekeeper since he was a child, but beyond the safe realm of family, he didn't do emotion any more.

Or hadn't up until now, when the figure of a little girl earnestly practising the word 'manipulator' had stolen his heart.

'Right, I've run cold water in the tub—actually, it's lukewarm and she probably doesn't need too much hot in it.'

Caroline was standing behind him in the small kitchen area, Ella on her hip, a small, super-absorbent towel and a wash-bag in one hand.

'I can do better than that for towels,' he said, trying to come to terms with the sheer normality of Caroline's behaviour. She was calmly going about what had to be done as if she hadn't just arrived from halfway around the world and been reunited with her former lover, who had shown no sign of welcome, and now had to bathe her daughter in an outside tub.

Though the Caroline he'd known had rarely let anything faze her so it was only to be expected that she was calmer than he was, which, in itself, was enough to stir his anger again.

He carried the kettle out to the tub and poured the hot water in, a little at time, testing it in between. That done, he took the kettle back inside, away from small probing hands—fear again—and went to the big camphor-wood chest that had been his mother's, finding a thick, soft, white towel for his daughter.

Thoughts of his mother stilled his anger. How she would have loved this grandchild who might, in some way, have made up for the fact that she hadn't been able to have more children after him. He tucked the towel under his arm and went out to face the two females who had turned his life upside down. He couldn't be angry with the small one, but reserved the right as far as Caroline was concerned.

'Wow! Lovely white towel, so much better than our make-do ones.'

Her delight seemed genuine, and she finished washing

the soap off Ella and lifted the little girl out of the tub, handing her to him, so he wrapped her tightly and carried her inside, a warm, damp, squirming bundle of delight, chatting to him about the bath and ears and a towel she had at home.

'With princesses on it,' she finished, as he set her down on the big armchair to dry her properly.

'Princesses?' he queried.

He heard a soft warning, 'Don't ask,' from behind him, but it was already too late.

Ella was telling him about the princesses she knew, Cinderella—'that's like my name'—Ariel, and someone else he couldn't make out.

She hadn't realised how much it would hurt, Caroline thought, as she rummaged through the backpack for Ella's pyjamas, to see Jorge interacting with her daughter.

Their daughter.

She wasn't jealous, or at least she didn't think she was, but seeing them together made her ache for all the time the pair had missed out on—all the bath times and story times and playtimes—the good times and the not so good.

'No sense in getting maudlin,' she muttered to herself, and she left the sanctuary of the bedroom and returned to the living room, handing the pyjamas to Jorge and trying not to be affected when his hand shook slightly as he took them.

But that slight tremor in his hand made her realise just how great an emotional upheaval this must be for him, finding out he had a daughter, seeing the child, interacting with her.

Now, don't go feeling sorry for him. The mental warning was firm, but it didn't hold much strength. In fairness, she had to admit that he seemed to be handling the situation superbly.

The thought saddened her. His interaction was all with Ella—he was doing all he could to win her confidence—which, she thought gloomily, was wonderful. She, Caroline, might not have existed, except as someone to field his anger when he allowed emotion to creep through his iron-hard control.

Back when he'd touched her in his office, she'd thought that control might crack—had sensed something arc in the air between them—but she'd obviously been wrong and it was just as well because had they kissed, how well could she have hidden her own feelings?

Dismissing kisses from her mind, she concentrated on practical things.

'A meal? You said you have food, but I have some packages of noodles that only need boiling water added. I can fix that for Ella.'

'Noodles, noodles, I want noodles,' the little girl sang.

Her father looked up from the pyjamas he was turning over in his hands, Ella still towel-wrapped in front of him.

'Pyjamas?' he queried. 'It is only six o'clock.'

'She goes to bed at seven,' Caroline told him, though now she was remembering other things Jorge had told her about his country—about people not eating dinner until nine or ten at night, nightclubs opening at midnight but people rarely going there before two in the morning.

'But then there'd be no time for a promenade and ice cream,' he protested.

And right on cue, Ella bounced up and down, dropping the white towel on the packed earth floor of the hut, shouting, 'Ice cream, ice cream!'

'Tonight she will have to promenade in pyjamas,' Caroline said firmly. 'We have limited clothes and I washed the ones she had on today while she was in the bath and she'll need the clean set for tomorrow. Two clean sets tomorrow, judging by today's playtime.'

Jorge nodded and began the task of getting an excited, squirming child into pyjamas and finding the right holes for the right buttons in a garment that seemed to be nothing but holes and buttons.

'She's a restless sleeper—that's why she needs a sleepsuit.' Caroline knelt beside him to change a few buttons into the right holes, but it was a mistake. Try as she might to deny it, the attraction she had felt towards Jorge almost from their first meeting was still as strong as ever—perhaps even stronger, now that he was off limits.

Was he off limits?

He was as far as she didn't intend revealing her feelings for him, but personally off limits? Was he in a relationship? And if so, how would the revelation of Ella's existence affect it?

The thought of him in a relationship—normal though that would be—sent an icy chill racing through her blood. She straightened up and told Ella to get a book from her backpack then faced her child's father.

But how to ask?

'Is this going to be a problem for you in your personal life?'

She blurted it out, and could practically see the question hovering in the air between them so hurried on. 'I mean, the article said you were a bachelor but that doesn't mean— I mean, you might have married and divorced, have other children. Is this a personal disruption for you?'

He scowled at her.

'You mean is finding out I have a child not enough of a personal disruption, but might it affect a whole family? And you didn't consider that before your mad dash across the Pacific?'

'The article *said* you were a bachelor!' Caroline repeated, standing up for herself, although inwardly cursing herself for not thinking it through before she'd rushed into her arrangements. 'And if you have a girlfriend or a partner, surely that's okay. Even other children. Eventually Ella would have to meet them and they meet her, so what harm is done?'

His scowl deepened, but as the room had grown shadowy she could barely see his eyes, let alone read any expression in them.

'I have no wife, no current lover, no—no *other* children. Satisfied?'

And with that he stalked out of the hut.

Why was he letting her upset him this way? Jorge asked himself the question as he strode towards the clinic. Why had questions about his private life angered him so much?

He'd have liked to think it was because she was so insensitive she hadn't considered how unlikely it was for a man who looked like him to find love, but that would be a coward's way out. His visible scars were only reminders of the deeper ones—of the damage the explosion had left inside him, physically and mentally, of the darkness that had come upon him and the long struggle he'd had to come to terms with the man he was now.

He'd had women love him since the accident, he just hadn't been able to love them back. And *that* was what had angered him! That the woman against whose love he'd measured other loves should ask such questions—that was what had hurt!

All was quiet at the clinic, the boy gone home, the place lit but only a nurse on duty for emergencies. He had no reason to linger there, although there was always paperwork, but back at his hut his daughter would be eating her dinner…

Caroline was waiting for the kettle to boil when he walked back into the hut. He looked across at her and some trick of the late afternoon light coming through the square hole in the wall that served as a window showed the depth of the scarring on his cheek.

Once again she longed to press her hand against it, while her mind raced through the likelihood of other scars, picturing them on his body—his beautiful body—not to mention the damage beneath the skin, physical and mental damage too terrible to contemplate…

Determined not to give in to the ache inside her, especially now Jorge had lifted Ella from the chair and had sat down with her on his knee to read the story to her, Caroline poured water onto the noodles and while she waited for them to swell and cool, she crossed to the stacks of books and pulled out the biggest of them, setting them down on a chair in the kitchen and putting her absorbent towel over them to protect them from spilled noodles.

'When the story's finished,' she said to the pair in the armchair, pleased she sounded so calm when inside her mind and body emotions whirled in senseless twists and turns—pleasure at the domesticity of the scene in front of her, slight envy that Ella had adopted Jorge as a friend so easily, the agony of realising her love for him was still so strong and, worst of all, the stress of hiding how she felt.

He carried Ella into the kitchen and set her down on the raised-up seat.

'Is she safe there?' he asked, and Caroline felt a pang of sympathy for him. If *her* insides were in turmoil, how must his be?

'She sits on books at home,' she replied. 'Fat telephone books.'

Ella was spooning noodles into her mouth, taking her time because she hated spilling any.

'She's a neat freak when it comes to eating,' Caroline explained, but even as she said the words she realised that every tiny detail she revealed must cut deeply into Jorge's emotions, that she knew these things about their child while he'd been cut off from learning them as she'd developed.

'I'm sorry,' she said quietly, remembering she'd said it earlier, and now, as then, she wasn't entirely sure what she was apologising for.

But he seemed to understand for he nodded, but not before she'd seen the pain in his eyes and read there his very real regrets.

'Finished!'

Ella set down her spoon and looked at Jorge.

'Ice cream now?'

Caroline had to laugh. She hoped it wouldn't take too long for Jorge to learn not to say anything he didn't want repeated in his daughter's hearing.

'Ice cream,' he agreed. 'We need to walk a little distance. Perhaps you would like to ride on my back.'

'Piggyback?' Ella asked, her delight at this idea obvious.

Caroline lifted her off the chair and settled her on Jorge's back, then for one craven instant considered telling them to go without her. The togetherness of it all—the family thing that was happening already—was upsetting her in ways she didn't understand.

But though she knew Jorge and would trust him with her daughter's life, he was still a stranger to Ella, for all she'd taken to him.

She followed them out the door and into the dusk.

'Look!' he said, jerking her out of thoughts she didn't want to have.

He was pointing west to the vivid colours splashed across the sky, the bare branches of a leafless tree making a tracery of black patterns against the scarlet, pink and orange.

'It's beautiful,' Caroline murmured. 'We don't look up enough, too busy looking where we're going next to appreciate what's here around us now.'

He looked at her and smiled, and the pain of her love for him all but exploded in her chest. Yes, his smile was a little lopsided now, and there was grey in the prickle of hair on his close-cropped head, but he was still Jorge, the man she'd loved.

Still loved…

She looked so beautiful, standing there looking at the sunset, that Jorge had to move away. To stay would be to fall in love again—if he'd ever fallen out of love with her. And while he might want her with every fibre of his being, he couldn't saddle her with the man he had become—couldn't trust that all she had to give him would be pity, for to be pitied by Caroline would surely kill him.

CHAPTER FOUR

'ICE CREAM!' his daughter reminded him, patting him on the head. He headed down the alley towards the main road where a small ice-cream cart usually stood at this time of the evening.

The van was there but it was the white pole on the pavement close by that attracted Caroline's attention.

'What is this?' she asked, studying the side of it that had its message in the Toba language.

'Walk around it. You will understand when you find the Spanish.'

'"May peace prevail on earth",' she read. 'How lovely. The other languages?'

'One in Toba, one in Guaran'—Toba is a sub-language of Guaran'—and one in Italian, representing the cultures that have contributed to the development of the neighbourhood. There is another such pole near the National Flag Memorial. They are called Peace Poles.'

He had squatted down to allow Ella to climb off his back and now he lifted her so she could see the variety of ice creams available. Caroline was still walking around the pole, reaching out to touch the words painted on it.

'We have to believe it will happen, don't we?' she

said quietly, and he remembered that there was so much more to her than her beauty—so much more that he had fallen in love with.

'I'll have choc'late,' Ella announced, breaking into his thoughts, which was just as well. He ordered her ice cream and made sure he grabbed a handful of napkins to mop up any spills. He carried the ice cream for her across the road to a small park bench and when she'd settled on it, handed it to her.

To his surprise she was as careful eating ice cream as she was eating noodles, both messy dishes for a child, but the little pink tongue licked around the edge, never allowing a melting drop to trickle down the thick waffle cone. He was so fascinated by her actions he didn't realise Caroline wasn't with them until she joined him, a cone in each hand.

'I didn't know what you'd like so I went for coffee and strawberry. Which do you want?'

It was too domestic to be true—too huge a leap in his life—so it seemed as if he'd been transported to another place in time, another world where nothing was quite real. But he'd lived with pretence for a long time—pretence that he wasn't in pain, pretence that his scars didn't matter, pretence that he didn't love—

No, he wasn't going there.

'Coffee would be great,' he said, no pretence needed but guessing she'd like the strawberry.

She handed it to him and sat down beside her daughter—their daughter—and he saw immediately where the 'neat freak', as Caroline had called Ella, had got her ice-cream eating techniques. For Caroline licked just as neatly, turning the cone in her hand, catching any potential drip before it could cause a mess.

He stood and watched the pair of them, so different in looks, licking at their ice creams, his own melting so sticky liquid was running down his fingers.

This was definitely an out-of-body experience, a dream, but if it wasn't, what next? There might be a temporary truce between himself and Caroline, but where did they go from here?

Anger, although tamped down, still burned inside him. It was where to aim it that bothered him. At fate? Too easy! At himself? Of course, this situation was, at least in part, his own fault for being so determined to return all her mail unopened.

But try as he may, he couldn't help but direct most of the anger at her. She'd kept his child from him then staged this grand reconciliation scene. There had to have been another way to have done this! And how hard had she really tried to contact him?

'Your ice cream's melting all down your hand.'

He looked at her and realised *all* his anger should be directed at himself. At himself for still loving her…

Watching him standing there, looking down at her and Ella, the ice cream melting in his hand, Caroline felt a surge, not of love this time but of pity for him. To have had so much emotion dumped on him, a man, she suspected, who had avoided any emotional connections for the past four years!

'It's impossible to even try to absorb it all at once,' she said quietly. 'Let's just take one day at a time. Can you tell me a little about the settlement and the clinic?

I know the people came from up north, but apart from that…'

'Floods and mechanisation in agriculture in the north left a lot of the Toba people without homes or jobs. Why they came to Rosario I'm not sure, but they settled in this area, building, as you saw, basic shelters. At first the government's reaction was to build affordable housing, but there was never enough. Now it's different.'

She remembered things they'd spoken of in Africa, how giving people things—housing, food, clothing—was not as effective as helping them arrange it for themselves.

'Enabling?' she queried, using a word that had been coming into vogue back then.

Now he smiled and though her heart leapt she reminded herself it wasn't personal. He, too, was remembering.

'Yes, the government is taking that attitude,' he told her. 'They are trying to develop an environment where the people, using their own resources, can find solutions to their housing problems in particular. The government is there to offer resources and technical help, but the movement is being generated by the people themselves.'

'And your work here is done?'

Ella had finished her ice cream and was nodding sleepily, but Caroline was reluctant to return to the hut where the four walls enfolded Jorge and herself in false intimacy. She lifted the tired child onto her knee, holding her gently, rocking slightly, knowing Ella would soon be asleep.

Jorge looked down at what could be a picture entitled *Mother and Child* and sadness overcame the simmering anger. He threw the soggy remainder of his ice cream into a bin, wiped his hands on the napkins, and returned to the bench.

'I will carry her home,' he said, and though he sensed Caroline wanted to protest, she stood up and handed the child to him. The little girl was heavy with sleep, and slumped against his chest, but the warmth of her body, the trust in the little arms that snaked around his neck, brought back the disturbance of feelings he'd had earlier when he'd seen her body and felt the connection between them for the first time.

The connection of blood!

Back at the hut, Caroline opened the door.

'I should have looked properly earlier. Is the bed in the spare bedroom made up? If it is we can slide her straight into it. It's not worth waking her to clean her teeth.'

Teeth-cleaning? For the first time in that momentous day it occurred to Jorge that there was more to fatherhood than falling in love with his daughter. He'd have to think about things like teeth-cleaning and a properly balanced diet—noodles and ice cream surely didn't count—and then there'd be kindergarten and school and—

'Bed? Made up?' Caroline repeated, and he shook away the myriad questions that were threatening to swamp him. How *often* should she clean her teeth? After every meal? Every snack? And was kindergarten good or bad for little people? *He'd* gone when he was three…

'It's made up,' he told Caroline, and followed her as she walked to the second bedroom, pleased he'd installed solar panels on the roof of his hut so she could turn on lights to see her way. She folded back the bed covers and he placed the sleeping child in it, pulling the sheet up over her then brushing the wayward curls off her face.

'That's her done till morning,' Caroline said, leading him out of the room, although he'd have liked to stay and just looked at the miracle that had come into his life—no matter she had brought such troubling questions. 'Most nights she sleeps right through, which is a blessing.'

He forced himself to leave the room, thinking maybe an early dinner would be the best idea. Caroline would be tired. She could eat and go to bed. Once again he thanked the heavens that he'd put in solar power. To have to eat with her by lamplight would have been too much to handle, for lamplight threw shadows as powerfully beguiling as a magician's tricks.

In the kitchen, he found the makings for *carbonada*—dried beans instead of beef, but he had corn and pumpkin and some other vegetables for the stew. With some flatbread Juan's wife had made only that morning, it would do for dinner.

He felt rather than heard her come out of the bedroom and not wanting to look at her again, even in electric light, said, without turning, 'Did you see the shower out the back when you were exploring earlier? It's fairly rudimentary but the water should be warm—I made my own solar water-heating system with a big rubber bag that sits on the roof of the bath-house. Test the water as sometimes it gets too hot, and don't drink it—don't even clean your teeth in it. I buy it from a truck that comes around but although it's meant to be safe I don't trust it. Our drinking water comes in large plastic drums. You might have noticed one by the outside tubs.'

He'd shut himself away again, Caroline realised as she returned to the bedroom and dug into her backpack for her toiletries bag.

Why?

Had putting Ella into bed upset him?

Did he fear *any* kind of sentimentality?

Yet earlier they'd shared the beauty of the sunset and she'd believed he'd opened himself up, just a little, to her. Was he closed off now because he feared a fleeting moment might break through whatever barriers he'd erected within himself?

She dug further into her backpack and found the long, loose cotton pyjama pants, black with yellow bananas on them, and the yellow T-shirt she wore with them. Good thing she hadn't splurged on sexy lingerie.

The bath-house was out the back, he'd said, which meant she'd have to walk past him to go through the back door. Or she could go out the front and walk around, which would be plain stupid and a dead giveaway that he was affecting her far more than she was, apparently, affecting him. So deep breath, and here we go!

Another loud cry from outside caught her in mid-stride.

'Jorge, Jorge!'

The desperation in the cry made Caroline drop her clothes and follow him through the door. A light above the clinic door showed a macabre scene, two small men, supporting between them a third, all three seemingly covered in blood.

Jorge had reached the trio, speaking to them in what must be their native language, helping them into the clinic.

'Only this man is injured,' he said to Caroline when he realised she'd followed him. He was lifting the patient onto the table in the treatment room as he spoke, shooing the others out.

Caroline looked with horror at the man's left leg, which was minus half a foot.

'They've tied a tourniquet around his leg but he's still losing far too much blood. I'll get some fluid running into him then tidy up the main wound. If you could suture the cuts on his hands and arms, it would be a great help.'

'But, Jorge, he needs a hospital,' she objected. 'There are hospitals here, five, I think I read, in the city and in the outlying areas as well. You can't expect to care for him here.'

Jorge's dark eyes glanced briefly at her.

'Later!' he said firmly. 'I will explain later. In the meantime, if you will help, Juan will sit with Ella.'

Apparently taking her agreement for granted, he spoke quickly to Juan who'd appeared from out the back, then unlocked and opened the tall metal cabinet, waving his hand to show her it should contain whatever she might need. Knowing Jorge's task was urgent, she searched for what she'd need herself. A couple of pairs of gloves, saline for flushing out the wounds, antiseptic for cleaning the skin around them, local anaesthetic and sutures. She found a tray leaning against the cabinet and stacked the things she needed on it, then carried it to the head of the table, setting it down beside the man's head.

His skin was grey—probably with pain as well as loss of blood—and she knew they had to work swiftly. But as she unwound the dirty cloth wrapped around his arms and hands she felt nausea rise in her stomach.

'These are defensive wounds,' she whispered to Jorge. 'He's been attacked.'

'Just stitch him up.' Jorge spoke quietly, calming her with his voice, and she remembered that first and foremost she was a doctor. It wasn't her business how a patient came to need her skills, only that she must help him. This had been her weakness in Africa, wanting to do more to help the refugees they'd treated there. Yes, they'd been able to improve their lives in small ways and certainly improve their health, but she'd had to learn not to get involved in their struggle to return to their homelands, or to try to understand the reasons they had fled.

She wrapped a clean cloth around one of the man's arms and concentrated on the other, swabbing the area around the deep cuts, shuddering as she imagined the axe or machete—what else could make such wounds?—cutting into the man's flesh.

'I'm giving him a general anaesthetic. It will be more effective as we'd need more locals than we have on hand. This is Lila, one of our nurses. She will watch him.'

Caroline said hello to the middle-aged woman who was placing a mask over the patient's mouth and nose as calmly as if a man minus a part of his foot was an everyday occurrence in the clinic. She had also, to Caroline's surprise, produced a monitor and was attaching leads to the man's bare chest so they could read his heart and lung movements as they worked.

'Right to go,' Jorge said, and Caroline saw him carefully pulling back the skin on the man's foot, flushing the wound, preparing to cut away more bone so it wouldn't protrude as the healing skin shrank.

She knew the horror she was feeling was probably reflected on her face so wasn't surprised when Jorge's next reminder was far harsher.

'Go,' he ordered, and she turned her attention to her own job, flushing the gaping wounds before carefully drawing them together, suturing the skin, aware, as she'd always been in Africa, that supplies were probably limited so she had to space the sutures close enough to hold the skin closed but not so close she wasted precious resources.

But as she worked, although ninety-nine per cent of her concentration was on her patient, that one per cent sped away, back to a street scene in Africa where, in Jorge's company, she'd once recoiled from the sight of a badly maimed beggar. She'd tried to explain to Jorge that it wasn't revulsion that had made her flinch but the helplessness she had felt at the fact that some scars and malformations couldn't be fixed and how unfortunate it was that so much of a person's self-worth was tied up in how he or she looked.

Had Jorge remembered that flinch as he'd lain in

hospital in France? Had he imagined she'd flinch from him? Did that explain why he'd pushed her away?

She finished with the deep wound at the base of the man's thumb, probing first to see if there might be nerve or tendon damage, wondering at the same time if it had been the memory of her recoil—and his reading of it—that had determined Jorge to send the email.

'All we can do is sew him up,' Jorge said quietly to her, apparently looking up from his task to see her hesitation. 'It is likely he will have it cut open again next week. See the other scars he has?'

So Caroline once again pushed the past back where it belonged and sewed, putting dressings over the wounds as she completed her stitching. She moved around the table and unwrapped the other arm, and began again, unaware of the passing of time until she was done, and Jorge touched her arm and she stepped back from the table.

'Lila will clean up here and move him into our little ward and we have a night nurse who will watch over him and call if we are needed. I've given him a massive dose of antibiotics and have prepared morphine for him if he wakes in pain. We'll go home and eat our dinner if it hasn't completely spoiled.'

Caroline had stripped off her gloves and was using a wet cloth Lila had handed her to wipe her arms, but what she needed most badly was a shower.

Not to mention an explanation!

The shower took precedence.

'Will dinner spoil more if I take five minutes for a shower?' she asked, and Jorge smiled at her.

'Could I deny it to you when you have helped me out this way? I, too, need a shower, but I can have one here. We'll meet back at the hut.'

There had been absolutely nothing in his tone of voice to suggest that the idea of showering together, as once they would have done, had even flashed through his mind, but as Caroline made her way back to the hut she had a stupid longing for what might have been.

Except if he *hadn't* ever loved her they probably wouldn't still be together, let alone sharing a shower.

Jorge stood beneath the tepid water, running the soap over the puckered skin on his torso. Caroline had begun her journey back to Australia, frantic with worry over her mother's diagnosis of breast cancer, when the rocket had hit their small hospital. He knew only what he'd been told of the accident, remembering nothing until he'd woken up in hospital in France, his body broken in so many places he'd wondered if it would ever heal. He'd been splinted and bandaged from head to toe, but not for long, the bandages being removed so he could be plunged into a bath where dead burnt skin was carefully peeled away.

This treatment had been agonising, but no more agonising than his decision to break up with Caroline. Uncertain not only whether he'd live or die, but whether he *wanted* to live or die, his one seemingly rational decision had been to send her the email that would keep her from rushing to his side at the first available opportunity. He'd told himself it was because he knew her mother needed her but he knew the motivating factor had been not wanting to see horror and revulsion in her eyes, not wanting the burden of the pity he knew would be in her heart.

He turned off the water and dried himself, slipping on a loose T-shirt—all his clothes were loose these days, illness having stripped off the weight and physical labour replacing it with muscle—and a pair of *bombachas*, the baggy cotton trousers worn by horsemen and outdoor workers all over the country.

Now to face the woman who had brought such chaos into his life and such confusion to his mind.

She was already in his small kitchen area, stirring the mixture in the pot, wearing long, loose pants not unlike the ones he wore, only hers had bright bananas all over them, and on top she wore a faded yellow T-shirt.

'Very fetching,' he remarked, determined to keep the conversation light. Back when he'd mentioned showers so many memories had flashed through his mind he'd thought he might lose it altogether, but he was back in charge of his thoughts and feelings now—touching his own scarred skin usually had that effect.

'What would they have been fighting about?' she asked, moving away from the cooking pot as if ceding his right to be in charge. She perched on one of his chairs, propped her elbows on the table and rested her chin in her hands as she waited for his answer.

'A bit of tin for a roof, perhaps a scrap of pipe one of them found, a woman? Who would know?'

'I thought the other men, the men who brought him in, would have told you. You spoke to them for some time.'

She hadn't changed much, Jorge realised. She'd

always questioned everything, especially things she probably shouldn't question.

And persistent!

He'd forgotten how persistent she could be, although her arrival here should have reminded him. Once she got an idea in her head, she followed through with it. Back in Africa she'd pushed and worked and wound officials around her little finger until she'd been allowed to run her clinic for the women in the village near the refugee camp, only to have to leave it when called home to her mother.

'Well?'

Yes, persistent!

'I gather it was about a woman,' he said, adding, 'Isn't it always,' with considerable asperity, for his thoughts had led him back down paths he hadn't wished to travel.

'He was attacked with an axe or machete over a woman?'

She'd lifted her head, her eyes watching him more closely now, as if she might read a lie or evasion in his reply.

'I suppose the other man just grabbed whatever was handy.'

'But the hospital? You didn't want to send him there.'

He turned the gas down under the pot and leaned against the small kitchen bench.

'Sending him to a hospital would involve the police. These people have a fear of being locked away and they also do not fare well in a general prison population. They are small, and too fiery for their size. The settlement has its own wardens—the two men who brought him to me are wardens—and they will deal with him and with his attacker in the appropriate way.'

Caroline shuddered at his words, although she knew Jorge wouldn't condone further violence as 'an appropriate way'. There was more to the story than Jorge was telling—perhaps more than he knew—but here she was, again wanting to probe deeper, to learn more, when it was, as he had used to say, none of her business. Only he'd always said it in Spanish, *Qué te importa*, so it sounded as if her query had been rude, his words a 'stay out of it' command.

Well, she'd stay out of local affairs—after all, it seemed as if she wouldn't be here even for a full month. Where she'd be when Jorge left she wasn't certain, but it would be somewhere near where he was. She hadn't come all this way to give in easily. Besides, now he'd met Ella, Caroline was reasonably sure he'd want to get to know her.

Perhaps it was time to talk about the future. Surely she could do that without being told, '*Qué te importa*'!

'You said you wouldn't be here for much longer. Where will you go? To another squatter settlement like this in another city?'

He looked blankly at her, as if he hadn't understood a word she'd said, but then blinked himself back from wherever he had been.

'Home,' he said, but there was little joy in the word.

'Home to your father? He is ill?'

She sounded concerned but, then, she'd always been

empathetic and perhaps not having known her own father had listened avidly to stories of his. But Jorge had to answer her, and how to answer when he wasn't one hundred per cent sure of his motives himself?

'He is not ill—the very opposite—but he is not getting any younger and I feel not a duty to return but something pulls me back there. He gave so much of his time to me, bringing me up when my mother died, taking time out of his day to do it when he could have left it to Antoinette, that I feel the least I can do is give him a little of my time.'

'Did you go straight home to his place from the hospital in France? Did you recuperate there?'

Caroline sounded interested enough for Jorge to explain further. Besides, talking about his father—about that time—took his mind off the other things he was feeling with Caroline here in his little hut.

'I stayed until I could walk again and my internal wounds had healed. Then I came up here. My father understood my need to get away for a while, to rebuild myself, both physically and mentally, and he would accept my absence if I felt my work here was necessary—if there was no one else who would do it. But the article you must have read on the internet was old, and now I have the clinic operating, the government is happy to step in and staff it.'

'And back in Buenos Aires, you have a job to go to?'

She was watching him closely, as if sensing that returning to the city of his youth, back among people who had known him as a handsome man, working with people with whom he had trained, was going to be hard for him, and because he knew himself well enough to accept that it was nothing more than pride that would make it difficult, he hoped his face was as unrevealing as the words he used.

'As you said earlier, doctors are always in demand.'

Was that enough?

Would she stop questioning him now?

Move so the ray of light from the lamp above her—the ray that had found a strand of silver hair to reflect off—would not be picking up the colour?

Silky!

Her hair had felt like silk—or maybe softer still, water washing through his fingers. They had loved with a fierce passion but had shared tenderness as well, not worshipping each other's bodies but learning them, giving and receiving caresses as soft as angels' wings.

He had the feeling he'd been split into levels like some multi-storied building, one level in the past with silky hair and angels wings, another, above that, the hidden fire that attraction had reignited in his belly, and on the top level the person he was pretending to be, talking calmly—he hoped—operating normally, keeping up the pretence that his world *hadn't* shifted beneath his feet, and his life *hadn't* been thrown into disarray.

Up on the top level he returned to stir the pot.

'Do you want to eat now? I imagine you must be exhausted.'

How was it possible to make such conversation, sound so normal, when his mind was replaying images of long ago—a film of love and longing, of passion and then pain—such pain—emotional and physical…?

Now he'd mentioned exhaustion. It dropped down on Caroline like a shroud but, tired as she was, she couldn't help but wonder if Jorge's offer to feed her now wasn't simply because he wanted to get rid of her, if only for the night.

She'd once thought she could read his mind, but probably she'd only imagined what he had been thinking—certainly imagining he'd loved her. Although that had been more than imagination for he'd said the words.

But words were empty things without emotion, deceiving those who wanted to believe them.

Was that how it had been?

She'd believed he'd loved her because she'd wanted to believe it?

She shook her head, angry at her thoughts. She was here to find a father for her daughter, not a lover, for all she might have imagined other scenarios. And the fact that Jorge had made it obvious he didn't want her here only made her more determined.

'Now? You are ready to eat?'

His voice jerked her out of the half-dream state into which she'd sunk.

'Sorry! Yes, please,' she replied. 'I must be more tired than I realised. I thought I'd answered you earlier.'

She had to stay awake long enough to eat. Talking would help. What *had* they been talking about?

Certainly not love.

Work, that was it. Even in her befuddled state she could manage work conversation.

'Do you want to specialise in anything when you get back to Buenos Aires?'

He was serving the stew onto two tin plates so didn't reply immediately.

'I'm going into research.'

He said the words with the same abruptness that he dumped her plate of stew onto the table in front of her, turning away before returning with two spoons.

'What a waste! You're the most empathetic doctor I've ever met!' She knew he'd intended the manner of his reply to cut the conversation off, but the scar on his face was the proverbial elephant in the room, there but unmentioned.

Time to point at it—to talk about it!

'If you think people would be repulsed by your scar, you're being precious,' she declared.

'Only some scars are visible!' he growled, glaring at her across the table, his dark eyes as hard as stones.

'Of course,' she agreed, hearing pain he'd probably never spoken of in his voice. 'But unfortunately it's the visible ones people react to. They don't see the broken bits inside or the mess terrible injuries can cause in the way a patient thinks of himself. But it seems to me in just the few hours I've been here that you've risen above that—that you've rebuilt yourself the way you built this house, bit by bit.'

Had she made too light of it that he pushed his plate away and walked out of the room, out of the back door of the hut?

Should she follow him? Put her arms around him?

Kiss the scarred skin and show him how little it meant to her?

But if he didn't love her—if his words had been the truth—how humiliating that would be for both of them, and she sensed he'd suffered enough humiliation already, enduring people's stares and carelessly hurtful remarks.

So much for pointing at the elephant!

She ate her stew, which was extremely tasty, scraped his back into the saucepan and put the lid on it, then washed both plates. She found an earthenware pot, painted with broad white and black stripes, perhaps local pottery, and filled it with water from the container outside, sneaking looks into the darkness to see if Jorge was lurking somewhere.

Lights were on in the clinic so presumably he was over there. Perhaps their patient had a fever. Perhaps he had to talk to the people he called wardens.

Sighing with frustration—there was nothing she could do—and a little disappointment as well—she'd have liked so much to sit and talk with Jorge—she brushed her teeth, drank some water, then went to bed, pulling a book out of her handbag but finding it too difficult to concentrate on the words, so letting it slide and remembering instead…

Her light was on but she was asleep, asleep as he'd so often seen her, with an open book resting on the bed covers, a little bundle beneath the quilt beside her showing where Ella lay. He should have turned out the light and walked away, but he indulged himself for a moment, doing nothing more than looking, not at the bundle that was his daughter but at Caroline as she slept. Her silvery hair was splayed across the pillow, and her pale eyelashes rested on faintly pink cheeks, but it was her mouth that drew his gaze—that wide, generous mouth with the full, rosy lips.

Jorge sighed. He knew about physical attraction, had shared it with the women he'd had in his life since Caroline, not many but enough to know that physical attraction without love was not enough—well, not for him.

But another love had come into his life as well—a simpler love to feel, though perhaps a far more complex love in the long term.

He looked from the mother to the child, the only visible bit a tangle of brown curls.

'Que te duermas con los angelitos,' he murmured, using the saying first his mother and then his father had used to him as they'd turned out his light at night.

'I hope you sleep with little angels.'

It sounded just as good in English.

CHAPTER FIVE

To CAROLINE'S surprise, Jorge made no objection to her attending the clinic the following day. In fact, he offered a young female nurse as an interpreter for those who didn't speak Spanish and suggested Caroline conduct the mothers' and children's clinic due to start at 8:00 a.m.

'The nurse usually conducts it,' Jorge had explained over a breakfast of fresh sweet pastries and delicious, milky coffee. They were on their own as Ella had woken with the birds and insisted on being taken outside to explore her new surroundings.

'Go back to bed,' Jorge had told Caroline. 'I will take her to the bakery up on the main road. If she tires, I can carry her on my shoulders.'

He'd not only bought the pastries but had fed Ella then watched her play with the children who had gathered outside until Mima had appeared to take over her child-watching duties, and Caroline, feeling jet-lagged and heavy-eyed, had dragged herself out of bed.

'The young nurse who runs the clinic comes to me if she needs medical help or will send a woman or child to me if necessary, but we have been encouraging the women to come so they and the children become used to the place in case they have to use it in the future. I suppose it is a form of a well-women's clinic.'

To Caroline's surprise, it seemed more like a play-group—a chance for the mothers to get together while the children played. The topics of conversation were mainly health-related—how to prevent infection developing from minor cuts and scratches, how to teach their children to always wash their hands after going to the toilet and before eating—but some of the women brought up personal problems as well.

'It's the same the whole world over,' she said to Jorge later. They were back in the hut, Ella asleep after a hectic morning, the two of them stepping back from the doorway where they'd been watching their sleeping daughter. At times like this, Caroline found herself relaxing, just slightly, in Jorge's presence, professionalism keeping her emotions in check.

'Actually, I think there's a song like that,' she continued. 'My grandmother used to sing it. But those women worry about making sure their children get the proper food they need to grow and while their worries are more basic—is there enough food?—mothers in the Western world are worrying that their kids might be hooked on junk food.'

She stopped, thinking back, then frowned at Jorge.

'*Is* there enough food?' she asked.

He nodded, but so slowly she had to wonder.

'Well?' she finally demanded, and he smiled, melting her insides and showing her how thin the crust of professionalism was. She strengthened it with willpower.

'There were times when a lot of the health problems

these people had were perhaps not caused by malnutrition but lack of a balanced diet was certainly a contributing factor. It was one of the reasons so many of the Toba moved south.'

'And one of the reasons you became involved with the settlement here? Because you could see more needed to be done to stabilise their lives?'

'Many people have worked, and still work, to help the Toba. I am only one small cog in the wheel. Other people see different needs, some put an emphasis on accommodation, others on education. I learned that although there are plenty of excellent medical facilities in the city, these people, for a variety of reasons, didn't like to use them, hence the clinic.'

'And now you have the structure in place, you'll move on. But will whatever you intend to do be enough of a challenge for you?'

Persistent again, Jorge thought.

But did he have to answer?

He looked at the woman who had chased him halfway across the world. Yes, she'd had a reason, wanting her daughter—his daughter—to know her father, but it still must have taken a lot of guts to do it—even to face up to him again after he had treated her so cruelly.

So, didn't she deserve an answer?

He offered a smile first, although painfully aware that smiling drew attention to his ruined face. Ruined face? That was vanity talking when it was the internal scarring—the mental scarring he'd suffered when he'd thought he'd never recover—that had really affected his life and made him deny his love for this woman.

Not that he intended to admit it…

'Don't you think going to work in the city, working with other people, getting again used to the stares and murmurs and, yes, kindness won't be enough of a challenge?'

'Oh, Jorge,' she whispered, but as she stepped towards him, her intention to put her arms around him and hug him quite clear, he stepped away. It broke his heart to do it—quite literally, it felt, from the pain that stabbed his chest—but he couldn't bear her pity—couldn't accept it—not from Caroline…

'We've the afternoon off—do you want to drive into the city and have a look around? There are any number of new high-rise buildings but in amongst them some wonderful examples of early twentieth-century architecture, and great *plazas* along the river bank.'

The stricken expression on her face, the one he'd put there with his rejection, eased and he saw her almost physically pull herself together, straightening her shoulders, lifting her head, tilting her chin.

'If you've the time to spare, it would be wonderful,' she told him. 'Ella usually sleeps for an hour. We can go when she wakes up. Will we be able to get lunch somewhere in the city?'

He'd regretted the offer almost as soon as he'd made it as they'd be sitting in the car together for three-quarters of an hour each way and being anywhere in Caroline's vicinity was causing his body enough tumult without plunking them both in a car together.

'We'll stop on the waterfront—near the river, the

Paraná. There are many beautiful parks along the river bank.'

Apparently his reluctance and regret hadn't manifested themselves in his voice for Caroline showed every indication of excitement as she said, 'I'll get changed,' before disappearing into the bedroom.

He could tell her he'd changed his mind, plead paperwork—there was plenty with the handover of the clinic looming—but now he'd suggested it he realised just how badly he wanted go somewhere—anywhere—with Ella, and this need to be with her was proving stronger than his need to avoid Caroline.

Ella!

His child—his daughter.

'Mi hija.'

He whispered words he'd never thought to say and felt a swell of what could only be pride.

And love!

But the idea of having a child—a daughter—terrified him as much as it thrilled him. He knew children were far more accepting of people who were 'different' than most adults were, but again he felt actual pain in his chest at the thought of his daughter seeing him as ugly and therefore frightening.

Not that she'd shown any signs of it when he'd spent time with her so far, confidently going off down the road with him that morning, chatting away, drawing his attention to this bird or that flower, her happy 'Look, Hor-hay!' filling his heart with love every time she said it.

Would her calling him Papá give him more joy?

Could it?

'Well, I'm ready, so all we need to do is wait for Ella to wake up.'

Caroline was back, changed out of the trousers she'd been wearing earlier into faded—from age, not fashion, he imagined—jeans, the neat navy blouse replaced with a bright pink T-shirt with a huge glittery butterfly on it.

'Ella's Christmas present to me,' she said, pointing at the shirt with a slight colouring of embarrassment. 'Of course, she picked it out herself and insisted we buy it so I could hardly refuse to accept it.'

'It suits you. You should wear pink more often,' Jorge found himself saying, which deepened the colour in Caroline's cheeks.

But she brushed the compliment aside.

'I haven't changed much since you knew me. Clothes shopping is still so far down my list of favourite things to do it might as well not be on it. I still buy half a dozen navy blouses at a time for work, and half a dozen—usually navy because they don't show the dirt—T-shirts for casual wear. A couple of pairs of trousers for work, a pair of jeans, a few pairs of shorts for summer and that's my wardrobe.'

With most women he'd have considered that an exaggeration, but he knew how Caroline had grown up, her mother working hard to give them both a decent life, and then to make sure Caroline's dreams of becoming a doctor came true.

'But surely now if your father left you money,' he protested as he watched her check necessities in a small backpack—filling a bottle with drinking water, slipping a small packet of tissues and some snack bars into the pack, 'you can afford—was "fripperies" the word you used for anything you considered inessential?'

She laughed and the soft musical notes caught in the air and blended with the pink and glittering butterfly in the usually stolid atmosphere in his adobe hut, turning his world to magic for a moment.

'Fancy you remembering that,' she said, totally unaware she'd given him an almost out-of-body experience. 'Fripperies! It's what my mother called them.'

She finished her preparations and looked up at him.

'You know, I never missed them. Even as a teenager I never longed for the latest fashion or secretly envied things, particularly clothes, my friends had. When I talk to teenagers today I wonder if I must have had something wrong with me, a missing gene perhaps, because the things they want seem so vital to their lives. I still don't have one of those music things you plug into your ears, which all my friends believe is indispensable to life itself. They say things like "But how do you exercise without one?" while I find exercising—well, walking, which is the only exercise I do—is thinking time, not listening time. Do other people need to think less, I wonder?'

Now he really regretted suggesting the jaunt to town, for it was Caroline's take on the world that had first beguiled him. She seemed to look at it in a different way from other people he knew, and it was in learning more of her view of the world that he had fallen in love with her. He'd worked in other places with women and they'd become nothing more than friendly co-workers, but there'd been something about Caroline, a layering effect, so the more he'd peeled back of the layers, the more he'd wanted to go deeper.

But not now!

Not this time!

He'd not be beguiled again.

Although he had to answer.

'Perhaps some people like something to do—something to listen to—to stop them thinking.'

She nodded, a slight frown between her eyebrows, as if he'd said something very profound.

'If you're right, that's fairly scary because we all need to think from time to time, although perhaps the music-in-the-ears people think at other times—in bed at night.'

The moment she said it, Caroline would have liked to take the words back. In all probability Jorge wouldn't think anything of them, but, like the conversation they'd had about showering the previous evening, the mention of bed had brought a series of images flashing through her mind, and the longing for the love they'd shared swamped her body. So it might have been nothing more than physical attraction but at the time it had felt like love and it had filled her life with a happiness she had been sure would last for ever.

'What a stupid conversation,' she muttered, as the strain of trying to paste over her churning, changeable emotions snapped her equilibrium. So much for aplomb! Although there was one conversation she could have—a professional conversation.

'How's your patient?'

She could tell from the expression on Jorge's face that he hadn't expected the switch of subjects, but she also read relief in his eyes, as if the strain of trying to pretend they were nothing more than polite old acquaintances was wearing thin with him as well.

'Why do you ask?'

She frowned at him.

'Why do I ask?' Okay, so this was a legitimate reason to let a little of the pent-up anger go—just a little. 'Why on earth do you think I ask? I'm interested in him. I was there, too, stitching him up. Do you think I need to know so I can report him to some authority? Is it such a hard question to answer?'

Was she as uptight over this reunion as he was? Was her outward control as fragile as his pretence at normality?

Jorge had no idea—he no longer knew her well enough to guess—but there'd been an edge of anger in her words as if it had escaped from somewhere deep within her.

It was hard to believe she had as much right to be angry over this ridiculous situation as he did, but she *had* been left, literally, holding the baby so he supposed he had to cut her some slack.

'I'm keeping him well sedated, so his body has time to get over the worst of the pain and shock of the amputation before his mind has to battle with accepting it.'

'And repercussions?' she asked. 'No one has reported it to the police?'

The question, from anyone else, might have seemed

intrusive, but he knew Caroline's mind liked all the ends tied up.

'They are a close-knit community,' he explained. 'One of the wardens is sitting with him and the man who caused the injury has been sent back up north, with his wife. In time, they might return, perhaps when our patient has recovered and moved on himself. I used to wonder about the rights and wrongs of the people in the settlement taking control of their own—I suppose judiciary is the word—but now I try to keep out of things like that mainly because I don't understand the history behind the decisions the wardens and the other leaders here make.'

A cry from the bedroom saved them from further awkward conversation, and Ella appeared, sleep-rumpled, her curls tangled around her head, and once again Jorge felt his heart melt at the sight of her.

'Come on,' Caroline told her, catching her up in a hug, 'let's tidy you up then we're going for a drive.'

'With Hor-hay?' Ella demanded.

'With Hor-hay,' Caroline confirmed, and Jorge wondered if perhaps he needed to be called Papá at all, so delighted did he feel by the way Ella said his name.

They disappeared into the bedroom, returning minutes later, the tangled curls only slightly tamed and the little purple shoes replacing the small sneakers Ella had been wearing earlier.

Such small feet.

How could he feel such joy, yet still be angry underneath—and apprehensive as well? Too many emotions in the mix, like a dish with too many ingredients.

He led the way to where he'd parked the car under the jacaranda tree, feeling a sense of other-worldliness again as he walked, with Caroline and his daughter, through the lavender-tinted world.

'She should have a car seat,' Caroline said, sounding hesitant about mentioning this but worried all the same.

'I have borrowed one,' Jorge told her, lifting Ella into his arms and opening the car door, then settling her into the seat, adjusting the straps for comfort and safety.

They drove slowly down the narrow lane, but once on the main road it seemed to Caroline that Jorge drove like all the other drivers on the road, at pace but with a skill that had him avoiding any accidental touches.

'Is it to do with the Latin temperament that you all drive as if you're competing in a Grand Prix?' she asked, as they skated around a particularly hairy bend and cut in front of a large bus.

He turned to her and grinned.

'Nervous?'

She shook her head. She probably was a little nervous but that grin, that one short, seemingly happy smile, had struck deep into her heart for that was the Jorge she had loved so desperately. That was the man who could make the unbearable almost acceptable, who could tease her out of despair when the poverty and helplessness of the lives of their patients had got her down.

Was he still in there, the man she'd loved? She hoped he was—though she had to admit to herself that even if he was, he was probably not for her. Not by the slightest word or glance had he revealed that he still felt anything for her. Or that he had *ever* felt anything for her, come to that!

She was here for Ella—she had to remember that—even if being in the enclosed space of a smallish vehicle with Jorge was testing her body to its limits.

And Ella was no help. The only time she didn't chatter was in a car, seeming to go into some kind of trance as she watched the passing scenery outside her window.

Think! Caroline told herself.

Talk!

Break the silence.

There were a million questions she could ask him, well, maybe a dozen. She wasn't usually prone to exaggeration. It had to be the discomfort of sitting in the car with him, of feeling his body so near hers.

Back to questions.

What would happen to them when he went south? Would he take them willingly to meet his father, or would she have to fight him over continued contact?

Did he want to get involved with Ella on a permanent basis?

Could they work something out?

She had no idea what, but her natural optimism—and her mother's upbringing—told her anything was possible if one was willing to work for it.

'I will be driving home a week on Saturday,' he said into the silence.

Had he read her thoughts?

'I would like to take Ella to meet my father. You, too, of course, but if you don't wish to accompany me on the drive, I can book flights for you.'

The idea of driving and seeing more of this country was appealing but the thought of meeting Jorge's adored father made Caroline's stomach knot so she didn't really consider the alternative to driving, too busy wondering just how the meeting would go.

'Of course we'll be willing to go with you,' she said. 'It's why we're here, so you can get to know Ella, and you can hardly get to know her if we're up here and you're down there. Oh…'

'Oh?' he echoed.

'I've just thought. I was to work here for a month. Do you think whoever is taking over the clinic might need me?'

Now he laughed and the sound of Jorge's laughter made her want to cry. It was such a joyous sound and it cut into her, reminding her so strongly of how they'd always laughed together.

'Conscientious Caroline,' he teased. 'If *I* didn't know you were coming and, believe me, I didn't, then none of the new people coming in will know they had a doctor willing to work with them for nothing for a month.'

He turned towards her and she saw the smile lingering on his face, and the knot in her stomach grew tighter. Her fingers ached to touch him, her skin burned with knowledge of his closeness, her body so aware of his it was a wonder she could sit still in the seat.

The car had slowed. Was he feeling it as well? Might he open a crack in his defences, touch her, kiss her even? Give her leave by any gesture that she could touch him?

Disappointment flooded her as she realised he'd

slowed to turn in between ornate stone gateposts, but common sense told her this was certainly for the best—as if she could handle touching him right now—while as for kissing…

'It is a very popular *plaza*. The land along the river has been redeveloped so there are plenty of recreation areas for the people of the city.'

He pulled into a parking area and stopped the car, turning to Caroline.

'You do realise that once my father meets Ella…'

Jorge wasn't certain how to go on—to explain.

'Will he be shocked? Will he not want to get to know her?'

'*Dios mio*, Caroline, it is just the opposite. That is the trouble. He'll be delighted. He'll be overwhelmed. He'll celebrate. He'll want the whole world to know. Within minutes of setting eyes on her, Ella will be the—how do you say it, some fruit of his eye?'

'Apple,' Caroline supplied obligingly, before adding, 'But isn't it good that he'll be happy? I can't believe you'd be jealous of a child being the apple of your father's eye so I really cannot see the problem.'

'You wouldn't,' Jorge told her, the gloom persisting, then, as he got out of the car to lift Ella from her car-seat, he couldn't help but add, 'Just you wait and see.'

The conversation ended, for it soon became obvious to him that taking a small child to a park was a full-time occupation. Any discussion centred on the safety of the various swings and slides she wanted to experience, while rescuing her from the dangers of falling head first into fountains, racing after her as she took off to chase a stray dog and tactfully removing her from where she'd stopped to observe the antics of a courting, kissing couple kept him from thinking of anything beyond the immediate or next likely danger.

Caroline, once satisfied Jorge had taken on the task of Ella-control, relaxed and looked around. She was startled by the enthusiasm of the courting couples who seemed to occupy every park bench and quite a lot of the grassy spaces. The park itself was beautiful. Wide, tree-shaded paths led to beautiful statues, some in fountains, some standing alone, huge stone sculptures, bronze and brass contortions, simple marble shapes, all art that pleased the eye and added another dimension to the extensive but beautifully planned parklands.

'Oh, wow!'

They were closer to the river now and a huge boat was floating past, seeming close enough to reach out and touch, although well out in the water.

'It's incredible,' she murmured, feeling the buzz of life in the park, hearing music and laughter and the shouts of young men kicking a football, seeing the smiles on the faces of the people, smelling the ripe, wet smell of the river and some perfumed flowers in the air.

A wave of well-being washed over her and as Jorge led her towards an outdoor restaurant she felt a sense of rightness in the situation, as if in some way she'd come home.

Not, she accepted, to the home she wanted—the home she still, deep down, hoped to find in Jorge—but a sensation of belonging, as if this country with its smiling people, beautiful parks with their statues and towering trees could be her home, hers and Ella's, no matter what happened between Jorge and herself.

'*Tostado* for Ella—a toasted sandwich with ham and cheese—yes?'

Jorge had lifted Ella onto a chair at a table that looked out across the park to the river. He looked enquiringly at Caroline, who realised she must have been lost in her thoughts of an unfamiliar sense of homecoming for too long.

'She'd like that and maybe she'd like some *dulce de leche*—the sweet milk you used to speak of,' Caroline replied.

Jorge, who was pulling out a chair for her, hesitated, looking directly into her face, frowning slightly.

'Did you think I'd forget things like that and *mate*?' she asked him, disturbed by something that had flickered in the air between them, not like the arc of attraction of the previous day, something different.

He didn't answer but continued to frown, making her wonder just what was going on in his head. It caused an ache deep within her that she didn't know.

'You might like to try a *super-lomito*,' was all he said, dashing any hope she might have had that he'd been thinking anything personal or had felt the flicker. 'It is a steak sandwich with a slice of ham and a fried egg on top of it.'

Caroline managed a nod, while inside she was smiling sadly. Here she was, thinking attraction—that was what the flicker had been—and he was thinking ham and eggs. Served her right.

CHAPTER SIX

IT WAS an idyllic afternoon. Looking back, it seemed to Caroline that both she and Jorge had set aside the past and all its pain and problems and lost themselves in the joyousness that filled the air throughout the *plaza*. Ella took it all in, watching the make-up football games, joining children on the slides and swings, throwing sticks into the river and watching them float, throwing stones to see the splash.

By the time they returned home, Ella was sleepy so for a second night she had noodles for tea, a quick bath, then into bed, not even staying awake to the end of the story Jorge was reading her.

Not wanting to see him sitting on the bed with Ella nestled up to him as he read, Caroline had walked across to the clinic to check on their patient. Juan was there, an anxious look in his eyes, although he hesitated when Caroline questioned him.

'He's had more antibiotics,' he said. 'He shouldn't be suffering from an infection.'

He was! The man's pulse was racing, his face flushed, his wounded foot swollen to almost twice its size. Caroline checked the dressings, picking up signs of a nasty ooze, and knew immediately that an infection had taken hold.

'I think Jorge might have to operate again. I hate asking you to watch Ella for me, so perhaps there's someone else. I'm happy to pay someone to—we call it babysit—if you can find someone you trust.'

'Mima will do it—but not for money. She is happy Jorge has helped us so much here in the settlement and she likes little Ella. I will get her and take her to the hut and tell Jorge what you think.'

By the time Jorge and Juan returned, Caroline had updated their patient's status, filling in her findings on the file by the side of the bed. She was bathing him with wet flannels, hoping to lower his temperature, not wanting to give him drugs before Jorge decided what he'd do.

'I'll have to open up the wound and clean it out,' he said as he examined the stained dressings. 'You will assist?'

He looked at Caroline and she read his distress. An infection could kill the man, and Jorge would surely blame himself for not having headed it off.

'Of course,' she said, and knowing how he thought added, 'and it wouldn't have made any difference if you'd been here all afternoon. Juan said he only developed the fever in the last hour.'

Jorge nodded, accepting her words, although she knew he'd still be wondering…

He and Juan shifted the man into the treatment room, Juan taking up his position at the man's head, ready to watch over the anaesthetic and the monitor. Jorge opened the big cupboard and began to pull out what he'd need, while Caroline unwrapped the injured foot, grimacing as she saw the swollen, angry wound.

'I wanted to keep his heel if possible as it would give him more stability, but the blood supply to the foot is so poor it might not be possible.'

It was an exercise in patience and precision and Caroline could only watch in wonder as Jorge probed and cut. She was kept busy swabbing and flushing, doing all she could to keep the intricacies of the wound clear for his scalpel. Juan reported the monitor findings—the man's blood pressure was stabilising, his temperature coming down.

'It's tricky,' Jorge said, 'because of the way the calf muscles hook onto the heel, but the smaller muscles hook further forward so they get better leverage. You have to balance the amount of bone you keep—all surgeons think more is better—against the amount of support the bone will get. I'm taking it further back towards the heel so he'll have good fleshy support but it means sacrificing some of the tendons.'

It was easy for Caroline to see that he was totally immersed in the surgery and it made her wonder just where his new life would take him.

'Have you seen many of these injuries or have you been reading up on amputations?' she asked, her fascination in the operation taking precedence over all the emotional stuff she'd been battling since she arrived.

'Making mud bricks, building and reading,' Jorge said lightly. 'That's been the pattern of my life lately.'

Then, as if sensing that she wasn't going to accept so easy a reply, he looked up at her.

'I've been reading widely,' he admitted, 'across a multitude of medical disciplines. I know myself well enough to know that whatever I do next, it will have to be a challenge—a real challenge.'

He carefully attached a tendon to the tarsal bone, saying, almost under his breath, 'I don't think this will do much good.'

That done, he straightened for a moment while Caroline swabbed and flushed.

Working with her like this, Jorge decided, was exciting somehow. The agonising emotions her sudden arrival had stirred back to life were set aside more easily while they worked as professional colleagues. And probably because of this professional closeness, he found himself telling her things he'd only, at this stage, discussed in his head.

'Given the state I was in when I returned home, I suppose it was natural I looked at psychology first, working my own way through the change in my life and wondering if it was in me to help others.'

He glanced up and saw the interest in her blue eyes—interest only, not a hint of pity. Was he wrong in thinking that was what she'd feel? Had he been wrong all along?

No! This was definitely not the time to be distracted by 'what ifs' so, resolutely, he turned his attention back to the probing and stitching.

'Burns, naturally, seemed a good idea, but so much good work is already being done in research and development there, particularly in growing new skin from the patient's own skin cells. Surgery had always interested me, and with landmines still littering the ground in many countries, I knew I could always be useful there.'

'Hence your knowledge of foot amputation,' Caroline put in. Although he couldn't see her mouth because of the mask she wore, he knew she was smiling as she spoke for the smile shone in her eyes and lilted in her voice, a perilous distraction.

Caroline!

Her name sighed through his head and whispered in his heart, so it took all his attention to focus once more on his patient, although once he was back on track with the operation, he could continue his conversation.

'I'm thinking genetics. I know it's the buzz word these days, and it's an infinite field, but I would like to tie it into racial differences. We've known for a long time about some genetic abnormalities in particular races and scientists have been working to change the genes that cause these but I'm more interested in the genetics of our indigenous population—the similarities and differences. We are in a unique situation as there are pockets of indigenous people who have never intermarried with the migrants who settled here.'

It made sense, Caroline decided, but knowing how well Jorge interacted with patients, she knew that shutting himself away in a laboratory would be, in some ways, a loss to medicine.

'It would also give me time to spend among these people,' he added, looking up at her, the twinkle in his dark eyes telling her he'd guessed what she'd been thinking.

Again.

But the discomfort she was feeling had nothing to do with his prescience, more to do with the twinkle that had sliced through her professional façade as easily as a scalpel through flesh. One glimpse of smiling eyes and she was thrust back into the emotional storm she'd been determined to hold at bay.

It fanned the embers of her anger that he could slide beneath her poise so easily. She should be stronger than this, more in control of her feelings, but how could she remain detached when every moment in his presence held reminders of what had been between them, even the very professional conversation they'd been having? His interest in every aspect of the medical world was one of the things that had drawn her to him, fascinated by the breadth of his knowledge and his determination to keep adding to it.

'There, I think I've got all the infected tissue, but I'll leave a new drain in place, higher up this time, just in case.'

He stepped back and Caroline read pain in the way he moved and tried to straighten.

'I'll sew it up,' she said, telling him, not offering. 'Needlework was my best subject at school.'

She moved so she was closer to the table, closer to Jorge as well but now was not the time to be considering closeness or the manifestations of it. Right now she needed to do her best to make the truncated foot as neat as possible, to close the wound tightly to prevent new infection, yet to sew it up in such a way that their patient would have some padding beneath the bones, and be able, in time, to learn to walk on it.

Jorge had stepped back to give her room, and although in some inner corner of her mind she continued to be aware of his presence, she concentrated on her job, pleased when, more than an hour later, Jorge said, 'Well done, that's a splendid job. Let's hope this time it will begin to heal.'

He touched her lightly on the shoulder, guiding her away, telling her that he'd dress it and help Juan take their patient back to the small 'ward', but Caroline was reluctant to move.

Once out of the small treatment room, all her concerns and worries about the future would return. It was all very well for Jorge to talk of taking them to Buenos Aires, but what then? The way Jorge spoke, his father could be a problem in some way and on top of that there'd been no indication from Jorge by either word or deed that she was important to him except as the mother of his child.

So she couldn't stay on for ever in his father's house. She'd have to find a home nearby for herself and Ella. She'd have to find a job because she loved her work and believed she should continue it.

She'd have to—

'There is something wrong? You've left something in the wound? We've forgotten something?'

Jorge's questions brought her abruptly out of her thoughts and she turned towards him.

'Nothing in the wound—I was just thinking…'

Was she frowning that he touched her gently on the arm?

'Juan and I will take care of him from here. There is food in the hut, maybe not much variety but certainly eggs if you would like to make an omelette. I will wait with our patient until he comes out of the anaesthetic and possibly relieve Juan from duty tonight. You will be all right in the hut?'

The twinkle was long gone from his eyes but Caroline thought she read anxiety there in its place. Was he worried that she'd been standing feeling lost while he and Juan prepared to shift their patient?

Or concerned about abandoning his role of host? Although she understood, after this setback, why he'd want to remain with the patient.

'I'll be fine,' she told him, and she hurried away, cursing herself for the muddle in her mind, for the mess she seemed to have landed in by jumping on a plane in such a rage and not thinking far enough ahead to at least have some kind of plan.

Back home it had seemed so easy. In her mind, Jorge, badly injured and fearing her pity, had rejected her with enough cruelty to convince her he hadn't ever loved her. Seeing the scars in the picture, she'd immediately decided he'd rejected her out of pride, hence her anger and the mad flight to Argentina. She'd had enough functioning brain cells to realise her assumptions could be wrong, but had decided that working with him for a month would be enough time to suss that out.

What she hadn't expected was to have so little time alone with him. Neither had she expected to be swept off to his father's house and into a wider web of complications in a situation already complicated enough, given that every moment in his presence was a kind of torture.

The moon was out and she paused to look up at it, nearly full, shining through the branches of a tree, a stark, spiky, possibly unattractive tree, although in the moonlight it had a peculiar beauty.

She sensed rather than heard Jorge's approach.

'I thought I should see you safely settled back at the hut,' he said quietly, moving up beside her where she was gazing at the tree.

'I can manage,' she told him. 'I know where things are. But what is that tree?'

'It's a thorn tree, a native of the Grand Chaco where the Toba people come from. There are two or three in the settlement, the seedlings brought out of sentiment, I suppose, by families when they came south.'

'I should have guessed,' Caroline replied. 'They're very similar to the thorn trees in Africa. I've always liked them, so persistent, growing where it seems nothing much should grow.'

He's like those trees, she thought to herself as she continued to admire the bare black branches outlined against the deep purple of the sky. Prickly, thorny, keeping people at bay, yet there's a strange beauty in the trees, especially when seen in silhouette, and Jorge's inner beauty won't have changed. He just doesn't realise it…

Jorge watched the woman, her hair more silvery than

ever in the moonlight, studying the thorn tree as if it was giving her some message.

He smiled to himself. Of course she'd like the thorn trees for she was equally persistent.

Music blasted from a nearby dwelling, the rich, vibrant notes of the tango, turned up, perhaps, so someone could dance, and the moonlight, the thorn tree and the music took him back…

'Remember?' he said quietly, and even as he said it, although remembering was what he was doing most of the time, he knew this remembering could be fatal, for this remembering meant touching her, holding her…

She turned to him, her face lit by an inner radiance—or maybe just the moon.

'When you taught me the tango? By moonlight? Near the thorn tree?'

She came into his arms as easily as if she'd never left them, as if he'd never pushed her out of them, but he knew that had been before, not now—knew they were both back in the past, in happier times.

If only for a few minutes…

He held her to his chest, for the Argentine tango was chest to chest—the only real tango in his opinion—and she followed his steps, their feet kicking up dust from the street as they swept back and forth, letting the music thrum through their blood, carrying them to another place—another time.

Then, as abruptly as it had started, the music stopped. For a moment it seemed to Jorge as if his heart, too, had stopped, for he'd been lost in the delight of holding Caroline in his arms, of feeling his body come to life with an urgency he'd forgotten could exist. Desire had pounded, hot and heavy, in his blood, the music driving his need and memory feeding it.

'Gracias,' Caroline whispered to him, but she didn't move away. Maybe because his arms still held her, chest to chest, kissing close—more than kissing close.

To kiss her would be worse than dancing with her. His head retained enough composure to remind him of that, yet would it be so wrong to touch his lips to hers?

Just once?

'And thank you too,' he said, and because he knew once would never be enough, he dropped his arms, stepping back out of temptation's way, returning to the clinic, his idea of seeing her safely into the hut, maybe organising some dinner for the pair of them forgotten, or at least set aside while he fought temptation on his own.

But the beat continued to course through his body, rattling his brain so when Juan asked him a question about their patient, Jorge had to shake his head to clear it before he could reply.

'Go home,' Juan said to him. 'You have done all you can for the man. Go home and feed your woman.'

'She is not my woman.' The denial was automatic, but saying the words made him wonder.

Could she still have feelings for him?

Yes, she'd come so Ella would know her father—knowing Caroline he believed that implicitly—but was it possible that he *hadn't* killed the love they'd shared?

In one part of his brain he was aware that even thinking of these things was putting his defensive structure in danger—he could all but hear the walls he'd built around his emotions cracking—yet he couldn't help but wonder.

And wondering he left the clinic, not going home to his woman but drawn to be where Caroline was…

It was too much! She couldn't go on with this—being with Jorge, near him, working with him, living in his house and pretending all the time she felt nothing for him. It was just too darned hard. Caroline sat in the comfy old armchair, her elbows resting on her knees, her head in her hands, despair in her heart.

She'd survived without a father, so surely Ella could!

Dancing with him had been the last straw. Being held in his arms, being carried back with the music to such blissful times, moving with him, feeling his body against hers, longing to be lost in it, longing for the touch of love, a gentle kiss perhaps, something—anything—to show he still felt something for her.

Could it be one-sided, the burning heat of desire that swept through her body when they touched, that had all but melted her brain when he'd taken her in his arms?

She'd stayed there, unable to push away, thanking him, wanting more, wanting so much to kiss him or be kissed that she was surprised her need hadn't been visible in a cloud of steam above her head.

And all he'd said had been, 'Thank you.' Then he'd dropped his arms and she'd stood there like a big galoot with her desire, and need, and wanting.

She'd go away, go back home, go tomorrow, for this pretence was killing her. Jorge didn't want her, that was obvious, and if he didn't want her then for sure he didn't love her, and if he didn't, perhaps he never had…

Her thoughts floundered, maudlin self-pity, something she abhorred, sneaking dangerously close.

Action, that was what she needed. She'd thanked Mima and sent her home as soon as she'd come in. Now she'd look in on Ella, find something to eat, and if Jorge returned she could leave him with Ella and go for a walk—a promenade.

That might not be a sensible idea at night in a strange place, although from what she'd seen everybody promenaded so it wasn't as if she'd be walking deserted streets.

She'd straightened in the armchair as she pondered these decisions so wasn't sitting slumped in despair when Jorge walked in.

'Have you eaten?'

The question was so abrupt she peered at him but the lighting in the hut was dim and she couldn't read any expression on his face.

Not that she cared any more what he was thinking or feeling, she told herself, and answered just as abruptly, 'No.'

'I will fix us an omelette,' he said, and moved into the kitchen where the light was slightly better so she could see that, although he was fighting to carry himself as upright as a soldier on parade, there was a tilt to his shoulders and a slight slump to his back.

She closed her eyes against the emotion that seeing his pain had caused, then reminded herself she was done with emotion.

'I can do omelettes,' she said, standing up and joining him in the kitchen. 'You sit down. We walked for hours by the river, you carried Ella, you were bent over your patient for another ninety-minutes, it's obvious your back's giving you hell.'

She put her hand on his chest and gave him a slight push, not much but enough to get him down onto a stool.

'Just tell me what you want in it, the omelette, then you can tell me about your health. Just how badly are you still affected by your injuries?'

She'd lifted the big cast-iron frying pan from the open shelves and set it on the gas ring as she spoke, then added a little oil and reached for a bowl and the basket of eggs.

He hadn't answered so she turned her attention from beating eggs and looked at him.

'Well?' she demanded.

'There are peppers in a basket under the gas ring, and brown onions, and I think in the refrigerator you'll find a chorizo to slice and throw in.'

'Very helpful!' Caroline snapped. 'But that wasn't the real question and you know it.'

She said no more, assembling the ingredients he'd suggested and beginning to peel and chop. The oil sizzled in the pan and she added the eggs, pushing them in at the sides so the omelette would thicken.

'Your injuries,' she reminded him.

'Are my business,' he said, so coldly she knew immediately she should stop probing, but her despair of earlier—the no-kiss despair—had stirred her anger again, and although she wasn't angry she definitely wasn't full of sweetness and light or about to be put off by coldness.

'Of course they are,' she said, as she tipped the colourful mix of vegetables and sausage into the pan on top of the eggs. 'You're lifting Ella, carrying her, driving her. Does pain immobilise you at times? Are you on strong painkillers? What should we avoid—long walks, or standing for any length of time? You're a doctor, you must realise I'm not asking you because I'm sorry for you—heaven forbid—you're the most self-reliant, self-contained, self-confident man I've ever met, the last man in the world anyone could feel sorry for.'

Did she mean it?

Jorge sat on the stool in his own kitchen, his back aching so badly that even sitting was an effort. He watched the woman busy with the omelette, not as he'd have made it but doing not too bad a job, and wondered if she spoke the truth.

To a certain extent he accepted what she'd said, but for too long he'd hidden the pain he'd suffered as a result of the broken bones and torn muscles and ligaments, refusing to talk about it to anyone, fearing the only way it could be borne was to keep it hidden, even, at times, from himself. He was aware that didn't make much sense but he'd devised ways of distracting himself from it when it was bad, and some instinct told him that if someone else knew of it—perhaps could see it or divine it in some way—then he'd no longer be able to escape it.

'I don't take strong drugs—some mild ones from time to time.'

She'd found plates and had flipped the omelette so it was folded in half. Now she slid it onto one of the plates, divided it in two with the spatula, served it out and handed him one of the plates. She settled on a stool across from him and pushed a fork towards him, saying nothing as she tasted her dinner.

He looked across the table at her—intent, it seemed, on the food in front of her. Would it help to share his pain?

The thought was startling—he, who'd shared so little of the whole episode of his accident even with his father, thinking such a thing. It must be because tonight the pain was bad, although when he'd danced…

'You must have medical reports, X-rays and things.'

She'd put down her fork and was leaning on the table, close enough for him to see the slight flecks of gold in her blue eyes, mesmerising him.

'So if you don't want to talk about it, maybe I could take a look at them and figure out the ongoing damage for myself.'

Mesmerising him was bad—probing into his pain, which was very personal to him, was even worse.

'It was four years ago,' he said, looking away from her eyes, turning his thoughts away from her probing. 'They are long gone.'

'I don't believe you. You're a doctor. You've permanent injuries so you must have regular—yearly or two-yearly—checks and X-rays and, being you, you'd want to compare them to the originals, if only to see if there's been degeneration.'

She lifted her fork and began eating again, but the questions hovered in her eyes every time she glanced up at him, curiosity, not pity, in that steadfast blue gaze.

'I don't talk about it.'

Would that stop her?

Knowing Caroline, probably not, but it might bring him enough respite to get his omelette—which was delicious—eaten. She'd finished hers and had stood up to rinse her plate then bring two glasses and the water jug to the table. She poured the water and pushed one glass across to him, lifting hers and saying, 'Cheers,' before drinking from it.

So much for a respite. He put down his fork and just looked at her, the desire that had shaken him to his core as they'd danced now flooding back.

Dios mio, why now? They were at odds, barely civil with each other, yet watching her raise that glass and draw water into her mouth had set fire to his groin so now new pain rattled his body and set alarm bells clanging in his mind.

Eat.

Had she said it or was it his bewildered brain giving the order? The word echoed in his head for a moment, and finally lodged where it needed to, telling his hand to pick up his fork, his lips to open and close, his throat to swallow.

'Thank you,' he managed as he finished the meal and in turn stood up to rinse his plate. She'd moved away and stood near the door, looking out at the moonlit area beyond his hut, so he busied himself boiling water and washing the dishes properly, the silence growing heavier and heavier in the air between them.

Should he tell her about his injuries, share things with her he'd not shared before?

He could understand where she was coming from. She was asking out of concern for Ella, not for herself, and that, though he hated to admit it, cut into him more than it should, if he really was all the things she'd called him—self-reliant, self-contained, self-confident.

Once he might have been all of these, back when she'd known him he'd have to say he *had* been, but now, he knew, they were largely pretence—a costume of self he wore for the world, hiding the wounded, broken man within.

'There was a time I thought I'd never walk again—never work again.'

He said the words very quietly, testing them out, talking to her back. She was turning towards him when a cry from the bedroom brought Caroline back through the kitchen, heading for the bedroom, and something he had to call fatherly instinct had him following close on her heels.

Ella was sitting up in bed, obviously distressed, although when Caroline lifted her, her crying ceased.

'Bad dreams?' he asked quietly, and Caroline nodded. She was rocking back and forth, the movement obviously soothing as Ella's eyes were closing again.

'She has them sometimes when she's overtired,' Caroline explained, speaking quietly. 'I suppose I should have expected it. The good thing is she goes right back to sleep after a cuddle and they don't seem to recur.'

Was it hearing her mother's voice that made Ella open her eyes?

Probably, but for whatever reason, to Jorge's delight, she looked right at him when she did and murmured a sleepy 'Hor-hay?'

'Yes, I'm here,' he said gently, moving closer and holding out his arms. To his delight, without a qualm, Ella slid from her mother's arms to his.

Jorge felt the little body settle confidently against his and something he'd never felt before surged through him. This was *his* child, *his* flesh and blood, and just like that he recognised the surge as love, a love so deep and profound he knew he'd do anything in his power to stay in her life.

And not as a bystander—a weekend father. Oh, he knew full well that could and did work in many families, but it was not for him. Somehow he and Caroline had to come to some arrangement where they could live together and share one hundred per cent in Ella's upbringing.

'Te quiero, mi hija.' He whispered the words of love—words she wouldn't understand—into the soft curls and rocked her in his arms until she grew heavy with sleep.

CHAPTER SEVEN

THEY drove south to Buenos Aires ten days later, Caroline more nervous than she'd been in the taxi on the way to the clinic to face Jorge in the first place. How he felt was anybody's guess, for he'd shut himself away from her again over their remaining days at the clinic, keeping busy anywhere but where she was. In return, she'd busied herself, helping nurse the man who'd lost his foot, accompanying the nurse when she visited people deep into the warren of lanes, seeing more of the settlement beyond the clinic and learning more of the people it served.

'Does your father know you are bringing us?' she asked Jorge as they eased off the freeway and onto more congested city streets—Buenos Aires streets.

'He knows I bring guests,' Jorge told her, then resumed his concentration on the road, weaving through the traffic as if their lives depended on reaching their destination in the shortest possible time.

Realising he must be as nervous as she was, perhaps more so—*Hi, Dad, here's my old lover who turned up with a daughter for me!*—she turned her attention to the scenery. She knew from the guide book she'd read on the first long flight that Buenos Aires was laid out in a grid pattern in very even squares, with plenty of green spaces marked.

'This is one of our biggest big *plazas*.'

Was he starting to read her mind?

Huge trees provided shade throughout the area, statues presiding beneath them, spray from fountains catching the sunlight, people parading, many with *mate* gourds, ornately decorated in silver, people sipping as they walked.

'I want some *mate*,' Ella announced, and Caroline, who'd thought her daughter was dozing, looked at her in surprise.

'Do you like it?' she asked, turning again to see Ella nod.

'Hor-hay makes it nice for me.'

Caroline knew Jorge had been spending a lot of time with Ella, and she, Caroline, had deliberately kept out of the way so the pair of them could begin to bond, but sharing *mate*—he never did that with her, not after that first day.

She gave an inward groan and assured herself she couldn't possibly be jealous of her daughter, but the niggle she felt could hardly be anything else.

Except perhaps longing, for that was what she felt every time she looked at Jorge, a longing she knew would remain just that—the ache of yearning, unspoken and unrequited.

'You will have some when we reach the house.'

Jorge answered Ella, turning briefly towards his

daughter. The little girl nodded again, obviously content with the reply.

But the simple phrase 'when we reach the house' had restarted the butterflies that were cavorting in Caroline's stomach. She knew Jorge was apprehensive about introducing them to his father, but as he hadn't explained why, she kept imagining the worst possible scenarios.

His father might hate foreigners.

He might hate children. No, it couldn't be that. From things Jorge had said, Carlos would adore a grandchild. Was Jorge worried his father might make too much of a fuss of Ella?

Or maybe he had someone picked out for Jorge to marry and the sudden arrival of a three-year-old daughter would spoil his plans.

Marriages were still arranged in many countries, mostly for business reasons. As Caroline's turbulent imagination raced ahead, she saw the man's business ruined, his life in tatters.

'We are here.'

Jorge had driven in through the wrought-iron gates held open by urns containing cascades of vibrant petunias. A longish drive, poplar lined, then a wide, rambling house of creamy stucco, carved wooden railings on the sandstone patio that stretched along the front, huge timber doors with ornate metal hinges and clasps, heavy timber beams holding up the red-tiled roof that overhung the patio, which was lined with neatly clipped trees in pots.

Olive trees? Something with fine, silvery leaves at any rate.

Her worries were forgotten—or, if not forgotten, shelved for the moment.

'What a magic place,' Caroline breathed. 'The building looks as if it grew here among the plants and bushes.'

'It is a popular style of architecture, old Spanish. There is another patio along the back, hidden from the street.'

He stopped the car, and turned towards her.

'But I told you that four years ago, no? Back when I promised to bring you to my home.'

There was no joy in his voice. In fact, he spoke as if the memory hurt him, while what lay ahead—the actual introduction to his father—was something to be faced with the strongest apprehension.

She reached out to touch him, but only very lightly, and only on the shoulder.

'Lighten up,' she ordered. 'It's not as if you're going to the gallows. I can't believe your father won't be pleased to know he has a granddaughter, so surely this should be a happy occasion.'

'You don't know my father,' Jorge responded, still obviously sunk in gloom.

'You think he won't be pleased?' Caroline demanded.

Jorge shook his head.

Her panic returned but before she could question the headshake he was out of the car and striding up the steps.

Caroline unstrapped Ella from her car seat and followed, though more slowly. Jorge had reached the landing at the top, and, as if someone had been spying from inside, the front doors opened as he reached them. A tall, imperious-looking woman in a black dress was holding one of the big doors, but the bulky man behind her soon pushed forward, enveloping Jorge in his arms, tears in his voice as he welcomed his son home.

Caroline walked more slowly—tentatively—up the steps, Ella in her arms. Jorge was talking now, his words too fast for Caroline to follow, although she heard enough to know he was explaining his visitors.

Then the cry '*Mi nieta*?'—the words loud with disbelief—the Spanish phrase for 'My granddaughter', repeated more huskily as the man came towards Caroline, but with eyes only for Ella.

Jorge was there before him, taking Ella from Caroline, talking quietly to her.

'This is your *abuelo*, your grandfather, Ella. Abuelito is a good name to call him—can you say that?'

'Ablito,' Ella, ever game to try a word, repeated.

'That will do, my princess,' the old man said, reaching out and cupping his hand to Ella's cheek. 'We will take time to get to know each other. You can call me Ablito and I will call you Princesa, okay?'

'*I'm* not a princess,' Ella told him. 'I'm just a little girl.'

'You will be my princess,' her grandfather told her, and Caroline, although things could not have gone better, felt a sense of doom descend upon her.

Somehow they all got through the afternoon and early evening, being shown to rooms, exploring the house, trying new foods—eating ice cream to die for—and finally, when Ella was tucked into bed, Caroline sat with Carlos and Jorge on the patio behind the house, admiring the soft lights in the formally laid-out garden, sipping a local white wine.

But not relaxing. The tension she'd been feeling had intensified when she'd seen Carlos's delight in his granddaughter. Now it was so strong it was a wonder she could swallow.

'You must marry, of course.'

Carlos's remark was so unexpected—mind-boggling might be a better word—Caroline couldn't reply.

'Not a man to beat around a bush, my father.' Jorge's words dropped into the sudden silence, and from the dry tone of his voice Caroline knew that *this* was what he had feared—*this*, not rejection, had been on his mind.

'You do not want my granddaughter growing up a bastard,' Carlos continued, as if this was a perfectly normal and logical conversation.

'Nobody cares about that kind of thing any more, Papá,' Jorge protested.

'*I* care about it,' Carlos retorted, and although he didn't raise his voice Caroline read not only truth but determination in the words.

'We will work it out between us, Caroline and I. After all, it is our business,' Jorge told him.

'And the child's,' Carlos pointed out, and the sinking feeling in Caroline's stomach told her she knew she'd lost.

But lost what?

She'd admitted to herself that she still loved Jorge so surely marriage to him wouldn't be a problem?

Except it would be if he didn't love her and so far she'd had no indication that he did.

The physical attraction was still there—she knew that—felt it in every nerve in her body whenever he was near. And she knew from his reaction to her presence that he wasn't immune to it either. Several times they'd nearly kissed—or so she'd thought—but…

What must she be thinking, sitting there so quietly, listening to my father's outrageous suggestion, to his reasoning that marriage was the only answer? Jorge tried to read Caroline's face, but it revealed nothing.

Neither did she show any signs of arguing with his father, although she must have been equally shocked by the old man's abrupt suggestion.

'I would never hurt Ella, but I must do what's right for Caroline as well,' Jorge told his father. 'And it is for she and I to decide what is best.'

'You *know* what is best, my son,' Carlos said. 'Now, I wish to speak to Antoinette about dinner and look in my princess. Why don't you take Caroline for a promenade in the *plaza* until it is time for us to sit down?'

He stood up and walked away, leaving Jorge wondering what to say to the woman who'd been on the receiving end of his father's proclamation.

Caroline solved that problem by speaking first.

'Does it put Antoinette out to have more people in the house, more people for dinner?' she asked, and the words stabbed into him, shocking him into speech far more effectively than his father's words had done.

'Is that where we have come to, you and I, mundane

conversation about Antoinette and dinner when my father has demanded we marry?'

To his surprise, Caroline laughed.

'What did you expect me to say? Something along the lines of how dare your father interfere in our lives? He has said what he said out of love, Jorge, love for a child he's met only once. And don't try to tell me you didn't suspect he'd react like this because you've been teetering on a tightrope since you first considered introducing Ella to him. I thought you were thinking, Will I, or won't I? tossing up about telling him at all, but now I realise you knew him well enough to have guessed how he'd react.'

Jorge stared at her, her usual attire of dark trousers and top making her all but invisible in the shadows, except for her face with its silvery halo of hair, luminous in the lamplight.

She smiled again, and stood up.

'Well, come on, you're under orders to take me for a promenade around the *plaza*.'

Dumbfounded again—it was a good thing he'd learned that descriptive English word—he joined her, following her through the wide hall to the front door, opening it for her, then taking her elbow as they walked down the steps.

'It's this way,' he said, but Caroline had halted at the front gate, and was looking around her in amazement.

'Earlier,' she said, nodding in a friendly fashion at people walking past, 'I held Ella up to the window to show her the moon and stars. She likes to see them before she goes to sleep. And from up there, in her bedroom…' Caroline turned to look up at the upper storey of the house '…the streets were deserted. I thought it odd because I've grown used to the custom of having dinner late in the evening and I wondered where everyone was, but now the streets are full of people strolling…' she grinned at Jorge '…or *promenading* along the pavement.'

He *had* to smile. How could he not, when her delight in this custom of his country was so obvious? But even smiling hurt when he considered how he should have brought Caroline home—how he'd intended bringing her home—four years ago.

He turned to practicality to hide the pain. At least that was something he was good at, hiding pain.

'They stay indoors until the heat of the day has passed. I think that's where this custom came from. Then in the cool of the evening they stroll out to meet their friends.'

'It's a lovely idea,' she said, and she sounded so pleased by everything around her that he set aside the past and all that belonged there and took her hand, tucking it in the crook of his arm.

'Shall we promenade, my lady?'

Big mistake. Now that her body was pressed close against his side, his left side—he'd made sure of that—his father's idea of marriage came rushing back into his head, his body telling him it was the best idea it had heard in a long time.

The physical attraction between them had been slow-growing—back then. Awareness had quivered from the beginning, but they'd come to like each other as friends, delighting in talking, discussing, even arguing together, until it had seemed only natural that they should take what they'd both recognised as something special to another stage.

'Are you thinking about sex?'

Caroline's question startled him so much he stopped, halting her progress so suddenly she stumbled against him.

He opened his mouth to deny it, then laughed.

'Why on earth would you ask that?'

'Because I was,' she admitted with a rueful laugh. 'About us, and the past, and how good our love-making always was, and it seems to me that lately you've been… not reading my mind perhaps, but definitely on the same wavelength, so I thought I'd ask.'

What could he reply?

What he'd have liked to say was, 'Oh, Caroline,' then he'd have liked to take her in his arms and hold her close, perhaps whisper of the things he would do to her later in the privacy of a bedroom, but that was hardly appropriate given how she must feel about him.

How he'd treated her…

But she'd brought it up—the past and their love-making…

Desire and panic squirmed inside him. He tucked her arm back into the crook of his elbow and resumed walking.

'It's because of my father's ridiculous assertion that we should marry,' he said. 'That's what's got us thinking this way.'

This time it was Caroline who stopped their progress.

'Ha!' she said, poking him in the chest. 'You *were* thinking about it! You said *us*.'

'Of course I was thinking about it,' he muttered at her, dragging her to one side of the pavement so people could pass. 'How could I not think about it when my body remembers how good it was between us? Physical attraction is a chemical thing, like magnetism—magnets attract. It's a fact, and we just happen to be the negative and positive of a very powerful magnet.'

'Oh!' she said, and he had a feeling she might be smiling at him but they'd stepped back into deep shadow and he couldn't really tell although he was sure he'd heard a smile in the exclamation. But when she added, 'Well, that explains it,' he *knew* the smile was there and no power on earth could have prevented the kiss he pressed on her lips.

'We'll never get to promenade,' she whispered against his cheek, his scarred cheek, some time later. 'And your father is sure to ask what I thought of the *plaza*.'

'Tell him you liked the statue of the three gods playing in heaven,' Jorge told her, intent on reclaiming her lips, for even just kissing Caroline was filling his soul with peace.

'Best I see it,' she said, speaking as gently as she moved, easing herself out of his arms.

He felt bereft—there was no other word—but he shut the loss away with so many other losses and continued their promenade, acutely aware that while she might think he could read her mind he didn't have the faintest notion of what she could be thinking, or even how she felt about the kiss.

Although she *had* kissed him back—he knew that much.

She shouldn't have kissed him back, Caroline told herself, but knew no power on earth could have stopped her once their lips had touched.

What had happened to her since arriving at the house that had changed her from a tense, unhappy wreck into a smiling, joking, kissing, for heaven's sake, woman like the person she'd been four years ago?

Had Carlos's declaration that they marry freed her from all the constraints that had been binding her—don't touch him, don't show your feelings, don't embarrass yourself and him?

Or was it the relaxed feeling in the air, the beautiful surroundings, the smiling people and music spinning through the air?

Caroline hadn't a clue but although she was thoroughly enjoying the moment—and had more than enjoyed the kiss!—she knew she should be wary. Just because things were peaceful between Jorge and herself right now, it didn't mean the armistice would last. Self-preservation dictated she keep her feelings in check—well, some of them—particularly the love that both sang and wept inside her. It was okay to show her attraction—how could she avoid it when they kissed? But love—love was dangerous. Love made people feel uncomfortable, especially the object of the love if love was not returned, and Jorge had enough discomfort in his life.

Her thoughts flitted like demented dragonflies in her head while she walked, pressed too close to Jorge's side. Now he stopped and she looked around, taking in her immediate surroundings for the first time.

'Three gods playing in heaven?' she queried, looking at the tangle of what might be figures in the fountain. But the man with whom she'd joked, the man she'd kissed, had gone and the closed-off stranger was back in his place. One look at his face was enough to tell her that.

'You need not be intimidated by my father, neither would I press you into anything you don't wish to do, but did you have ideas, when you came, of what you wished for in our reunion? Apart from a father for Ella?'

He'd released her hand from the crook of his arm and turned to face her—perhaps deliberately standing in the light from a lamppost so his scarred face was cruelly visible.

'I thought we'd have a month,' she admitted, knowing he deserved her honesty. 'I thought that would give us time to work out a plan for the future—to work out together what would be best for Ella, and for all three of us.'

She watched him closely as she spoke but there was no hint of a reaction, although what she'd said had been as bland as custard, so why would he react?

'You must have had some ideas,' he persisted, and the anger that was never far beneath the surface of her composure flared again.

'Of course I had some ideas,' she snapped. 'I had stupid, foolish, idiotic ideas that somewhere beneath the closed-off, self-pitying wreck you have become some spark of what we'd shared might have lingered. But one day with you was enough to know you'd chosen defeat over life—you'd shut yourself off with your injuries and your pain, shut yourself in on them and held them close, using them as a wall to hide behind, terrified you might see pity in the eyes of someone who loved you.'

She spun away, aware she'd said too much but not caring, the tension of the past weeks finally catching up with her.

Except she couldn't walk away; that was as feeble a behaviour as his was, so she turned back to him.

'And, yes, I've thought,' she said. 'I'll get a flat, I'll get a job, I'll settle Ella into kindergarten—you can have just as much say in that as I do. We'll be close, you can work out the shared parenting however you like, and as long as Ella is happy and settled I'll be content.'

'Content? You'd settle for content?'

His voice was harsh with anger but her own was still hot.

'Are you telling me you haven't?' she demanded, and this time when she turned she continued walking, back along the avenue of trees in the big *plaza*, past the smiling faces and the ice cream and *mate* stands, stalking out onto the boulevard, desperate to get back to the house, to her room, where she could give way to the torrent of emotions cascading through her mind and body—where she could have a damn good cry…

Jorge let her go and followed more slowly—keeping her in sight although he knew she'd be safe in this neighbourhood, with people strolling through the streets, unaware of the emotional storm in two of their number.

Or maybe there were storms in other hearts and heads.

Not that it mattered. What mattered was what Caroline had said—the words she'd flung at him. Was she right? Had he been hiding behind his pain?

He could think of a dozen ways to deny it, but the words prickled at his skin, or maybe at his conscience. Was fearing pity the weakness she obviously considered it? Was it weakness, not strength, that made him turn away from it?

Dinner with Carlos that evening, Caroline realised later, was a harbinger of things to come. He was congenial, charming and so obviously delighted by the revelation of an instant family that Caroline forbore arguing when he talked of marriage, thinking she'd take it up with Jorge when they were alone.

The problem was exacerbated the next day as she watched Carlos play in the garden with Ella, devoting himself wholeheartedly to her game of hide and seek. Ella was always the one to hide, Carlos pretending not to see her where she stood, usually in plain view, behind a tree or shrub.

Caroline saw the joy on the man's face and read the happiness in his eyes. His hands trembled slightly when he touched Ella, as if he was afraid he'd break this precious new being who had come into his life.

Not having known him from before, she couldn't say

for certain he seemed to be getting younger, but the man who carried Ella to her bath a few days later was certainly a more carefree man than the man she'd first met.

Of Jorge she saw little. Having delivered a grandchild to his father, did he feel his duty was done? Or was he out of the house with genuine purpose, following through on his desire to find work in genetics?

The other alternative—perhaps the obvious one—was that he was avoiding her, and though it upset Caroline to think that, she was honest enough to admit she couldn't blame him, for she'd thrown some harsh words at him on their promenade.

'I have been talking to my father's doctor.' Three days after their arrival Jorge sought her out, finding her in the beautiful, book-lined library where she retreated when Ella played with Carlos. Jorge settled opposite her in a leather armchair and continued talking. 'I noticed a change in him on our arrival and wondered, but he, the doctor, has confirmed he's been having a series of TIAs.'

Transient ischemic attacks—the words of the acronym sounded in Caroline's head. Small strokes, really, lasting only a minute or two, leaving the patient feeling confused and tired. The problem was that a third—she thought it was a third—of people who suffered them could go on to have a full-blown stroke.

'Is he taking some kind of anti-platelet therapy? Aspirin at least?' she asked, and Jorge nodded.

'And lifestyle changes? I've noticed he doesn't smoke, and as far as I've seen he only has a couple of glasses of wine in the evenings. Does he have a history of heart disease or carotid artery disease?'

To Caroline's surprise, Jorge didn't answer, smiling at her instead.

'Are you aware you clicked straight into medical mode then?' he asked.

She frowned at him, upset by the smile but not willing to let it show.

'Why wouldn't I?' she demanded.

He shrugged but as his smile had faded she didn't push for an answer. It was easier to cope with a non-smiling Jorge, so she didn't have to hide behind medical questions—although she'd grown fond enough of Carlos, and not only because of his devotion to Ella, to be genuinely concerned.

'Is he handling it well? What did the doctor say?' she persisted.

'Well enough, but you know they could be a precursor to something more serious,' Jorge replied. 'It is that I wished to discuss with you.'

'The possibility of your father having a stroke?' Caroline studied him, aware she was frowning, then shrugged her shoulders. 'I don't know any more than the experts—probably less.'

'You know about the lifestyle changes. Yes, he did smoke cigars but no longer does; yes, he liked his drink before dinner and wine with dinner and a brandy after it, and has cut right down, but stress is another factor and right now, although he doesn't show it, I know he must be stressed.'

Admittedly she barely knew the man but what she

did know of him she liked. In fact, the more she saw and learned of him the more she liked him. He was the kind of man who showed his feelings, particularly his love, and his love appeared to be all-reaching—a huge umbrella he spread across his family, warming, protecting, oozing love.

Concern made her voice sharp as she asked, 'Is it us being here? Is it too much for him?'

Jorge looked uncomfortable. He fidgeted in the chair, eventually standing up and taking a turn around the room, pausing by his father's desk, touching things on it—a pen set, an old-fashioned blotter in a leather case, a matching leather tray of mail.

'It is the opposite,' he finally admitted. 'Us being here—Ella being here—has given him a new lease on life, trite though that might sound. It is for that reason I would want him to live as long and as healthily as possible, that he might enjoy her company for many years to come.'

'And she his,' Caroline put in, still uncertain where this conversation was going. 'She already adores him. I hate to say it, but if you don't come home early one afternoon to play in the garden with her, then her Ablito, as she calls him, will replace you in her affections.'

Jorge took another turn around the room, pausing this time at the deep window embrasure, peering out through the slightly open and heavy velvet curtains into the garden.

'They are playing there now. Even through the window you can hear their laughter.'

He turned back to Caroline.

'He brought me up himself when my mother died, although he could have left the task to Antoinette and servants. He put me back together when I came home from France, held me in the night when I cried out in pain. I rewarded him by going away—by leaving him here, worrying all the time about my health, both mental and physical—yet he made no move, spoke no word, to hold me near him.'

Caroline found herself swallowing hard, images of Carlos as the father Jorge had known so vivid in her head she could have wept for him.

Wept for Jorge as well, for he was looking pale and strained—wretched, in fact, although the tell-tale tilt to his back wasn't there so she doubted it was pain bothering him.

'You're telling me this because you feel you owe him something? And I can help you repay him in some way?'

'You can,' Jorge said, coming closer and taking both her hands in his. 'I know it is a lot to ask of you, but you must know it is his dearest wish. You must know that, being the old-fashioned man he is, he frets about it.'

Caroline shook her head.

'You've lost me,' she said, although she had guessed where the conversation was going. Maybe it was because Jorge was touching her, actually holding her hands, and her brain had gone into a whirl that she felt she could not cope with it just now.

'He mentioned it the first afternoon you were here,' Jorge said.

'I was in such a daze that first afternoon,' she said,

removing her hands from that tempting grasp, 'I doubt I remember much of it. Your father calling Ella his princess, she telling him she was a girl. We walked, we argued.'

Jorge looked at her. For some reason, today she was wearing the pink T-shirt with the bright butterfly on it and she made a splash of colour in the dim library. He looked away again, the pain of looking at her too real. Did she really not remember? They'd had a long drive, she would have been apprehensive about meeting his father, concerned about Ella…

'He thinks we should marry.' Jorge blurted out the words then knew they weren't enough. 'It pains him to think of Ella as a bastard and while you and I know that is a very old-fashioned take on things, it's *his* take on it, and it worries him, probably enough, though he wouldn't mention it again, to exacerbate his condition.'

He *had* to look at her. Had to try to read her reaction on her face, but it was blank, as if all emotion had been wiped away by the shock of his revelation. Then, as he watched, she nodded.

'I suppose it's easy enough to do—we marry. Do you have registry offices here? We can do it in a few minutes, although I'll have to check on the legalities as far as being an Australian is concerned. The embassy could tell me. It's no big deal, Jorge. We'll sort it out—you can tell him that we're onto it.'

Could she really be so casual about it?

Worse, could she really believe a couple of minutes in front of a judge or priest would satisfy his father as a marriage?

Of course, she didn't know his father as he did. She had no idea what a wedding here entailed.

And knowing it would pain his father more to believe the marriage was a sham—to see it as a sham—he, Jorge, had to somehow backtrack along this conversation and bring the marriage in from another angle.

A marriage of convenience?

Convenient certainly, but a true marriage?

No matter how much he might wish to hold himself apart from Caroline—to continue to hide behind the barriers he'd built up—he couldn't be part of a sham played out for his father. He also had no doubt the attraction that had existed between them from their first meeting was as strong as ever, so why *not* a marriage in every sense?

But how to put this to Caroline?

Caroline sat very still, thinking maybe if she didn't move, the world would return to normal.

Although she'd tried to sound as casual as possible, flippant even, as if she fronted up to a judge to get married every day of the week, the thought of marrying Jorge, even if it wasn't real, made her feel as if a hand had reached inside her body and clutched at her intestines. It clenched around them, tightening her lungs as well, fingers squeezing at her heart.

Marry Jorge—a dream, yet not a dream. Without love would it be a nightmare?

Or could it work?

Could she make it work?

She had no idea.

And from what she could see, watching him go back

to pacing around the library, he didn't seem overly delighted by her calm acceptance of the strange proposal. In fact, he seemed more perturbed than he had earlier, pacing, muttering under his breath, frowning ferociously as, every now and then, his gaze darted towards her.

'Sit!' she finally ordered, and though he started at the command, he eventually sat—directly in front of her once again.

'What's the problem?' she asked him, speaking calmly, ignoring the turmoil in her body and the questions battering her brain. 'You want us to marry to please your father, I've said yes. What's bothering you now?'

He looked at her in silence for a long moment, then he smiled and her intestines tightened some more, while her heart began to beat out a rhythm she didn't want to analyse.

Though maybe it was a tango…

'May I kiss you?' he said, so formally she wondered if she'd heard the words aright.

Did she nod?

Say yes without realising it?

Was that why he was standing now, his hands holding hers, drawing her up out of the chair, his head bending and his lips brushing hers, feather-soft at first then demanding, seducing, conquering.?

She fell into the kiss with a hunger she couldn't believe existed, a hunger she'd managed to keep hidden since they'd met again, a hunger that could no longer be denied…

It was only because, in some dim recess of her

brain, she remembered Ella and Carlos, not to mention Antoinette, being in the house that she didn't begin to rip clothes off—hers, his. Who cared?

This kiss spiralled deep into her body, pushing heat and frustrated desire before it, trailing need and want and passion in its wake. Her blood thundered in her ears, deafening all common sense—all warnings to step back, be sensible, take this one step at a time.

Had that first kiss in the street primed her for this? She had no idea, she only knew that kissing Jorge here and now was like coming home. His body anchored hers, solid, firm, hard where she was soft. His hands roamed her limbs, her back, her waist, her breasts, fingers edging between their bodies to move against her nipples.

Words whimpered from her lips, pleas for more, words of love only just caught back by her teeth—some remnant of common sense must remain! But no other limit held them back as they explored each other's bodies, touching, pressing, gliding, Jorge's lips now on her throat, now at her temple, her teeth biting into the hollow of his shoulder as he teased her to madness with his tongue against her ear.

Yet even as the kiss—the word hardly seemed appropriate for the conflagration in the library—reached a panting, breathless, close-to-exhaustion peak, Caroline felt part of herself detach and stand there, watching.

He's doing this to prove something, that other self whispered, knowing that she was helpless, so when he finally let go of her and stood back a little, his fingers trailing over her flushed face and undoubtedly swollen lips, and said, 'Well?' quite quietly, she allowed herself to nod, knowing the question he hadn't asked, knowing her response to his kiss had already given him his answer.

CHAPTER EIGHT

CARLOS took over their lives. Barely able to believe that Caroline had agreed to a marriage in every sense, Jorge continued to keep out of her way, half fearing too much exposure to him might change her mind. Half hoping she might change her mind for marriage would certainly break through his defences—physically at least.

Emotionally, could he retain his detachment? Keep at least his heart and all it held hidden from her?

Avoiding Caroline was easy. Ella, though, was a different matter, and he made sure he spent time with her every day—special time when he showed her old toys he'd played with as a child. One day, he took her up into the attic and removed the covers off a dolls' house that had been his mother's.

'Can I play with it, Hor-hay?' she asked, her voice barely above a whisper as she took in all the details of tiny, perfect furniture—upholstered chairs, beds made up with impossibly small silk sheets and coverlets, tiny dolls that fitted in the rooms, even a baby in the nursery.

'You can,' he told her. 'I will carry it downstairs into

the room where my old toys are and Antoinette will clean it up for you.'

'Oh, Hor-hay!' Ella cried out her delight, and flung her arms around his neck, her little body pressed against him, her lips soft against his scarred cheek.

'But she might break things,' Caroline protested when she saw the incredible miniature house.

'I do not think so,' Jorge argued, 'but if she does, would it matter so very much? Could we not get them fixed? Is it not something to be used, rather than hidden away in an attic?'

Caroline looked at him and shrugged, but before she could turn away he caught her hand, and while Ella knelt in front of the little house, watching Antoinette lift out each piece and put it on a table, he touched the face of the woman he was to marry soon.

'You are pale. Is this all too much for you? You only have to say and we can do it more simply.'

Her smile was as pale as she was, a shadowy replica of her usual bright grin.

'Now? When Carlos has ordered up not only food but clothes and guests, and wedding presents arrive on the hour every hour? I think not, Jorge.'

'But it is getting you down.' He was facing her, studying the faint lines drawn beside her lips, the shadows beneath her clear blue eyes. 'I did not wish for that.'

She touched his cheek with cool fingers.

'I'll survive,' she said, 'and now I have to go. I have an appointment with a seamstress, would you believe? I didn't know such people still existed, let alone made house calls.'

Jorge watched her walk away, his body aching with desire for her, the skin on his cheek burning where she'd touched it, his mind a chaos of memory and foreboding. Yes, he wanted this marriage for many reasons, not least of them physical, but what of Caroline? She was too honest to deny the attraction between them, but surely he'd killed the love she'd had for him?

Love wasn't the issue, he reminded himself, so why did it keep creeping into his mind?

Because he loved her and if she knew or guessed it, would it be a burden to her?

Love.

Back when he'd broken off their relationship, using words so cruel she had to hate him, he'd looked ahead to years of operations, to the possibility of never walking again, to years of being a deadweight on her. His pride had refused to let her see the broken man he'd become, and that same pride was now the cause of his foreboding.

He'd seen her flinch—once long ago—seen horror in her eyes as she'd looked on a man so badly deformed it was a wonder he'd survived, and it was the memory of that flinch that had confirmed he was doing the right thing when he'd pressed the Send button on the email program.

Would she flinch again?

Some wedding night to look forward to, with his mind following these lines!

'See, Hor-hay! The baby has a little cot all of his own.'

Ella's voice brought him out of the deep pit of despair

his thoughts had dug for him, and her little hands, as she handed him the tiny cot, made the breath catch in his throat.

He had to forget his own feelings and forebodings. They were doing this for their precious child—for Ella—and as he turned the cot in his hands and helped her fit the baby into it, he knew he had to hide the doubts and pain he felt and go forward into this marriage with, if not confidence, at least a semblance of it.

Caroline stood in her allotted bedroom, the pure white silk of Jorge's mother's wedding dress falling almost to the floor. The original Ella must have been shorter and plumper than Caroline, but not by much, so the seamstress had little to do.

Where the dress had come from, Caroline had no idea. She only knew Carlos had handed her the big box, once white but yellowing with age, and though he hadn't said anything, she knew, when she saw the dress, exactly what he wanted of her.

Part of her wanted to protest, to tell him it was too much. She was already doing this—getting married—for him, but to wear the dress? Pretend it was a real wedding for a real marriage? Surely that was too much to ask of her?

Ella had clinched the deal, coming in as Caroline opened the box with a photo in her hands.

'Here's a picture, Mummy, of Ablito and my grandma who's a star—my first grandma—getting married, and Ablito says you'll wear this pretty dress and he'll get a pretty dress for me, like the one the little girl in the picture is wearing.'

Caroline had looked at the picture and realised that for Ella, to be dressed in layered frills like a doll on the top of a wedding cake would be a dream come true.

So, now she stood, pins going in around her waist, thinking not of marrying Jorge but of what would come after it.

Had he been keeping away from her deliberately, knowing that her desire would build and build? Knowing that the kiss had fired her senses to the point where the next kiss would inevitably lead to bed?

Oh, they still promenaded in the evenings, but with Carlos and with Ella, whose bedtime had slowly but surely grown later and later. The night before last they'd even danced in the paved square beyond the gods playing in heaven, danced to the music of a busker with a guitar. And as she'd strutted through the steps of the tango, feeling the heat of the dance, the to and fro of the dangerous flirtation it represented, she had wanted nothing more than to be held in Jorge's arms for ever.

It's a pretence, she reminded herself, pulling away as the music ended and other couples moved into the deep shadows of the trees.

'Is it danced at weddings?' she asked, hoping he would take the flutter in her voice for pre-wedding nerves, not wound-tight wanting—lust, almost. Although she hadn't ever thought to feel something as earthy as the word lust suggested.

'Of course,' he said, leading her back to where Ella and Carlos waited by the fountain. 'It is like foreplay.'

His eyes held hers as he said the word, the glint in them telling her he, too, was tightly wound. Caroline shivered in the warm night air. It was okay for a man to feel lust, but for a woman? Weren't women supposedly beyond such basic emotions? And was it an emotion or simply a biological imperative?

'You are cold. We will return to the house.'

Jorge slipped his jacket around her shoulders and the smell of him—man-smell, definitely earthy—nearly proved her undoing. She clutched the lapels, pulling them close, hoping he wouldn't see the trembling of her body as she imagined not the jacket but the man himself, wrapping around her, enveloping her this way.

Somehow she got back to the house. Somehow she sat on Ella's big four-poster bed while Jorge read her nightly story. Somehow she held her child up at the window while she said goodnight to the moon and stars, but when it came to going down to dinner, to sitting with Carlos and Antoinette and Jorge and pretending life was normal, Caroline backed out.

She found Antoinette in the kitchen.

'I know I have to eat something,' Caroline told her, 'but my stomach isn't up to dinner. May I take some biscuits and cheese up to my room?'

Antoinette turned around and, to Caroline's surprise, gave her a big hug.

'Everyone is pretending a wedding is just another business activity while for you it is emotional storm, no?' she said, and it took Caroline all her willpower to hold back her tears. She was *not* going to her wedding with red eyes.

'I'll be okay,' she assured Antoinette, who moved away, fussing in the pantry, pulling out tins and bottles, assembling a tray of tasty treats for Caroline to take up to her room.

'And wine,' Antoinette said firmly. 'A mellow red to help you sleep. See, a small bottle, you must drink it all. Tomorrow there are caterers for the party so I will help you dress and take care of Ella too.'

Then, to Caroline's surprise, the housekeeper cupped her hands around Caroline's face and looked into her eyes.

'There are worse things than marrying when unsure about love,' she said. 'At least you are getting a chance to show him how you feel.'

The words rang in Caroline's head as she carried the tray up to her room.

Was her love for Jorge so obvious that Antoinette had picked up on it? And could she, Caroline, afford to show Jorge how she felt? Might he not reject her love again?

Could she take that kind of risk when he'd rejected her once before?

And had it been her father's earlier rejection that had made her take Jorge's rejection so hard? Made her so afraid of being rejected again?

She had no answers to any of her questions so she turned her thoughts back to Antoinette and realised something she had missed, so caught up had she been in her own thoughts and feelings. Antoinette loved Carlos, and probably had for some time. Antoinette knew the pain of unrequited love, of love that couldn't be shown, or celebrated.

And Carlos?

Ws he still pining for his Ella?

Antoinette was an attractive woman—did he not see that?

'You are not coming to dinner?'

Jorge was in front of her, having emerged from his bedroom—a sanctum she had yet to see but was reasonably sure would be her bedroom tomorrow night.

'I'm a little tired and not hungry, although Antoinette has fixed more in snacks than I'd eat in a full meal.'

'I am sorry to have put you through all of this production,' he said quietly, taking the tray from her hands and turning to lead her to her room. 'But—'

'But it pleases Carlos,' Caroline finished for him as Jorge set the tray down on the small table by the window. She touched his arm. 'It's no big deal,' she added, but he'd moved into the light and she saw the strain on his face too.

'No big deal?' he queried, his voice rough with emotion. 'No big deal when my body aches for you every minute of every day? When I can't sleep for thinking of you in bed only metres from my room? When I replay our kisses in the library over and over in my head, wondering how I had the strength to not lock the door and finish what we'd started? Are you so immune to me now—did I hurt you so badly—that you can step out of my arms after a tango and carry on a normal conversation while my imagination is stripping off your clothes and slathering your naked body with kisses?'

Caroline stared at him, unable to believe the closed-off man she'd been coming to know over the last few weeks was talking like this. It wasn't love, that much was obvious, but if he wanted her as much as she wanted him, then might not love find a way back into their relationship?

She stepped towards him and put her arms around him, kissing him gently on the lips.

'One more night,' she whispered, then she pulled away, using her hands on his shoulders to turn him and guide him towards the door. Then, with her heart full of hope, she ate some of Antoinette's carefully prepared snacks and drank the wine.

She could make this work.

She *would* make this work!

At times it seemed the minutes flew, while others dragged out to hours. She'd vetoed the cathedral, settling for the local church, next to the school Jorge had attended, the school Ella would probably attend.

Clad in a frilly white dress with a crown of roses in her hair, Ella danced through the morning in such a welter of excitement Caroline *had* to forget her own reservations and laugh at her daughter's antics.

But when Antoinette pinned a mantilla of fine old Spanish lace into Caroline's hair, all she'd wanted to do was cry. Here she was, the very vision of a bride, but a bride should go in joyous love down the aisle to the man who loved her, while she, for all the love she felt for Jorge, was going with fear and trepidation in her heart.

Red eyes! she reminded herself.

Enjoy Ella's delight.

Remember it is only a couple of hours out of your life—nothing more.

But as she repeated age-old, solemn vows she knew it was a whole lot more. To love and to cherish—oh, how she longed to do just that to Jorge so *her* promise, though wavery, was heartfelt.

But his?

Oh, she had no doubt about the cherish part for he would look after her in every way, but love?

Once again the question of whether it had ever existed on his part slipped into her head, and the rest of the ceremony passed in a blur. He'd said not, told her he'd never loved her, and for all she could make up excuses why he'd do that, she couldn't know for sure.

Maybe tonight…

He was shifting her mantilla, pushing it back so it framed her face, his fingers trembling, as were the lips that touched hers, but behind them the guests had erupted into loud applause and cheering and probably some lewd remarks, although Caroline's grasp of Spanish seemed to have disappeared, so lost was she in her emotions.

Her beauty had overwhelmed him so he'd had to hold back tears as she'd approached the altar, but now the lost look in her eyes cut into his heart.

She's doing this for me—for Papá.

I've forced her into it, into a marriage without love.

Would telling her I love her still—that the hateful, hurtful words were lies—help or make things worse?

Make things worse, undoubtedly, if the words I used as swords to cut through the bond between us worked and she no longer loves me. Then she'll have the burden of a maimed, diminished husband *and* a love she can't return. And surely the latter would be the heaviest of loads.

The added complication of talking love was if she said it was returned.

To have her say she loved him. Would that hurt most of all—because would he ever know if it was truly love or pity?

Best let things lie.

With the papers signed he led her back down the aisle, the triumph of the music diminishing him more with every step he took.

'Smile!' his new wife ordered, and the word shocked him out of his gloomy thoughts.

She was smiling.

Looking so radiant—so beautiful—his heart stopped beating.

'Look how Ella is enjoying all of this,' Caroline added, pointing to their daughter with her basket of rose petals, strewing them down the aisle ahead of them. 'If we're not careful she's going to grow into a right little miss with Carlos and Antoinette doting on her so much.'

'Can a child have too much love?' Jorge asked, although watching his daughter's antics *had* brought a smile to his face.

'I suppose not,' Caroline agreed, 'as long as she doesn't take advantage of it.'

'We'll see she doesn't,' Jorge assured her, and felt his worries and concerns drop from his shoulders. They were marrying for Ella and the shared responsibility of silly things, like seeing she wasn't spoiled by too much attention, was surely more important than love. He and Caroline would be good in bed—their mutual enjoyment a given, not only from past experience but from what he now thought of, in capital letters, as The Library Kiss!

Yes, things would be okay, and now he really smiled.

'Ella is going to fall asleep in her ice cream,' Caroline whispered to Jorge when the speeches were made and the toasts were done and tiredness was making her think she, too, might fall asleep at the table.

'We will take her up to bed, then retire ourselves. Papá will excuse us.'

Retire ourselves. How civilised it sounded, yet Caroline's skin prickled at the words, goose-bumps forming in the most unlikely places.

She glanced towards Carlos, who nodded in reply to her unspoken question, and as Jorge lifted Ella, her ruffles crushed and her face wreathed in chocolate ice cream, Caroline rose, said goodnight to the guests who'd come to share their dinner, and followed him upstairs.

Bath, teeth, bed, story, say goodnight to moon and stars, then she and Jorge were alone, standing in the doorway of Ella's room, their child already asleep.

'Come,' Jorge said, his voice a husky whisper. He put his arm around her shoulders and led her past the door of the room where she'd been sleeping, to his suite of rooms further along the corridor.

Inside he unpinned the comb that had held her mantilla in place and set the old lace carefully down on the top of a heavy wooden dresser.

'You looked so beautiful I could barely breathe,' he said, and Caroline, feeling the tension tightening in her body, knew she had to break it somehow or shatter into pieces herself.

'You polished up okay yourself,' she said lightly, kicking off her shoes, then bending to lift her skirt to undo the clasps that had held her stockings in place.

Had she lifted her skirt too far that Jorge stepped towards her?

'A suspender belt? You wore a suspender belt?' Awed was the only way to describe his voice.

'I suppose a pair of garters would be more symbolic but I thought—'

He stopped her with a kiss.

'No more talk,' he commanded when they could both breathe again.

Jorge turned her around to get at the million tiny buttons running down the back of the silky gown and with fumbling fingers began the task of undoing them, easing the gown, as it opened, first off her shoulders, then letting it slide to her waist, fighting the last buttons until eventually it slid down over her hips, leaving her standing in a pool of white silk, a lacy bra, matching lacy panties and a frothy confection of a suspender belt, white strips of satin ribbon running down to the top of lacy-topped stockings.

He walked around to see her from the front and shook his head.

'I have always known you were beautiful, but now you steal my breath, my mind, my—'

He stopped himself before the word 'heart' erupted from his lips, substituting 'power of words'.

She stepped out of the puddle of white froth, bending to lift it, giving him a tantalising glimpse of thigh, before she spread the gown over the mantilla on the dresser.

His body was burning with such desire he knew he was likely to make a fool of himself if he touched her, so he simply looked, watching as she sat down on the bed and now slid off the stockings.

He should be doing that!

He moved, turning on a bedside light, dimming it, then turning off the main light so although she shone in the gloom of the darkened room, he felt less embarrassed about his own body—about the scars she had yet to see.

He knew it was pride that bothered him—foolish pride—yet Caroline had loved his body—his old body—so how would she feel? How would she react?

Could he go through with this?

Other women had seen the scars, one had even seemed to be turned on by them in some macabre way, but…

He tried to rationalise his fears which came down to…

What?

Losing her?

She was made of sterner stuff.

Yet fear and, yes, stupid pride still held him in their thrall.

Now she unclipped the suspender belt and tossed it lightly onto a chair, then stood up and came towards him.

'Fair's fair,' she said, and moved close enough to pull his bow-tie undone, removing it, then starting on his shirt buttons, her fingers sliding into the opening of his shirt, undoing the cuff links, finally easing it off his shoulders, not pausing to gaze at the ravages the explosion had left on his body, calmly undoing his belt now, sliding down his zip.

'You will have to do some of this yourself and as it's been a very long day, I would really like a shower before we go to bed.'

She pressed a kiss on his lips.

'Can I leave you to get naked on your own?' she teased, and as if he wasn't hard enough his groin tightened even further—agonising…

He'd shower in the guest bathroom. Sex in the shower was all very well, but this first time—this new first time—with Caroline—well, she deserved a bed. They both deserved a bed.

He wasn't sure of the logic of this, but his mind was racing around like a rat in a maze so logic didn't stand a chance. He'd shower, put on a nightshirt—Antoinette had produced a new silk one as a pre-wedding gift. Had she guessed how apprehensive he was about leaping the hurdle of a 'real' marriage?

Or had Antoinette, who'd bathed his injured, battered body, thought he should wear it for Caroline's sake?

Not that he didn't want to wear it—appearing naked in front of Caroline would break down the last of his carefully erected barriers and fear of her revulsion tamed his lust.

But Caroline had said get naked, so wouldn't she

expect to find him that way, not in a nightshirt, even if it was silk?

The rat kept running into walls, hopelessly trying to learn the escape route. Once Caroline would have laughed if he'd told her about the rat in his head—would she now?

He had no idea—no idea how to begin to think it through, think anything through.

'You're not naked!'

She was back!

She couldn't be back.

And *she* wasn't naked, though she might as well have been for he could see right through the diaphanous gown she was wearing to the pale, slim, shapely body beneath—the body that had haunted his dreams for four years.

It came to Caroline, standing there, feeling foolish in the nightdress Antoinette had given her—a nightdress Caroline suspected had long lain in Antoinette's hope chest until hope had faded into sadness—that Jorge was even more uptight than she was about the night ahead of them.

'Beautiful gown,' he murmured, but the words rough as if his throat was dry, his mouth devoid of moisture.

She grinned at him.

'Antoinette took one look at my banana pyjama pants and took over my night-time wardrobe,' she said, coming closer to where her husband stood. He looked so incredibly foolish with his shirt half-off and his trousers around his knees that it was all she could do not to laugh.

She kissed him lightly on the lips.

'Go have a shower,' she told him. 'You'll feel much better. You know this isn't a regular wedding night. You're under no pressure to perform. Just shower and come to bed.'

CHAPTER NINE

HE CAME to bed, a silk nightshirt covering his body, and slid in beside her, turning off the bedside light. Caroline wanted to protest, to strip off her gown and his so they'd be naked together, but through the silk she felt the damage to the skin on his torso—damage she'd carefully not looked at as she'd unbuttoned his shirt.

Tears filled her eyes, a bone-deep sadness descending on her. That Jorge, whom she'd loved more than life itself, should shield his scarred body from her… That he did not trust her to love him, scars and all, or even accept him as a lover, scars and all, seemed so overwhelmingly sad she couldn't help but cry.

Had he heard her sniff or felt the tears on her cheeks that he put his arms around her and held her to him, patting her shoulder, whispering to her in Spanish? Although her Spanish seemed to have deserted her because she didn't understand the words.

'It is all right,' he finally said in English. 'We married for our daughter, nothing more, so I do not expect more of you. We can share the bed without sex, or I will sleep on the couch tonight and tomorrow make arrangements for us to have separate rooms. This is a suite, there's another bedroom right next door. My father knows I sleep badly. He will accept the separate rooms.'

The spate of tears had passed. She'd lived with sadness before, she could do it again. Besides, now there was a diversion for her thoughts. Held close against Jorge's body, the heated desire that had been building since they'd kissed in the library flared back to life.

Yet he was talking so dispassionately about them *not* having sex, she could hardly insist on it.

Maybe he didn't want to.

Too bad?

Wasn't she entitled to a say?

She moved against him, experimentally.

Felt him stiffen then his body responding.

Whether he wanted it to or not?

Caroline decided she didn't care. She shifted so she could kiss his lips, moving her mouth against his until she felt his response.

'It would be a pity to not use the foreplay of the tango, surely,' she murmured, and his kiss deepened, his tongue probing into her mouth so she was tasting him, feeling his heat.

She slid her hands beneath his nightshirt, feeling the soft silk ruffle upwards as her fingers splayed against his body. Smooth skin, rough skin—she could feel both but this was Jorge and it didn't matter. Brushing her fingers across his nipples, she felt his response, hardness pressed against her belly. His kisses slithered down her neck, licks and kisses, teasing her nerve endings, causing a shivery excitement in her skin.

Now she was trembling against him and through the

fine silk of her gown his mouth found her breasts, teasing first one nipple then the other, teasing, teasing, the rasp of the silk intensifying the sensation. His hands wandered lower, not through silk but under it, finding her moist and ready for him, so ready she gasped as he touched her and trembled some more.

She reached for him and guided him into her body, rising to meet him, opening to him, so full of love it was hard to hold back the words she longed to say.

But love could be a burden—and didn't he have enough burdens to carry?

He was moving deep inside her now, and as she moved with him her thoughts were consumed by feeling, by the need and hunger and the race towards fulfilment.

'Slow!' he ordered, and though she wondered at his restraint—was the man made of steel?—she slowed her movements, letting him take control, driving their pace, teasing her towards orgasm then drawing back, until she flung all caution to the winds and moved again, her turn to take control as she worked towards the final moment when her body imploded, reverberations travelling to the tips of her toes, again and again until he cried out, too, and slumped against her, so she held his weight and blinked away more tears.

Different tears this time. Tears of joy that once again she was holding Jorge. That once again that had been joined in love.

Love?

Where had that come from?

It wasn't love, it was attraction—the magnet with opposing poles.

As her mind got back into gear, the argument began.

You don't need love, one side said.

And sex without it? queried the other.

Didn't it count that she loved him? the first voice cried.

Not really, said the killjoy.

For his part, Jorge seemed unbothered by questions of love. By questions of anything judging by the soft, not-exactly-snoring but definitely snuffling sounds coming from him. He had rolled over on his side and gone straight to sleep.

Once they would have held each other and talked—really talked—but thinking about that time was a sure way to bring the stupid tears on again and she'd cried enough for Jorge. She turned so her back was to him and tried to sleep herself but the distraction of his body, so close, made sleep impossible.

It wasn't going to work. For all he'd been the one to insist on a 'real' marriage—as if!—he'd obviously been reluctant to consummate it, first standing there half-undressed, later wearing his nightshirt to bed. Her heart ached at the thought that he feared her revulsion when she saw his scars. Surely they'd been close enough for him to know—

Go to sleep.

Ordering sleep didn't work and after another fruitless hour, lying motionless because she was unwilling to toss and turn fearing she'd wake him, she got out of bed, slipped on a robe that matched her nightgown—a second gift from Antoinette—and walked quietly out of the room, down the corridor to check on Ella.

The little girl was curled into one corner of the big four-poster and it took only seconds for Caroline to slip in beside her. Surely here, away from Jorge, she would sleep.

He knew before he was fully awake that she was gone. How had he slept so deeply that he didn't hear her depart, he who slept in snatches of restless stupor these days? Jorge rolled over and felt the space beside him. The sheets were cold so she'd been gone for some time.

He thought back to the tears she'd shed and cursed himself for putting her in this situation. She'd agreed to marry him for his father's sake, but *he'd* been the one to push the physical side of their union.

Why?

What had prompted him?

Surely more than the fact that his body ached for her and had since the day he'd cut her from his life, unwilling to burden her with a permanent invalid, yet perversely, in the present, he'd pushed for a 'real' marriage, then panicked when she'd suggested he get naked, afraid of what she'd think of the scarred shadow of the man she'd known.

Was it his obvious reluctance that had caused her tears?

His stupid pride in wearing that ridiculous nightshirt?

Or had she seen enough of his scarred body to be repulsed?

The rat was back in the maze.

And his wife was gone!

Knowing his father would accept it if neither of them appeared for breakfast but deciding he'd make the effort anyway, Jorge climbed out of bed, showered, shaved and dressed, then, knowing there'd be wondering looks and questions if he appeared alone, went in search of his wife.

She was wearing a robe over the beautiful nightgown but it didn't conceal much more than the gown did and his body leapt in response to the pale shape of her beneath the layers of silk. Memories of the passion they'd shared the previous night—hard, heated sex—had desire stirring again.

Hardly appropriate thoughts in front of their child, who was bouncing up and down and making it very difficult for Caroline to drag a wide comb through the tangled curls.

'I'm ready for breakfast, Hor-hay,' Ella announced, 'but Ablito says I can call you Papá. Do you want me to call you that?'

Papá!

Jorge felt as if his heart might break in two, while his throat tightened, making speech impossible.

He nodded at the little girl, who gave a cry of delight and flung herself into his arms, chanting, 'Papá, Papá, Papá!' in shrill, excited tones.

'I'll take her down to breakfast?' he asked Caroline as Ella's little arms fastened around his neck.

Caroline, still kneeling where she'd been while she'd dressed Ella and struggled to tame her hair, nodded.

'And you?' Jorge continued. 'Would you like something sent up?'

Something like a miracle? Caroline thought, though what kind of miracle she needed she wasn't sure.

Maybe the kind that turned back time—turned it back four years to before the accident so they could change the way their lives had played out.

Aloud she said, 'No, I'll be down in a few minutes,' and she rose to her feet, aware of Jorge's eyes on her—aware he was trying to read her thoughts.

But if she couldn't work out what she was thinking, what hope did he have?

Jorge left the house after breakfast, something about an appointment muttered into the air above Carlos's and Caroline's heads.

'I will take you and Ella to look at the kindergarten,' Carlos told Caroline.

So, the honeymoon is over, she thought, sadness welling inside her once again as she thought of what might have been. In spite of all the fuss of the big wedding, nothing had changed.

And everything had changed.

The day played out, Ella delighted with the kindergarten and seemingly unconcerned that the children all chattered at her in Spanish, although, Caroline realised as she heard her daughter answer, Ella was picking it up amazingly quickly.

'Do you wish to leave her here today to have a little play, perhaps until siesta time—one o'clock?'

Caroline asked Ella what she thought, although she

read the answer in her daughter's excited face before Ella said, 'Oh, yes, please, Mummy.'

'I'll walk back to the house from here,' Caroline told Carlos, knowing he'd already given up a lot of his time to plan the wedding.

'You are sure?' he asked, his eyes searching her face as if the question might mean something more.

'I'm sure,' she told him, and wished she could give him other assurances—assurances about his son and promises to make Jorge happy, but as she couldn't reach behind the mask with which Jorge faced the world she couldn't hope to heal whatever torment that mask hid.

She walked along the boulevard, enjoying the shade of the spreading trees above her, drinking in the atmosphere of a place where even the air seemed to tingle with the liveliness of the people who lived here. She remembered Jorge describing his homeland and the city he swore was the most wonderful in the world, and, remembering, she knew she had to do something to break down the barriers that still existed between them.

Surely if she loved him enough, she could…not make him love her but at least find some place where they could live in harmony.

If she stopped expecting love from him, that would make things easier. And if she accepted that perhaps he'd never loved her, then she *could* stop expecting love.

Arriving back at the house, full of resolve, she went straight to the room that had been 'hers' since her arrival in Buenos Aires. Her apprehension about their marriage had meant she'd left all her belongings in this room—seeing it as a refuge. But now she'd given herself permission to love Jorge, it was time for change.

There wasn't much to move, and once she'd put what few clothes she had into Jorge's wardrobe and her few toiletries into his en suite bathroom she decided more change was needed.

'Where do I shop?' she asked Antoinette. 'You took me to that gorgeous boutique for my undies for the wedding, but where would I go for everyday clothes that aren't jeans and trousers and T-shirts?'

Antoinette's eyes lit up.

'I know just the place,' she said. 'It's a new boutique that has opened not far from here. I believe it has some beautiful clothes—one-off pieces that you won't see everywhere.'

'You'll come with me?' Caroline asked, and Antoinette beamed her agreement.

But when they reached the little mall that held the new boutique, Caroline had second thoughts. For so long she'd refused to think of clothes as anything but serviceable coverings for her body and although she splashed out on pretty things for Ella to wear, she'd never spent money on what she thought of as 'tarting herself up'. Now, just looking at the colourful array of clothing in the window of the boutique, she felt a surge of panic.

'Hmm.'

Antoinette's doubt was reflected in the single syllable, and Caroline realised that the housekeeper was probably thinking exactly the same thing. Where she, Caroline, stuck to navy tops and trousers or jeans, Antoinette's 'uniform' appeared to be black—though skirts and shirts, or dresses, rather than the more casual trousers and jeans.

In the end it was the thought of seeing Antoinette dressed up in something different that made Caroline put her arm around the older woman and urge her through the door.

Once inside, she completely lost her reason.

'We both need some beautiful clothes,' she announced. 'My friend here has been so good to me and given me some beautiful things so I want her to have whatever she wants—whatever looks good on her—and I need a whole new look as well.'

She turned to Antoinette and took both her hands.

'You game?' she asked, and was delighted when Antoinette's face lit up and the woman gave a little skip of excitement.

'Let's do it,' she said.

The two saleswomen entered into the spirit of the adventure and after two hours of trying on just about every garment in the shop and parading in the ones they liked, the two women departed, heavily laden with bags and both wearing bright skirts and matching tops, Antoinette in red and Caroline in an icy blue, the exact colour of her eyes.

'We should go out to lunch to celebrate,' Caroline said, 'but I have to collect Ella from kindergarten.'

Antoinette looked stricken.

'Lunch!' she muttered. 'I have done nothing about lunch. Carlos will be home soon and nothing is prepared.'

Caroline hugged her hard.

'You have more food in your refrigerator and larder than most small hotels,' she reminded Antoinette. 'We'll throw together a salad and maybe a quick onion and tomato tart. Anyway, he'll be so stunned by how gorgeous you look he won't notice what he's eating.'

'Oh, but I'll have to change when I get home,' Antoinette protested.

'No way!' Caroline told her. 'Tomorrow, if you like, you can go back to your black for breakfast and lunch but for dinner every night I want to see you in your new clothes. *And* today for lunch! We'll explain to Carlos we've been shopping and he'll be as pleased as we are. You know he will.'

Caroline saw doubt and hope vying for victory in Antoinette's eyes and knew exactly how the older woman felt. She, Caroline, had no doubt that her fine clothes weren't going to make Jorge love her, but if they made him look at her more closely, that was enough to be going on with.

They met Carlos at the kindergarten.

'I wasn't sure if I was to collect Ella,' he explained after he'd declared delight at their new finery. 'But as we're all here now, and you two look so glamorous, we should all go out to lunch.'

He chose a restaurant in a park where Ella could run around, and Caroline was delighted to see that his eyes kept straying to Antoinette, puzzlement and a little disbelief in his expression, but certainly drawn to look at her again and again.

Once home, with Ella sleeping, Caroline unpacked her new clothes in Jorge's room, then walked down the road to the small local shopping mall and splurged on beauty products—scented bubble bath, new shampoo, moisturiser, body lotion, hand cream—things that hadn't fitted into a backpack.

Jorge spent the morning at the laboratory where he'd been offered work, but his mind wasn't on the guided tour he was being given, his mind was on the woman he'd left back at the house—his wife.

Had she simply got out of bed a little earlier than him to check on Ella, or had sleeping beside him proved impossible so she'd moved as soon as he'd fallen asleep?

Did it matter?

He thought it did, although he couldn't put into words quite why…

Also niggling at him were Caroline's words—things she'd said when he'd talked about working on genetics—talk of wasting his people skills.

He'd still see people.

'Of course,' he said to his guide, and hoped that was the right response for he'd lost track of the explanation the man had been giving.

'We'll see you next week, then,' the man said, and Jorge realised he must have agreed to start work, more or less immediately.

He drove home, telling himself it was a good thing—it would get him out of the house. He'd come home to be close to his father so he could hardly go haring off to some other place that needed a new clinic, people skills or not.

The house was deserted, although laughter from the garden suggested at least Ella was out there. He'd shed his suit—it felt like a straitjacket but he'd have to get used to it as his position in the laboratory would entail meeting businesspeople to plead for donations—and play with his daughter.

A faint and unfamiliar perfume hung in his room, stronger near the bathroom where he found, to his surprise, a line-up of feminine beauty products.

His heart gave such a leap he had to put his hand on the doorjamb to steady himself.

Get a grip! Just because she's moved stuff in doesn't mean anything.

It means she must intend staying, hope argued. Not just in the house but in his bedroom.

No, it was too much—too intrusive—not what he wanted…

'No?' He asked the question aloud because maybe that way he could make sense of his tortured feelings.

He wanted Caroline more than life itself, wanted to love her and be loved by her, yet it was the very depth of that wanting that made him reject the current situation—this pretence of love.

He could hardly shift her things back to the guest room she'd been given when she'd arrived.

He could sleep in his spare bedroom—plead the nightmares.

Or he could—

Be a man and stand before her—what did they say—warts and all! He had more than warts, he had scars that made doctors cringe when they first saw them.

Could he bear to see her cringe?

He rested his head against the doorjamb, breathing

in the softly scented air, his body stirring just thinking of the woman he had married.

If she hadn't cried…

Cursing his foolishness, he pushed away, stripped off and showered, scrubbing at his puckered skin until it felt raw. Then he pulled on jeans and a sweatshirt and went to play with his daughter in the garden.

In the garden where an Antoinette he'd never seen before—a regally lovely Antoinette—was cutting roses as red as the outfit she wore, placing each bloom into a shallow basket held by his father, while further off, a splash of blue he first took to be Ella turned out to be his wife, in a shirt the colour of her eyes and a skirt with rainbow colours chasing up to match the blue.

As he watched—well, stared really—she bent to lift Ella high into the air, her face uptilted as she laughed at her daughter's delight. It was a picture of happy families, Jorge realised, something beautiful enough for an artist to paint. The red, the blue, the flowers, the smiling, laughing people—family.

'Papá!'

Ella saw him first and her delighted cry broke the spell that held him in its thrall. Caroline set Ella on the ground and the little girl raced towards him, flinging herself the last metre, confident his arms would catch her and hold her safe. She cupped her hands around his head so she could kiss both cheeks the way she'd learned, then she kissed him on the lips, petal-soft baby lips touching his with such trust and love his heart began to hurt again.

Now his wife was walking towards him, a Caroline he didn't know.

'Isn't Mummy pretty?' Ella demanded. 'And 'Toinette?'

'They are both looking extremely beautiful,' he assured Ella, giving Antoinette a perfunctory glance before settling his gaze back on Caroline.

'Successful visit?' she asked as she came closer, and he smelt the scent he'd picked up in his room wafting in the air around her.

Something else seemed to waft in the air around her.

Happiness?

Why?

It wasn't that he didn't want her to be happy, but this new Caroline was so far beyond his comprehension he had no idea how to take her.

'Reasonably,' he said, deciding the least he could do was answer her question. 'They would like me to start next week.'

'So soon?' she said, which made him even more puzzled.

'You'd prefer I didn't? Would you like to spend some time with me? Like me to show you around the city, perhaps take you out to the mountains?'

She shook her head and smiled, making his stomach knot with anxiety because—well, he didn't know why but it was knotted. Things were wrong—just look at Antoinette. And when had Caroline ever worn anything other than navy blue? Serviceable, she'd always said…

'I thought you might need more time to think it

through,' she said, as he set Ella on the ground so she could answer Carlos's call to come and see a grasshopper on the rose bush. 'More time to consider if working with microscopes rather than people was really what you wanted.'

How dared she pounce on the one issue that bothered him about the job? Righteous anger replaced the anxiety in his intestines, but then she touched his arm and added, 'But you must do as you think best,' which was so unlike his usual assertive Caroline that he gave a snort of laughter.

'Oh, yes?' He didn't sneer but it was close and he saw the glint of reaction in her eyes.

'Well, you know how I feel!' she muttered. 'It's not as if I haven't told you what a waste of talent and empathy it will be for you to make such a radical shift.'

It was the opening he wanted and he reached out to touch her shirt.

'And this? Is this not a radical shift?'

He saw anger flare but she quickly doused it, actually laughing as she admitted, 'This is just the beginning. You've no idea what two women not into fripperies can do when let loose in a new and utterly beautiful boutique. Antoinette and I went mad.'

She was so beautiful, laughing there in front of him, he wanted some way to grasp the moment and hold on to it for ever.

Could they ever reach the stage where they laughed like that together? Where they were at ease with each other instead of being so tense and touchy it was uncomfortable to be close for long?

She'd moved her clothes into his room.

'I saw some of the purchases,' he said, speaking carefully because he had no idea what had been in her head when she'd made the decision, or what it might mean.

'Of course you would have,' she said easily, and it seemed as if she might say more, but Ella called to him to come and catch the grasshopper for her and the moment passed.

Dinner was an unusually joyous affair.

Because the two women were still wearing their bright clothes?

Jorge couldn't make it out, but it seemed as if the atmosphere—usually relaxed and pleasant at dinner—had taken on an extra spark. Ella showed off her manners, excusing herself when she gave a little cough. Carlos told a joke he'd heard at work, but had seemed more pleased by Antoinette's laughter than by the general appreciation.

Antoinette and his father?

He must have been frowning over this—well, it was hardly a revelation but certainly a development—for he felt Caroline's foot bump against his shin, and looked at her in time to catch a quick smile and a whispered 'Later'.

The word brought goose-bumps out on his arms, although he knew it was a foolish reaction—all she meant by later was that they'd talk.

Talking was good.

'We might take our coffee into the garden if that's all right with you, Antoinette?'

Caroline asked the question when they returned downstairs after saying goodnight to Ella, leaving Carlos, who was designated story-reader that evening, with the little girl.

'I will bring it out for the two of you,' Antoinette said. 'Carlos will have his in the library as usual.'

And ask you to join him, Caroline hoped, but she didn't say it, not wanting Antoinette to know she'd guessed her secret love.

'For any particular reason?' Jorge asked as they settled in the deep padded wooden chairs on the back patio.

'Because it's pleasant, and some flowering plant here perfumes the air at night and, to be honest, because it offers privacy in a neutral situation.'

'Neutral situation?' he queried.

'As in not a bedroom,' Caroline qualified, although she thought he would have guessed, and on top of that she was now feeling extremely nervous about the conversation she felt they had to have.

Would she have to start it?

He'd seen the clothes—mentioned them—so surely he'd bring the subject up again.

He didn't, of course. Nothing was ever that easy.

'I thought if we were to have a real marriage I should share your bedroom, that's why I moved my clothes.'

The words blustered out and hung in the scented air, sounding pathetic as their echoes rang in Caroline's ears.

Silence stretched.

Jorge was in touching distance. She could reach out

and take his hand, but something in the silence kept her still, as if movement of any kind might break something fragile.

'Why did you cry?'

The question was so totally unexpected it took her a moment to work out what it meant.

Cry?

When had she cried?

Back when she'd had that cruel rejection for sure, but recently?

In front of him?

'Last night!' he clarified, and she felt a rush of shame that she'd forgotten how pathetically she'd reacted to him coming to bed in a nightgown.

'Oh, Jorge,' she whispered, and now she did reach out and take his hand, coffee forgotten. 'How could I not cry, remembering how it had been between us? How could I not cry when what I wanted more than anything in the world—even more, perhaps, than finding a father for Ella—was to lie in bed with you again, skin to skin, and there you were in a nightshirt.'

'You wore a nightgown!' he retorted, his voice harsh though why she couldn't tell.

But she smiled as she answered him.

'And fully expected you to tear it off me—or at least remove it somehow. Such a flimsy garment would have been no challenge to the man who could strip me naked within seconds when we were both excited.'

More silence told her she'd done the wrong thing,

reminding him of what had been between them, but they couldn't stay in the hole they'd dug for themselves, and it seemed she was the one who had to climb out first.

CHAPTER TEN

'YOU need to know some things,' she said, letting go of his hand and standing up so she could move as she talked, the emotion churning inside her too strong for her to be still.

'The first is that your email struck so deep into my heart I thought I would never recover. The things you said, the words you used—they were good, Jorge, if your intention was to kill my love for you. But without that love I was lost, while finding that love had been false—if I believed your words—was even more shattering, soul-destroying. Discovering I was pregnant meant I had to find a way back into the real world, which I did.'

She paced some more, knowing this next bit was where she gave her heart away, where she opened herself up to more pain if Jorge's words had not been false.

'I suppose my life was settling into some kind of a pattern when my mother died and it took another turn, especially when I came into money from my father. Then I read the article about the clinic on the internet—yes, I ran a search on your name from time to time, pathetic though that might sound. It wasn't so much the story of the clinic that got to me, but the picture.'

He should walk away now, Jorge decided. Make an excuse. Get away from her. Already her words had brought back so much remembered pain, both physical and emotional, he was wound as tight as a tourniquet.

He didn't *have* to listen.

Didn't want to hear the pain in her voice, pain he had caused.

But she was speaking again—speaking of the article, the picture.

'I read the article, saw the picture, and I knew,' she said, coming to stand directly in front of him. 'I knew the day they told you the extent of your injuries you'd decided I'd pity you and you sent that email.'

Now she knelt before him, not touching him but close enough to touch.

'I was so angry with you, Jorge, so angry with your stubborn Latin pride, that you'd hurt me and deprive Ella of a father, and turn your back on people because you weren't as whole or as beautiful as you once had been. And don't try to deny it. Oh, some of the words you wrote might have been true—maybe you didn't ever love me—but you turned away from me because of something as superficial as a few scars. You thought my love was so weak? Did you think it couldn't cope with a man injured helping others to a better life? Did you think so little of me?'

He couldn't speak, certainly couldn't deny her accusations for he'd thought all those things—except the one about not loving her. He couldn't let that go.

'I lied about not loving you,' he said quietly, and she stood up and paced again.

'Lied to hurt me?' she demanded, anger radiating from her.

'Lied to keep you away. Lied because…'

He couldn't say it.

He had to say it.

'It was more than burns I had, though they were the obvious injuries. For months I wondered if I'd walk again, work again, be anything but a burden on anyone I loved.'

She turned on him, her anger like an aura around her in the dim light.

'And you thought if I came to you, stood by you, helped you through, it would be out of pity?' she stormed. 'Admit it—that's what you thought. That's why you turned me away. As if I'd pity you. You were the strongest man I'd ever met—the strongest and the gentlest. You were still you inside that injured body. The bomb blast hadn't changed the man you were. Pity was the last thing I'd have felt for you, but your stupid pride wouldn't allow you to think that. Your stupid pride blew us apart, depriving all three of us of years of happiness.'

'There was nothing happy in my rehab,' he muttered at her, unable to answer her other accusations because he had feared pity more than anything.

'There would have been if I'd been there, and don't tell me you wouldn't have worked harder at it, knowing Ella was on the way.'

Was she right?

Of course she was, although at the time he'd pushed

himself to the limit every day—but knowing Caroline was there beside him *would* have made things easier.

He tried to think, tried to sort out the myriad thoughts racing through his head—dozens of rats in the maze now.

'I cannot help my pride,' he finally declared, because he sensed this was the last hurdle in the way to an understanding between them.

More than an understanding?

There had to be for even as they'd argued and she'd yelled at him he'd been so aware of wanting her he'd felt ashamed.

'Even if it's false pride?' Caroline asked quietly, sensing they were at some kind of crossroads and not knowing which way things would go. 'Pride should be about who we are, not about our physical weaknesses or how we look. I know that's easy to say and much harder to live by, but do you think Ella notices your scars when she rushes into your arms for a hug? You're her father, her *papá*—that's all she sees.'

She took a deep breath, knowing this was a commitment she couldn't retract.

'It's no different for me, Jorge. No matter what your body looks like, no matter what injuries it carries, it's you the person that I love. That I have always loved.'

She stood in front of him for a moment, but when he didn't respond she wandered deeper into the garden, seeking a place where she could hide her aching heart.

Surely that had been his opportunity to admit his love for her, and his silence told her more than words could ever tell. Having married her, he could hardly come right out and say he felt nothing for her. She'd put him in an impossible position and, to make matters worse, she'd ripped out her own heart to lay before him, and for nothing.

Except embarrassment.

Embarrassment! She'd shifted all her clothes into his bedroom.

She turned back towards the house, hurrying now. Okay, so he'd seen the clothes, but no one else would have. The cleaning lady who came in had been and gone before Caroline had shifted things.

He caught her hand as she was hurtling through the door.

'Where are you going?'

She spun to face him, angry to be halted in her resolve.

'I'm going to move my clothes back into my bedroom,' she snapped. 'I'll stay married to you, Jorge, but I'm not going to live a lie. In bed together, in the past, we made love. Now it would be sex and while, because of that magnet-like attraction you spoke of, it would be good, it's not enough for me.'

She tried to jerk her hand out of his but he held it firmly, using it to draw her closer, walking backwards so she had to follow, reaching a shadowy arbour where the perfume of the garden was headily strong.

'And if I said I loved you?' he asked softly, still holding only her hand but standing so close she could feel the heat radiating off his body, weakening her bones so staying upright was difficult.

'Words are easy to say,' she managed to get out. 'Do you mean it?'

'With every fibre of my being,' he replied, his voice husky again. 'With every cell of my body—always and for ever, Caroline.'

He drew her closer now, enclosing her in his arms.

'Sending that email was the hardest thing I ever did in my life. Writing those hateful words—even thinking them—hurt me more than all my injuries, but at the time...'

He paused and she knew she had to wait, knew she had to know just what had led the man she loved to hurt her as he had.

'You are right—it was pride. At the time I told myself it was the only thing to do—that I was doing it out of love, that I couldn't allow you to throw your life away on a broken shell of a man, that I couldn't tie you to someone who might be an invalid for life.'

He tilted her head up and looked into her face.

'And you'd have done it, don't deny it. You'd have stuck with me even if your love for me had died, and died it surely would have had you seen me back then.'

'Never,' she whispered, shaking her head, while Jorge smiled his disbelief.

'We've both seen it happen—watched love die between a couple where one is so badly injured the treatment goes on for ever, operation after operation, struggling through physio and occupational therapy. Love needs a response and the injured person is too self-focussed, has to be to get where he or she wants to get, so there's nothing to give back.'

'And we've seen it survive and flourish,' Caroline argued, stepping back from him, not willing to let him get away with this. 'You couldn't know how it would be for us.'

He put his hands up to cup her face.

'I couldn't bear to take the risk,' he said. 'Couldn't bear to see the love die out of your eyes, to see pity sneaking in to replace it.'

He kissed her, gently, as if to emphasise his words, then added, 'I was wrong. I wronged you and in wronging you I wronged myself, but at the time…'

Could she understand?

Wouldn't she have reacted the same way?

Probably, but she wasn't going to admit it.

'And now?' she whispered against his lips, *she* kissing *him* this time.

She felt his response.

'Perhaps we should get naked together,' he whispered back.

EPILOGUE

THE baby gurgled in the little hammock Carlos had slung between two trees for him, waving chubby fists at the shadows of the leaves in the shady part of the garden. Somewhere in the bushes Ella was calling to her grandfather, 'Find me, Ablito, find me!'

Caroline settled into a chair beside Antoinette, who was knitting as she watched baby Charlie explore the wonders of his hands—opening and closing them, gurgling his delight.

'It's not making you too tired, working part time at the hospital?' Antoinette asked, pouring fresh-made lemonade from a crystal jug and handing a glass to Caroline.

'I love it,' Caroline admitted, 'and though I miss being with the children, it does keep my mind off missing Jorge when he's up in Salta, working at the new clinic.'

'He'll be home soon,' Antoinette reminded her, although just mentioning his name had sent a shiver of anticipation through Caroline's body. *It* knew he'd be home soon.

'Is it working, the Salta clinic?' Antoinette asked, and Caroline couldn't help but smile, for they'd set up the

Salta clinic together, their little family of three moving up to the far north of the country to improve the medical facilities for the indigenous people in the area.

'So well, Jorge's job is nearly done. We'd started to work with the local government before I came back here to have Charlie, that was, when—five months ago? What we've got to think about is where we go next. It's been great living here while I had the baby with you and Carlos to mind Ella and help out with Charlie, but now you two are married, you don't want other people in the house.'

'It's a big house,' Antoinette reminded her, then she leaned over and kissed Caroline on the cheek. 'As if we'd turn you out when you've brought Carlos and me such happiness,' she added. 'And as if he'd want you to take the children out from under his wing. You are happy here, please tell me?'

'Yes, but—'

Caroline got no further for footsteps were echoing through the tiled entrance, firm footsteps she recognised immediately.

As did Ella apparently, for her cry of 'Papà' and her headlong dash into the house beat Caroline to the first hug.

But she could wait.

She could stand and watch the man she loved lift their daughter into the air and kiss her on both cheeks, then hold her close against his body, love and pride radiating from him, although now, over Ella's shoulder, his eyes sought his wife, found her, and transmitted even more love, deep and resonant, the kind of love that would last for ever.

'Mi esposa.' The words were hoarse with longing as he pulled her into his arms, a three-way cuddle, but her body felt his warmth all along one side and desire vied with love to be expressed.

'Best you see your *hijo*, too, *and* your *papá*!' Caroline reminded him, breaking the kiss Jorge had pressed on her lips—the kiss she really didn't want to break.

Together, the three of them walked into the garden, stopping by the hammock. Charlie looked up at them for a moment, before gurgling delight spread across his face and the little arms lifted towards his father.

Caroline lifted him and settled him in Jorge's arm, and he carried both children out into the garden to find his father.

She watched them make their way through the beautiful plants and shook her head in wonder that so much happiness could have come her way. A son, a daughter, a man to love and a family complete with two very loving grandparents. What more could any woman want?

'We'll get naked soon?'

Jorge was back, whispering against her neck, Carlos following with Charlie in his arms, Ella trotting along behind, telling some story about her kindergarten friends.

Caroline turned and kissed her husband quickly on the lips.

'Very soon,' she whispered.

SMALL TOWN MARRIAGE MIRACLE

BY

JENNIFER TAYLOR

To Pam and Dudley. Thank you for always being there.

First published in Great Britain 2011
by Mills & Boon, an imprint of Harlequin (UK) Limited,
Eton House, 18-24 Paradise Road, Richmond, Surrey TW9 1SR

ISBN: 978 0 263 88593 4

Harlequin (UK) policy is to use papers that are natural, renewable and recyclable products and made from wood grown in sustainable forests. The logging and manufacturing process conform to the legal environmental regulations of the country of origin.

Printed and bound in Spain
by Blackprint CPI, Barcelona

Her voice was so low that it was a moment before Daniel realised what she had said. He frowned, unsure where this was leading. 'You're sorry?'

'Yes. About the way I…I've behaved recently.' She tipped back her head and looked him squarely in the eyes. 'I agreed to call a truce and I haven't kept to that. I apologise.'

'I know how difficult this situation is, Emma,' he said quietly, more touched than he cared to admit. 'I find it hard, too.'

'Do you?' She looked at him in surprise and he sighed.

'Yes. I can't just forget what happened five years ago. You meant a lot to me, Emma.'

'Did I?'

'Of course you did.' He frowned when he saw the uncertainty on her face. He had never tried to hide his feelings—how could he have done? She had meant the whole world to him, and all of a sudden it seemed important that she understood that.

'I cared a lot about you, Emma,' he said quickly, wishing that he didn't have to use such a milk-and-water term to describe how he'd felt. Claiming he'd *cared* barely touched on the way he had really felt about her—but what else could he say? Admitting that he had loved her with every fibre of his being wasn't what she wanted to hear. His heart ached as he repeated it with as much conviction as he dared. 'I really and truly cared about you.'

Jennifer Taylor lives in the north-west of England, in a small village surrounded by some really beautiful countryside. She has written for several different Mills & Boon® series in the past, but it wasn't until she read her first Medical™ Romance that she truly found her niche. She was so captivated by these heart-warming stories that she set out to write them herself! When she's not writing, or doing research for her latest book, Jennifer's hobbies include reading, gardening, travel, and chatting to friends both on and off-line. She is always delighted to hear from readers, so do visit her website at www.jennifer-taylor.com

Recent titles by the same author:

THE MIDWIFE'S CHRISTMAS MIRACLE
THE DOCTOR'S BABY BOMBSHELL*
THE GP'S MEANT-TO-BE BRIDE*
MARRYING THE RUNAWAY BRIDE*
THE SURGEON'S FATHERHOOD SURPRISE**

**Dalverston Weddings*
***Brides of Penhally Bay*

CHAPTER ONE

'I feel terrible about what's happened, Emma. You came home for a rest, not to be faced with this.'

'It doesn't matter. Really it doesn't.'

Emma Roberts smiled soothingly as she led her aunt, Margaret Haynes, over to a chair. She sat down beside her, seeing the strain that had etched deep lines onto the older woman's face. Her aunt had aged a lot since the last time Emma had seen her and she couldn't help feeling guilty. She should have realised that something was wrong and returned home sooner than this.

'Now tell me what the consultant said,' she ordered gently.

'He said that it's imperative your uncle has a coronary artery bypass done as soon as possible. If Jim waits any longer, there will be no point doing it.'

'Wait? Do you mean that Uncle Jim has been putting off having it done?' Emma queried in surprise.

'Yes. I'm afraid he has.' Margaret Haynes sighed. 'His angina has been getting worse for some time now. Even his medication doesn't always help when he has a really bad attack. I kept nagging him to have the bypass done, but you know how stubborn he can be.'

Emma smiled. 'I do indeed. Once Uncle Jim gets an idea into his head, it's impossible to shift it.' She sobered abruptly. 'But from what you've said, it sounds as though the situation is extremely urgent now.'

'It is.' Margaret gave a little sob. 'I thought I was going to lose him yesterday. He was in such terrible pain…'

'Shh, it's OK. He's going to be fine,' Emma assured her. She put her arm around the older woman's shoulders, wishing she were as certain of the outcome as she was trying to appear. Her aunt and uncle had brought her up after her parents had died and she loved them dearly. The thought of anything happening to Uncle Jim was almost more than she could bear.

'Of course he will. I'm just being silly, aren't I?' Margaret blew her nose. 'The consultant told me that he has high hopes the operation will be a complete success, so I have to remember that and not get upset. I certainly don't want your uncle to see me weeping and wailing.'

'It's the last thing he needs,' Emma agreed, admiring her aunt's steely determination. 'Uncle Jim will need plenty of rest after he's had the operation, though. I hope he understands that.'

'Oh, I shall make sure he does,' Margaret said firmly. 'He'll be in hospital for about twelve days and after that I intend to take him away to the cottage. Jim will need at least six weeks to recover from the operation and I won't be able to keep him out of the surgery for that length of time if we're at home.'

'Which is where I come in,' Emma said quickly, stifling a small pang of regret. Maybe she had been looking forward to a much-needed rest after a gruelling six months spent working overseas, but this was an emergency. If she ran the practice while her uncle recuperated, he would be less likely to worry. It was a small price to pay for all the love her aunt and uncle had lavished on her over the years.

'I'll take charge of the surgery while you're away,' she began, but her aunt shook her head.

'Oh, no, you don't need to do that, dear. Daniel will be here, so if you could just help out if it gets really busy, that would be more than enough.'

'Daniel?' Emma repeated, somewhat at a loss.

'Yes. I'm sure I told you last night when you phoned that Daniel had agreed to step in earlier than planned… Or did I? I was so worried, you see…'

'Daniel who?' Emma put in hurriedly before her aunt could drift off at a tangent again.

'Daniel Kennedy.'

Emma swung round when a deep voice answered her question. Her green eyes widened when she saw the tall, dark-haired man who was standing behind her. Just for a moment shock stole her ability to speak as she stared at him in dismay. It had been five years since she'd last seen him, and a lot had happened during that time, yet all of a sudden it felt as though she was right back to where she had been all those years ago—madly in love with the man she wanted to spend her whole life with. The thought scared her witless.

'Hello, Emma.' Daniel smiled at her but there was a wariness about the look he gave her, Emma realised, as though he wasn't sure how she would feel about seeing him again.

He was right to wonder, too, Emma thought grimly as she rose to her feet. Maybe she *had* believed at one time that Daniel was the man for her, but she didn't believe it any longer. The truth was that Daniel had used her, slept with her and then cast her aside when he had discovered she'd been getting too serious about him. It had taken her a long time to accept what he had done, but nowadays she was under no illusions. Daniel had never truly cared about *her.* He'd only ever cared about himself.

Emma took a deep breath. Maybe she hadn't expected to see him here, but she would deal with it. She was no longer the naïve and trusting young woman she had been back then. She had grown up now and she had seen too much of the world to be dazzled by a man like Daniel Kennedy ever again!

Daniel felt as though his smile had been pasted into place. He had been dreading seeing Emma again for a number of reasons, although he wasn't about to delve into them right then. He held out his hand, playing the role of old friend to the best of his ability even though he knew it wasn't true. He and Emma had been a lot more than friends at one time.

'It's good to see you again, Emma. How are you?'

'Fine, thank you.'

She shook his hand and a frisson ran through him when he felt the coolness of her skin. Just for a moment he was reminded of all the other occasions when he had touched her. Her skin had been cool then but it had soon warmed up as he had stroked and caressed her. The memory sent a surge of heat coursing through him and he hurriedly blanked it out, knowing how foolish it was to go down that route.

'This must have come as a shock to you?'

'It has.' She glanced at her aunt and drew him aside. 'Aunt Margaret just told me that Uncle Jim has been putting off having the bypass done. Is that true?'

'Yes, it is.' Daniel sighed. 'You know how dedicated Jim is. I expect he was worried about what would happen to the practice if he took any time off.'

'That's so typical of him. He puts everyone else's needs before his own.' She gave him a hard look. 'Did you know that he was delaying having surgery?'

'No. I knew Jim had angina, of course, but he never admitted how bad things had got until last week,' Daniel answered truthfully. 'I suspect he only told me then because he needed my help. He'd finally agreed to have his op at the end of the month and he wanted me to cover for him.'

'Really?' Emma frowned. 'I don't understand why he asked you to take over the practice. He knew I was coming home, so why didn't he ask me?'

'I can't answer that. You'll have to ask Jim, although I suggest you leave it until after he's had his operation.' He shrugged when he saw her mouth tighten. It was obvious that she didn't appreciate his advice but he refused to let it deter him. 'Jim needs peace and quiet more than anything else at the moment. What he doesn't need,

Emma, is for us to be conducting some sort of personal vendetta.'

'Don't flatter yourself,' she snapped back. 'The days when I cared enough to fight with you, Daniel, are long gone.'

'Good. Then it won't cause any problems if I'm in charge of the practice in your uncle's absence.'

'The only problem I have is understanding why you've agreed to do it. I mean, working in the middle of nowhere is hardly a step up the professional ladder, is it, Daniel?'

Daniel flinched when he heard the scorn in her voice. It didn't make it any easier to know that he only had himself to blame for it either. He'd been so desperate to convince her that there was no future for them that he had led her to believe that all he was interested in was his career. Now he was reaping the consequences.

'It's all good experience,' he said quietly. 'Plus, I'm very fond of your aunt and uncle. I'm happy to help in any way I can.'

'How very altruistic of you.' She smiled but her green eyes were chilly. 'Of course a cynic would wonder if there was an ulterior motive to your generosity. Still, I'm sure the truth will come out at some stage.'

She turned away before he could reply, not that he could think of anything to say in his defence. Emma wouldn't believe him if he told her that he wasn't interested in personal advancement and never had been. All of a sudden he bitterly regretted those claims he had made about going into private practice one day, but what else could he have done? Accepted what she'd been offering him, knowing that it could ruin both their lives?

Daniel's heart was heavy as he excused himself and made his way along the corridor. There was a coffee machine at the bottom of the stairs and he fed some coins into it. It disgorged a stream of insipid-looking liquid into a plastic cup but he didn't care how it looked or tasted even. He took it over to the window and stood there staring out across the town. Avondale was a pretty little market town in the middle of the Yorkshire Dales. During the summer months, the population virtually doubled thanks to a steady influx of tourists, but at this time of the year there were few tourists willing to brave the inclement weather. He had first come to the town to do his GP training and that was how he had met Emma. She had just completed her rotations and was enjoying a well-deserved break before she took up a junior registrar's post in Scotland with a top surgical team.

Daniel knew that competition for surgical posts was always fierce, and that it was particularly hard for a woman to break into that field. Whilst most consultants paid lip service to the idea of equality between the sexes, far too many refused to accept a woman as part of their team. The old prejudices were still rife: what was the point of training a woman when she would only leave to have a family? That Emma had overcome such narrow-minded thinking and secured a prestigious post for herself proved how hard she must have worked. He was impressed. He was also deeply attracted to her.

Almost before he'd realised what was happening,

Daniel had fallen in love with her and she with him. It had been a gloriously blissful time for them both until Emma had announced one day that she had changed her mind about going into surgery. She no longer wanted such a demanding career, she'd claimed. She wanted a private life, time for them, so she would stay in England and train as a GP instead. That way they could be together.

Daniel had realised immediately that he couldn't allow her to sacrifice her dreams for him. Although she might truly have believed that she was happy to give up her plans to become a surgeon, he knew how much it meant to her and that it would drive a wedge between them eventually if she didn't fulfil her goals. He had seen it happen to his own parents, watched as his mother's resentment at forsaking her career had eaten away at their marriage, and he had sworn the same thing would never happen to him.

For Emma to succeed in her chosen field, Daniel knew that she would need to focus all her attention on her training for the next few years. Even though he could have found a job in Scotland easily enough, he realised that it wasn't the answer. She would be working long hours and wouldn't have time to devote to a relationship. He would be a distraction for her, a hindrance, and he couldn't bear the thought that she might fail because of him. Although it was the hardest decision he had ever made, he decided that he had to give Emma up rather than run the risk of her ending up hating him.

He sighed as he recalled her shock when he had told her curtly that he had no intention of making a commitment at that stage in his life. He had plans for the future and they were far more important than their relationship. The contempt in her eyes as she had told him that she understood had devastated him. He had almost weakened at that point and admitted that he'd lied, but somehow he had managed to hold back. She had packed her bags and left that same night and he hadn't seen her again until today.

The sound of footsteps made him look round and he felt pain stab his heart when he saw her coming along the corridor. She must have come straight to the hospital from the airport because her clothes were crumpled after the long flight, her red-gold hair lying in tangled waves around her shoulders, but that didn't matter. She was still the most beautiful and most desirable woman he had ever seen. It was only when she drew closer that Daniel could see the lines of strain that tugged down the corners of her mouth.

He knew from what Jim Haynes had told him that she'd been working overseas for the past six months and could imagine how hard it must have been, working under the most gruelling conditions. However, he also knew that it wasn't the work or the shock of learning that her uncle was ill that made her look so drawn. It was seeing him again that was the problem. In that second Daniel realised that he had to make the situation as easy as possible for her. He couldn't bear to think that he might end up hurting her again as he had hurt her once before.

Emma took a steadying breath as she stopped in front of Daniel, but she could feel her heart racing. Seeing him again had been a shock—she had admitted that—but she could handle it. She certainly didn't intend to go to pieces just because the man she had once mistakenly thought she'd loved had reappeared in her life.

'Aunt Margaret has gone in to see Uncle Jim,' she said coolly. 'They'll be doing the bypass later today and she wants to sit with him until it's time for him to go to Theatre.'

'The sooner it's done, the better.'

There was a roughness to Daniel's voice that troubled her until she realised how stupid it was to let it worry her. Daniel Kennedy was part of her past, nothing more than a memory she had long since relegated to the darkest reaches of her mind.

'Definitely.' She glanced along the corridor, giving herself a moment to absorb that thought. When she turned to face him again, she was pleased to discover that she didn't feel a thing. 'I'm not sure how long it's going to take, but there doesn't seem any point you hanging around here.'

'It isn't a problem.' He checked his watch and shrugged. 'I don't need to get back to the surgery for another couple of hours yet, so I'll stay a bit longer.'

'There's no need. Aunt Margaret will be fine.' Emma stood up straighter, determined to get her own way. 'I'm more than capable of looking after her.'

'I'm sure you are.' He smiled, his hazel eyes skimming over her face before they came to rest on her mouth, and despite her resolve, Emma felt a little flutter of awareness in the pit of her stomach. She took a quick breath, determined that it wasn't going to grow into anything bigger. The days when one of Daniel's smiles could turn her insides to jelly were long gone!

'You always were very good at looking after other people, Emma, but you need to think about yourself for once. You've had a long journey to get here and you must be tired. Why not let me stay with your aunt while you go home and get some sleep?'

'I don't need you to tell me what to do!' she shot back, terrified by the speed of her response. One minute she'd had herself under control and the next….

She shivered as a wave of fear swept over her. She couldn't bear to think that Daniel still had an effect on her. Five years ago she would have done anything for them to be together, but he had made it clear that all he'd cared about was his career. It had been a devastating blow but it had taught her a valuable lesson: she would never make the mistake of falling in love again.

'I am not trying to tell you what to do. I'm just making a suggestion. It's entirely up to you whether you stay here or go home.'

His tone was reasonable in the extreme and she felt her face heat. She knew she was overreacting and she hated to think that Daniel might read anything into it. She didn't care about him any longer, but if she carried on this way, he would never believe that.

'I apologise. I shouldn't have jumped down your throat like that.'

He shrugged. 'It doesn't matter. It's little wonder that you're stressed after everything that's happened. All this coming on top of the journey you've had would be a lot for anyone to cope with.'

It was on the tip of her tongue to deny it until she realised that she was in danger of digging an even deeper hole for herself. Did she really want to admit that it was seeing him again that was causing her to behave so irrationally?

'Probably.' She glanced at her watch and came to a swift decision. 'If you're happy to stay then maybe I will go back to the house. I need to unpack and get settled in.'

'It's fine by me,' he agreed equably.

'Right, that's what I'll do, then. I'll just let Aunt Margaret know what's happening first.'

'I'll come with you.' He shrugged when she glanced sharply at him. 'I'd like to see Jim before he goes down to Theatre, set his mind at rest that the practice is in safe hands. You know what a worrier he is.'

'That's true.' Emma headed back along the corridor, very conscious of the fact that Daniel was just a step behind her. She paused outside the door to the private room where her uncle had been taken and glanced at him. 'It would be best if Uncle Jim didn't have to worry about anything at the moment, so I suggest we call a truce.'

'That's fine by me.' He smiled at her and Emma felt her breath catch when she saw the warmth in his eyes. She had never expected him to look at her that way and it threw her for a moment. It was an effort to concentrate when he continued. 'I don't want to fight with you, Emma. It's the last thing I want, in fact.'

'Me too,' she replied stiffly.

'Then we'll agree to set our differences aside, shall we?'

'Yes.'

She turned away, struggling to contain the emotions that were welling up inside her. It had been months since she'd even thought about Daniel, although in the beginning the memory of what had happened had tormented her. She had kept going over everything he'd said, reliving the pain of discovering that she had meant less to him than his precious career had done. Only by immersing herself in her work had she got through that terrible period and she refused to place herself in the same position again.

She squared her shoulders. No matter what Daniel said or did, no matter how convincing he sounded, she would never trust him again.

CHAPTER TWO

BY two o'clock Emma had finished unpacking and put everything away. She looked fondly around the room that had been hers since childhood. It had changed very little over the years and she found it reassuring to see her collection of stuffed toys on top of the wardrobe and the shelves of books she'd read while she had been growing up. She had moved house several times in the past few years and although it had never bothered her, it was good to know that there was somewhere permanent she could return to.

She sighed softly as she stowed the canvas hold-all in the bottom of the wardrobe because if Uncle Jim was forced to give up the practice, there would need to be a lot of changes made. The surgery was attached to the house and it was unlikely that her aunt and uncle would want to carry on living here. Nothing was truly permanent and she had to get used to the idea, even though she hated the thought of not being able to call this place her home.

Emma closed the wardrobe door and headed downstairs to make herself a cup of tea. She glanced at the clock as she filled the kettle. Uncle Jim should be leaving

Theatre soon, so she would drink her tea then go back to the hospital to keep her aunt company. It would give Daniel time to get back for evening surgery.

'I wouldn't say no to a cup of tea, if you're making one.'

As though thinking about him had somehow conjured him up, Daniel suddenly appeared. Emma looked round in surprise when she heard his voice. 'What are you doing here? I thought you were going to stay at the hospital until I got back.'

'I was, but your aunt insisted that she'd be all right by herself.' He grimaced. 'I tried to persuade her to let me stay but she wouldn't hear of it. I think she was worried in case I was late for evening surgery.'

Emma sighed. 'She's as bad as Uncle Jim. Their lives revolve around the practice and have done for years. It isn't right that it should come first, especially not at the moment.'

'It certainly isn't.' He pulled out a chair and sat down. 'They need to concentrate on making sure that Jim makes a full recovery and that's where we come in.'

Emma wasn't sure she appreciated that *we*, although she didn't correct him. She poured boiling water into the pot then went to fetch the milk out of the fridge. The days when she and Daniel had been a couple were long gone and she, for one, wouldn't wish them back again.

'So what do you suggest?' she asked, adopting a deliberately neutral tone to conceal the pain that thought had aroused, oddly enough.

'Basically, what we agreed on today. We make sure we do nothing to cause your aunt and uncle any concern.' He shrugged. 'Margaret told me that she's hoping to take Jim to their cottage on the coast while he recuperates, but he'll refuse to go if he thinks you and I are at loggerheads.'

'I can assure you that I have no intention of causing a disruption,' Emma said sharply, trying to ignore the squirmy feeling in the pit of her stomach. It was one thing to agree to a truce but it could be something entirely different to stick to it. Could they really maintain a wholly professional relationship when they had once been lovers?

The fact that she should be experiencing such doubts when she was determined not to let Daniel affect her in any way annoyed her and she glared at him. 'I said it before but obviously it didn't sink in so I'll repeat it. I don't *care* enough to fight with you, Daniel. OK?'

'Good.' He smiled calmly back at her. 'It should make life a lot simpler for all of us.'

Emma didn't say anything as she poured the tea. Daniel obviously believed her and that was all that mattered. She certainly didn't want him to suspect that she had doubts, not that she really did. She had moved on from the days when splitting up with him had left her feeling utterly devastated.

Of course it must have been easier for him to get over their break-up, she thought as she placed the cups on the table. He had never invested as much of himself into their relationship as she had done. Although he had told her at the time that he loved her, it patently hadn't been true. He would never have chosen his career over her if he'd felt even a fraction of the love she had felt for him.

She frowned. It made his decision to work in Avondale all the more difficult to understand. Taking time off to come here didn't make sense when he was so keen to pursue his ambitions. *Did* he have an ulterior motive? It was what she had accused him of earlier in the day, although she hadn't seriously believed it. Now she found herself wondering if it was true. As she knew to her cost, Daniel's career meant more to him than anything else.

Daniel wasn't sure what was going through Emma's mind, but he could tell that it wasn't anything pleasant. He bit back a sigh because he had a nasty feeling that it had something to do with him. Once again he found himself wishing that he hadn't misled her five years ago, even though he knew that he'd had no choice. He had loved her far too much to let her sacrifice her dreams for him.

'Are you still working in London?'

He looked up when she spoke, trying to control the surge his pulse gave as his eyes alighted on her face. Although he had been out with a number of extremely attractive women since they'd parted, he had never been tempted to have a long-term relationship with any of them. A few dates and that was it: *finito.* In fact, he'd gained a bit of a reputation amongst his friends as being a 'love them and leave them' kind of guy. He always laughed off the accusation by claiming that he simply hadn't met the right woman, but now he realised the truth was far more complicated. He had never met anyone who could match up to Emma.

It was an unsettling thought and he tried not to dwell on it as he answered her question. 'Yes. It's a busy practice, lots of variety, and I get on well with the rest of the team so I've not been tempted to leave.'

'And they don't mind you taking time off to work here?'

'No. They were very sympathetic, in fact,' Daniel replied, wondering what was behind her sudden interest.

'It must have caused a problem when you had to drop everything without any warning, though,' she persisted. 'Didn't you say that Uncle Jim had asked you to cover from the end of the month originally?'

'That's right. Fortunately, our practice manager was able to juggle the timetable and fit it in.' He shrugged. 'It's worked out quite well, actually. I had some leave owing, so I'm using it up.'

'Really?' Her brows rose. 'You had six whole weeks of leave stored up?'

'One of the senior partners was pregnant last summer and we couldn't get locum cover for part of her maternity leave,' he explained. 'I offered to carry my leave forward. It's lucky I did as it turns out.'

'Hmm, very lucky indeed.'

Daniel frowned when he heard the scepticism in her voice. He wasn't sure what had caused it and before he could ask, the telephone rang. He stood up before he was tempted to explain that it wasn't the first time he hadn't taken his full holiday entitlement. It always seemed like a waste of time, taking time off, when he could be working. Although he had never been driven by personal ambition, he wanted to learn all he could so he could help the people who relied on him for their care. That aim had become even more important since he and Emma had parted.

'I'll get that,' he said briskly. It wouldn't help the situation to dwell on how much his life had been influenced by what had happened between him and Emma. 'It's probably Ruth checking that there'll be a surgery tonight. Morning surgery had to be cancelled so I expect it will be busy this evening.'

'I'll give you a hand when I get back from the hospital,' Emma offered.

'That would be great.' He smiled at her, relieved that she was willing to do her bit to maintain the peace. 'Thanks.'

He went out to the hall to take the call. As he'd expected, it was the practice receptionist, Ruth Hargreaves. He assured her that surgery would go ahead as scheduled and hung up. There was no sign of Emma when he went back to the kitchen but he heard a car starting up and looked out of the window in time to see her driving away. She hadn't bothered saying goodbye but why should she? So far as Emma was concerned, she would do what had to be done and that was it. She wasn't going to suddenly want to become his best friend and he didn't blame her. He had hurt her badly and the worst thing was knowing that he could never atone for what he had done. Even if he told her the truth, and even if by some miracle she believed him, it was far too late to get back what they'd had.

* * *

The waiting room was packed when Emma got back shortly after five p.m. Aunt Margaret had decided to stay the night at the hospital so Emma had come back on her own. Ruth was on the phone when she went in, looking unusually harassed. Emma waited until the receptionist finished the call.

'Problems?'

'Oh, just the umpteenth person phoning to see if we're open.' Ruth rolled her eyes when the phone rang again the second she put down the receiver. 'That'll be another one. I'm sorely tempted to take the wretched thing off the hook!'

'I don't blame you.' Emma smiled sympathetically. 'I'm helping out tonight so you can send the next patient in to me when you get the chance.'

'Will do.'

Ruth snatched up the receiver as Emma made her way along the corridor. There were two consulting rooms and she guessed that Daniel would be using the one her uncle normally used. She made her way to the other room and switched on the light. The room hadn't been used very often since her uncle's partner had retired some years ago. Although Uncle Jim had tried to find a replacement, few doctors had been keen to relocate to the area. The younger ones thought the town too quiet to consider living there permanently, while the older ones weren't willing to cope with the difficulties of the job.

As well as caring for the townsfolk, the practice provided care for the people living on the outlying farms. Some home visits could be extremely difficult to reach, especially during the winter months. The few candidates who had applied for the post had soon lost interest when they'd discovered what the job had entailed, so in the end her uncle had given up advertising and run the surgery single-handed. However, if the number of patients in the waiting room was anything to go by, it really needed more than one doctor to run the practice.

It was something that needed thinking about in view of her uncle's health, Emma decided. However, there was no time to worry about it right then. A knock on the door heralded the arrival of her first patient, a young woman who looked vaguely familiar. Emma smiled at her.

'Please sit down. I'm Dr Roberts. I'm helping out while my uncle is in hospital.'

'Oh, I remember you!' the young woman exclaimed. 'You were in the same class at school as my sister—Cathy Martindale. Remember her?'

'Of course I do.' Emma laughed. 'No wonder you look so familiar. You're very like Cathy. How is she, by the way?'

'She's fine. She lives in Leeds now with her husband and her two little boys.'

'Tell her I was asking about her, will you?' Emma picked up the folder of notes that the girl had brought in with her. 'So, Judith, what can I do for you today?'

'It's my periods, Dr Roberts. They're so heavy and irregular that they're causing me a real problem. I also suffer the most awful pain in my tummy and lower back each time it happens.'

'I see. How long has this been going on?' Emma asked.

'About a year now. I came off the Pill eighteen months ago because my husband and I want to start a family. My periods were very erratic after I stopped taking it, but I thought everything would settle down once the drugs were out of my system. Instead, it's just got worse.'

'Have you had any other symptoms? Pain on having intercourse, perhaps?'

'Yes.' Judith blushed. 'I've never had a problem before, but recently I dread making love with David because it's so uncomfortable.'

'Which doesn't help when you're hoping to have a baby,' Emma said sympathetically, standing up. 'I'll just check your blood pressure and then I'd like to examine you, if that's all right?'

'Oh, yes, of course it is.' Judith sounded relieved as she slipped off her coat. 'I've been putting off coming for weeks, to be honest. Dr Haynes is lovely, but I felt so embarrassed about having to explain it all to him. I couldn't believe my luck when Ruth told me I'd be seeing you tonight!'

'Good.' Emma laughed, although she couldn't help wondering how many other women were delaying making appointments because they felt uncomfortable about discussing their problems with an elderly male doctor.

She checked Judith's BP, which was fine, then asked her to undress and lie on the couch while she examined her. She gently palpated her abdomen and then performed an internal examination but could find nothing to indicate what was causing the problem. Judith had had a smear test the previous month and that had come back clear.

'And there's been no other symptoms at all?' she asked after Judith had got dressed again. 'Not even something that is apparently unrelated?'

'No…well, apart from the fact that I've had several bouts of diarrhoea. It's not something I've ever suffered from before, but it's happened a few times lately. Either that or I get constipated,' Judith added, grimacing.

'I see.' Emma frowned thoughtfully as she considered what she'd heard. 'It's possible that you're suffering from endometriosis, although I wouldn't like to make a final diagnosis without sending you for some tests first. However, the symptoms you described could point towards it being that.'

'Endometriosis?' Judith repeated. 'What's that? I've never heard of it.'

'It's when tiny pieces of the lining of the womb, the endometrium, are shed during menstruation but don't pass out of the body. Instead they travel up the Fallopian tubes into the pelvic cavity and attach themselves to the pelvic organs. They continue to respond to your menstrual cycle so each month they bleed, but because the blood can't escape, it causes cysts to form. And they're the cause of most of the pain and discomfort.'

'How weird!' Judith exclaimed. 'And you think that's what is wrong with me?'

'I think it's worth investigating further.' Emma brought up the relevant document on the computer and filled in the patient's details. She glanced at Judith. 'You need to be seen by a gynaecologist so I'll organise an appointment for you. Basically, what it means is that your pelvic cavity will need to be examined. It's done by using a laparoscope, which is a special instrument that's passed through the wall of the abdomen. There's a tiny camera on the end of it so the gynaecologist can see what's going on inside you.'

'It sounds horrible,' Judith said, shuddering.

'It'll be fine,' Emma assured her. 'And it will be worth having it done if it means we can sort out this problem you have.'

'If I do have this endometriosis, how will you treat it?'

'It depends how severe it is. Drugs can be very effective in some cases. In others, where the cysts are very large, surgery to remove them is the best option. Pregnancy can also suppress the condition.'

'So I can still have a baby?' Judith asked anxiously.

'Yes, although it's only fair to warn you that endometriosis can affect your fertility. However, let's find out if my diagnosis is correct before we worry about that.' Emma tried to sound as positive as she could but she could tell that Judith was upset by the thought that she might not have the baby she longed for.

Emma saw her out and buzzed for her next patient. The evening flew past and before she knew it, it was time to pack up for the night. She collected up the files she had used and took them into the office. Ruth looked up from the computer and smiled at her. She had worked at the practice for many years and had watched Emma growing up so there was no question of her standing on ceremony.

'I bet you're sorry you came home now, aren't you, love?'

'It did cross my mind,' Emma replied, jokingly. She held up the files. 'You'd think we should be able to do away with all this paperwork now that we have computers to help us.'

'I wish!' Ruth replied cheerfully. 'The trouble is that computers have a nasty habit of breaking down, so we need the files as back-up.'

'I suppose so.'

Emma looked round when she heard footsteps in the corridor, feeling her pulse surge when Daniel appeared in the doorway. She had been too stressed about seeing him again to take much notice earlier in the day, but all of a sudden she found herself taking stock of the changes the past few years had wrought. Although he was still extremely good looking with those craggy, very masculine features and that thick dark hair, there were lines on his face that hadn't been there five years before, an underlying sadness in his hazel eyes that surprised her. Daniel looked as though he had suffered some kind of sorrow in his life and she couldn't help wondering what had happened. Was it possible that he had fallen in love and been let down?

The thought sent a shaft of pain searing through her. Emma bit her lip to contain the cry that threatened to emerge. That Daniel might have experienced the same kind of unhappiness as she had done when they'd parted should have filled her with a certain satisfaction, but it didn't. All she felt was an overwhelming sense of grief that he might have loved some other woman more than he had loved her.

'I hope it isn't always as busy as that?' He grinned at Ruth. 'Sure you didn't ring round all the patients and ask them to call in tonight so you could put me through my paces?'

'How did you guess?' Ruth winked at Emma. 'Drat! We've been found out.'

'I…um…it looks like it.' Emma did her best to respond to the teasing comment but it wasn't easy. The thought of Daniel loving another woman was more painful than it had any right to be. She was over him and it shouldn't matter, but it did. She took a quick breath to control the pain when she saw him look at her in surprise. 'We're only joking, Daniel.'

'That's good to hear.' He smiled coolly. 'I'd hate to think you had it in for me, Emma.'

Emma flushed when she heard the irony in his voice. She turned away, busying herself with placing the files she'd used in the tray. By the time Daniel added his, it was brimming over. 'Do you want me to put these away so you can have a clear run in the morning?' she offered.

'There's no need. Dr Haynes took on a part-time receptionist at Christmas,' Ruth explained. 'There was some sort of wretched tummy bug doing the rounds and I was snowed under with all the extra paperwork. Claire comes in three mornings a week and helps with the filing, et cetera. We'll soon get everything sorted out between us.'

'Oh, right. That's fine.' Emma placed the referral letter she'd printed in the tray for posting. 'There's just the one letter that needs sending as well.'

'And I've got another one here.'

Daniel leant past her and dropped his letter on top of hers. Emma tried not to flinch when his shoulder brushed against her but he must have felt the small involuntary jerk she gave. He stepped back, his face betraying very little as he told Ruth that he would lock up and set the alarm.

Emma took it as her cue to leave. She murmured a general goodbye and hurriedly left. Although the surgery was attached to the house, it was completely self-contained and she had to walk round to the front door to let herself in. She hung her coat in the hall then made her way to the sitting room to turn on the gas fire. Although the central heating was switched on, the house still felt chilly.

She sighed. It probably felt chilly because her body hadn't adjusted to the change in temperature yet. When she'd left South Africa early that morning the temperature had been in the high 30s, so it was bound to be a shock to her system to be plunged back into the tail end of a British winter. Still, she would soon adapt…

Emma looked round in surprise when she heard the front door open. It slammed shut and a moment later she heard footsteps crossing the hall. Her heart was already racing when Daniel appeared, even though she had no idea what he wanted.

'Oh, good. You've got the fire going. It's a lot colder

up here than it is in London,' he observed, crossing the room to warm his hands.

'I suppose it is,' Emma agreed uncertainly. She frowned when she realised that he wasn't wearing a coat. He'd had it on earlier so why had he taken it off? A horrible suspicion started to rear its head and she stared at him in alarm. 'What are you doing here, Daniel?'

'At this precise moment, I'm trying to warm up. But give me a couple of minutes and I'll make myself useful.'

'Useful?'

'Uh-huh. I'll cook dinner tonight. It doesn't seem fair to expect you to do it after the day you've had.'

'Cook dinner?' Emma took a quick breath when she realised that she was repeating everything he said. 'Why on earth would you want to cook dinner?'

'Because we both need to eat,' he replied reasonably. He glanced at her, the light from the fire reflecting in his eyes so that she found it impossible to read his expression. 'We can work out a rota if you prefer, but tonight I'll cook.'

He straightened up and headed for the door but Emma knew that she couldn't let him leave before she found out what was going on. 'Why do we need a rota? Surely you'll be having dinner wherever you're staying? Most of the guest houses will provide an evening meal if you ask them to.'

'Your aunt hasn't told you, then?' He stopped and

turned, and she could see the concern on his face. It made her feel even more alarmed.

'Told me what?' she snapped.

'That I'm staying here.'

CHAPTER THREE

'EVERYTHING happened so fast that there was no time to arrange accommodation before I left London. I was going to sort something out when I got here, but Margaret insisted that I stay at the house.'

Daniel shrugged but he could tell from the frozen expression on Emma's face that the news had come as a shock to her. 'I can't see that it will cause a problem, Emma, but if you aren't happy with the arrangement then, of course, I'll find somewhere else.'

'There's no need,' she said stiffly. 'If Aunt Margaret invited you to stay, I'm certainly not going to object.'

'Fine. If you change your mind, though, just let me know.'

Daniel managed to maintain an outward show of indifference as he left the sitting room, but he sighed as he headed for the kitchen. Emma's reaction to the news that they would be sharing the house was upsetting but what did he expect? It might have been different if her aunt and uncle had been there, but she probably didn't relish the idea of them being on their own. All he could do now was monitor the situation and find somewhere else if it looked as though it was going to create friction.

It was the logical solution, although it didn't make him feel good to know that he was *persona non grata* so far as Emma was concerned. He tried not to dwell on it as he made a start on dinner. He was just mashing the potatoes to go with the lamb chops and green beans he had cooked when Emma appeared.

'I'll set the table.'

She busied herself with place mats and cutlery, glasses for water and condiments. Daniel suspected that it was displacement activity, aimed at taking her mind off the thought of eating with him. He couldn't help feeling sad as he remembered all the other meals they had shared—impromptu picnics in the country, lunches in one of the local pubs. It hadn't mattered what they'd eaten or where because they'd always enjoyed it. Just being together had added extra zest to the food.

'Remember that meal we had at the Golden Goose?'

Emma's voice cut into his thoughts and he felt a tingle run through him. That she had been recalling the good times they'd had seemed too much of a coincidence, yet why should it be? It wasn't the first time their thoughts had been so in tune. Maybe there was still some kind of connection between them.

Daniel hurriedly quashed that thought. He couldn't allow himself to think like that; it was too dangerous. 'Not really,' he replied offhandedly.

He spooned mashed potato onto the plates, ignoring the flicker of hurt that crossed her face. He was doing this for her sake. They couldn't go back and they couldn't go forward either. Not together. Leaving aside the fact that Emma no longer loved him, the old objections were as valid today as they had been five years ago. He knew from what Jim had told him that Emma was determined to make consultant one day. If that was to happen then he knew that she needed to remain completely focused. If she failed to achieve her goal, she would regret it just as much as she would have done if she'd given up surgery all together.

Daniel's heart was heavy as he carried the plates over to the table. Even if Emma was prepared to give them a second chance—which she wasn't!—there was no future for them. 'I hope this is all right for you. There's no gravy, I'm afraid. I've never mastered the art of making decent gravy.'

'It's fine. Thank you.'

Her tone was painfully polite and it cut him to the quick to know that she was deliberately distancing herself from him. He didn't react, however, as he pulled out a chair and sat down because there was nothing he could do that would help. Emma sat down as well and began to eat. Apart from the faint clatter of cutlery, the room was silent and Daniel could feel the tension mounting as the minutes passed. He searched his mind for something uncontroversial to say, but all he could come up with was work. Still, it was better than nothing.

'How did you get on tonight?'

'Fine, thank you.' Emma forked a little potato into her mouth. She chewed and swallowed it then looked at him. 'How about you?'

'Oh, yes, fine. Thanks.' Daniel inwardly groaned when he heard the stilted note in his voice. This was hardly the best way to improve the atmosphere, was it?

He cleared his throat and tried again. 'I was surprised by how busy it was, to be honest. I know morning surgery had to be cancelled, but even so I didn't expect that many patients to turn up. Did you?'

'No.' She scooped a little more potato onto her fork then hesitated. Daniel held his breath, hoping that she would find something else to say. If the next few weeks weren't to be an ordeal for them both, Emma needed to meet him halfway.

'To be frank, I don't know how Uncle Jim copes on his own. It was obvious from the number of people we saw tonight that it needs more than one doctor to run this practice.'

Daniel felt like punching the air in relief, but managed to control the urge. Two sentences didn't make a conversation. And they definitely didn't make up for past hurts. 'I agree. The workload is way too much for one person, especially when that person has health issues of his own,' he agreed soberly, trying to ignore the pang of guilt he felt. He had never set out to hurt her, far from it. He'd done what was necessary to safeguard her happiness and he had to remember that, even though it was hard.

'We have to find a way to make Uncle Jim understand that.' Emma sighed. 'It won't be easy, though. You know how independent he is and admitting that he needs help will be extremely difficult for him. Then there's the problem of finding someone suitable who's willing to work here. That will be another major hurdle.'

'Jim told me once that he'd not had much luck finding a replacement after his partner retired,' Daniel said quietly.

'No. There were very few applications when the post was advertised, so he wasn't exactly spoiled for choice. And the couple of candidates he interviewed changed their minds when they discovered what the job actually entailed.' She shrugged. 'It takes a certain type of person willing to go out to a call at one of the farms in the middle of winter.'

'Not many doctors are as dedicated as Jim is, but he has to face facts. He's not getting any younger. Even without this operation, he would have had to think about at least scaling back even if he doesn't intend to retire. Quite frankly, he can't go on working as hard as he's been doing.'

'We know that, but convincing Uncle Jim is another matter. The practice means everything to him,' she added worriedly.

'I know it does, Emma, but somehow we have to make him see that he needs to think about himself for a change. And about your aunt, too. She must be worried sick about him.'

'She is.' Tears welled to her eyes and she looked away.

Daniel reached out and laid his hand over hers, hating to see her looking so upset. 'We'll work something out, Emma. Promise.'

He gave her hand a gentle squeeze, his heart lifting when he felt her fingers curl around his for a moment before she pulled away. Picking up her cutlery, she started eating again and he knew that the all too brief moment of togetherness had passed. They finished the meal as it had begun, in silence. Daniel knew there was no point trying to draw her out again, even if he'd had the heart to try. Emma was deliberately shutting him out and although it hurt like hell, he understood why. She didn't trust him after what had happened and he couldn't blame her.

Emma refused both dessert and coffee. Her nerves were stretched so tightly by then that she would have been sick if she'd consumed anything else. She stacked her plate and glass in the dishwasher then went upstairs to her room. Daniel had mentioned something about watching television in the sitting room, but she had no intention of joining him. Dinner had been enough of an ordeal.

She sighed as she lay down on the narrow single bed. The thought of having to spend the next few weeks making stilted conversation wasn't appealing, but what choice did she have? If she asked Daniel to find somewhere else to live it would only arouse her aunt and uncle's suspicions that things weren't right between them. Although Aunt Margaret and Uncle Jim knew that she and Daniel had spent a lot of time together five years ago, they had no idea just how serious the relationship had been or, rather, how much it had meant to *her.* As far as the older couple were concerned, it had been nothing more than a summer romance and she didn't intend to disabuse them of that idea. She and Daniel would have to muddle through as best they could, although one thing was certain—if he tried to touch her again, she would make it clear that he was overstepping the mark.

Emma tried to ignore the tingle that shot up her arm as she recalled the warm grip of his fingers. She got up and went to the bookshelves, selecting a well-worn copy of *Black Beauty*, a childhood favourite. Curling up on the bed, she proceeded to reacquaint herself with the familiar characters. She must have drifted off to sleep at some point because the next thing she knew, the telephone was ringing.

She got up and hurried out to the landing, but Daniel had beaten her to it. He had already lifted the phone off its rest and was holding it to his ear. Emma felt her breath catch when she discovered that all he was wearing was a pair of pyjama pants resting low on his narrow hips. His chest was bare, the thick, dark hair outlining the solid strength of his pectoral muscles before it arrowed down to disappear tantalisingly beneath the waistband of his pants. It was only when he dropped the receiver back onto its rest with a clatter that she managed to drag her gaze away.

'That was Harry Groves from High Dale Farm. Apparently, his wife has gone into labour and the midwife is at another call. Harry has phoned for an ambulance but it will be at least an hour before it gets there,' Daniel explained. 'I said I'd go over there straight away.'

'High Dale Farm is right up in the hills. It's a long drive even from here, so no wonder the ambulance will need time to get there,' Emma agreed worriedly.

'Is it marked on the map?' Daniel asked, referring to the Ordnance Survey map they kept in the surgery.

It showed the location of every farm in their catchment area, with the roads leading to it marked in red.

'It should be. It's certainly one of the most difficult places to find if you don't know the area.' Emma hurried back into her room and slipped on her shoes. 'I'll fetch it while you get dressed.'

'Thanks. Oh, and can you bring me a printout of Mrs Groves's most recent notes? I don't want to go unprepared.'

'Will do.'

Emma ran down the stairs. There was a set of keys for the surgery on the hook by the door and she picked them up then snatched her coat off the peg. Although it was the end of March, the air felt frosty as she made her way to the surgery and let herself in. Once she'd turned off the alarm, she found the map and checked that the farm was marked on it. She groaned as she traced her finger along the route. As she'd thought, it was one of the most difficult places to reach.

After printing out a copy of Sarah Groves's notes, she ran back to the house. Daniel had started his car and was ready to leave by the time she got there. Emma hurried round to the passenger side and opened the door. 'Turn left as soon as we leave here, then right at the crossroads.'

'You don't need to come, Emma. So long as I have the map, I should be able to find the place.'

Emma shook her head as she slid into the seat. 'You can't map-read and navigate these roads. They're little more than cart tracks in places.'

She fastened her seat belt, hoping that he wasn't going

to argue with her as she really didn't feel like a confrontation at this time of the night. It was a relief when he put the car in gear and headed out of the drive.

'Seeing as you're here, can you read through Mrs Groves's notes,' he suggested as soon as they were on the road. 'Her husband said that it had been a textbook pregnancy so far, but I'd like to be sure. There's a torch in the glove box. You can use that instead of turning on the interior light.'

Emma nodded as she found the torch. It would make it easier for Daniel to see where he was going if he didn't have to contend with the glare from the interior lights. She shielded the end of the torch with her hand as she quickly read through the notes that had been made when Sarah Groves had last visited the surgery.

'There's nothing here to indicate a problem,' she told Daniel as they reached the crossroads and turned right. 'She was seen last week and her BP was fine. Nothing showed up in her urine sample either, and there was no sign of oedema.'

'How many weeks is she? I asked the husband but he was in such a state he couldn't remember.'

'Thirty-five,' Emma told him, checking the woman's chart.

'That's not too bad, is it? I know that technically a baby is considered premature if it's born before thirty-seven weeks, but it should be a decent enough weight by this stage.'

'I wonder why she's gone into labour. Did the husband say if she was bleeding?'

'No. I did ask him, but he was almost incoherent

and didn't seem to be taking much in. He just kept asking how soon I could get there.' She felt him glance at her. 'You're wondering if there's a problem with the placenta?'

'Yes.' Emma felt a shiver run down her spine when he correctly interpreted her thoughts. Once, the fact that they'd been so much in tune had delighted her, but now it filled her with alarm. She didn't want to share that kind of closeness with him ever again.

'It's one of the causes of premature labour so we certainly can't rule it out.' He slowed down and peered through the windscreen. 'There's another junction coming up. Which way now?'

'Straight on for about ten miles then we'll need to turn off the main road and head into hills,' she told him, checking the map.

'That's when the fun really starts, is it?' he asked with a laugh as he picked up speed again.

'It will be fine.'

'Spoken like someone who's used to tearing around the back of beyond. Jim told me that you've done several stints overseas in the last couple of years. How did you get into that sort of work?'

'Richard suggested it. He worked for an aid agency when he was a junior registrar and said it was invaluable experience.'

'Richard?'

'Richard Walker, my boss,' she explained.

'You obviously get on well with him,' he observed, and she frowned when she heard the edge in his voice.

She had the impression that something had displeased him, but had no idea what it could be.

'Yes, I do,' she said a shade defensively. 'All the team think very highly of him, in fact.'

'I see.' He changed gear then glanced at her and there was no sign of anything other than friendly interest on his face. 'Working overseas must be challenging, I imagine.'

'Sometimes.' She shrugged. 'It all depends where you're working. If you're based at a clinic, like the one I've just worked in, then it tends to be easier. The facilities are better, and there's usually more staff to help out than if you're working at a field hospital.'

'And do you enjoy surgery as much as you thought you would?'

Emma frowned. She had the strangest feeling that her answer was important to him and couldn't understand why. Why should it matter to Daniel if she was happy or not? He certainly hadn't cared about her happiness five years ago, had he?

The thought pierced a hole right through the protective shell she had built around her heart. It was an effort to respond when it felt as though it was in danger of cracking wide open. It was only pride that gave her the strength to carry on, pride plus a desire not to let him know how badly he had hurt her.

'Yes, I do. It's everything I hoped it would be.' She laughed wryly. 'I suppose I should thank you, Daniel. If you hadn't been so committed to your own career, I might have turned down the chance to become a surgeon and that would have been a huge mistake. I don't doubt that in time I would have come to regret my decision.'

CHAPTER FOUR

DANIEL drew up in front of the farmhouse and switched off the engine. Emma hadn't faltered as she had directed him along a series of increasingly narrow tracks. He knew that he would have had a much harder time finding the farm without her help but, contrarily, wished that she had stayed at home. At least then he wouldn't have to face up to the realisation that he had been right all along. Their relationship would never have survived if she had given up her dreams to be with him.

'I'll let Harry know that we're here.' She got out of the car and ran over to the house. The door was open and she didn't waste time knocking before she hurried inside.

Daniel got out and took his case out of the back. He also lifted out the pack of medical supplies that Jim kept ready for just such an emergency as this. There was no sign of Emma when he let himself into the house but he could hear voices coming from upstairs so headed in that direction and soon found himself in the main bedroom. A fair-haired man in his thirties, whom he assumed must be Harry Groves, was holding the hand of the woman lying on the bed. She was very pale and obviously in a great deal of pain. Emma was in the process of checking her pulse so Daniel left her to deal with that while he introduced himself.

'I'm Daniel Kennedy. I'm covering for Dr Haynes while he's in hospital.'

'So Emma said,' Harry replied. He looked anxiously at the door. 'Did you pass the ambulance on your way here?'

'No, but it may have taken a different route from us.' Daniel smiled reassuringly at the couple. 'Can you tell me exactly what's happened?'

'I started having pains after tea but thought it was because of the way the baby was lying,' Sarah Groves explained. 'I lay down on the settee for a while and that seemed to help, but then the pains started again, worse than ever. That's when I discovered I was bleeding. I told Harry to phone the midwife, but she was out at another call so he phoned for an ambulance.' Her voice shook. 'When they said it would take over an hour for it to get here, he rang the surgery.'

'You did exactly the right thing,' Daniel said soothingly. He glanced at Emma, hoping his feelings didn't show. Maybe it was foolish to feel upset but he couldn't help it. In a tiny corner of his heart, he had nurtured the hope that their love could have overcome any obstacle. Even though he hadn't been prepared to take that risk, it had been something to cling to, but now he could see how stupid it had been. His relationship with Emma would have ended the same way as his parents' had done if they had stayed together.

'We need to know how much longer the ambulance is going to be,' he said with a heavy heart.

'I'll get onto Ambulance Control and see if they can give us an update,' Emma offered immediately.

She left the bedroom and Daniel turned his attention to Sarah again, relieved to have something to focus on apart from his aching heart. 'Has the bleeding stopped now?'

Sarah shook her head, her pretty face clouded with worry. 'No. In fact, I think it's got worse in the last ten minutes or so.'

'I'll just take a look, if that's all right with you.'

Daniel drew back the bedding, struggling to hide his dismay when he saw the bright red pool that had collected on the sheets. He fetched the foetal stethoscope from the pack of emergency medical supplies and listened to the baby's heartbeat. It was slightly slower than it should have been but not worryingly so, which was a relief. He had just finished when Emma came back and he could tell immediately that it wasn't good news when she beckoned him over to the door.

'What's happened?' he demanded.

'Apparently, the ambulance has had a puncture. They're waiting for the breakdown truck, so Ambulance Control has dispatched a second vehicle.'

Daniel rolled his eyes. 'Which means we're starting from scratch. It could be another hour before an ambulance gets here.'

'It looks like it.' Emma looked at Sarah. 'How is she?'

'She's lost a lot of blood. I'm going to set up a drip,

which should help, but I'm not happy with the way things are going.'

'How about the baby?'

'Foetal heartbeat is slightly slower than I would like it to be. We'll need to keep a close check on what's happening.'

'It looks like a placental abruption, doesn't it?'

'Yes, that's my guess too. At least part of the placenta has become detached from the wall of the uterus.' He sighed. 'If we were able to perform an ultrasound scan then we could tell how bad the abruption is, but at the moment we're batting in the dark.'

'What's going on, Doctor? I may not have seen a human baby being born before but I've delivered umpteen lambs and I know this isn't normal.'

Daniel turned when Harry came to join them. The farmer was obviously worried and Daniel led him out onto the landing. The last thing he wanted was to upset Sarah any more. 'The bleeding could be a sign that the placenta has become partially detached from the wall of the uterus.'

'But why?' Harry demanded. 'Sarah's been fit as a fiddle up to now, so why on earth should this have happened right out of the blue?'

'It's impossible to say. These things just happen sometimes and there's no explanation as to why.'

Daniel glanced back into the room. Emma was bending over the bed while she inserted a cannula into the back of Sarah's hand. Her face was set with concentration, even though she must have performed the procedure many times before. Daniel felt a wave of emotion wash over him as he watched her. He might regret having to let her go but he knew that he would do the same thing all over again. He simply couldn't bear it if Emma ended up hating him for ruining her life.

Emma could feel Daniel watching her but she didn't look up. She felt too emotionally raw to take that risk. Had Daniel ever regretted breaking up with her? she wondered as she taped the cannula into place. Had he ever missed her? Even though she knew how stupid it was, she couldn't help wishing that he'd felt *something*.

Sarah moaned softly, clutching her stomach, and Emma quickly returned her thoughts to what was going on. 'Are the pains coming at regular intervals?' she asked, placing her own hand on the woman's distended abdomen.

'I don't know…they seem to be coming closer together,' Sarah murmured.

Emma kept her hand on Sarah's abdomen and felt it tense as her uterus contracted. There was no doubt in her mind that Sarah was in labour. She reached for the foetal stethoscope and checked the baby's heartbeat, frowning when she discovered how slow it was. It was a sign that the baby was in distress and that they needed to take immediate steps to help it. She beckoned Daniel over to the bed.

'The baby's heartbeat has dropped. We need to deliver it as soon as possible.'

'A Caesarean section, you mean?'

'Yes. I know it's not ideal to do it here, but we don't have a choice,' she said, hoping he wouldn't disagree with her. 'Even if the ambulance arrives in the next few minutes, it will take at least another hour to get Sarah to hospital. That's way too long in my opinion.'

'You're right, we can't afford to wait that long.' His dark brows rose. 'It's been ages since I did my obstetrics rotation. I assisted with a couple of sections then but I've not done any since. How about you?'

'I did one a couple of weeks ago,' Emma told him.

'Great! You lead and I'll assist.'

It was all arranged with the minimum of fuss. Although it made sense for her to take the lead in view of her surgical background, Emma was a little surprised that Daniel had suggested it. It certainly didn't gel with the idea of him wanting to cover himself with glory, did it?

There was no time to dwell on the thought, however. Emma unpacked the emergency medical supplies while Daniel explained what they were going to do. Sarah and Harry were naturally concerned, but once Daniel had told them that their baby was in distress, they agreed to go ahead. In a very short time, everything was organised.

Emma draped the bed with clean sheets while Daniel attended to the anaesthetic. Harry showed her where the bathroom was so she could scrub up. Daniel did the same and then they helped each other glove up. Harry had elected to stay with his wife so once Emma had swabbed Sarah's abdomen with antiseptic solution, she set to work, knowing there was no time to lose.

Daniel handed her a scalpel, standing back as she made a horizontal incision just above the bikini line.

Any qualms she may have had about carrying out the procedure soon disappeared as she focused on what needed doing. Within a very short time she was able to lift the baby out of Sarah's womb and hand it to Daniel, who wrapped it in a clean towel and carried it over to the chest of drawers that was doubling as an examination table. There was a moment when they all held their breath and then the baby cried, a tentative sound at first that soon grew louder.

'Congratulations!' Emma smiled at the couple. 'You have a lovely little boy.'

'A boy?' Harry repeated. He appeared completely shocked after what had happened and stared at her in confusion. 'We decided that we'd wait until the baby was born to find out what it was, but we were convinced we were having a little girl. Are you sure it's a boy?'

'Oh, yes, there's definitely no mistake about that. He's got all the necessary bits and pieces,' Emma replied with a laugh. She delivered the placenta and checked that there were no bits missing from it then set about stitching up the wound. Daniel brought the baby over to the bed while she was doing so.

'So who gets first go at holding him?' he asked.

'Sarah,' Harry said promptly. He bent and kissed his wife tenderly on the cheek. 'If it wasn't for Sarah, we wouldn't have this little fellow.'

Daniel placed the tiny mite in his mother's arms, smiling as he watched Sarah pull back the folds of towel to perform the age-old ritual of counting his fingers and toes. Emma looked away when she felt a lump come to her throat. Once upon a time she had imagined just such a scene, only the baby whose toes were being counted had been hers and Daniel's. That was how much she had loved him, enough to want to give him a child.

Tears stung her eyes as she busied herself, stitching up. Even though she was over him, it still hurt to recall how much she had once loved him. She had wanted the whole lot with Daniel—marriage, motherhood, years and years of happily-ever-after as a family.

Would she ever have a family now? she wondered suddenly. Ever experience the joy of holding her own child in her arms?

She tried to picture it but it was impossible to imagine a life not dictated by her work. It made her question if she was right to devote every waking minute to her job, and it was worrying to be beset by doubts. For the past five years her work had been what had kept her centred, what had given meaning to her life, but all of a sudden she found herself wanting more, a life that wasn't shaped by the demands of her profession, and it was unsettling. However, the worst thing of all was that it was being around Daniel that had triggered such thoughts.

It was an effort to push it to the back of her mind as she finished off. She made Sarah comfortable and then Daniel helped her clear everything away. By the time they'd finished, the ambulance was pulling up outside. Sarah was reluctant to leave the house at first until Emma gently explained that she and baby Thomas needed to be checked over in the hospital's maternity unit. Although little Thomas appeared to be fit and healthy, technically he was premature, and Sarah herself had lost a lot of blood: it would be foolish to take any risks at this stage.

She and Daniel waited while the family were loaded on board the ambulance then they got into the car and followed it back to the main road. It roared away, taking the opposite direction from where they were heading.

'All in all, I'd say that was a good night's work, wouldn't you?'

Daniel's voice echoed with satisfaction and nothing else. If he'd experienced even a fraction of the anguish she had felt earlier then it certainly wasn't apparent, Emma thought sickly as she murmured her agreement. Maybe they had never discussed having children but in her mind the two were linked—when you loved someone, you wanted to have a child with them. It proved beyond any doubt that Daniel's feelings for her hadn't been what he had claimed. Although she should have felt glad that she was rid of him, oddly enough it hurt to have yet more proof of the way he had lied to her.

Daniel knew that he would remember that night for a long time to come. Seeing little Thomas make his appearance in the world had touched him in a way he had not expected it to. All he'd been able to think about was how wonderful it would have been if he'd been watching his own child—his and *Emma*'s son—being born.

He glanced at her as they reached the outskirts of the town but she wasn't looking at him. Her eyes were closed, although he didn't think she was asleep. Had she been moved by tonight's events, wondered how it would have been if it had been their child? He doubted it. Emma had made her feelings perfectly clear when she had told him that she was glad they had parted. She certainly wasn't wasting her time by thinking about what might have been!

A feeling of dejection swept over him as he drew up in front of the house. He'd known it would be difficult to see Emma again when he had agreed to run the practice, but he had never imagined that he would feel this wretched. The only way he could hope to get through the coming weeks was to forget what had happened in the past and focus on what was happening at the present moment. And the one thing that was crystal clear was that Emma had moved on.

Daniel followed her into the house and headed straight for the kitchen to make himself a cup of tea in the probably vain hope that it would give him a much-needed boost. He hadn't expected Emma to join him and looked round in surprise when he heard her follow him into the room. 'Would you like a drink as well?'

'Please. I don't know if it's the excitement of what happened tonight or the fact that all that travelling has upset my body clock, but I'm too wide awake to sleep.' She tossed her coat over a chair and went to the cupboard. 'I wonder if there's any hot chocolate... Ah, yes, there it is.'

She stood on tiptoe to try and reach the jar of drinking chocolate but it was just out of her grasp. Daniel crossed the room and lifted it down off the shelf. 'Here you go, shorty,' he said without thinking.

'I'm not short, just tidily packaged,' she retorted, as

she'd done so many times when he had teased her about her height.

Daniel felt the blood rush to his head. He remembered only too well what came next, how he would apologise for the supposed slight with a kiss. His eyes flew to Emma's face and his blood pressure zoomed several more notches up the scale when he saw that she too remembered what had used to happen. Whether it was that or the fact that his emotions were already in turmoil he didn't know but all of a sudden he found himself bending towards her until he was close enough to feel the moistness of her breath cloud on his lips.

'Emma.'

He wasn't sure if he actually spoke her name out loud or not. He was beyond hearing by that point, beyond everything including reason. What did it matter if he had just resolved to forget about the past? It wasn't a sin if he changed his mind, was it? All he wanted was to feel her lips under his once more, taste their sweetness, savour their warmth and softness. One kiss was all he asked for, just one kiss to stave off the pain that was gnawing away at his heart. Surely it wasn't wrong to allow himself this one brief moment of pleasure?

His head dipped until merely a millimetre separated them. Daniel could feel the heat of her skin now, smell the scent of the soap she'd used. Memories crowded his mind but he no longer needed to recall the past when he had a chance to create a whole new delicious present…

His mouth touched hers and the shock of the contact almost brought him to his knees. He could feel the blood rushing through his veins like liquid fire, feel the heat that invaded every cell in his body, and groaned. His hands lifted as he went to draw her closer so that he could feel the soft curves of her body moulding themselves against the hardness of his, but he never got the chance. With a tiny cry of alarm, Emma pushed him away and ran from the room.

Daniel leant back against the worktop, needing its support as all the strength suddenly drained from his body. He desperately wanted to go after her but he knew it would be the wrong thing to do. Maybe he could persuade her to let him kiss her again—possibly even do more than kiss her—but it wouldn't be fair. Perhaps there was still some vestige of attraction between them, but it didn't alter the fact that he could so easily ruin her life even now. Emma needed to focus on her job now more than ever or she could end up losing everything she had worked so hard for. Nothing was worth that risk, certainly not his own selfish desires.

Emma slammed the bedroom door, scarcely able to believe what had happened. She wanted to blame Daniel for it but she was too honest to claim that she hadn't been partly at fault. She had wanted him to kiss her, wanted it so much that her cheeks burned with shame. Hadn't she learned anything from past experiences? Did she really want to find herself right back where she'd been five years ago, her life in tatters, her heart broken?

She pressed her fist against her mouth to stem the sob that threatened to escape it. She refused to cry, refused to risk her hard-won composure by breaking down. So what if she had been tempted for a moment? She had come to her senses in time, hadn't she? If anything, it proved that she could handle this situation. Daniel's kiss may have been tempting but she had realised the risks, assessed the damage it could cause, and taken steps to stop what was happening. She should be proud of herself for what she had done.

The thought steadied her. She quickly undressed and got into bed, pulling the quilt up to her chin. It was gone midnight and she needed to get some sleep if she hoped to be fit enough to help out at morning surgery…

The sound of footsteps climbing the stairs made her eyes fly open. She hadn't thought to ask Daniel which room he was using and found herself holding her breath as she waited for him to reach the landing. The house was large and there were a number of empty bedrooms, including the room next to hers.

Her breath whooshed out in relief when she heard his footsteps fade. He was obviously using the guest room, which was on the opposite side of the house. For some reason, she felt safer knowing that he wasn't sleeping in the room next to hers. She had resisted temptation once tonight and she didn't intend to put herself to the test again. She might not like the idea, but she had to face the fact that she might not have the strength to hold out a second time.

CHAPTER FIVE

'THAT'S excellent news. Thank you for letting me know… Yes, of course. I'll pass on your message.'

Daniel replaced the phone and leant back in his chair. Morning surgery had ended and he'd been getting ready to go out to some house calls when Harry Groves had phoned to tell him that Sarah and baby Thomas had been given a clean bill of health by the consultant at the hospital. Harry had asked him to pass on the news to Emma, which he would do, but he needed a few minutes' breathing space before he sought her out.

He sighed as he tipped back his chair and stared at the ceiling. The memory of what had happened the previous night had continued to haunt him. He kept remembering that kiss and how sweet it had been, even though he knew how stupid it was. He had made a mistake by kissing her and he had no intention of repeating it, so it would be better if he put it out of his mind; however, it was proving to be easier said than done. Every time his thoughts wandered, he could feel Emma's mouth under his and it was driving him mad!

'Ruth said there's quite a lot of calls to do today, so do you want me to help?'

The sound of Emma's voice almost made him tip over the chair. Daniel hurriedly returned it to all four legs as he turned towards the door. He'd made a point of leaving the house extra early that morning so it was the first time he'd seen her that day. Now he found his senses running riot as he took stock of her slender figure encased in a neat grey skirt and a crisp white blouse. It may not have been the sexiest of outfits, granted, but it definitely did something for him.

'No, it's fine.' Daniel dragged his unruly thoughts back into line again and prayed they would stay there. That sort of thinking wasn't going to help one jot. 'I imagine you want to visit your uncle this afternoon, so I'll do the calls.'

'Well, if you're sure?' She gave him a moment to reconsider then shrugged. 'I'll do them tomorrow, then. OK?'

'Fine, although don't feel that you have to. After all, Jim asked me to cover for him.'

He'd only meant to point out that she wasn't under any obligation to work in the surgery. Although he appreciated the offer, she had come home for a holiday and it seemed a shame that her plans should be scuppered. However, that obviously wasn't how she took it. Daniel's heart sank when he saw the mutinous set to her mouth.

'I'm very much aware of that, thank you. Don't worry, Daniel, I don't intend to step on your toes. So far as my aunt and uncle are concerned, you're the knight in shining armour who's come to rescue them. Let's just hope they still feel the same way in a few weeks' time.'

'Meaning what precisely?' he demanded, stung by the comment.

She shrugged. 'That I still find it hard to believe it was purely altruism that brought you here. There has to be something in it for you, personally or professionally, otherwise why would you give up so much of your free time to work in the back of beyond?'

'I see. So what do you think I'm hoping to gain from it?' he asked, refusing to let her see how much it hurt to hear her judge him so harshly. Maybe it was his own fault that she had such a low opinion of him, but if she had loved him—as she'd once claimed—surely she shouldn't have been so willing to believe the worst?

'I don't know. I haven't worked that out yet.' She gave him a cool smile. 'But when I do, you'll be the first to know.'

She left the room, leaving the door wide open. Daniel listened to the sound of her footsteps receding along the corridor and sighed. He could go after her and tell her that she was wrong, that his motives were of the very highest order, but she wouldn't believe him. She wanted to think badly of him, wanted to bury any feelings she'd had for him under a blanket of mistrust. It shouldn't be that difficult, not after what he had done. She must be ninety-nine per cent certain that he was a rat of the first order, but obviously she was keen to add that precious last one per cent to the score. And finding out that he had an ulterior motive for offering to cover for Jim would be the perfect way to round up the total, so help him.

Emma went back to the house and made herself a sandwich. She took it up to her room, unwilling to stick around in case Daniel decided to have his lunch before he did the calls. She was still smarting from their most recent confrontation and needed time to calm down before she saw him again.

She sighed as she took a bite of the bread. It would take more than a few hours to soothe her feelings where Daniel was concerned. Every time she spoke to him, she felt so churned up inside that it was hard to maintain an outward show of composure. Maybe it was always difficult to relax with someone you'd once been heavily involved with—she really didn't know.

Although she'd been out with several different men in the last few years, she had never had a serious relationship with any of them. She had told herself that she was too busy with her career to worry about that side of her life but it wasn't true. Her experiences with Daniel had put her off, made her wary of getting involved with anyone again. However, she couldn't allow the past to continue influencing her or she would never be truly free of him. She had to put what had happened behind her. And mean it.

Emma finished her lunch, wondering if this might prove to be a turning point. Discovering that Daniel was working here had been a shock but it could turn out to be a good thing. Seeing him again had awoken a lot of feelings she'd thought were dead and now she would be able to dispatch them for ever. And if she did find out that he had his own agenda for agreeing to cover for her uncle then so much the better. It would put the final nail in the coffin of their relationship.

* * *

Daniel got through the house calls faster than he'd expected. He checked his watch after he left his final call and realised that he had time to drop into the hospital. It would only take him ten minutes or so to drive there and he would like to see how Jim was faring.

He started his car, refusing to speculate as to how Emma would feel about him joining her at her uncle's bedside. She'd made it perfectly clear yesterday that she hadn't wanted him there, but it was hard luck. He just wanted to reassure the older man that everything was going smoothly, or at least everything to do with the running of the *practice*. So far as his relationship with Emma, well, it would be better not to mention that.

He managed to find a parking space close to the main doors, which was a minor miracle. Hurrying inside, he made his way to the lift and pressed the button. It arrived promptly and he was about to step inside when he heard someone calling his name. Glancing round, he spotted Emma crossing the foyer, carrying two cardboard containers of coffee. She glared at him as she drew closer.

'What are you doing here?'

'I came to see how Jim was doing,' he replied evenly, putting out his hand to stop the lift doors closing.

'He's fine,' she said shortly, stepping inside. 'I had a word with his consultant and he's very happy with how things went.'

'That's good to hear.' Daniel stepped into the lift. Pressing the button for their floor, he turned to her. 'Your aunt must be very relieved.'

'Of course.' Her tone was clipped. 'What Uncle Jim

needs now is plenty of rest. What he doesn't need is a lot of people visiting him.'

'I agree. However, he'll be able to rest more easily once he's sure that everything is running smoothly at the surgery.'

'I've already assured him that everything is fine.' She tipped back her head, a hint of challenge in her eyes. 'It doesn't need both of us to give him a progress report, Daniel. I'm perfectly capable of doing that by myself.'

'I'm sure you are, but knowing Jim he will still worry in case you're keeping something from him.' He shrugged. 'Jim knows that I'll tell him the truth.'

'Tell the truth and shame the devil. Is that the maxim you live by, Daniel, or only when it suits you?'

'I do my best to be truthful at all times,' he said quietly.

A flash of hurt crossed her face. 'Really? Then all I can say is that there must be more than one version of the truth in your world.'

The lift came to a halt and she got out before he could reply, although what he could have said was open to question. Daniel's heart was heavy as he followed her because he knew what she was alluding to. Five years ago he had told her that he'd loved her, but he'd also told her that his career had meant more to him than she would ever do. No wonder she was so reluctant to believe him.

Jim Haynes was in the intensive care unit where his heart and other bodily functions were being closely monitored. He was awake and looked remarkably chirpy for someone who had undergone major surgery in the past twenty-four hours. He smiled with genuine pleasure when he saw Daniel. 'Ah, good to see you, Daniel. At least I know you won't fuss over me like these two insist on doing.'

Daniel laughed. 'I shall try my very best not to fuss, I promise you.' He pulled up a chair and sat down, trying to ignore the fact that Emma was sitting next to him. He had to stop being so aware of her and treat her as he would any colleague, politely and civilly. If he could stick to that there wouldn't be a problem.

'Good.' Jim frowned. 'So how is everything at the surgery? Emma insists that it's all going swimmingly but I doubt if she'd tell me even if it weren't. The main thing is, are you coping?'

'Yes, we are.' Daniel leant forward, feeling heat flash along his veins when his arm brushed against Emma's. Even though he was wearing a jacket he could feel the contact in every cell. He cleared his throat, keeping his gaze centred on the other man so that it wouldn't wander in her direction. It would be silly to check if she had felt that same flicker of awareness run through her.

He gave Jim a complete rundown about what had been happening. He sensed that Emma wasn't happy about him going into so much detail but he guessed that it would worry Jim more if he tried to gloss over how busy it had been. He realised he was right when he saw the frown disappear from the older man's face after he finished.

'Excellent. It's good to know the practice is in such safe hands,' Jim declared. 'Now I can let Margaret whisk me away to the cottage to recuperate without having to worry about what's going on here.'

'How did you know that I was planning on taking you to the cottage?' Margaret demanded. 'I've never even mentioned it!'

'After forty years of marriage, my dear, I can read you like an open book,' Jim told her, winking at them.

Everyone laughed at that and then Daniel stood up. 'I don't want to tire you out so I won't stay any longer. Take care of yourself, Jim, and do what your doctor orders.'

'Oh, I shall.' Jim raised his eyes to the heavens. 'I don't have a choice with this pair standing guard over me!'

Daniel was still laughing as he left ICU. He made his way along the corridor, pausing when he heard Emma calling him. He waited for her to catch him up, wondering what misdemeanour he was guilty of this time. He was already steeling himself for another tongue-lashing when she came to a halt.

'I just wanted to say that you were right. Uncle Jim did need to hear it from you that everything was all right at the surgery.'

'Oh…right…thank you.'

Daniel was so shocked that he couldn't think of anything else to say. She gave him a tight little smile then turned and hurried away. He carried on walking, only realising that he must have walked straight past the lifts when he came to the end of the corridor and could go no further. He turned around and went back the way he'd come, thinking about what Emma had said.

Maybe he was reading too much into it but it was good to know that she thought he'd done something right for a change.

He groaned as he punched the button to summon the lift. How pathetic was that? A few words of praise from Emma and all of a sudden the world seemed like a much brighter place!

Emma was home well in time for evening surgery. Her aunt had returned with her but only to pack a bag. Margaret Haynes had decided to stay at a friend's house close to the hospital to save her having to make the journey back and forth. It meant that Emma and Daniel would be on their own again that night and for many more nights to come.

Emma washed her hands and then made her way round to the surgery, determined that she wasn't going to waste her time worrying about it. They were both adults and more than capable of sharing the house for the next few weeks. She was due back in Scotland in just over a month's time so it wasn't as though the situation was going to last indefinitely. Obviously, if she'd needed to take over the practice while her uncle recuperated, she would have had to arrange compassionate leave, but with Daniel here that wouldn't be necessary. He would be able to run things until Uncle Jim was well enough to return to work.

She frowned, wondering once again why Daniel had agreed to give up so much of his time to help. Although she knew that he had got on well with her uncle while he'd been doing his GP training, she hadn't realised the two men had kept in touch. Her aunt and uncle had never mentioned Daniel over the years and she certainly hadn't asked about him. She had wanted to expunge the whole unhappy episode from her life rather than dwell on it. It made her feel uneasy all of a sudden to wonder if Daniel had ever asked about her.

Emma quickly dismissed the thought as she pushed open the surgery door. Daniel had demonstrated his lack of interest five years ago in the most effective way possible!

'I'm afraid evening surgery doesn't start until four.'

Emma glanced up when she realised someone was speaking to her. She smiled at the young woman behind the reception desk. 'You must be Claire.'

'That's right. How did you know…? Oh, you must be Emma!' The other woman blushed. 'I'm so sorry. Ruth told me that you'd probably be coming in tonight, but I was expecting someone *much* older.' She clapped her hand over her mouth, obviously wishing she hadn't said that, and Emma laughed.

'Thank you. I shall take that as a compliment. Believe me, some days I feel as old as Methuselah, so it's nice to know that I don't actually look it!' She glanced around the waiting room. 'Is Ruth not in tonight?' she asked, neatly changing the subject to spare Claire's blushes.

'Yes, but she might be a bit late. A filling fell out of one of her teeth and the dentist could only fit her in this afternoon as he's on holiday for the rest of the week,' Claire explained. 'She asked me if I'd hold the fort until she gets here. I hope that's all right.'

'Of course it is.' Emma smiled at her. 'If you have

any problems, give me a buzz. I used to work on the reception desk when I was a student and I might be able to help.'

'Thanks. That's really kind of you.' Claire beamed at her. 'Daniel told me the same thing, to buzz him if I got stuck. It's the first time I've manned the desk on my own, so it's a relief to know that I can call on you two.'

'No problem.'

Emma drummed up a smile, although she could feel her hackles rising. Trust Daniel to try and worm his way into the receptionist's good books, she thought sourly, then realised how two-faced that sounded when it would appear she had done the same thing. However, her offer had been a genuine one, she assured herself as she made her way to the consulting room, aimed at making life simpler for all of them. Whereas Daniel's had undoubtedly been a way to curry favour.

She sat down at the desk, refusing to admit that she was being unfair to him. Maybe she didn't have any proof, but everything Daniel did, he did for a reason. Look at the way he had pursued her five years ago. At the time, it had seemed that their feelings had arisen so spontaneously that she had never questioned if his were genuine. Even after they'd parted she had clung to the belief that he had genuinely felt something for her, although obviously not enough to put her before his precious career. It had taken a while before she had accepted that he had merely used her feelings for him to get her into his bed.

Emma bit her lip. It might have happened a long time ago, but it still hurt to know that she had been nothing more to him than a convenient and willing bedmate.

CHAPTER SIX

THE week came to an end and Saturday arrived. As Daniel made his way downstairs, he couldn't help wishing there was a morning surgery that day. At least if he was working, he could stay out of Emma's way.

He sighed as he went into the kitchen. To say that relations between him and Emma were strained was an understatement. She only spoke to him when it was absolutely necessary and even then it was hard to get more than a dozen words out of her. He had hoped that her attitude towards him might be softening after he'd been to visit her uncle, but obviously not. He wished he could think of a way to ease the situation but it was impossible when every time he tried to talk to her, she cut him dead.

He filled the kettle with water and popped some bread into the toaster, wondering for the umpteenth time how he could gain her trust. He wasn't a threat to her, yet she insisted on treating him like some kind of pariah, and it was very hard to take. He knew that he had hurt her but he'd been hurt too; it didn't seem fair that he should have to suffer when he had been trying to do what was right.

Daniel gave himself a brisk mental shake. Feeling sorry for himself wouldn't help. What he needed was something to take his mind off the situation and put him in a more positive frame of mind. It was a glorious day and a good long walk in the hills should blow away a lot of cobwebs.

He made himself a pot of coffee then sat down at the table to eat his breakfast. He had almost finished when Emma appeared and he sighed when he saw her stop as soon as she spotted him sitting at the table. Even the local axe murderer would receive a warmer welcome than him! He dropped the last piece of toast back onto his plate and stood up.

'Just give me a couple of seconds to wash my dishes and I'll get out of your way.'

'There's no need,' she said sharply. 'You're perfectly entitled to finish your breakfast.'

'Thank you.' It was impossible to keep the sarcasm out of his voice. 'However, I seem to have lost my appetite all of a sudden.'

He carried his dishes over to the sink. He knew that Emma was still standing in the doorway and felt pain stab through him. Had it reached the point now where she couldn't even bear to be in the same room as him?

The thought seemed to set light to his temper and he turned on the tap with far more force than was necessary. A jet of water hit the edge of his cup and bounced back up, soaking the front of his T-shirt. Daniel cursed under his breath as he hastily turned off the water. That was all he needed!

'Here.'

A hand suddenly appeared, offering him a towel. Daniel took it, trying to hide his surprise at such a conciliatory gesture. He mopped the front of his T-shirt then glanced round. Emma was standing beside him and for the first time in days she wasn't giving off the usual icy vibes. She looked up and his breath caught when he saw that her lips were twitching.

'That tap's always been a nuisance. I've had the odd soaking over the years,' she told him, struggling to contain her amusement.

'I doubt if you've been as wet as I am,' he replied drolly, shaking his head so that beads of water flew out of his hair.

'No, I haven't.' She gave a choked little gurgle. 'I know I shouldn't laugh, but if you'd seen the expression on your face…'

She burst out laughing and Daniel felt the cold knotty feeling that had been building up inside him for days suddenly start to unravel. He grinned at her, his hazel eyes sparkling with amusement.

'Think it's funny to see someone almost drowning, do you?'

'Yes… I mean, no. Of course not.' She bit her lip, doing her best to behave with suitable decorum.

Daniel chuckled wickedly. Turning on the tap, he scooped up a handful of water. 'I wonder how funny you'd find it if you were on the receiving end of an impromptu shower?'

'Daniel, you wouldn't!'

'Oh, wouldn't I?' He let a few drops of water dribble

onto her bare arm, grinning when he heard her squeal in alarm. 'Are you sure about that?'

'Yes, I am.' She stared up at him and he could see the conviction in her eyes. 'You wouldn't be that cruel!'

'No, I wouldn't.' He opened his hand and let the water flow into the sink, feeling the knotty feeling start to build up inside him again. 'It's good to know that you don't think I'm completely rotten to the core, Emma.'

She didn't say anything to that and he didn't wait around while she thought of something either. He left the kitchen, taking the stairs two at a time as he headed for his room. Why in heaven's name had he said that, let her know how much it hurt to be treated as an outcast? It wouldn't achieve anything, definitely wouldn't improve her opinion of him. The last thing he wanted was for it to appear as though he was looking for sympathy!

He cursed roundly, stopping dead when he heard a knock on the door. Striding across the room, he flung it open, too angry with himself to care about putting up a front. 'Yes?'

'I just wanted to say that I'm sorry.'

Her voice was so low that it was a moment before Daniel realised what she had said. He frowned, unsure where this was leading. 'You're sorry?'

'Yes. About the way I...I've behaved recently.' She tipped back her head and looked him squarely in the eyes. 'I agreed to call a truce and I haven't kept to that. I apologise.'

'I know how difficult this situation is, Emma,' he said quietly, more touched than he cared to admit. 'I find it hard, too.'

'Do you?' She looked at him in surprise and he sighed.

'Yes. I can't just forget what happened five years ago. You meant a lot to me, Emma.'

'Did I?'

'Of course you did.' He frowned when he saw the uncertainty on her face. Surely she must know how he had felt, even though he had pushed her away? He had never tried to hide his feelings—how could he have done? She had meant the whole world to him and all of a sudden it seemed important she understood that.

'I cared a lot about you, Emma,' he said quickly, wishing that he didn't have to use such a milk-and-water term to describe how he'd felt. Claiming he'd cared barely touched on the way he had really felt about her but what else could he say? Admitting that he had loved her with every fibre of his being wasn't what she wanted to hear. His heart ached as he repeated it with as much conviction as he dared. 'I really and truly cared about you.'

'But not as much as you cared about your career.' She smiled and his heart filled with sadness when he saw the bleakness in her eyes. 'Don't worry, Daniel, I understand. And as I said the other day, it's probably a good thing that we parted. Oh, I won't pretend that it didn't hurt at the time because it did. A lot. But I'm both older and wiser, and I can see the problems it would have caused if we'd stayed together.'

'You would have regretted giving up your dreams of becoming a surgeon?' he said flatly.

'Yes. I love my job and I'm good at it, too.' She gave a little shrug. 'It was the right decision for both of us.'

'I'm glad you think so,' he said roughly. Maybe he should have been relieved to hear her say that, but all he felt was a terrible emptiness. He couldn't help wishing that he had been brave enough—or foolish enough—to take a chance and see what would happen, and it shocked him to find himself entertaining such a crazy idea. It was an effort to concentrate when she continued.

'I do. I have a job I love, good friends and a nice home. I have everything I want, in fact.'

'How about love and marriage?' he asked, then could have bitten off his tongue for asking such a personal question. Emma's love life had nothing to do with him.

'Not on my agenda at the present time. It's hard enough for a woman to establish herself in surgery without adding a husband and a family to the equation, although I haven't ruled them out completely.' She shrugged. 'If they happen at some point down the line, that's fine, but if not then I can live with it. How about you? Is there anyone special in your life?'

'No. My job seems to take up most of my time, too,' he said, not willing to admit that he had never considered the idea of marriage after they had parted.

'Still determined to set up in private practice one day?' She smiled but he could tell from her tone what she thought of the idea.

'Maybe.' He shrugged, unable to add to his guilt by deliberately misleading her again. 'Who knows what could happen in the future?'

'Who, indeed? But I'm sure you'll do everything in your power to achieve your ambitions, Daniel, won't you?'

Daniel's heart sank when he heard the suspicion in her voice. It seemed that their brief moment of harmony was over and they were back to where they had started, with Emma mistrusting his motives. Suddenly, he couldn't bear it any longer. He had to set matters straight and to hell with the consequences. 'Look, Emma, you're completely—'

He never had a chance to finish because at that moment the phone rang. Emma excused herself and went to answer it. Daniel guessed from what she said that it was her aunt calling so went back into his room. He found himself a sweater and a waterproof jacket because the weather was very changeable at this time of the year. Emma was still on the phone when he headed to the stairs; she gave him a curt little nod as he passed her then turned away, concentrating on what her aunt was saying.

Daniel left the house and walked into the town centre; there was a footpath beside the church that led up into the hills. He set off at a brisk pace, hoping the fresh air and exercise would soothe him, but it was hard to enjoy the peace and quiet when his mind was in turmoil. He hated to think that Emma was so suspicious of him but what could he do? He had forfeited her trust when he had told her that his career had meant more to him than she had done, and it was doubtful if he could win it back. Although it hurt like hell, he had to accept that Emma would never trust him again.

Emma found it hard to settle after she'd spoken to her aunt. Aunt Margaret had told her that two of her uncle's friends were planning on visiting him that afternoon. As the number of visitors to the IC unit was strictly limited, Emma had immediately offered to wait until the following day. Now she had a free day ahead of her and suddenly found herself wondering what to do. Although there were jobs that needed doing in the house, she felt too restless to spend the day indoors. Maybe a walk would help to work off some of her excess energy.

She fetched her jacket and found an old pair of walking boots in the hall cupboard. Although she wasn't planning on going too far, she found herself taking all the usual precautions that her aunt and uncle had drummed into her over the years. The weather in the Dales could be very changeable and it was better to be prepared rather than come unstuck.

She made some sandwiches and a flask of coffee and packed them into a small haversack. After adding a map and a compass, she checked that her mobile phone was charged. Although reception was patchy in the Dales, it could come in useful. As she let herself out of the back door, she could feel her spirits lifting. It had been ages since she'd been for a good long tramp across the hills and she was suddenly looking forward to it.

The air was cool as she set off across the stile that led to the lower slopes of the hills. There were dozens of footpaths criss-crossing the area, but Emma didn't hesitate. She'd done this walk many times before and remembered the route even though it had been at least five years since she'd last been along it. She and Daniel had come this way one Sunday morning and had had a picnic at the top of the hill. And after they had finished eating they had made love, right there in the open with only the blue sky above them.

Emma blinked when she realised that she couldn't see properly. Running her hand over her eyes, she wiped away tears. She wasn't going to cry, certainly wasn't going to waste the day by thinking about the past. It was the present that mattered, nothing else. As she'd told Daniel, she liked her life the way it was and was glad that she hadn't given up her dreams for him.

She walked for almost two hours then decided to stop for a break when she reached Pilgrim's Point, a local beauty spot. Finding a sheltered area in the lea of the huge rock that marked the spot, she unzipped her jacket and laid it on the ground then sat down. Uncapping the flask, she poured herself a cup of coffee, sighing appreciatively as she inhaled the fragrant aroma. Without the usual traffic fumes to clog up her nose, everything seemed to smell so much better.

She had almost finished the coffee when she heard someone coming along the path close to where she was sitting. It was a popular route with walkers and she wasn't surprised that someone else had decided to take advantage of the weather. Glancing round, she caught a glimpse of a figure heading towards her before he disappeared into a dip in the land, but it was enough for her to recognise him. What on earth was Daniel doing here? Surely he hadn't followed her, had he? Emma's temper was already creeping up the scale when Daniel reappeared. He stopped dead and she saw the surprise on his face when he spotted her.

'Emma! What on earth are you doing here? I thought you were going to visit your uncle this afternoon?'

'Some friends of Uncle Jim's are visiting him so I decided to go for a walk instead,' she replied curtly. Although it was obvious from his reaction that he hadn't followed her, she still felt annoyed. She had been hoping for a few Daniel-free hours and it was irritating to have him turn up like this. She glowered at him. 'I was hoping to enjoy a bit of peace and quiet on my own.'

'Don't let me stop you,' he said calmly, but she saw the hurt in his eyes and immediately felt awful about being so rude. Maybe there wasn't any love lost between them nowadays but that was no excuse for the way she was behaving.

'You're not.' She gave a little shrug, unable to bring herself to actually apologise. 'I just stopped for a drink.'

Daniel sniffed the air. 'Ah, so that explains it. I thought I could smell coffee as I was coming along the path but decided I was hallucinating.' He smiled at her and her heart lifted when she saw the warmth in his eyes. 'I don't think any of the coffee-house chains has set up an outlet in the hills yet, have they?'

'Not so far as I know. It must be an oversight on their behalf,' Emma said, chuckling.

'Oh, I'm sure they'll realise that they're missing a trick,' he assured her. 'Give it a few more months and I expect you'll be able to buy your double cappuccino with hazelnut syrup on the slopes of Mount Everest!'

Emma laughed out loud. 'It wouldn't surprise me. It never fails to amaze me just how many coffee shops there are. Every town and city seems to be awash with them.'

'I have a theory about that,' Daniel said gravely. He bent towards her and lowered his voice. 'I think they're a front for alien invaders. I mean, think about it. All those hissing and gurgling machines can't just be making cups of coffee, can they? They're probably powering up the spaceships that are hidden in the basements.'

It was so ridiculous that Emma couldn't stop laughing. She clutched her aching sides. 'Don't! I feel sick from laughing so much.'

'Sorry.' Daniel didn't sound the least bit repentant. He grinned down at her. 'I won't tell you my theory about burger bars, then.'

'Oh, please, don't! I don't think I can take any more.' Emma wiped her streaming eyes and smiled up at him, feeling her breath catch when her gaze met his. Why was Daniel looking at her that way? she wondered dizzily. He didn't love her; he never had loved her. And yet there was something in his eyes that made her heart start to race…

'Looks like the weather is about to change.'

He turned to stare across the hills and the moment passed. Emma shuddered as she looked at the black clouds that were amassing on the horizon. Had she imagined it or had Daniel really been looking at her as though she meant the whole world to him?

She took a shaky breath when she realised how ridiculous that idea was. Daniel might care about her but only in the sort of impersonal way he would care about any woman he'd had a relationship with. She would be a fool to imagine it was anything more than that.

Emma stood up abruptly and shrugged on her jacket. Although the sun was still shining, she felt chilled to the bone and knew that it had little to do with the impending storm. Picking up the flask, she offered it to him. 'There's some coffee left if you want it.'

'Thanks.' He took the flask from her with a smile that held nothing more than gratitude. Unscrewing the lid, he filled the cup and offered it to her first. 'Do you want some more?'

'No, thank you. I've had more than enough.'

Emma could hear the edge in her voice and hated it because of what it represented. She wanted to remain indifferent to Daniel, to not allow him to affect her in any way, but it was proving impossible to achieve that. It worried her that she was so responsive to his every mood. If she was over him then she shouldn't care how he felt about anything. Including her. The thought was too much to deal with on top of everything else.

'I think I'll head back,' she informed him coolly. Bending down, she picked up the haversack and went to swing it over her shoulder, stopping abruptly when he put out his hand.

'I know this is really cheeky but those aren't sandwiches, are they?' He pointed to the package sticking out of her bag and Emma nodded.

'Yes, I thought I might have my lunch while I was out.'

'But you've changed your mind?' he suggested.

Emma could tell that he suspected he was the reason for her change of plans and shrugged. The last thing she wanted was for Daniel to think that he could exert any sort of influence over her. 'I'd prefer to get home before the rain starts.'

'Of course. But if those sandwiches are going spare, I wouldn't mind them. I'm afraid I'm not as well prepared as you are.'

He gave her a tight little smile and Emma knew immediately that he hadn't believed her excuse. She handed him the sandwiches, refusing to dwell on the thought. Let him think what he liked—she didn't care!

'Thanks. I'll see you later, I expect.' He sat down in the spot she'd recently vacated and opened the package. Emma watched as he selected a thick ham and cheese sandwich and bit into it with relish. If he was at all disturbed about ruining her plans for the day, it certainly didn't show, she thought bitterly.

'Actually, I'm going out this evening,' she said abruptly. Although she hadn't planned on going out, the thought of spending the evening with him was suddenly more than she could bear, and she hurried on. 'I don't know when I'll be back, so I'll see you tomorrow.'

'Right. Have fun.'

Whether or not he believed her was open to question and Emma didn't waste any time worrying about it. She made her way back along the paths until she reached the stile. It had started to rain now, a fine drizzle that obscured the view of the hills. As she stepped down from the stile, she couldn't help wondering if Daniel would be all right. Although he had enjoyed walking in the area when he'd done his training here, it was easy to get lost. Maybe she should have made sure that he got back safely?

She took a deep breath. Daniel had made it clear five years ago that she had no rights where he was concerned. He wouldn't thank her for worrying about him now!

CHAPTER SEVEN

DANIEL finished the sandwiches and wadded the cling film into a ball. Tucking it into his pocket, he drained the last dregs of coffee from the cup. The clouds were fairly scurrying across the sky now and he guessed it wouldn't be long before the rain started. Maybe he should follow Emma's example and head back?

He sighed as he set off along the path. Once again he'd thought he was making headway with her and once again he'd been mistaken. It was a case of one step forward and two back, and it was difficult to explain how frustrated he felt. Maybe it was foolish to hope that she would accept him as a friend after what had happened in the past, but he couldn't bear to think that she would continue to think so badly of him.

Daniel's heart was heavy as he climbed out of the dip. The path skirted an area of loose shale and he picked his way around it, wary of slipping. The first drops of rain started to fall as he cleared the area and he picked up speed, hoping to avoid getting soaked. Although it would have been quicker if he'd taken the path Emma had used, he wasn't sure if he could remember the way.

The last thing he needed to round off the day was to get himself lost!

He must have gone about a mile or so when all of a sudden he heard someone shouting. He stopped and looked around but it was difficult to see now that the rain was falling in earnest. Cupping his hands around his mouth, he shouted as loudly as he could, 'Hello! Where are you?'

'Over here,' the reply came back immediately.

Daniel turned towards the direction from where the sound seemed to be coming and frowned when he caught a glimpse of a figure frantically waving to him. What on earth was going on?

He hurriedly changed course, his heart sinking as he got closer and discovered there were actually two people, both teenage boys, and one of them was injured. 'What happened?' he demanded, crouching down beside the injured boy.

'We were just messing about, having a sword fight with a couple of sticks, when Jack slipped. I thought he was kidding at first when he didn't get up, but then I saw all the blood…' The boy gulped, obviously too shaken by what had happened to continue.

'I see.' Daniel didn't press him for any more details as he carefully eased the boy's blood-soaked T-shirt aside so he could examine the puncture wound in his chest. Although it wasn't very large, it was obviously deep and had bled copiously. He could hear the boy struggling to breathe and placed his hand over the wound. Even if the lung itself wasn't damaged, this type of injury—where air was being drawn directly into the chest cavity—could cause it to deflate

'How long ago did it happen?' he asked, glancing up.

'I'm not sure. Half an hour, maybe longer—I seem to have been shouting for ages.' The boy wiped his eyes with the back of his hand. 'I didn't know what to do. I tried to get Jack to stand up but he couldn't, so I thought about going for help. But even if I'd managed to find someone, I wasn't sure if I'd be able to find my way back here.'

'You don't have a mobile with you?' Daniel queried, dragging over a haversack and using it to support the boy's head and shoulders. He inclined the teenager's body towards the injured side so that the sound lung was uppermost then dug in his pocket and took out a clean handkerchief plus the piece of crumpled cling film. Sealing the wound to stop any more air entering the chest cavity would help the boy to breathe more easily.

'Yes, but there's no signal out here. I've tried it dozens of times but my phone just won't work!'

'Typical.' Daniel sighed as he placed the handkerchief over the hole in the boy's chest. 'Can you hold that there while I unravel this piece of cling film?' he instructed. Once he had smoothed out the plastic wrapping, he placed it over the handkerchief, pressing it tightly against the boy's damp skin. He was pleased to hear that the teenager's breathing sounded a little less laboured after he'd finished.

Standing up, he stripped off his jacket and laid it over

the boy. Hypothermia was a very real concern in a situation like this and he needed to do whatever he could to avoid it. Once he was sure the boy was protected from the rain, he turned to his friend again. 'What's your name, son?'

'Ryan.'

'OK, Ryan. I'm Dr Kennedy. I work at the surgery in Avondale—do you know it?'

Ryan shook his head. 'No.'

'So can I take it that you don't live round here?'

'No. We're on a school trip. We're staying at the outward bound centre near Malham.'

'I see. So is there anyone who's likely to be looking for you right now? Your teachers, for instance?

'No. They don't know we're out here,' Ryan mumbled, looking sheepish.

'What do you mean, they don't know you're out here?'

Ryan shrugged. 'Most of the teachers have gone to Settle with the rest of the group. They're going on a train ride. Jack and I weren't allowed to go because we smuggled some beer into our dormitory last night. A couple of the boys were sick and things got a bit messy, so we had to stay behind to clean up as a punishment.'

'Surely you weren't left on your own?'

'No, one of the teachers stayed with us, but he had to go to the office to deal with a query.' Ryan looked even more uncomfortable. 'Jack and I decided to sneak out while he was gone and that's how we ended up here.'

'And found yourself in an even bigger mess from the look of it,' Daniel declared, sighing. He quickly considered their options but it was obvious what needed to be done. 'We can assume you'll be missed at some point but it could take a while before the alarm is raised and even longer before they send someone out to look for you. Quite frankly, we can't afford to wait around too long so here's what we're going to do. I'm going to stay here with Jack while you go for help. It's better if I stay with him in case anything happens.'

'But what if I can't find my way?' the boy exclaimed.

'You'll be fine,' Daniel assured him, hoping he wasn't being overly confident. 'I'll take you back to the main path and show you which way to go. So long as you stay on the path and don't wander off it, you'll be perfectly all right. It brings you out into the centre of Avondale and once you're there, just ask anyone you meet to help you.'

'But how about finding my way back here?' Ryan asked anxiously. He glanced around and shuddered. 'All this countryside looks the same to me.'

'Have you got a watch?' Daniel unfastened his own watch when the boy shook his head and handed it to him. 'Put that on and use it to time how long it takes you to reach the town. That should give the search and rescue team a rough idea of where we are. You can also tell them that we're about a mile or so from a large rock and that Dr Roberts at the surgery can probably help to pinpoint our location if they ask her. Think you can remember all that?'

'I think so.' Ryan took a deep breath. 'Do you want me to go now?'

'Yes. Oh, and also tell them that we'll need an ambulance on standby and that they should inform the hospital to be prepared for a serious chest trauma. OK?' He smiled when Ryan nodded. 'Good. Let's get going, then. The sooner we get your friend to hospital, the better.'

Daniel led the boy back to the path and pointed him in the right direction, repeating his instruction to stay on the path and not wander off it. He frowned as he watched him set off, hoping he was doing the right thing by sending him for help, but what choice did he have? He couldn't go because he needed to stay with Jack.

He sighed as he made his way back to the injured boy. What was that saying about the road to hell being paved with good intentions? Although his intentions may have been good five years ago, look how badly things had turned out then. Hopefully, there would be a happier outcome this time.

Emma decided to go to the cinema in the end. Although it was a bit of trek to the nearest town that boasted a cinema, it would be worth it. If she set off early, she could do some shopping first and then watch the film. She may as well go for a meal afterwards too. Then she could keep out of Daniel's way for the rest of the day.

She groaned as she stepped into the shower. She couldn't continue avoiding him. Whether she liked the idea or not, she and Daniel were going to have to get along for the next few weeks both in and out of the surgery. Maybe there was a lot of history between them but the key word in that statement was *history*. Their relationship was in the past and it shouldn't have any bearing on what happened at the present time. She'd been out with other men in the past few years and remained on good terms with them too. If she could get it into her head that Daniel was just someone she had once dated, she could put it behind her.

She got dressed and went downstairs. She was just unhooking her jacket off the hall peg when she heard a car pull up outside and frowned. She wasn't expecting visitors and had no idea who it could be. Opening the door, she blinked in surprise when she saw one of the local search and rescue vehicles parked outside. Although her uncle had been a member of the team for many years, he had been forced to retire when his health had started to deteriorate. She couldn't imagine what they were doing here and waited expectantly as Mike Harding, the team leader, hurried towards her.

'Looks as though we've arrived in the nick of time,' Mike observed jovially. A pleasant man in his forties who ran the local pub with his wife, April, he'd been leading the local team for the past ten years. 'I take it that you were on your way out?'

'I was,' Emma agreed. 'I was just about to head off to the cinema, in fact. Why? Is there a problem?'

'Seems like it.' Mike pointed towards a boy sitting in the front passenger seat. 'According to that young fellow, his friend is out in the Dales somewhere, injured, and Dr Kennedy is with him.'

'Daniel!' Emma exclaimed. 'Are you sure?'

'As sure as I can be. The lad came stumbling into the pub about ten minutes ago and told us that his friend was hurt and that there was a man with him who said he was a doctor.' Mike shrugged. 'April asked him to describe him and she said that it sounded very much like Dr Kennedy.'

'She's probably right,' Emma said slowly. 'Daniel did go for a walk this morning. In fact, I met him while I was out.'

'And where was that?' Mike said quickly. 'Apparently, Dr Kennedy told the lad to tell us that he was about a mile from a large rock and that you'd know where it was.'

'He must mean Pilgrim's Point,' Emma told him. 'I was sitting there when I saw Daniel.'

'Great!' Mike beamed at her. 'It doesn't half help when folk are able to narrow down the search area. I'll get on the radio and let the others know where we're heading.'

Emma followed him back to the car, waiting quietly as he put through a call to the rest of the team. 'Do we know how badly injured the other boy is?' she asked as soon as he finished.

'Chest injury, apparently. Your Dr Kennedy told the lad to tell us to have an ambulance on standby and to inform the hospital to prepare for a serious chest trauma.'

Emma felt her face heat. He wasn't *her* Dr Kennedy; he never had been hers in any way, shape or form. It was on the tip of her tongue to point that out until she realised how silly it was to make a fuss. She was supposed to be trying to think of Daniel as just another ex-boyfriend!

'It might be best to have the air ambulance on stand-by,' she suggested, confining her thoughts to the matter at hand.

'We've already done that,' Mike informed her. 'Air Ambulance Control has logged the request, although they can't guarantee another call won't come in in the meantime.'

'Of course not,' Emma agreed, shivering as she glanced towards the hills. The rain was much heavier now, a heavy blanket of clouds overhead stealing the light from the day. Although it was barely the middle of the afternoon, it looked more like evening. She knew that the longer Daniel and the boy were missing, the greater the risk of them not being found before night fell. The thought spurred her to a swift decision.

'I'm coming with you.' She held up her hand when Mike started to protest that it wasn't necessary. 'No, I want to come. I'll be able to help with the boy if nothing else. Give me two minutes to change and I'll be right with you.'

She ran back into the house, quickly exchanging her lightweight jacket for something more suitable. Her walking boots were on the mat where she'd left them and it took only seconds to slip them on. She knew the team carried basic medical supplies as a matter of course so didn't need to worry about that. Within a couple of minutes she was back at the Land Rover.

'Ready,' she told Mike as she climbed into the rear seat. She could feel her tension building as they drove into the centre of the town. The rest of the team was gathered outside the church. There were about a dozen altogether, all of them volunteers.

Emma nodded hello then stood to one side while Mike spread an Ordnance Survey sheet on the bonnet of the car. He ringed Pilgrim's Point in red then turned to the boy. Emma bit her lip when Ryan explained that it had taken him just over two hours to reach the town. It was already three o'clock, which meant it would be going dark before they got back to where Daniel was waiting and that was assuming they could pinpoint his location. Finding people lost in the Dales wasn't easy, as any member of the team would confirm.

She took a deep breath as Mike folded up the map. The thought of Daniel being at risk was more than she could bear, even though she refused to ask herself why.

Without a watch to refer to, Daniel had no idea how much time had passed since Ryan had gone for help. It seemed to be hours since the boy had left yet he knew that it was probably his mind playing tricks. As he checked Jack's pulse again, he found himself praying that help would arrive soon. The boy had lapsed into unconsciousness a while ago and there was no doubt that his condition was deteriorating. He needed to be admitted to hospital as quickly as possible if he was to have any chance of pulling through.

The thought had barely crossed his mind when the boy suddenly stopped breathing. Daniel quickly rolled him onto his back and checked his airway. Once he was sure it was clear, he pinched Jack's nostrils closed and breathed into his mouth, sharply, four times to inflate his lungs. He then checked his pulse and was relieved to find that his heart was still beating. He breathed into his mouth again and continued doing so for several more minutes until Jack started breathing for himself again.

After placing the boy in the recovery position, Daniel stood up, groaning as he stretched his aching limbs. He was soaking wet, thanks to the rain, and freezing cold too. He jumped up and down to try to generate some warmth in his body, flapping his arms as well for good measure. It helped a bit but he knew that the effects wouldn't last. Night was drawing in and the temperature would drop even lower then. What wouldn't he give to be sitting in front of a roaring fire with Emma curled up beside him…?

He blanked out that thought. He was feeling miserable enough without making himself feel even worse because the chances of Emma ever curling up beside him were nil!

Although Emma must have walked along the route dozens of times before, she had never attempted it in such appalling weather. The rain was beating down now, turning the path into a sea of mud in places, so that it was difficult to keep her footing. It didn't help either that some of the streams had burst their banks, forcing them to wade ankle deep through icy-cold water. It was only the thought of Daniel and the injured boy waiting for them that kept her going. They had to find them.

'OK, let's stop for a moment while we get our bearings.' Mike called the group to a halt, waiting until they had formed a circle before he continued. 'By my reckoning, we should be fairly close to where young Ryan here said he left his friend so we'll split up into groups and see if we can find him and the doc.'

Everyone nodded. Within a very short time they had formed four groups. Mike turned to Emma. 'You and the lad can come with me. They can't be far from here so let's hope we can find them pretty soon.'

He didn't add anything else as he started walking again but he didn't need to. Emma knew that once it got dark, the chances of them finding the pair were very slim. She and Ryan followed the others along the track, scouring the land to right and left in the hope of spotting them. They came to a slight rise in the ground and Ryan suddenly stopped.

'I remember this bit!' he exclaimed excitedly.

'How far is it from where you left your friend?' Mike demanded.

'Not very far, I think…ten, twenty metres, something like that,' the boy told him.

'Right then, let's start shouting and see if they can hear us.' Mike cupped his hands round his mouth. 'Hello! Can you hear us? Are you out there, Doc?'

Emma held her breath. Ryan seemed so certain that surely he couldn't have been mistaken? Mike shouted again but there was still no reply and her heart sank. They carried on for another few minutes and then Mike stopped and repeated the process. When a voice suddenly shouted back she didn't know whether to laugh or cry because she felt so overwhelmed with emotion. It was all she could do to stumble after the others as they hurried towards where the sound had come from.

'Am I glad to see you,' Daniel began, standing up. He suddenly caught sight of her and Emma saw the shock on his face. It was blatantly obvious that he hadn't expected to see her and all of a sudden she felt uncomfortable about her reasons for being there.

Crossing the narrow strip of ground that separated them, she crouched down beside the injured boy, busying herself with doing his obs while Daniel conferred with Mike. Although she could hear what was being said, it seemed to be happening at one step removed from her. It was only when Daniel crouched down beside her that everything snapped back into focus.

'I'll set up a drip,' she said crisply, starting to rise, but he caught her hand and stopped her.

'I didn't expect you to come, Emma.'

'No?' She gave a little shrug, hoping it would convince him that her reasons had had little to do with him. 'I thought you might need help, that's all. With the boy.'

'That was good of you. Thank you.'

His voice was low but she could hear the note it held and her heart reacted immediately to it. She stood up abruptly and hurried over to where Mike had left the bag of medical supplies. Saline, antiseptic wipes, cannula… She mentally listed all the things she needed because it was safer to concentrate on them than on anything else, far safer than letting herself think about the way Daniel had looked at her just now.

She took a deep breath, held it until she felt dizzy,

then let it out as slowly as she could, but the thought didn't flow away with it. It seemed to be stuck in her head, neon bright and incredibly scary: Daniel had been pleased to see her, surprised but pleased. What did it mean?

CHAPTER EIGHT

DANIEL could feel his heart thumping as he helped Emma set up the drip. It had been a shock to see her and there was no point denying it. Had she come purely to offer her services as a doctor, or because she had been worried about him?

His heart beat all the harder at that beguiling thought and he gritted his teeth. He was doing it again, letting himself hope for the impossible, and it was stupid to behave this way. Emma's reasons for being here had nothing to do with him and everything to do with their patient!

He stood up abruptly and turned to Mike. 'That's about all we can do for him. The sooner we get him to hospital, the better his chances will be.'

'The air ambulance is on its way,' Mike informed him. 'The problem is that it can't land out here in the dark—it's way too dangerous. We're going to have to carry the lad to the nearest stretch of road and have him picked up from there.'

'How long's that going to take?' Daniel demanded, his heart sinking at the thought of there being a further lengthy delay.

'Fifteen minutes max,' Mike assured him.

'But it takes a lot longer than that to get back to town,' Daniel protested.

'It does, but I expect the team will use a different route to get him to the road,' Emma said quietly beside him.

Daniel spun round, feeling his senses reel when he realised how close she was. Normally, she kept her distance, both physically and mentally, but she was standing so close to him now that he could feel the warmth of her skin. It was hard to concentrate when every cell in his body was so acutely aware of her.

'Do you mean to say that I could have got help here sooner if I hadn't sent Ryan into the town?' he demanded, the force of his reaction making him sound—and *feel*—distinctly tetchy.

'I doubt it. The nearest road to here is fairly isolated. There's very little traffic uses it, especially at this time of the year, so the chances of Ryan being able to flag down a car were pretty remote. You did the best thing by sending him back to town to get help,' she replied calmly, although Daniel couldn't help noticing that she avoided meeting his eyes.

Was she equally aware of him as he was of her? he wondered, then had to swallow his groan when his heart set off again, pounding away as though possessed. When Mike came over with a foil blanket for him to wrap around himself, he barely managed to nod his thanks. Forget about feeling cold and wet—it would be a miracle if he didn't have a heart attack at this rate!

It took them just under the allotted time to stretcher

the injured boy to the pick-up point. The police were already there and had set up a landing site for the helicopter in a nearby field. It arrived a couple of minutes later and Daniel handed over his patient, briefly explaining to the crew what had happened and what he had done. Five minutes later, it was on its way again. The police had also contacted the outward-bound centre where the two boys were staying and one of the teachers had come to collect Ryan. From the glum expression on the teenager's face as he got into the car, Daniel guessed that he wasn't expecting much of a welcome when he got back.

'That's it, folks. Let's just hope the lad will be all right, eh?'

Mike voiced everyone's opinion as they headed over to the vehicles. A couple of the reserve team had driven over to collect them and Daniel had to admit that it was a relief not to have to walk all the way back to town. Now that the adrenalin rush was dying down, he felt too cold and stiff to welcome the thought of a long walk home.

He slid into the back of one of the vehicles, moving over when Emma got in beside him. Another member of the team climbed in beside her so it was a bit of a squash. Daniel held himself rigid as they set off but it was impossible to avoid touching her as they swung around the bends.

'Sorry,' he murmured when once again he found himself cannoning into her.

'That's OK.'

She gave him a tight little smile then stared straight ahead, making it clear that she wasn't keen to start a conversation. He wasn't either, mainly because he didn't want anything he said to be misconstrued. He sighed wearily. When had life become so complicated that he had to watch every word he said?

Emma couldn't wait to get home. Sitting beside Daniel was sheer torture. Every time they rounded a bend, his shoulder brushed hers or his thigh pressed against her thigh and she didn't appreciate the feelings it aroused inside her. It was a relief when the car drew up outside the house.

Daniel got out and offered her his hand but she pretended not to see it. Sliding across the seat, she got out and thanked the driver. The car drove away with a toot of its horn, its taillights rapidly disappearing into the darkness. Emma headed towards the front door, feeling her tension mounting when she heard Daniel's footsteps crunching on the gravel behind her. All of a sudden she was achingly aware of the fact that there were just the two of them. She would have given anything to open the door and find Aunt Margaret at home but it wasn't going to happen so she had to make the best of things. Unlocking the front door, she summoned a smile.

'I'll put the kettle on while you get out of those wet clothes. Do you prefer tea or coffee?'

'Coffee, please.' Daniel grimaced as he stepped into the hall. 'I'm soaking. I'd better take my clothes off here rather than drip water all through the house.'

He shed the foil blanket then dragged his sodden sweater over his head. Emma just caught a glimpse of a broad, muscled chest before she hastily turned away.

'I'll get the coffee on,' she murmured, hurrying along the hall as though the hounds of hell were snapping at her heels. She filled the kettle then took off her wet coat and carried it through to the back porch so it could drip. When she chanced a wary glance along the hall there was no sign of Daniel, just a heap of sodden clothing lying neatly on the mat.

She ran upstairs to her room and changed into dry jeans then went back down and gathered up Daniel's clothing to take it through to the kitchen, putting his sweater and jeans straight into the washer. His boots were soaked so she stuffed them with newspaper and left them in the corner to dry. By the time she'd done all that, he reappeared, shaking his head as he came into the kitchen.

'You shouldn't have cleared up after me, Emma. I'd have done it myself.'

'It wasn't a problem,' she said lightly, not wanting him to attach any significance to her actions. She had done it purely because she liked order in her life, not because she'd wanted to help him, she assured herself. She headed towards the kettle then stopped when he waved her aside.

'*I'll* make the coffee. It's the least I can do.'

Emma opened her mouth then hurriedly shut it again. Arguing about who should make the coffee would be extremely childish. Walking over to the cupboard, she lifted out the biscuit tin and set it on the table. When Daniel brought over the tray, he looked hopefully at her.

'I hope there's some chocolate biscuits in there.

There's nothing like comfort food when you're feeling cold and miserable.'

'There should be.' Emma took the lid off the tin and nodded. 'You're in luck. There's a new packet of chocolate digestives—your favourites.'

'So you remember which biscuits I like?' His tone was even but she felt the blood rush up her face when she realised how revealing that had been. If she had erased him from her life then why on earth would she remember his taste in food?

'Yes,' she said firmly, knowing there was no point lying. She looked him straight in the eyes. 'I'm hardly likely to forget, bearing in mind the amount of biscuits you consumed when you worked here.'

'Hmm, I suppose not.' He grinned. 'I *could* claim that I'm a reformed character and only eat them in exceptional circumstances but that would be cutting off my nose to spite my face.' He helped himself to a biscuit. 'All I can say is that it's my only vice, or the only one I'm willing to admit to!'

He chuckled as he bit into the biscuit and Emma felt a little flurry of heat run through her veins. She had forgotten how endearing he could be when he was poking fun at himself.

The thought troubled her and she picked up the pot, quickly pouring coffee into two mugs. She didn't want to think about Daniel's good points, certainly didn't want to remember the reasons why she had fallen in love with him. She needed to focus on the way he had treated her. She had been willing to give up her dreams for him but it hadn't been enough. His career had meant far more to him than what she could have given him.

Pain lanced her heart and she took a gulp of her coffee then coughed when the hot liquid shot down the wrong way. Putting the mug down on the table, she tried to catch her breath but it felt as though her lungs had gone into spasm.

'Are you all right?' Daniel leant forward and looked at her in concern. 'Emma?'

Emma tried to answer but there was no way that she could force out even a single word and she saw him leap to his feet. Moving swiftly behind her chair he slapped her on the back and with relief she felt the constriction loosen. Sucking in a deep breath, she finally managed to speak.

'I'm all right now.'

'Sure?' He went over to the sink when she nodded and filled a glass with cold water and gave it to her. 'Take a couple of sips of this.'

Emma obediently sipped the water then set the glass on the table, feeling embarrassed about having caused such a fuss. 'Some of the coffee must have gone down the wrong way.'

'Easily done,' he said lightly, sitting down again. He slid the biscuit tin across the table. 'Aren't you going to have one?'

'I'm not sure if I should risk it after what just happened,' she said wryly.

Daniel laughed. 'Go on—live dangerously. Anyway, I'm a dab hand at the Heimlich manoeuvre if the need arises.'

Emma grimaced as she selected a biscuit. 'Let's hope it doesn't come to that.'

'Fingers crossed,' he said, suiting his actions to his words.

Emma chuckled as she bit into her biscuit. Daniel had a real gift when it came to putting people at ease. Some of the doctors she had worked with seemed to enjoy feeling superior, but Daniel wasn't like that. He cared too much about other people to want them to feel uncomfortable around him.

The thought surprised her because it didn't gel with the image she had held of him for the past few years. If Daniel was the single-minded, ambitious man she had believed him to be, surely he wouldn't care about anyone else's feelings?

'Penny for them.'

Emma looked up when he spoke, feeling her heart lurch when she saw the way he was watching her so intently. Why did she have the feeling that he really wanted to know what was troubling her? She had no idea but it was that thought which made her reply without pausing to consider the wisdom of what she was doing. 'I was just thinking what a contradiction you are.'

'Really?' His brows rose as he picked up his mug of coffee. He took a sip of the hot liquid then placed the mug carefully back on the table. 'In what way?'

'Well, you've never made any bones about the fact that you're very ambitious, have you, Daniel? And yet in some respects you don't fit that bill.' She shrugged when he looked quizzically at her. 'You genuinely seem to care about people and it's rare that the two go hand in hand.'

'Of course I care. I wouldn't have gone into medicine if I hadn't.'

Emma frowned when she heard the edge in his voice, wondering if she had touched a nerve. 'One doesn't always follow the other,' she pointed out. 'I've worked with a number of doctors who openly admitted that they decided on medicine purely because it seemed like a good career choice.'

'They're the exceptions. Or I hope they are.' He stared down at the mug he was holding. 'In my opinion you can't do this job properly unless you genuinely want to help people.'

'So how does your desire to help people equate with wanting to go into private practice? Surely you could help far more people by working for the NHS?'

'Rich people get sick too, Emma.' He glanced up and she was surprised when she saw the sadness on his face because she wasn't sure what had caused it. 'Having money doesn't protect you from all the usual ailments.'

'I know that.' She leant forward, suddenly impatient to get to the bottom of this mystery. The more she thought about it, the stranger it seemed that Daniel of all people should be so keen to follow this course. 'And I'm not suggesting that people who can afford it shouldn't have the right to choose to pay for their treatment. But setting yourself up in private practice doesn't seem like something you would want to do. I just can't understand it, if I'm honest.'

Daniel wasn't sure what to say. If he admitted that he'd never had any intention of going into private practice, he would have to tell her the truth. How would she feel if he admitted that he had deliberately misled her? Hurt, angry, upset; she was bound to feel all of those things. But would she understand that he had been trying to protect her, stop her doing something she would regret?

'What's to understand?' he said shortly, knowing it was a risk he wasn't prepared to take. 'Everyone has their aims in life, including you. What made *you* decide to become a surgeon?'

'Because I saw how surgery could improve people's lives when I did my rotations,' she said simply. 'That's why I chose it.'

'There you are, then. You chose your path and I chose mine. It's as simple as that.' He stood up abruptly, pushing back his chair so fast that the legs scraped across the tiles. 'I think I'll have an early night. Hopefully, a good night's sleep will ease some of the kinks out of my aching muscles.'

'Of course. I'll see you in the morning, I expect.'

'If I manage to drag myself out of bed.'

Daniel summoned a smile but it was a poor effort, he knew. He left the kitchen and headed upstairs to his room. Switching on the bedside lamp, he sank down on the bed, wishing with all his heart that he could have done things differently five years ago. Letting Emma go had been the hardest thing he had ever done yet he was more convinced than ever that it had been the right thing to do. Maybe they would have had a few years of happiness together, but eventually she would have regretted giving up her dreams to be with him.

He took a deep breath. No matter how hard it had been, it would have been so much worse if Emma had ended up hating him.

Emma spent a couple of hours watching television after Daniel retired to his room. The plans she'd made to go to the cinema had been put on hold because she couldn't be bothered getting ready to go out. However, by the time the old grandfather clock in the hall struck nine, she was bored stiff. She switched off the set and made her way upstairs. She reached the landing and paused to listen but there was no sound coming from Daniel's side of the house. Obviously, he was fast asleep, worn out after his exertions that day.

Emma went to her room and collected her toilet bag then made her way to the bathroom. She felt too restless to sleep and was hoping that a long, hot soak in the bath would help her relax. Turning on the taps, she added a generous dollop of bubble bath to the water then stripped off her clothes. Water had been in short supply where she had been working recently and it was a luxury to be able to fill the bath almost to the brim.

She slid into the scented bubbles with an appreciative groan and closed her eyes. Whether it was the warmth of the water or the silence, she soon drifted off to sleep only to awake with a start when the bathroom door suddenly opened. Emma's eyes shot open as she stared at Daniel in dismay.

'What are you doing? Get out!'

'I'm sorry. I had no idea you were in here. The door wasn't locked,' he began, then stopped.

Emma saw him swallow and looked down, feeling her heart leap when she realised that all the bubbles had melted away while she'd slept. Without them to conceal her, her body was naked to his gaze and she could tell that the sight was having an effect. Water sloshed over the side of the bath as she scrambled to her feet and reached for a towel off the rail, but Daniel was ahead of her.

'Here.' He passed her a towel then turned away while she wrapped it around herself.

Emma stepped out of the bath, shaking her wet hair out of her eyes. She felt both cold and shivery, and it owed little to the fact that she'd been lying in the cooling water for too long. Daniel wanted her: she had seen it in his eyes, seen the desire that had filled them just now. The thought should have repulsed her but it didn't—just the opposite, in fact. Heat suddenly scorched along her veins when she realised with a jolt of shock that she wanted him too….

Afterwards, she was never sure what happened next, whether she made some sort of small betraying sound or it was sheer coincidence that he turned at that moment. There was a second when their eyes locked and held before he slowly reached out and touched her cheek.

'Emma.'

Her name sounded so different when he said it that way, his deep voice throbbing with hunger and need. Emma wasn't aware of moving yet all of a sudden she was standing in front of him, so close that she could feel the tremor that passed through his body. When his hand lifted to her face again, she didn't move, just stood there while his fingers grazed along her jaw, gliding so lightly over her skin that it was hard to know for sure if he was actually touching her.

'Your skin's so soft,' he whispered as his fingers came to rest a millimetre away from her mouth.

Emma knew that if she dipped her head the barest fraction she would feel them on her lips and the thought was the sweetest kind of torment. She wanted him to touch her mouth but she wasn't sure where it would lead if he did. Could she allow Daniel to touch her, caress her, *make love* to her, and not feel anything except desire? Maybe it was what she needed to finally get him out of her system. Although she had been out with other men since they had split up, she had never wanted to sleep with any of them. In the beginning she had been too wary of getting hurt to risk getting involved and, more recently, she had been so busy in work that she'd had no time for a private life—or so she had told herself. Now Emma found herself wondering if the truth was far more complicated: she had never really drawn a line under her affair with Daniel so that she could move on.

This could be the perfect opportunity to do so, but still she hesitated. Her feelings for Daniel were so muddled up. Although sleeping with him might give her the closure she needed, it might achieve just the opposite result. What if she found that the old feelings she'd had for him, the ones she had thought were dead and buried a long time ago, were still very much alive?

It was the uncertainty that scared her, the thought that she might regret whichever decision she made for the rest of her life.

CHAPTER NINE

DANIEL could feel his heart racing. It wasn't just this desire he felt to take Emma in his arms and make love to her that was causing it to happen but fear as well. For the past five years he had kept his emotions strictly under wraps. It hadn't been difficult. He had never had a proper relationship with another woman since they had split up and had never wanted one. Although he dated frequently, he steadfastly avoided commitment. Whenever he made love to a woman, it was a purely physical experience: he had remained emotionally detached. However, he knew he wouldn't be able to do that with Emma.

Fear turned his guts to ice and he froze. Emma was standing stock still as well and he sensed that she was fighting her own inner battle about what should happen. He was already preparing himself for the inevitable rejection when her head dipped just a fraction. He sucked in his breath when he felt her mouth brush his fingers. Heat surged through his veins, melting away the fear that had filled him only moments before. He wanted her so much, wanted to bury himself in her softness and sweetness while they made love. Maybe it was madness and maybe he would regret it later but right now he needed this more than he had needed anything in his life!

He drew her into his arms and it was like coming home. Her body felt so sweetly familiar as it nestled against him, each soft curve fitting so perfectly that he didn't have to think how he should hold her—he just did. He could feel her breasts pressing against his chest and closed his eyes as a wave of pure pleasure swept over him. She felt so right in his arms that the years they'd spent apart might never have happened.

'Daniel?'

Her voice was low, the uncertainty it held filling him with tenderness. Bending, her touched her mouth with his in a kiss that was meant to reassure and calm her fears. However, the moment his lips tasted hers desire took over. He pulled her to him, letting her feel the effect she was having on him, and felt her tremble. There wasn't a doubt in his mind that she was equally affected and his heart overflowed with joy. Even after everything that had happened, Emma still wanted him!

He kissed her again with a passion that immediately had her clinging to him. When her lips opened, inviting him to deepen the kiss, he groaned. He was shaking by the time he drew back but so was she. Cupping her face between his hands, he looked deep into her eyes, hoping she could see how much this meant to him.

'I want to make love to you, Emma, more than anything, but are you sure it's what you really want?'

'Yes.' Her voice was still low but there was a conviction in it now that reassured him she knew exactly what she was doing. 'It's what I want too, Daniel.'

'Good.'

He smiled as he bent and kissed her again. When he lifted her up into his arms, she rested her head on his shoulder. He carried her back to her room and laid her down on the narrow single bed then sat down beside her. Reaching out, he tugged gently on the folds of damp towel, feeling his breath catch when they parted to reveal her body to his gaze. Her breasts were high and full, the rose-pink nipples standing erect and proud beneath his gaze. Her waist was narrow, her hips curved, her thighs smooth and firm. Every tiny inch of her was so perfect that for a moment he was overwhelmed by her beauty and couldn't move. It was only when she placed her hand on his that the spell was broken.

He lifted her hand to his mouth and pressed a kiss against her palm. 'You're beautiful, Emma,' he whispered, his voice grating with the force of his desire.

'Am I?' She smiled at him, her green eyes heavy with passion.

'Yes. More beautiful than any woman I've ever known.'

He kissed her palm again then gently placed her hand by her side while his fingers trailed across her wrist and up her arm. He paused when he came to her shoulder. Her skin was still slightly damp from her bath and he allowed himself a moment to savour its warmth and moistness under his fingertips. When his hand moved on, following the line of her collarbone, he heard her murmur and smiled. This was one journey they were both enjoying making together.

His fingers traced the delicate bones until they came

to her throat where once again they lingered. Daniel could feel her pulse beating, could feel it racing, in fact, but as his was racing too it didn't seem strange. Bending, he let the tip of his tongue touch the spot where it beat so strongly and felt her shudder, and shuddered too, more affected by her response than he would have believed. In that second he realised just how different it was making love to Emma than to any other woman. Whatever she felt, he felt too; they were that much in tune.

The thought almost blew him away but there were more delights awaiting him and he wanted to savour them all. His hand glided down her throat, following the lines of her body as it skated over the swell of her breasts, the dip of her waist, the curve of her hips. He could have stopped at any one of those places, and remained there quite happily too, but he was greedy to reacquaint himself with every inch of her delectable body.

Her thighs came next, then her knees and her ankles followed by her feet. As he caressed her toes, Daniel knew that he would never feel this depth of desire for any other woman. It was only Emma he had ever wanted so totally, only Emma he had ever loved so completely.

Emma could feel the desire building inside her as Daniel continued to stroke and caress every inch of her body. He had always been a considerate lover, taking time and care to ensure that she enjoyed their love-making as much as he did. She'd had a couple of brief affairs before she had met him, but nobody had ever made her feel as loved and as cherished as Daniel did. When his hand began its upward journey, retracing the route it had taken, she closed her eyes, relishing the touch of his fingers as they glided over her skin. She knew that she had given in to temptation and that she might regret it later, but at that moment it didn't seem to matter. All she wanted right now was to feel: his hand on her thighs, on her belly, her breasts….

Desire shot through her, red-hot and urgent, when his hand was replaced by his mouth as he took her nipple between his lips and suckled her, and she gasped. She had forgotten how intensely Daniel could make her feel, how he could carry her to a peak of need and then take her even higher. No man had ever done that apart from him. No man ever would.

Pain lanced her heart at the thought but there was no time to dwell on it because his mouth had moved to her other breast. Once again there was that surge of desire that made her stomach muscles clench and her senses reel. When he raised his head, Emma was no longer capable of thinking, only feeling, and he must have realised that. His mouth skimmed up her throat and captured hers in a kiss so raw, so filled with passion that it seemed to consume her totally. She could barely breathe when he drew back but, then, neither could he. They looked at one another for a long moment and she could see the same wonderment in his eyes that she knew must be in hers.

'Emma, I…'

He stopped and shook his head, although whether it was because he couldn't find the words to describe how he felt or because he was reluctant to say them, she wasn't sure, and maybe it was for the best. Even though she had no idea what would happen later, she knew that this wasn't the start of something more. Passion was one thing but love was something completely different and she knew for certain that Daniel didn't love her.

Tears filled her eyes but she blinked them away. She refused to cry. The past was over, the future unknown; it was the here and now that mattered. When Daniel stood up and stripped off his clothes, she focused on the moment, nothing more. And when he lay down beside her and took her in his arms, she let their passion sweep her away to a place where nothing else existed except her and Daniel and the magic they were creating together.

The air was cool when Daniel awoke the following morning. The central heating hadn't switched on yet and the temperature had dropped considerably through the night. Leaning over, he carefully drew the quilt over Emma's shoulders, resisting the urge he felt to kiss her awake. They had made love several times during the night and it wouldn't be fair to wake her when she needed to sleep.

He sighed as he swung his legs out of bed and stood up. Had it been fair to make love to her in the first place? Last night he'd been carried away by his desire for her but now it was time to face up to what he had done. He had made love to Emma when he had known in his heart that it was the last thing he should have done. It made no difference that she had been as eager and as willing as he'd been; he should have had the strength to resist temptation. He would never forgive himself if he ended up hurting her through his selfishness.

Daniel's heart was heavy as he made his way to the bathroom. Switching on the shower, he let the hot water pound down on his head and shoulders. However, if he'd hoped that it would wash away some of the guilt he felt then he was disappointed. Last night shouldn't have happened and there was no excuse for his actions. All he could do now was to try and lessen the damage he may have caused.

He went to his room and dressed then made his way to the kitchen. As soon as the kettle boiled he made himself a cup of instant coffee and sat down at the table while he tried to work out how he should handle things. So much depended on how Emma felt about the situation, of course. Would she be stricken with guilt too? He hoped not. Emma wasn't to blame for the fact that he had been unable to control himself!

'Stop it, Daniel.'

The sound of her voice brought his head up. Daniel's heart gave an almighty lurch when he saw her standing in the doorway. She was wearing a thick towelling robe and he knew without having to be told that she wasn't wearing anything under it. Heat scorched along his veins and he cursed soundlessly. He couldn't afford to dwell on thoughts like that when he had to make sure that Emma didn't come to any harm.

'I don't know what you mean,' he said, his voice sounding unnaturally gruff as he tried to work out how to salvage the situation.

'Of course you do.' She came into the room and stood in front of the table. 'You're sitting there, wallowing in guilt because of what happened last night, and it's so typically arrogant of you.'

'Arrogant?' His brows shot skywards and he looked at her in surprise.

'Yes.' Resting her hands on the edge of the table she bent so that she could look straight into his eyes. 'You didn't coerce me into bed, neither did you have your *wicked way* with me. I made love with you because I wanted to. If I hadn't wanted to, it would never have happened. Is that clear?'

'Yes.' He was so stunned by her forthright approach that he couldn't think what else to say but Emma didn't seem to expect him to say anything.

'Good. The last thing I need is you thinking that I'm holding out for a reconciliation.' She gave a sharp laugh. 'Last night was fun and I enjoyed it but that's as far as it went. It certainly wasn't the start of something more.'

'That's how I feel too,' Daniel said thickly. Even though he knew he should be relieved that she felt this way, he couldn't help feeling hurt that their love-making had meant so little to her.

'It seems we're in agreement, then.' She gave him a cool little smile and went to switch on the kettle.

Daniel finished his coffee in a couple of quick gulps and excused himself. Emma was making toast when he left the kitchen, acting as though everything was completely normal, and maybe it was for her. Maybe she'd had a string of lovers in the past few years, men she had enjoyed the odd night of passion with. She'd mentioned her boss, hadn't she? Richard something-or-other. Maybe he was one of them, although there could be a long line of past and present suitors for all he knew. Although he hated the idea, what right did he have to criticise how she lived her life? The truth was that he had forfeited any rights where Emma was concerned five years ago. She was free to do whatever she wished.

The thought was so agonising that Daniel knew he had to get out of the house before he made a fool of himself. Unhooking his coat off the peg, he let himself out of the front door. His car was parked in the drive so he got in and started the engine. When he reached the main road, he headed towards Harrogate purely because it was somewhere to aim for. He wasn't heading *to* somewhere but away from a place where it was too painful to be. The trouble was that no matter how many miles he put between himself and Emma, it didn't stop him thinking about her, definitely didn't stop him wishing that things could have been different.

Emma managed to maintain her composure until she heard Daniel's car driving away. She sank down onto a chair, feeling sick and shaken by what had happened. She had known the moment she had seen him sitting at the table that he had regretted what had happened the night before. It had been pride that had helped her deal with the situation, pride plus the fear of what might happen if he realised how much it had meant to her.

She bit her lip, overwhelmed by a sudden feeling of dread. Making love with Daniel had been everything she could have wished for but she wasn't foolish enough to think that it had meant anything special to him. Maybe he had desired her but that was all it had been. Whilst she had tried to convince herself that it would be the ideal way to draw a line under the past, she doubted if Daniel had viewed it that way. He hadn't needed to because he had got over her a long time ago. There was no way that had he been celibate for the past five years, and last night she had been just another in a long line of women willing and eager to give him pleasure.

The thought of Daniel making love to all those other women was incredibly painful, so Emma tried not to dwell on it. There were just two weeks left of her stay and after that she would return to the life she had built for herself. It had taken her a long time to get over Daniel the last time and she couldn't bear to think that she would have to go through that kind of heartache again, so she would make sure he didn't gain any kind of hold over her. And that meant there must never be a repeat of what had happened last night.

Daniel was snatching five minutes' break in the middle of what had turned out to be an extremely busy Monday morning surgery when Emma knocked on his door.

'Ruth said you didn't have a patient with you at the moment,' she explained as she came into the room.

'I was just taking a breather,' he replied, hoping he sounded calmer than he felt.

He had managed to stay out of her way for the remainder of the weekend. It had been almost midnight when he'd got back to the house and she'd been in bed. There'd been no sign of her when he'd got up that morning either, although he hadn't lingered. He had skipped breakfast and come straight to the surgery, making do with a cup of coffee to tide him over. If he'd had his way he would have avoided seeing her for the rest of the day too, but obviously that wasn't to be. Now all he could hope was that the decision he'd made yesterday to behave calmly and professionally around her for the next couple of weeks would see him through.

'It has been busy,' she agreed evenly. Closing the door, she came over to his desk and handed him a file. 'Would you mind taking a look at this for me? I'm afraid it's got me stumped.'

'Of course.' Daniel took the file and quickly read through the patient's notes. His brows rose when he noted how many times the man had visited the surgery in the past two months. 'Alistair Grant is either an extremely sick man or he's a complete hypochondriac. You could fill a textbook with the variety of symptoms he's presented with recently.'

'Exactly.' She leant across the desk and selected a sheet from the file. 'Uncle Jim sent him for a whole battery of tests last month and they all came back clear.'

'Hmm.' Daniel placed the file on the desk, trying to ignore the leap his heart gave when her hand brushed his as she passed him the test results. Ruthlessly, he battened it down, refusing to allow himself even the tiniest leeway. He was going to treat Emma as a colleague from now on, even if it killed him!

'Does he seem genuine to you?' he asked, sticking determinedly to the matter under discussion.

'It's hard to say.' She grimaced. 'I only met him today so I don't have any real idea of what he's like as a person.'

'So he hasn't lived in Avondale all that long?'

'No. Apparently he moved here three months ago.'

'And almost immediately began visiting the surgery on a regular basis.' Daniel frowned as he picked up the patient's file again and flicked through it. 'How come we don't have any notes from his last GP?'

'He's been working abroad ever since he left university. He told me that he assumed his notes would be still at the practice his parents use but they've been unable to find them. Ruth has contacted the university to see if they were transferred to their medical centre but so far she's not heard back from them.'

'That's a shame. It would have been helpful to see if he had a history of visiting his GP on a frequent basis.'

'It would. To be honest, it's not a situation I've come across before. Most people who are undergoing surgery have been seen by several doctors before they reach us. That tends to weed out any malingerers.'

'Would it help if I had a word with him?' Daniel offered. 'I'm not saying I'll be able to tell if he's making it up, but it might deter him if he knows we're dubious about the claims he's been making.'

'Would you mind? I'd hate to make any hasty assumptions about his credibility and overlook something serious.'

Daniel heard the relief in her voice and immediately stood up. He would do anything to help her, he thought as he followed her to the door. He sighed as they walked along the corridor together. If only he'd thought about that on Saturday night. Making love with Emma may have been wonderful, but it had caused problems for him if not for her. She might be able to chalk it up to experience but he certainly couldn't. Just for a second his head reeled as he recalled how sweetly responsive she had been when he'd held her in his arms before he forced the thought to the deepest, darkest reaches of his mind. He couldn't afford to think about that or he wouldn't be able to function!

Alistair Grant was sitting in the chair exactly where Emma had left him. A thin young man in his late twenties with sandy-coloured hair and a pale complexion, he cut a rather pathetic figure. Emma smiled at him as she went into the room.

'I'm sorry to have left you sitting here, Alistair. This is Dr Kennedy. He would like to have a word with you to see if he can get to the root of your problems.'

'I hope somebody can.' Alistair stood up to shake hands. He sat down heavily again as though he didn't have the strength to remain on his feet for very long. Propping himself against the edge of the desk, Daniel regarded him thoughtfully.

'You seem to have been through the mill recently, Alistair. I've read your notes and you've had a lot of distressing symptoms in the last few months, it appears.'

Emma took her seat behind the desk, leaving it up to Daniel to take the lead. She had to admit that the case had her stumped and she would value his help. She listened attentively while he asked Alistair how his health had been in general over the past year.

'I was fine right up until a few months ago,' Alistair

assured them. 'I never had anything wrong with me before that apart from the odd cold.'

'Dr Roberts told me that you've been working abroad. Were you ill while you were there or did it all kick off when you came back to England?'

'When I moved to Avondale, actually. I'd only been here a couple of weeks when I started feeling really rough—tired and as though I had no energy. Then I started with all these aches and pains, the headaches, etcetera.'

He sounded really despondent and Emma frowned. If he was making it up then he was extremely convincing. By the time Daniel finished talking to him, she could tell that he was as perplexed as she was.

'I have to admit that it's got me baffled, Alistair. I know you've had a whole range of tests done, but I'd like to send you for more blood tests and see what they show up. Where were you working when you were abroad, by the way?'

'South Africa was the last place but I've been all over in the past few years—India, China, various parts of Africa. I'm a civil engineer so I go wherever the job takes me.'

'Are you working here at the moment?' Emma put in.

'Yes. I'm overseeing the building of a new wind farm. We're due to start in a couple of weeks' time so I've been doing a lot of the ground work beforehand.'

'I imagine there was opposition to building a wind farm around here,' Daniel suggested.

Alistair sighed. 'There was. It's taken years to get

the go-ahead and there's a lot of folk who still aren't happy about it. One of the local farmers in particular has caused us a great deal of trouble—dumping loads of manure and old oil drums in the middle of the track to block our access, that sort of thing. Last week he even warned some of the men off with a shotgun. When we called the police, he claimed it was all a misunderstanding and that he was out shooting rabbits.'

'It can't be easy, dealing with that kind of behaviour!' Emma exclaimed.

'It isn't, although it wouldn't be so bad if I felt a bit more up to it,' Alistair stated ruefully.

'Well, let's hope we can get to the bottom of this as soon as possible,' Daniel said encouragingly. 'Bearing in mind where you've been working recently, I'd like you screened for some of the more obscure tropical diseases as well. It could be that you've picked something up overseas and that's what's causing the problem. We'll arrange for a blood sample to be sent to the School of Tropical Medicine in Liverpool and see if they can come up with any answers.'

Emma printed out a form for bloods to be taken at the hospital, adding a request for samples to be sent straight to Liverpool. She handed the form to Alistair who thanked her rather wearily and left. She frowned as the door closed behind him. 'I don't think he's making it up, do you?'

'No. It didn't seem like it to me either,' Daniel agreed. 'Let's hope something shows up in the next lot of tests because it's very puzzling.'

'Fingers crossed.' She reached for the button to buzz

through her next patient, not wanting to appear as though she was keen to detain him. However, he was way ahead of her.

'Let me know when the test results come back, will you?' he asked as he strode to the door.

'Of course.'

Emma summoned a smile but it was galling to know how eager he was to avoid spending any time with her. He had stayed away from the house all day on Sunday, only returning when he'd been sure that she would be in bed. She had heard his car turn into the drive well after midnight and had hurriedly switched off her lamp, afraid that he would think she was waiting up for him.

It was obvious that Daniel was keen to avoid a repeat of what had happened on Saturday night. She was too but for a different reason. She was afraid of getting emotionally involved but that wasn't something he would worry about. Daniel simply didn't want any complications in his life. Maybe he *had* told her that she was more beautiful than any woman he had ever known but talk was cheap: actions said far more. And he had proved beyond any doubt that he didn't care a jot about her.

CHAPTER TEN

THE week wore on and Daniel found to his dismay that he couldn't stop thinking about what had happened between him and Emma. It wasn't so bad while he was working, he could focus on his patients then. However, when he was on his own, that was when the real problem started.

It was as though Emma had invaded his mind and every time he relaxed his guard, thoughts of her popped into his head. He kept remembering in glorious detail how it had felt when they'd made love and it was driving him mad. He longed to tell her how he felt yet he knew he couldn't do it. How could he confess that making love to her had touched his heart and his soul when it was clear that she didn't feel the same way?

In an effort to retain his sanity he spent an increasing amount of time away from the house. Fortunately the weather had improved and with the nights getting lighter, he was able to go walking after evening surgery ended. He became quite familiar with the various footpaths surrounding the town, although he was careful not to stray too far afield. It was while he was out one evening that he came across the search and rescue team tending an injured walker. When Mike Harding asked him if he would take a look at the woman's ankle, Daniel readily agreed.

'It looks to me very much like a Pott's fracture,' he declared after he'd examined her. He glanced at Mike and grimaced. 'When she fell, she broke her fibula and either broke the tibia as well or tore the ligaments, resulting in a dislocation of the ankle. It's a nasty injury.'

'Can you help us put a splint on it, Doc?' Mike asked. 'We certainly don't want to cause any more damage.'

'Of course.' Daniel gave the woman some Entonox™ to help with the pain then helped Mike fit an inflatable splint to support her ankle. He accompanied the team back to their Land Rover, shaking his head when Mike thanked him profusely. 'I was happy to help.'

'I still appreciate what you did, Doc. That's twice in a very short time that we've been glad of your services. How's that young lad doing, by the way? Have you heard?'

'Do you mean Jack? He's been moved from Intensive Care and by all accounts is making an excellent recovery.'

'Which he probably wouldn't be doing if you hadn't been on hand to help him.' Mike shook his head when Daniel demurred. 'No, credit where it's due, Doc. You saved that kid's life and that's a fact. It's just a shame that you aren't going to be here long term. We could do with someone like you to call on, especially as we're coming up to our busiest time of the year. I don't suppose you'd consider moving here permanently, would you?'

'Nice idea, although I'm not sure my colleagues in

London would appreciate me jumping ship,' Daniel told him with a laugh to disguise how touched he felt by the request.

'Pity. You've fitted in really well around here. Everyone's said so. And they don't always take kindly to outsiders, believe me.'

Mike sketched him a wave and drove off. Daniel made his way back to the house, thinking about what the other man had said. Despite the problems with Emma, he had enjoyed working in the town far more than he had expected. Not only had he enjoyed being part of such a close-knit community, he had dealt with a far wider variety of cases than he normally would have seen. With the nearest hospital being so far away, the surgery was the first port of call in an emergency and it had been good to test his skills.

He knew that if circumstances had been different, he would have been tempted to ask Jim Haynes if he was still interested in taking on a partner. There was certainly sufficient work for a second doctor; in fact, he couldn't imagine how Jim was going to cope on his own when he returned to work. However, he also knew how Emma would feel about the idea. He would be the last person she would want working here.

It was a dispiriting thought. Knowing how Emma felt about him hurt, even though he refused to examine the reasons why it was so painful. He knew that she would take care to ensure their paths never crossed in the future and it was hard to accept that once she left, he would never see her again. Even though he knew it was for the best, he was going to miss her.

* * *

Emma found it difficult to put what had happened between her and Daniel behind her. The fact that he never once alluded to it should have helped but it didn't. She found it deeply hurtful that he'd been able to dismiss the fact that they had slept together.

In an effort to make the remainder of her stay in Avondale bearable, she made a point of keeping out of his way outside working hours. It wasn't difficult. Daniel had taken to going for a walk after evening surgery finished, which meant he was rarely at home. She did wonder if he was avoiding her too but decided she was being fanciful. Daniel had demonstrated very clearly that he had very few feelings for her, so why would he feel that he needed to keep out of her way?

Another week passed and the surgery was busier than ever. There was a steady influx of tourists arriving in the area and they added to the number of people wanting to be seen. Emma couldn't help wondering how her uncle was going to cope when he returned to work. Although he was making excellent progress, according to her aunt, running a busy practice with all that it entailed was very different from convalescing. She couldn't bear to think that Uncle Jim might put his health at risk out of a sense of duty and decided to speak to Daniel about it. She managed to catch him on his way out to some house calls on Friday lunchtime.

'Have you got a minute?'

'Yes, of course. What's up? Problems?'

He put his case on the desk and turned to face her. Emma felt her heart give a little jolt and swallowed. The weather had been exceptionally warm that day and he'd shed his jacket and rolled up his shirtsleeves. The pale blue cotton set off his olive-toned skin and provided the perfect foil for his dark brown hair. He looked big and vital and so gloriously male that she was suddenly aware of her own femininity in a way she hadn't been since the night they had made love.

The thought wasn't the least bit welcome. She hurriedly drove it from her mind and concentrated on what she'd come to say. 'I've been thinking about what's going to happen when Uncle Jim comes back to work.'

'You mean how he's going to manage on his own?' Daniel said immediately, and she looked at him in surprise.

'Yes. How did you know that's what I meant?'

'Because I've been thinking about it too.' He gave her a tight smile. 'It doesn't take a genius to see that he's going to be pushed to keep up with the workload here. Quite frankly, it's way too much for one person.'

'It is. He needs someone to help him, ideally another partner, but I can't see that happening, can you?'

'It could take time to find the right person,' Daniel said slowly. 'And it isn't something we can organise without your uncle's consent.'

'No, it isn't. And if Uncle Jim is as choosy this time round as he was the last time he advertised, it could take for ever.' She sighed. 'It's hard to know what to do, isn't it?'

'How about a locum?' Daniel suggested.

'Do you think we'd find anyone willing to work here, though?'

'I can't see why not. Oh, I know Avondale isn't

exactly a mecca for bright lights and a wild social life, but neither is it the back of beyond. And at this time of the year—when the weather is fine—it might be an attractive proposition for someone.'

'It's worth a try,' she said slowly. 'I don't suppose you know any reliable agencies who provide locum cover? It's not something I've had to deal with.'

'I'll get onto our practice manager and ask her for some phone numbers,' Daniel assured her. 'We often need locum cover so she keeps a list of agencies.'

'That would be great. Thank you. Should we tell Uncle Jim what we're planning when he phones?'

'Oh, yes, I think so, don't you?' He shrugged. 'If I were in his shoes, I'd expect to be kept up to date with what was going on here.'

'I only hope he doesn't object,' Emma said anxiously. 'You know how touchy he can be about his patients, wants to be sure they receive first-class care, et cetera.'

'Leave it to me. I'm sure I can convince him it will be in everyone's best interests if he has help, if only during the summer months.'

'That's probably the best way to sell the idea to him,' Emma agreed. 'Even Uncle Jim will have to admit that it's hard to cope when there are so many visitors in the area.'

'And once he's admitted that, it should be easier to make him see that he needs help at other times of the year as well.'

'Take it one step at a time, you mean?' she said, frowning as she considered the idea and realised that it had a lot of merit.

'Yes.' Daniel sighed. 'Trying to push your uncle into admitting that he isn't up to running the practice on his own any longer will only make him dig in his heels, so we'll take things slowly, let him discover for himself that he needs help.'

'It makes sense. I'd hate it to look as though we doubt his capabilities.'

'Exactly. This way, any decisions that are made about the future of the practice will be his. He won't feel as though he's being pushed into doing something he doesn't want to do.'

'You're right,' Emma agreed, surprised by Daniel's astute assessment of the situation. She knew that her uncle would hate to feel as though he wasn't in charge any more, but it surprised her that Daniel had realised that too.

She turned to leave then stopped when Daniel said suddenly, 'Oh, by the way, those test results for Alistair Grant have come back. I was in the office when they arrived so I had a look at them. I hope you don't mind?'

'Of course not. What did they show? Anything?'

'According to the lab at Liverpool there are traces of pesticide in Alistair's blood.' Daniel shrugged. 'It would certainly explain the wide variety of symptoms he's presented with recently, wouldn't it?'

'It would. Do you think he's been in contact with pesticides while he's been here or did it happen while he was working overseas?' she queried.

'Liverpool seems to think the problem is recent. I've asked Ruth to phone Alistair and get him to make an appointment to see if we can find out how he may have come into contact with the chemicals. If we can't find an answer, I imagine environmental services will need to be alerted to see if they can sort it out.'

'Of course. If it is a local problem then we don't want anyone else being taken ill,' she said worriedly.

'Exactly.' He smiled at her. 'I'll mention it to your uncle when he phones. I'm sure he'd enjoy getting to the bottom of the mystery.'

'I'm sure he would,' she agreed quietly.

Emma sighed as she left the room. She couldn't help wondering how one person could be such a contradiction. On the one hand Daniel genuinely seemed to care about other people's feelings, but on the other hand he didn't seem to care a jot about hers. Even though she knew it was stupid, she couldn't help wishing that he would spare some of that concern for her.

The house calls had taken far longer than he'd expected so that it was after three p.m. by the time Daniel drew up in front of Niths Farm. He switched off the engine and reached for the printout that Ruth had prepared for him. According to the patient's notes, it had been over ten years since Harold Dawson had last visited the surgery. He'd suffered an injury to his left arm following an incident with some kind of farm machinery but had refused to go to the hospital. Jim had stitched his arm, given him a tetanus shot, and that had been it. Harold Dawson hadn't returned to have the stitches removed and had ignored several telephone messages asking him to contact the surgery. Daniel grimaced as he got out of the car. It didn't bode well for what was going to greet him today.

He rapped on the farmhouse door, glancing around while he waited. Although the farm was large, it was very untidy. Bits of rusty old machinery littered the yard and there was a pile of stones heaped up in the corner where one of the barn walls had given way. The whole place had a pervading air of neglect that saddened him. It seemed a shame that what had been once an obviously thriving concern should have been reduced to such a pitiful state as this.

'Aye? And what do you want?'

Daniel swung round when a gruff voice spoke behind him. He summoned a smile as he greeted the elderly man standing in the doorway. 'I'm Dr Kennedy. You phoned the surgery and requested a home visit.'

'I asked to see the real doctor, not some stand-in,' the man replied rudely. He glared at Daniel. 'Tell them I want to see Dr Haynes, no one else.'

'I'm afraid Dr Haynes is away at the present time,' Daniel explained quietly.

'Then I'll wait till he's back.'

He went to shut the door but Daniel put out his hand and stopped him. 'Dr Haynes won't be back for another month. Are you sure you want to wait that long, Mr Dawson?'

The man hesitated while he considered the idea. He scowled as he wrenched open the door. 'Suppose you'd better come in, then, seeing as you're here.'

Daniel sighed ruefully as he followed the old man into a dingy hallway. Not exactly the warmest welcome he'd ever received. Harold Dawson led him down the hall to the kitchen, which turned out to be equally neglected. Daniel's heart sank as he took stock of the piles of dirty dishes on the draining board and the inch-thick layer of grease that coated the top of the old-fashioned range. It didn't appear as though any cleaning had been done in the place for months, if not years. Pushing aside a stack of old newspapers, he placed his case on the table.

'So what exactly is the problem, Mr Dawson? You told Ruth it was something to do with your foot, I believe.'

'That's right, although I wouldn't have bothered phoning if I weren't in so much pain.' The man glared at him. 'I don't hold with all these pills you doctors hand out. Don't do folk no good, in my opinion.'

Daniel forbore to say anything, deeming it wiser not to get embroiled in an argument he was unlikely to win. 'I'd better take a look at your foot.'

Harold Dawson sat down heavily on a chair and started to peel off a filthy sock from his right foot. Daniel shook his head in dismay when he saw the how red and swollen it looked.

'When did this start?' he asked, kneeling down in front of the old man.

'A few weeks ago, mebbe a bit longer,' Harold replied curtly. He winced when Daniel touched the inflamed skin. 'It's real tender so don't you go poking and prodding at it.'

'I'll be as careful as I can,' Daniel assured him. He carefully felt the swollen foot, pausing when he discovered a strong pulse beating beneath the flesh because it confirmed his initial diagnosis. Standing up, he took a bottle of hand gel out of his case, deeming it more hygienic than using the sink to wash his hands.

'It looks to me as though you have immersion foot, Mr Dawson. It's a type of injury caused when feet are allowed to remain wet and cold for a prolonged period. You may have heard of trench foot which so many soldiers in the First World War suffered from? It's the same thing.'

'I've not been standing in any trenches,' Harold retorted scathingly.

'I'm sure you haven't. But if you've been outdoors and got your feet wet and not bothered to change your shoes and socks, that could have caused it.' Daniel tactfully didn't add that from the state of the man's socks there was no *could* about it. It was doubtful if Harold Dawson had put on clean socks or anything else for a very long time!

He took a prescription pad out of his case and wrote out a script for painkillers. 'I imagine your foot's very painful so these will help. You'll also need to bathe your foot in tepid water to cool it and reduce the swelling. Make sure you put on clean, dry socks and that your shoes or boots are dry too.' Daniel handed the man the prescription. 'If you notice any sores appearing, contact the surgery. Skin ulcers can develop and that's something we want to avoid.'

'So that's it, is it?' Harold Dawson slammed the prescription down on the table. 'Take some pills and put on dry socks. I could've worked that out for myself!'

Daniel smiled calmly, resisting the urge to tell

the man that if he'd done that in the beginning there wouldn't have been a problem. 'That's right. It's just a question of taking care of yourself.'

'I don't need any advice from you,' the old man responded belligerently. He shuffled towards the door, making it clear that he expected Daniel to leave.

Daniel picked up his case, knowing how pointless it was to suggest that he arranged for the community nurse to call and check how Harold's foot was healing. If the poor woman received the kind of reception he'd received, she would probably refuse to call a second time, and he wouldn't blame her either. He made a note to speak to Ruth about the old man when he got back to the surgery and headed out to the hall, pausing when there was a loud banging on the front door.

'What the dickens…!' Harold Dawson pushed past him and strode along the hall. Wrenching open the door, he glowered at the young man standing outside. 'You can take yourself off my property right now.'

'Believe me, I'd like nothing better than not to see hide nor hair of you or this place for the rest of my life,' the other man retorted.

Daniel frowned when he realised that the caller was Alistair Grant. It seemed a coincidence that he should turn up here when he needed to speak to him. However, he was less concerned about resolving Alistair's health issues at that moment than he was about defusing the situation.

He hurried to the door, hoping to avert a full-scale row.

'Hello, Alistair,' he said quietly, drawing both men's attention to him. 'I'm surprised to see you here.'

'I'm not here out of choice, believe me, Dr Kennedy,' Alistair replied angrily. He glared at the old man. 'If you don't stop dumping stuff on the road to the construction site then I warn you, Dawson, that the company I work for will take legal action. Carry on with your little games and you'll find yourself in prison. Is that clear?'

'Aye, it's clear enough. But if you think a young pup like you can come to my home and threaten me, think again.'

Daniel's heart sank when he saw Harold Dawson reach behind the front door and pick up a shotgun that had been standing there. He aimed it at Alistair Grant's chest. 'You need to learn some manners, lad, and I'm just the one to teach them to you.'

'Come on, now, let's all calm down,' Daniel said soothingly. He stepped forward then stopped when Dawson swung round and pointed the gun at him.

'I've told you once that I don't need any advice from you.' The old man scowled at him. 'You're no better than he is. Coming in here, thinking you can tell folk what to do. Well, I've had enough, do you hear me? It's 'bout time someone stood up to the likes of you. Inside, both of you.'

Dawson waved the shotgun towards the kitchen. Daniel hesitated but one glance at the old man's face warned him that it would be foolish to refuse to do what he asked. He headed back along the hall, wondering what was going to happen next. Maybe Dawson only wanted to scare them but he didn't think so—it looked far more serious than that.

He put his case on the table as Alistair followed him

into the room, seeing the sheen of perspiration on the younger man's face. It was obvious that he was scared stiff and Daniel didn't blame him. Harold Dawson was on the brink of losing control and there was no knowing what would happen then.

A picture of Emma suddenly appeared in his mind's eye and he felt a shaft of regret so sharp run through him that he winced. He couldn't bear to think that he might die without telling Emma that he loved her.

CHAPTER ELEVEN

'I DON'T suppose you've seen Daniel, have you, Emma?'

Emma paused when Ruth called to her on her way into the surgery that afternoon. It was five minutes to four and she was keen to get to her room before her first patient arrived. 'Not since lunchtime, I'm afraid.'

'Oh, right.' Ruth sighed.

Emma frowned. 'Why? Is there a problem?'

'No, not really. It's just that he usually pops in with his notes after he's finished the house calls, but he's not been in yet this afternoon.'

'Maybe he's running late,' Emma suggested.

'Probably, although there weren't that many calls to do today.' Ruth shrugged when the phone rang. 'Maybe he got held up. You know how some people love to talk—he probably couldn't get away.'

'I expect that's it,' Emma agreed as she carried on along the corridor, although she was surprised that Daniel would have allowed himself to be late. He was a stickler for punctuality and was usually at his desk well before his first appointment was due.

She booted up her computer then glanced through the list that Ruth had left on her desk. It wasn't too long for a change so, hopefully, she could finish on time for once. She buzzed through for her first patient, smiling when Judith Fisher walked into the room.

'Hello, Judith. How are you?'

'I'm all right, Dr Roberts.' The young woman sat down in front of the desk. 'I had an appointment at the hospital on Wednesday. The consultant did a laparoscopy and confirmed that I have endometriosis, like you suspected.'

'At least we know what we're dealing with now,' Emma said quietly.

'I suppose so,' Judith agreed wistfully.

Emma guessed that it had been a blow for Judith to have her suspicions confirmed and tried to focus on the positive aspects of the diagnosis. 'What did the consultant suggest by way of treatment?'

'He's put me back on the Pill to prevent me menstruating. It will help to control the pain and, hopefully, stop the cysts from getting any bigger. He also said that he might surgically remove some of the larger cysts at a later date.'

'And you're worried about how that will affect your chances of having a baby?'

'Yes.' Tears rose in Judith's eyes. 'I don't think I'll ever have a baby now, will I?'

'I haven't received a copy of your consultant's report yet, Judith, so there is no way that I can tell you that everything is going to be all right. However, what I can say is that between sixty and seventy per cent of women who suffer from endometriosis are able to have children.'

'That sounds much better than how the consultant put it.' Judith managed a watery smile. 'He said that thirty to forty per cent of women with endometriosis are infertile.'

'I suppose it's the glass half full or half empty scenario,' Emma said with a chuckle. 'It depends which way you choose to look at the figures.'

'Well, I prefer your way.' Judith sounded more optimistic all of a sudden. 'I have almost a seventy per cent chance of becoming a mum and that's pretty good odds, I'd say.'

'So would I.' Emma smiled at her. 'I know it must be hard but try to remain positive. Once you've completed the treatment, who knows what might happen? And the plus factor is that pregnancy is known to suppress the symptoms of endometriosis.'

'A case of fingers crossed.' Judith laughed as she stood up.

'Exactly.'

Emma was still smiling as she buzzed through her next patient. It was always good to know that you had helped someone be more positive about their life. That was one of the reasons why she loved surgery, of course, although she hadn't realised that she would derive the same pleasure from general practice work. No wonder Daniel enjoyed his job so much.

The thought startled her. Ever since Daniel had announced that he planned to go into private practice, she'd had a jaundiced view of his motives for becoming a GP. Now she could see that she may have misjudged him.

It didn't necessarily mean that it was purely financial gain that drove him.

It was uncomfortable to find her view of Daniel knocked off kilter. Emma found it difficult to push the idea aside as she dealt with her next patient, an elderly man who suffered from chronic bronchitis. She renewed his prescription for an inhaler and gently suggested that he might benefit from oxygen therapy. Once she had explained that oxygen cylinders could be delivered to his home, he happily agreed. She made a note to ask Ruth to contact the nearest supplier and saw him out. She was just about to sit down again when Ruth, herself, hurried into the room.

'I'm sorry to barge in, Emma, but Daniel still hasn't appeared. I'm getting really worried now, because it just isn't like him not to turn up,' the receptionist told her anxiously.

'No, it certainly isn't,' Emma agreed. 'Have you tried his phone?'

'Yes, but it goes straight to voice mail.' Ruth bit her lip. 'You don't think he's had an accident, do you? Some of the roads round here are a bit tricky if you don't know them that well.'

'I'm sure we'd have heard if he had,' Emma assured her, although her heart had started to race at the thought of Daniel lying injured somewhere. She took a deep breath before panic could set in. 'Do you have a list of the calls he was supposed to do this afternoon?' When Ruth nodded, she hurried on. 'Then I suggest you telephone everyone on the list and check what time he visited them. That way we'll have a better idea of where he might be.'

'Good idea!' Ruth exclaimed. She hurried to the door then paused. 'What about his patients, though? There's a real backlog forming.'

'I'll have to see them,' Emma told her. 'I'll see one of mine then one of Daniel's—that will be fairer than making his patients wait till I finish my list.'

Emma picked up the phone as soon as Ruth left and dialled Daniel's phone but the call went straight to voice mail again. She hung up, feeling her stomach churning with nerves. What could have happened to stop him even answering his phone? She had no idea but it was extremely worrying. Maybe they didn't see eye to eye on a lot of things but she couldn't bear to think that he may have been hurt or worse even.

Her heart suddenly seemed to shrivel up inside her. The thought of never seeing Daniel again was more than she could bear.

Daniel heard his phone ring and guessed that it must be Ruth calling to see where he was. He glanced at his watch, realising with a start that it was almost four-thirty. How much longer was Dawson going to keep them here? he wondered, glancing at the old man, who was standing guard by the kitchen door. He had no idea but something needed to be done to resolve this situation soon.

'Look, Mr Dawson, I know you're upset but this is crazy. Keeping us here won't achieve anything,' he said in his most reasonable tone. 'All you'll do is find yourself in a whole load of trouble and I'm sure that isn't what any of us wants.'

'I don't care how much trouble I'm in. It'll be worth it to put a stop to what's going on.' Harold Dawson raised the shotgun and pointed it at Alistair Grant. 'If him and his cronies think they can come here and tear up the countryside then they can think again!'

Daniel saw the colour drain from Alistair's face and quickly interceded. 'If that's the way you feel, you need to talk to someone, see if you can get the decision to build this wind farm reversed.'

'Talk! I've talked till I'm blue in the face and no one's listened to me.' Harold's face flushed with anger. 'No, it's actions that will get their attention, nothing else.'

Daniel opened his mouth to try again to make him see sense when the telephone rang. Harold Dawson lifted the receiver off its rest. Daniel could tell from what the old man was saying that it was the surgery phoning and guessed that Ruth must be checking up on his whereabouts. He was tempted to shout out that he was there but Dawson must have realised he might do that and swung the gun towards him.

'No, the doctor left a while ago. No, I don't know what time it was. I've better things to do than keep a check on folk's comings and goings.'

He went to slam the receiver back on its rest at the same moment that Daniel's mobile phone rang again. He let it go to voice mail once more, knowing it would be foolish to try and answer it. Dawson's mood was far too volatile to risk upsetting him any further. He glanced at Alistair and saw the fear in the younger man's eyes.

'What are we going to do?' Alistair mouthed desperately.

Daniel shook his head. Reasoning with the old man obviously wasn't going to work and using physical force was out of the question when Dawson had that gun. All he could hope was that Emma would call the police when he failed to turn up. So long as she didn't try tracking him down herself, of course.

The air seemed to lock in his lungs at the thought of her following him to the farm and placing herself in danger. He knew if that happened he would have to do something, no matter how risky it was.

He took a deep breath and his mind was suddenly crystal clear. He would give up his life to protect Emma because he loved her.

It was seven o'clock before the last patient left. Emma hurried through to Reception, not needing to ask if there was any news when she saw the worry on Ruth's face. 'Still nothing,' she said helplessly.

'No. I just don't know what to do next, Emma.'

'You've called everyone who'd requested a home visit?'

'Yes, and they all said that Dr Kennedy had left ages ago.' Ruth shook her head. 'Most of them were able to tell me almost to the minute what time he left too. It was only old Harold Dawson who refused to say what time Daniel left his farm but that's typical of him. A really awkward old devil, he is.'

'Harold Dawson from Niths Farm, you mean?' Emma queried.

'That's right. He's always been difficult but he's got worse since his wife died. He doesn't have any family and I doubt he's got any friends either...' Ruth paused and frowned.

'What?' Emma said quickly. 'You've obviously thought of something.'

'It's just that when I was hanging up the phone after speaking to him I could have sworn I heard a mobile phone ringing in the background.' Ruth shrugged. 'It just seems odd. I wouldn't have thought old Mr Dawson would be the sort to bother having a mobile.'

'Maybe he had somebody visiting him,' Emma suggested.

'Could be, although I doubt they'd get much of a welcome. He's not one to mix, believe me.'

Emma sighed. Although it did seem strange, it had nothing to do with what had happened to Daniel so there wasn't time to worry about it right then. She came to a swift decision. 'I'm going to phone the police and report Daniel missing. I'm not sure what they can do but we can't just sit here, wondering what's happened to him.'

'I think you should call them,' Ruth agreed, looking relieved. 'Daniel would have let us know if his car had broken down or if he'd had some sort of minor accident.'

Emma bit her lip as she reached for the receiver. Ruth was right. Daniel *would* have contacted them—if he could. She put a call through to the police station and told them what had happened. They promised to check with the various agencies in case Daniel had been involved in an RTA and get back to her. Ruth insisted on staying while they waited for the police to phone back and went off to make them a cup of tea. Almost as soon as she'd gone, there was a loud banging on the surgery door and Emma felt her spirits soar in relief. That had to be Daniel!

Hurrying to the door, she swung it open. 'And about time too—' she began, then stopped abruptly when she found Mike Harding standing on the step. 'Sorry, Mike. I thought you were someone else.'

Mike grimaced. 'And I'm sorry to turn up like this too but I noticed the lights were still on as I was passing.' He held up his hand, which was covered in a blood-soaked bandage. 'We've been out on a training exercise tonight and I managed to get my thumb caught in one of the ratchets we use to haul people up the hillside. It needs a stitch or two and I was hoping you might do it to save me having to trail off to the hospital.'

'I…um…yes, of course. Come in.' Emma led the way inside. 'Come straight through to my room while I take a look at it.'

Mike followed her along the corridor, glancing round when Ruth came rushing out of the staffroom. He must have seen her face fall because he grinned. 'Obviously, I'm not the person you hoped to see either.'

'No, you're not,' Ruth said bluntly.

Mike's smile faded as he looked from her to Emma. 'Is something wrong?'

'Daniel failed to turn up for surgery this evening,' Emma explained as she ushered him into her room. 'He hasn't phoned and he isn't answering his mobile either.'

'That's odd.' Mike frowned as he sat down and unwound the bandage. 'I wouldn't have thought there was a problem getting a signal in that part of the Dales.'

Emma stopped and stared at him. 'What do you mean, that part of the Dales? Have you seen him?'

'Yes, well not *him* but I've seen his car. It's parked outside old man Dawson's place—Niths Farm. You know.'

'What time was this?' Emma demanded.

'Oh, around six-thirty, give or take a few minutes.' Mike shrugged. 'I did my hand in soon after that so it can't have been much later.'

'But Ruth phoned Harold Dawson way before then and he told her that Daniel had already left!' Emma exclaimed.

'Well, it was definitely Dr Kennedy's car. You don't get many fancy motors like that round here and certainly not at Dawson's place. There was another car there too, now that I think about it, a site vehicle from that wind farm they're building on the edge of Dawson's land.' Mike looked worried now. 'Why on earth did Dawson say the doc wasn't there when he was?'

'I don't know but it needs checking.' Emma picked up a dish and filled it with saline then gently bathed Mike's thumb. She frowned when she saw the deep gash at its base. 'That looks nasty. It's going to need three or four stitches by the look of it.'

She numbed Mike's thumb with an injection of local anaesthetic then set to work. It only took her only a few minutes to complete the job and Mike shook his head in admiration. 'That was quick work. You've done that a time or two, by the look of it.'

'Just a couple of times.' Emma summoned a smile but it was hard to concentrate. She had a nasty feeling about what Mike had told her and wouldn't rest until she had paid Harold Dawson a visit to see what was going on.

'Dr Haynes told me that you'd gone into surgery.' Mike smiled at her as he stood up. 'He's every right to be proud of you.'

Emma merely nodded, her mind too busy churning over possibilities to focus on the compliment. She looked up when Mike sighed. 'If it's hurting I can give you some painkillers,' she offered, feeling guilty for neglecting her patient.

'It's fine. No, it's obvious that you're worried sick about Dr Kennedy, aren't you?'

Emma flushed. 'It just seems strange that he hasn't called us,' she demurred.

Mike gave her an old-fashioned look. 'Hmm. It does. Why don't we drive over there and see what's going on? It's the least I can do after you've saved me a long wait in Casualty.'

'Oh, I couldn't expect you to do that,' she began, but Mike shook his head.

'Of course you can. In fact, I'm going to get onto the rest of the team and tell them what's happened. If the doc's out there, we'll find him. That's a promise.'

He put a comforting arm around Emma's shoulders and she sagged gratefully against him. 'Thanks, Mike,' she murmured huskily.

'No sweat.' He gave her a brotherly hug then went to the door. 'I'll put through that call and see you outside. OK?'

Emma nodded then hurried to find Ruth and tell her what had happened. They agreed that the police should be informed that Daniel's car had been seen, although whether they would act on the information was open to question. Mike had the engine running when Emma hurried outside and as soon as she got into the Land Rover, they set off. It was a good thirty-minute drive to Niths Farm and Emma was on tenterhooks all the way. If Daniel had left the farm, she had no idea where to start looking for him.

They turned down the lane leading to the farm and Mike slowed as they reached the bottom. 'Look,' he said, pointing.

Emma's heart leapt into her throat when she saw Daniel's car parked in the yard alongside another vehicle, which bore the logo of the wind farm's contractors. Obviously he was still there despite Harold Dawson's assurances to the contrary. 'What should we do?' she asked anxiously.

'I don't know, but whatever we decide we need to be careful.' Mike's tone was sombre. 'Old Dawson is a bit of a loose cannon lately. Folk have seen him walking round with a shotgun. Let's not go rushing in until we know what's happening, eh?'

'But Daniel may be in danger!' she protested.

'Yes. And we don't want to make matters worse by forcing Dawson's hand.' Mike picked up the radio receiver. 'I'm going to call the police and get them over here right away.'

Emma opened her door and climbed out of the car while Mike made the call. There were only a few hundred yards between her and Daniel but the distance had never seemed greater. The fact that she had no idea what was happening to him was so painful that she felt tears well to her eyes. Maybe they weren't destined to spend their lives together, as she had once hoped, but that didn't matter. So long as she knew that he was safe and well somewhere in the world, that was enough. In that moment she was forced to acknowledge the truth. She loved him. She loved him with the whole of her heart and she always would.

CHAPTER TWELVE

DANIEL heard the sound of a car stopping in the lane and frowned. Was it possible that someone had come looking for him and Alistair? He glanced at Harold Dawson but the old man seemed oblivious to what was happening outside. Dawson had grown increasingly agitated in the past hour. He had placed the shotgun by the back door and started walking around the kitchen, muttering to himself. Daniel might have been tempted to make a grab for the shotgun if it weren't for the fact that someone could get hurt if there was a struggle. It had seemed safer to bide his time but he might not have that luxury for much longer. He turned to Alistair.

'There's a car stopped in the lane,' he mouthed.

'Do you think it's the police?' Alistair whispered, hopefully.

Before Daniel could answer, Harold Dawson swung round and glared at them. 'Don't you two start thinking you can get up to anything.' He grabbed hold of the shotgun and pointed it at them. 'I won't think twice about using this, I warn you.'

'And what will that achieve, Mr Dawson?' Daniel

said in sudden exasperation. 'You'll end up in prison and the wind farm will still go ahead.'

'At least they'll know they can't trample all over me,' Harold roared. He aimed the gun at the ceiling and pulled the trigger. Daniel ducked as bits of wood and plaster rained down on them. His ears were throbbing from the noise of the explosion so that it was several seconds before he could hear let alone speak.

'Force isn't the answer,' he told the old man grimly. 'The powers-that-be won't give in because you threaten them. You need to go through the proper channels.'

If Dawson was listening he gave no sign of it. Daniel realised that he was wasting his breath trying to reason with him. He glanced towards the window, mentally crossing his fingers that it was the police outside and not some other unsuspecting visitor. His heart turned over at the thought that it might be Emma before he realised how foolish it was to imagine she cared enough to try and find him. Emma may have contacted the police when he hadn't turned up for evening surgery but that would have been all. She certainly wouldn't be spending her time worrying about him.

Emma's heart seemed to stop when she heard the sound of a shotgun being discharged. Mike was speaking to the police on the radio and she saw the shock on his face as he looked up. He hastily finished his call and hung up.

'The police will be here ASAP,' he told her. 'They said that we're not to approach the house and that under no circumstances are we to try and contact either Dawson or Dr Kennedy.'

'But we can't just sit here,' Emma protested. 'Anything could be going on inside that farmhouse. We need to do something!'

'We daren't risk it, Emma. I know it's hard but we could make matters a whole lot worse if we go rushing in.' Mike patted her hand. 'Let's wait for the police, love. They know what they're doing.'

Emma bit her lip. She knew Mike was right but it was sheer agony to wonder if Daniel might be hurt. It seemed to take for ever before the police arrived. She and Mike told them everything they knew, which was very little. When the police insisted that they back up the lane, she protested, but the police were adamant. They couldn't risk there being any civilian casualties.

The time dragged after that. The police used a loud-hailer to speak to Harold Dawson, trying to persuade him to let the hostages go. He refused all their pleas, ending the negotiations by firing the shotgun out of the window. Armed police officers were deployed to surround the house and everyone looked very tense. However, by the time midnight arrived, little progress had been made.

Emma couldn't imagine what it must be like for Daniel and the other hostage being caught up in such a drama. All she could do was hope that Harold Dawson would come to his senses and let them go. And if he did then she intended to tell Daniel the truth about how she felt. She loved him and she wasn't going to lie about it, wasn't going to pretend any more. She would tell him the truth—and hope that it meant something to him.

* * *

Daniel could feel his nerves humming with tension. Ever since Dawson had fired that shot at the police, he had become increasingly unstable. Daniel knew that he was within a hairsbreadth of losing control and had no idea what would happen then. Somehow he had to get the old man talking and hopefully defuse the situation.

'Why exactly are you so against this wind farm being built?' he asked as Harold made another circuit of the room.

'Because it shouldn't be there, that's why.' Harold glowered at him but Daniel tried not to let it deter him.

'You think it will spoil the countryside?'

''Course it will. Who wants to look at dozens of great lumps of metal? My Mary wouldn't. That's for sure.'

'Mary's your wife?' Daniel said quickly, wanting to keep the conversation flowing.

'Was. She died six years ago.' Tears suddenly welled into the old man's eyes. 'She loved the view over those hills, did my Mary. There's a meadow there that's full of wildflowers in the spring and she always said it was the most beautiful place on God's earth. Even when she was so ill that she couldn't get out of bed most days, she'd ask me to take her up there. And now folks like him want to dig it all up and spoil it.'

He jerked his thumb at Alistair, who blanched. Daniel realised that he had hit upon the real crux of the problem. Harold Dawson's desire to stop the wind farm going ahead was all tied up with his late wife. He realised that he needed to tread warily.

'No wonder you're upset about what's happening,' he

said quietly. 'It must be difficult to accept that a place which meant so much to your wife is going to change. But do you think Mary would have been happy about what you're doing?'

'What do you mean?' Dawson demanded querulously.

'Keeping us here and threatening us. Shooting at the police.' Daniel shrugged. 'What would Mary say if she knew that was what you were up to?'

Harold Dawson stopped pacing; his expression was reflective. 'My Mary hated guns. She wouldn't even let me shoot rabbits when she was alive. Said it was cruel, she did.'

'Then I doubt if she'd have approved of this, would she?' Daniel held out his hand. 'Why not give me the shotgun, Mr Dawson. Let's stop this now before things get any worse.'

Harold Dawson hesitated then slowly handed over the shotgun. Daniel carefully ejected the cartridges then placed it against the wall and stood up. 'I suggest we tell the police that we're coming out.'

Dawson didn't try to stop them as he and Alistair walked along the hall. Daniel cautiously opened the front door, shouting out that he and Alistair were coming out. Everything happened at great speed after that. The police came running towards them, some of the officers going straight into the house while others hurried him and Alistair away to safety. People were firing questions at him from all directions and he did his best to answer them, but he had caught sight of a figure standing just beyond the police cordon. Emma was here? She had cared enough to come and find him?

His heart sang with joy as he walked straight past the policeman who was trying to speak to him. Emma had started walking too, ducking under the tape, so that they met in the middle of the lane. When he opened his arms, she stepped into them and it was then that he knew everything was going to be all right. How could it not be when the love of his life was here in his arms, her heart beating in time with his?

He bent and kissed her, uncaring that everyone was watching them. He didn't give a damn who knew how he felt so long as Emma knew it. Drawing back, he looked into her eyes, wanting there to be no more misunderstandings, either deliberate or accidental.

'I love you,' he said softly, his voice grating with emotion. He felt the tremor that ran through her, heard the sharp indrawn breath she took, and held her tighter, knowing it must be a shock for her to hear him say that. He had hurt her so much, seemingly thrown away her love, and it was a lot to ask her to believe him now, but he had to try. 'I love you, Emma. I always have.'

'Daniel, I…'

She stopped and swallowed. Daniel could see the uncertainty in her eyes and prayed that she would find it in her heart to give him another chance. He wanted to take her somewhere quiet and explain it all to her, but there was no hope of that right now. He sighed when the officer in charge came over and told him firmly that he needed to speak to him at the police station. It appeared that sorting things out with Emma would have to wait for now.

'I'll have to go,' he told her huskily, smoothing a silky lock of her hair behind her ear. He dropped a kiss on her lips then smiled at her. 'I'll be back as soon as I can. Will you wait up for me?'

'Yes.' She gave him a wobbly smile, her eyes holding his fast for a moment before she turned away.

Daniel watched her walk over to Mike, who put a friendly arm around her shoulders as he led her to his car. He would have felt better if they could have sorted things out immediately rather than wait, but there was nothing he could do. As he allowed the officer to lead him to the waiting police car he sent up a silent prayer that everything would be all right. He just needed Emma to give him a second chance.

It was five a.m. before Emma heard a car turn into the drive. She ran to the window, feeling her heart leap when she saw Daniel getting out of a police car. Hurrying into the hall, she flung open the front door, seeing the lines that fatigue had been etched onto his handsome face.

'I thought they were never going to let me go,' he said as he stepped into the hall. 'I must have gone over what happened a dozen times before they were satisfied that I'd told them everything.'

'Come into the sitting room.'

Emma led the way, waiting until he had sunk down onto a chair before she went back to the door. She had spent the intervening time wondering what would happen when he got back. He had told her that he loved her but was it true? She longed to know yet now that the moment had arrived, she was suddenly afraid. What if Daniel hadn't really meant it, what if it had been merely a reaction to the stress he'd been under? She wasn't sure if she could cope with the disappointment of having her hopes dashed a second time.

'I'll make you a drink,' she said hurriedly. 'What do you prefer—tea or coffee?'

'Neither, thank you. My stomach is awash with the foul brew that passes for tea at the police station.' He gave her a gentle smile as he held out his hand. 'Come and sit down, Emma. We need to talk.'

Emma bit her lip as she slowly sat down on the end of the sofa. She didn't know how she was going to bear it if Daniel told her it had been the stress of the moment that had made him say that he loved her. People said all sorts of things they didn't mean when they were under pressure, after all.

'Emma, about what I said before—' he began, but she didn't let him finish, couldn't bear to hear him say the words that once again would rip open her heart.

'I understand, Daniel. Really I do.' She gave a light laugh and saw him frown.

'You do?'

'Of course. You were under a huge amount of strain. It's perfectly understandable if you…well, if you said something you didn't really mean.'

'So you think that I didn't mean it when I said that I loved you?'

His tone was so devoid of expression that Emma found it impossible to guess what he was thinking. She shrugged, not wanting him to suspect how difficult this was for her. She loved him so much, had even planned to tell him that, but now she realised how foolish it would be. She simply couldn't bear to put herself in the position of having her heart broken all over again.

'I think it's perfectly natural that you reacted to the stress of the moment. People say the strangest things when they're under pressure.'

'I see. And you're not angry that I said what I did?'

'Of course not! We've all said things we've regretted, Daniel. It's part and parcel of being human, so please don't worry about it.'

'It's kind of you to take that view,' he said gruffly.

Emma frowned when she heard the roughness in his voice. He sounded upset but why should he be when she had offered him the perfect escape route? It was very strange but before she could work out what might be wrong, he stood up.

'I think I'll try and snatch a couple of hours' sleep or I'll be fit for nothing.'

He left the room before Emma could stop him. She followed him into the hall but he had already gone upstairs. She made her way to her room and lay down on the bed, fully clothed. She had done the right thing, she assured herself, given Daniel the let-out he'd needed. He didn't love her and it would have been a mistake to let herself believe that he did. Tears trickled down her cheeks but she didn't try to stop them. She needed to cry out all the disappointment and put it behind her if she was to get on with her life.

The sound of the door suddenly opening made her

jump. Pushing herself up against the pillows, she stared at Daniel in surprise. 'Daniel! What is it?'

'I'm probably about to make a complete and utter fool of myself but there is no way that I can let this go.' He came over to the bed and glared down at her. 'I didn't tell you that I loved you because I was under pressure, Emma—far from it. For the first time in a long while I was thinking clearly. Letting you go five years ago was the hardest thing I have ever done. Not a day has passed since then when I haven't wished that I could have done things differently. I love you, Emma. That's the plain and simple truth. It might not be what you want to hear but it's what I need to tell you.'

He spun round on his heel and strode out of the door but there was no way that Emma was prepared to let him leave after making such a mind-blowing statement. She scrambled off the bed and ran after him, catching up with him on the landing. 'Daniel, wait! You can't come barging into my room and tell me that and then just… *storm* back out!'

'Better I do that than commit another sin,' he ground out, his eyes blazing into hers in a way that made a shaft of heat sear through her.

Emma felt her breath catch when she saw the expression in his eyes. It wasn't anger that had driven him to such extremes of emotion, she realised, but desire, desire for *her*. Her hand half lifted in a gesture that could have been interpreted either way, as a rejection or as an invitation. Even she wasn't sure what it meant, but then Daniel took a step towards her so that she could feel the heat of his body burning into hers, and her mind was suddenly crystal clear. She wanted him. Only him.

Her arms wound around his neck at the same moment as he reached out and hauled her towards him so that their bodies collided with a small thud, as though they had been struck by a mini-earthquake. Emma could feel the aftershocks rippling through her, tiny flurries of sensation that made her feel wonderfully alive. As her fingers buried themselves in the crisp dark hair at the nape of Daniel's neck, she murmured softly—sounds, not words—because forming anything as difficult as a word was beyond her, but Daniel seemed to understand what she meant anyway.

His mouth found hers, his lips parting hers so that he could plunder her mouth, and she groaned. There was nothing gentle about the kiss, nothing tender. It was as though every scrap of raw passion had been distilled into this one kiss, so that she was breathless when it ended, her body throbbing, her mind numb, her heart awash with emotions.

'Emma, my sweet, sweet Emma.'

His voice was hoarse as he gently laid her down on the carpet and started to undo the buttons down the front of her shirt. Emma would have loved to help him but her hands wouldn't respond. They were locked around his neck, her fingers still buried in his cool crisp hair, and they refused to let go. She just lay there as he finished unbuttoning her shirt and parted the edges, lay there still as he reached beneath her and unclipped her bra. It was only when he lifted her right breast free of the lacy cup that the spell was broken and she was able to move but even then her hands remained locked around his neck as she drew his head down, inviting him to suckle her.

She gasped as a wave of intense pleasure rushed through her when his lips closed around her nipple. There was no slow build-up of passion, no need for caresses or time. She wanted him, right there, right now, this minute.

He lifted his head and must have seen how she felt because he shuddered. Emma could feel the tension in his body as he stripped off her clothes then shed his own. He made love to her there on the floor, his body pressing hers down into the carpet, but even though everything was heat and passion, there was tenderness, too. And it was that more than anything else that convinced her that Daniel had been telling her the truth. He did love her. Her heart soared at the thought.

Daniel could feel his heart pounding as he slowly came back down to earth. Making love with Emma had always been the most wonderful of experiences and this time they had reached new heights. Propping himself up on his elbows, he stared down into her face, feeling his love for her swamp him.

'Wow! I'm not sure how that came about but it was definitely something else,' he murmured, buzzing her lips with a kiss.

'It was.' She smiled as she cupped his cheek with her hand. 'A definite wow in my book too.'

'I'm glad to hear it.' Daniel laughed throatily. 'At least I don't have to apologise for not finding somewhere more comfortable.'

'Oh, it's comfy enough.' She wriggled a little and his breath caught when he felt her body moving beneath his. Even though it was only moments since they had made love, he could feel himself responding. 'Although I may need to check my backside for carpet burns.'

'If you do find any, I'll be more than happy to administer a little first aid,' he assured her, grinning.

'I'll let you know,' she told him, laughing.

Daniel kissed her lightly on the mouth then rolled to his feet. Although he could have happily stayed there all day, they needed to talk and they couldn't do it there. He offered her his hand, unable to resist pulling her into his arms when she stood up.

'I didn't plan for that to happen, Emma, but I'm glad that it did.' He raised her chin so that he could look into her eyes. 'I know you think that I was under a lot of pressure earlier but I'm not under any pressure now and I still feel the same. I love you and that's why I made love to you just now. I only hope that somehow, some way, I can make you believe me.'

'I do believe you, Daniel.' She gave a little shrug when he gasped. 'You couldn't have made love to me like that and not cared.'

'No, I couldn't,' he agreed, his heart overflowing with emotion. He kissed her on the lips then led her to her room and gently steered her through the door. 'We need to talk and I won't be able to concentrate if you're in that state of undress. Put something on and come downstairs. We'll talk then.'

She didn't say anything as she went into her room and closed the door. Daniel went back to his own room and quickly dressed, hoping he hadn't made a mistake by suggesting they waited. Would Emma start to have second thoughts while she was away from him? He hoped not but even if she did, he would convince her that he was telling her the truth. What would happen then was up to her, of course, and his stomach sank at the thought that his future was hanging in the balance. He might love Emma with his whole heart and every fibre of his being, but he had no real idea how she felt about him.

CHAPTER THIRTEEN

EMMA could feel her stomach churning as she made her way down the stairs. Now that the rush of euphoria had started to fade, she'd had time to think and there were a lot of questions that needed answering, the main one being that if Daniel had loved her five years ago then why had he let her go? Maybe he had been keen to further his career but surely he must have known that she would have supported him? After all, she had offered to give up her own dreams of becoming a surgeon so they could be together—how much more proof had he needed about her commitment to him? It was all very puzzling so it was little wonder her heart was racing as she went into the sitting room.

'That was quick.'

He stood up and came over to her, taking her hand to lead her over to the sofa. He had switched on the gas fire and the room felt warm, too warm, in fact. Emma sank down onto the cushion, feeling slightly faint, although maybe it was the ambiguity of the situation that was causing her to feel like this rather than the temperature. She needed answers and she needed them now.

'Look, Daniel, I…'

'I know how difficult...'

They both spoke at once and both stopped. Emma bit her lip in an agony of frustration. They would get nowhere if they carried on this way.

'You first.' Daniel sat back in his seat and regarded her gravely. 'What were you going to say?'

'Just that I don't understand why you pushed me away if you loved me, as you claim to have done.'

'The simple answer is that I was afraid,' he said quietly.

'Afraid?' Emma looked at him in confusion. 'What of?'

'Of hurting you. Of ruining your life.' He stared down at the floor for a moment and his expression was bleak when he looked up. 'Of you ending up hating me.'

Emma didn't know what to say. She stared at him in silence, too shocked by the statement to dispute it. Daniel sighed heavily as he reached for her hand and linked his fingers through hers.

'I decided it was better if I drove you away rather than run the risk of that happening, Emma. Maybe I was wrong but I did it with the best of intentions. I did it for you and I hope you will believe that.'

'It's hard,' she said shakily. 'You hurt me so much, Daniel. At the time I didn't know if I would ever get over what you'd done, and now you tell me that you did it for me—'

She broke off, unable to disguise her scepticism. She hated to think that he might be lying to her but what else could she think? She had offered him her love and he had rejected it in the cruellest way possible. How could that have been to her advantage?

She went to stand up, not sure if she could sit there and listen to any more, but he pulled her back down beside him. His tone was urgent now, the look he gave her filled with desperation.

'I'm not explaining this very well, so it's no wonder that you're confused. But what I said was true. Sending you away seemed like the only thing I could do to protect you.'

'Protect me? From what? I loved you, Daniel. I wanted to be with you and told you that. Surely you must have known I was telling you the truth?'

'Of course I did!' He gripped her hand so hard that she winced and he swore softly, under his breath, as he released her. Standing up, he went over to the window and stood there, staring out across the garden. And when he spoke his voice echoed with so much pain that it brought tears to her eyes.

'I knew you loved me, Emma, and that was what scared me, the fact that you loved me so much you were willing to give up your dreams to be with me.' He turned and she could see the regret in his eyes. 'I couldn't let you do that, my darling. It was too great a risk, you see.'

'No, I don't see. I don't understand what you mean, Daniel.' She leant forward beseechingly. 'I would have been happy to give up my plans to become a surgeon if it had meant we could be together.'

'I know you mean that but can't you see that it would have driven a wedge between us eventually?' He came back and knelt in front of her. 'You admitted only the other day that you would have regretted giving up surgery, so how long do you think it would have been before you'd blamed me for making that decision?'

She started to demur but he shook his head. 'No, I've seen it happen before, Emma. It was the reason why my own parents' marriage failed. My mother was just starting out as a barrister when she met my father. He was in the diplomatic service, which meant he was posted overseas for long periods of time. It would have been impossible for Mum to pursue her career after they married so she gave up the law.'

'But surely she must have thought it all through, weighed up the pros and cons before she made her decision?'

'Of course she did, and I suppose she thought that being with Dad was more important than anything else.' He shrugged. 'Sadly, it didn't work out that way. Mum became increasingly resentful about giving up her career. My childhood was one long round of arguments about it, in fact. It was a relief when I was sent to boarding school because it meant I didn't have to listen to my parents fighting.'

'It must have been horrible for you,' she said quietly, and he shrugged.

'It wasn't a happy time. Mum was bored and frustrated, and Dad felt guilty because if it hadn't been for him, her life would have been very different. The sad thing was that they really loved one another in the beginning but it wasn't enough.'

'And you believe it wouldn't have been enough for us either?' Emma said flatly.

'No, I don't think it would have been. I think that in time you'd have regretted giving up so much for me.' He squeezed her fingers. 'I knew how much surgery meant to you, you see. That's why I discounted the idea of moving to Scotland to be with you while you did your training.'

'You would have done that for me?'

'Yes, willingly, if it had been the right thing to do. The problem was that I knew you would need to devote all your time and energy to your work. Surgery isn't an easy option and I would have been an unnecessary distraction.' He sighed. 'That's why I told you that my career meant more to me than our relationship. I wanted to protect you, Emma, and, if I'm honest, I wanted to protect myself as well. I couldn't have stood it if one day I'd seen resentment in your eyes when you looked at me because you'd failed to achieve your ambitions.'

Daniel took a deep breath. He had no idea how Emma was going to react to what he had told her and the strain made him feel as though every nerve had been stretched to breaking point. He literally jumped when she finally spoke.

'Why didn't you tell me all this, about your parents and everything, five years ago?'

He looked up but it was impossible to guess what she was thinking and his nerves seemed to tighten that bit more. 'Because I was afraid that you would persuade me that none of it mattered, that what had happened to my parents would never happen to us,' he told her simply.

'Maybe it wouldn't have done. Maybe we could have worked things out somehow. The trouble is that you weren't prepared to give us a chance, were you?'

'I wasn't prepared to take any risks,' he corrected, his heart sinking when he heard the bitterness in her voice.

'But it wasn't just your decision, Daniel. It was mine too, only I wasn't allowed to decide what *I* wanted. You took things out of my hands and that was it.' She stood up abruptly. 'Maybe I can't say for certain that our relationship would have lasted, but I would have liked the chance to try and make it work. You denied me that opportunity and no matter how well intentioned your motives were, you didn't have the right to do that. You didn't trust me, Daniel. That's what it all boils down to. And that hurts more than anything else.'

She left the room and Daniel heard her footsteps walking along the hall. He wanted to go after her and beg her to believe that he had done it for her benefit but he knew how pointless it would be. She needed time to come to terms with what he had told her, time to work out how she felt about him now that she knew the truth.

He put his head in his hands as a wave of despair washed over him. He had to face the fact that Emma might not be able to forgive him for what he had done. He might lose her again for telling her the truth, just as he had lost her before for trying to protect her.

It was a busy morning. As well as having to deal with an exceptionally long list, Emma was summoned to the police station at lunchtime to make a statement about what had happened the previous evening.

She stuck determinedly to the facts. How she had felt when she'd realised that Daniel was missing wasn't the issue and the police didn't need to know about that. However, when she left the station an hour later she felt both physically and emotionally drained. Recalling the moments when she'd thought Daniel had been hurt had brought back all the horror.

She made her way to the nearest coffee shop and sat down at a table, wondering what she was going to do. She loved Daniel so much, but discovering that he hadn't trusted her to know her own mind five years ago hurt unbearably. The fact that he had chosen to end their relationship rather than try to make it work made her wonder if he really understood what love meant. Maybe he'd thought he'd loved her then as he thought he loved her now, but did he? Really? Was he even capable of the depth of love she felt for him?

By the time she left the coffee shop, her head was throbbing from trying to work it all out. It had started to rain heavily and the traffic was moving at a snail's pace as she drove through the town. Emma grimaced as she glanced at the dashboard clock. She was going to be late for evening surgery if she didn't get a move on.

She managed to pick up speed once she left the town. There were a lot of cars on the road, probably visitors to the area who were driving around to avoid getting soaked. She overtook a car and caravan combination then had to slow down again when she found herself stuck behind a tractor. The road was too narrow to overtake and she had to wait until it turned off before she could put her foot down. She crested the bridge over the river and breathed a sigh of relief. Just another couple of miles and she'd be home.

The thought had barely crossed her mind when she felt the car suddenly skid when the tyres hit a patch of mud lying on the road. Turning the wheel, she tried to correct the sideways movement but to no avail. There was a horrible scrunch of metal as the car hit the side of the bridge, followed by a loud bang as the driver's airbag exploded. The noise was deafening so that it was several minutes before Emma realised that someone was knocking on the side window. The man gestured for her to unlock the door, which she did.

'Are you all right?' he demanded, bending so he could peer into the car.

'I think so.' She tentatively tried moving her arms and legs. 'Yes. Everything seems to be working OK.'

'What about your neck?' he said quickly when she went to unbuckle her seat belt. 'You can't be too careful when it comes to neck injuries. That's what they say on the television, how you should always make sure a person's neck is properly supported. Maybe you should sit there until the ambulance arrives in case you do yourself any damage.'

'Oh, but I don't need an ambulance,' she protested. 'I'm fine, really.'

'Best to make sure,' the man insisted. 'Anyhow, I've phoned them now so it would be silly not to let them check you over.'

Emma sighed. She could hardly refuse to let the paramedics treat her, seeing as they'd been summoned. She dug her phone out of her pocket and called the surgery, briefly explaining to Ruth what had happened and that she would be back as soon as possible. She had just finished when the ambulance arrived so she turned off her phone while she answered the crew's questions.

They examined her thoroughly, checking how her pupils responded to light and making sure that she hadn't been unconscious at any point before finally agreeing to let her get out of the car. The driver's door was jammed against the wall so she had to slide over to the passenger seat to get out and was surprised to find how shaky she felt when she stood up. The accident had caused quite a long tailback of traffic on both sides of the bridge, too. Emma grimaced as she turned to one of the paramedics.

'I seem to have created havoc,' she began, then stopped when she spotted a figure running towards them. Her eyes widened in shock when she realised it was Daniel.

'What are you doing here?' she began, but he didn't let her finish. Sweeping her into his arms, he stared down into her face and she was stunned to see the fear in his eyes.

'Are you all right, Emma?'

'I'm fine,' she told him shakily.

'Are you sure?' He glanced at her car and she saw the colour leach from his face when he saw the state it was in.

'Quite sure. Aren't I, guys?' She glanced at the

paramedics, who added their endorsement to her claim. Daniel took a deep breath and she felt him shudder.

'Thank heavens for that. When Ruth told me you'd been in an accident…'

He couldn't go on but she understood. He'd been as terrified about her as she'd been about him the night before. All of a sudden the doubts she'd had melted away. Daniel loved her, he really and truly did. It was the most glorious feeling to know it for certain once more.

Reaching up, she kissed him lightly on the lips. It was no more than a token but she could tell he understood what it meant when she saw his eyes blaze with joy. Emma could feel the same sense of happiness and wonderment bubbling inside her as they thanked the ambulance crew. A couple of the other drivers helped Daniel push her car off the road so that the traffic could start moving again. Once that was done, Daniel phoned the local garage and arranged for the car to be collected.

'That's it, then. Let's get you home.' He put his arm around her waist as he led her back to where he had left his car part way up the lane. Emma slid into the passenger seat, smiling as he bent and dropped a kiss on her lips.

'Mmm, what have I done to deserve that?' she teased.

'Nothing. Everything.' He kissed her again then closed the door and walked round to the driver's side. He started the engine then turned to look at her. 'I love you, Emma. I know you were hurt this morning when I told you why I had ended our relationship. I did what I thought was right, although now I can see that I shouldn't have made the decision all by myself. I just hope that one day you can find it in your heart to forgive me.'

'There's nothing to forgive. You were trying to protect me, Daniel, because you loved me.'

'Yes, I was. Maybe I went about it the wrong way but it was the only way I could think of at the time.' He took her hand and raised it to his lips. 'You meant the world to me then, Emma, just as you mean everything to me now.'

'And you mean the world to me, too, so let's not waste any more time.' She leant over and kissed him softly on the cheek. 'From now on any decisions about our future shall be made together. Agreed?'

'Agreed!'

He gave a whoop of laughter as he planted a kiss on her mouth then put the car into gear. They headed back to the surgery and it felt to Emma as though they were floating on a cloud of happiness rather than doing anything as mundane as driving. Daniel refused to let her help him take evening surgery and dispatched her straight to the house with orders to put her feet up until he got back. Emma didn't protest because she wasn't sure she was in a fit state to be seeing patients while she was functioning at this level of euphoria.

She let herself into the house and waited for Daniel to return, knowing what would happen when he did, and it was just as she had expected. They made love to each other with a joy and intensity that brought tears to both their eyes.

'I love you, my sweet Emma,' Daniel told her as he

held her against his heart. 'I want to be with you for ever, if you'll let me.'

'It's what I want too,' she told him honestly. 'Although I'm not sure about the logistics of it, with you working in London and me in Scotland.'

'Trivialities,' he assured her airily. 'We have far more important things to worry about, like when we're getting married.'

'Married?' She sat up straight and stared at him. *'Married!'*

'Uh-huh.' He pulled her back into his arms and kissed her slowly, grinning wickedly when he heard her moan. 'That's what couples do when they're in love. They get married and live happily ever after.'

'So this is a proposal, is it?' she said when she could summon enough breath to speak.

'I suppose it is.' He suddenly rolled to his feet and knelt by the side of the bed, smiling up at her as he took her hand. 'I'd better do it properly so there's no mistake. Will you, Emma Roberts, do me the honour of becoming my wife?'

'Yes,' she whispered then repeated it much louder so there would be no mistake about her answer either. 'Yes, I will!'

EPILOGUE

Three months later...

EMMA stepped in front of the mirror and studied her reflection. It was her wedding day and she wanted everything to be perfect, even though it had been a rush to get things organised in such a short space of time. Now she smiled as she took stock of the dress she had chosen.

Made from pure silk in the palest shade of cream, it fell in soft folds to the floor. The cream rosebuds that the hairdresser had pinned into her hair that morning exactly matched the colour of the fabric. More rosebuds had been hand-tied to form a posy which she would carry up the aisle. She knew she looked her best and hoped that Daniel would think so too. They had waited so long for this day to come and she wanted it to be special, a celebration of their love for each other.

A knock on the bedroom door heralded the arrival of her aunt. Both her aunt and her uncle had been thrilled when she and Daniel had announced that they were getting married. It appeared that they had known all along how she had felt about Daniel five years ago. Although he would never admit it, Emma suspected that her uncle had been doing a bit of matchmaking when he had asked Daniel to cover for him.

It had been Uncle Jim who had suggested that Daniel should think about becoming a partner in the practice, an offer which Daniel had eagerly accepted, much to Emma's delight. It had solved the problem of where they should live as once they returned from honeymoon, she would be taking up a new surgical post at the local hospital. She and Daniel would start their married life in Avondale, where they had first met and fallen in love.

'Your uncle sent me upstairs to check if you were ready,' her aunt informed her, taking a tissue out of her bag. 'You look beautiful, Emma, really beautiful.'

'Thank you.' Emma gave her aunt a hug then smiled at her. 'Shall we go? I don't want to keep Daniel waiting.'

There was quite a crowd gathered outside the local church when they drew up a short time later. Emma smiled when she spotted Alistair Grant, who was acting as one of the ushers. The source of his problems had been traced to the old chemical drums Harold Dawson had used to block access to the wind farm. Environmental services had visited Niths Farm and removed a number of other drums containing hazardous liquids. It was good to know that the community she was going to be a part of once more was no longer at risk.

The organist struck up 'The Wedding March' as they stepped inside the porch and her uncle gave her hand a reassuring squeeze. 'All set, my dear?'

'Yes.'

Emma took a deep breath as they set off down the aisle but the moment she saw Daniel waiting in front of the altar her nerves disappeared. Here was the man she loved, the man she wanted to spend her life with. From this moment on they would be together for ever.

Daniel felt his heart turn over as he watched Emma walking towards him. It was as though every hope and dream he'd ever had had crystallised into this one moment. She stopped beside him and he saw the love in her eyes when she turned to look at him and knew she could see the same emotion in his. They loved each other. They trusted each other. They were meant to be together.

Taking her hand, he made himself a promise that no matter what happened in the future nothing would spoil what they had. Maybe he had been afraid in the past but he wasn't afraid any longer. He loved Emma and she loved him. They had everything they needed to guarantee a wonderful life together.

1_BOTM

are proud to present

June 2011

Ordinary Girl in a Tiara

by Jessica Hart

from Mills & Boon® Riva™

Caro Cartwright's had enough of romance – she's after a quiet life. Until an old school friend begs her to stage a gossip-worthy royal diversion! Reluctantly, Caro prepares to masquerade as a European prince's latest squeeze…

Available 3rd June 2011

July 2011

Lady Drusilla's Road to Ruin

by Christine Merrill

from Mills & Boon® Historical

Considered a spinster, Lady Drusilla Rudney has only one role in life: to chaperon her sister. So when her flighty sibling elopes, Dru employs the help of a fellow travelling companion, ex-army captain John Hendricks, who looks harmless enough…

Available 1st July 2011

Tell us what you think!

millsandboon.co.uk/community
facebook.com/romancehq
twitter.com/millsandboonuk